Outstanding praise for the novels of Holly Chamberlin!

THE SUMMER NANNY

"A satisfying and multifaceted story that keeps readers guessing. For fans of similar works by authors such as Shelley Noble and Nancy Thayer."
—*Library Journal*

THE SEASON OF US

"A warm and witty tale. This heartfelt and emotional story will appeal to members of the Sandwich Generation or anyone who has had to set aside long-buried childhood resentments for the well-being of an aging parent. Fans of Elin Hilderbrand and Wendy Wax will adore this genuine exploration of family bonds, personal growth, and acceptance."
—*Booklist*

SUMMER FRIENDS

"A great summer read."
—*Fresh Fiction*

"A novel rich in drama and insights into what factors bring people together and, juast as fatefully, tear them apart."
—*The Portland Press Herald*

THE FAMILY BEACH HOUSE

"Explores questions about the meaning of home, family dynamics and tolerance." —*The Bangor Daily News*

"An enjoyable summer read, but it's more. It is a novel for all seasons that adds to the enduring excitement of Ogunquit."
—*The Maine Sunday Telegram*

Books by Holly Chamberlin

LIVING SINGLE

THE SUMMER OF US

BABYLAND

BACK IN THE GAME

THE FRIENDS WE KEEP

TUSCAN HOLIDAY

ONE WEEK IN DECEMBER

THE FAMILY BEACH HOUSE

SUMMER FRIENDS

LAST SUMMER

THE SUMMER EVERYTHING CHANGED

THE BEACH QUILT

SUMMER WITH MY SISTERS

SEASHELL SEASON

THE SEASON OF US

HOME FOR THE SUMMER

HOME FOR CHRISTMAS

THE SUMMER NANNY

A WEDDING ON THE BEACH

ALL OUR SUMMERS

Published by Kensington Publishing Corporation

Seashell Season

Holly Chamberlin

KENSINGTON BOOKS
www.kensingtonbooks.com

KENSINGTON BOOKS are published by
Kensington Publishing Corp.
119 West 40th Street
New York, NY 10018

All Kensington titles, imprints, and distributed lines are available at special quantity discounts for bulk purchases for sales promotion, premiums, fund-raising, educational, or institutional use.

Special book excerpts or customized printings can also be created to fit specific needs. For details, write or phone the office of the Kensington Sales Manager: Kensington Publishing Corp., 119 West 40th Street, New York, NY 10018. Attn. Sales Department. Phone: 1-800-221-2647.

Kensington and the K logo Reg. U.S. Pat. & TM Off.

ISBN-13: 978-1-4967-0153-4 (ebook)
ISBN-10: 1-4967-0153-4 (ebook)

ISBN-13: 978-1-4967-2451-9
ISBN-10: 1-4967-2451-9
First Kensington Trade Paperback Printing: May 2020

10 9 8 7

Printed in the United States of America

As always, for Stephen
And this time also in memory of Cyrus Smith

Acknowledgments

Thanks once again to John Scognamiglio for everything. Also, my most sincere gratitude to the staff at Casco Bay Veterinary Hospital—especially to Dr. Marc Ouellette, Dr. Sara Leven, Heather Elliott, and Amanda Ellis—for their excellent care of Cyrus in his final weeks and moments.

Love is like quicksilver in the hand.
Leave the fingers open and it stays.
Clutch it, and it darts away.

—Dorothy Parker

Prologue

"Verity, have you finished collating that handout?"

Collating. *Didn't someone build a machine for that, like, thirty years ago?* I thought. "Almost," I told my boss. One of my bosses. When you're clerical staff, pretty much everyone else at the office is your superior, at least from nine in the morning until five in the afternoon. Below me in the hierarchy at Rowland Electronics are the cleaning staff, who come in at ten minutes after five every Wednesday, and the kid in the mail room. I say kid because he's just seventeen, a high school dropout who nevertheless is super efficient at his job, and for all of my time at the company at least he's never missed a day of work.

Amy frowned down at me where I sat at my tiny desk in a creaky, duct-taped chair that definitely predated my birth twenty-four years ago. "As soon as you can, please. My meeting starts in half an hour." Amy Howard, the least pleasant of my bosses, stalked off in the direction of her cubicle.

For a brief moment, as I looked down at the stapler and the short stacks of Xeroxed printouts before me, I felt an intense desire to overturn the desk (it probably wouldn't have been difficult, as it, too, was old and a bit shaky) and go running out of the building. That's what boredom can do to you, make you feel and act like a crazy person.

Of course, I did no such thing, and continued to organize

and to staple and to remind myself that I very much needed this job. My art had gotten me nowhere, at least in a financial sense, and with a baby to support pretty much on my own, any source of income was welcome.

The thought of Gemma, my daughter, instantly made me smile and sit up straighter and focus my attention on the task at hand, however boring. Gemma, who has the cutest little nose and the most adorable way of fluttering her little fingers while being fed, was with Barbara at the moment (it being Barbara's day off) probably sleeping—she usually slept from about eight to ten each morning, after which she would wake with a roar and demand her bottle. Barbara, my colleague here at Rowland Electronics, has generously taken Gemma and me in until I can afford a place of my own. Alan, Gemma's father, my former fiancé, is still living in the tiny apartment we shared for the past few years until I announced I was leaving him and taking Gemma with me.

The decision wasn't a snap one. No, it had been a long time coming, and I made up my mind only after I'd given Alan the benefit of the doubt time and time again, only after I'd made all sorts of excuses for his odd and controlling behavior, only after I'd finally worked up the nerve to disappoint my father and his mother by breaking things off. You see, from the outside looking in, Alan could be considered a doting and caring and utterly devoted man a woman would be crazy to reject. From the inside, well, from the inside it's different.

The crisis point came when one evening, Alan, under one of his weird delusions that I wasn't taking proper care of our infant daughter, attempted to snatch her from my arms, in the process of which, if I hadn't been agile and quick, she would have fallen to the floor.

Since then, since Gemma and I moved in with Barbara a few weeks ago, I've been seeing Alan on a somewhat regular basis. To talk, nothing more, and always in a public place, which was my mandate. And surprisingly, he's been acting, well, normally. Calmly. Rationally. He's apologized for various failings.

He's brought me flowers. His mother's told me he's vowed to make some big changes and work on his temper, his possessiveness about me that can lead to jealous rages, and get past the suspension he's currently under here at Rowland and never get suspended again. And last week Alan asked to see Gemma, and after some hesitation I agreed. "Always with you," he said, "always in a public place."

Things are going well. Don't get me wrong. I'm not saying I'll go back to Alan someday, put back on the engagement ring he insisted I keep, and start planning our wedding. No, I don't really see that happening, but what I do hope happens is that we three—our family—Gemma, Alan, and I, can really *be* a family, not estranged from one another, not just a family on paper.

Finished. I gathered up the stack of collated handouts and brought them to Amy's cubicle.

"All done," I said.

With a muttered word of thanks—I think—Amy took the stack and waved me off.

When I was a few feet from my desk, my phone rang. It was an outside line, not a call from one of my many superiors, who in fact usually prefer to give me orders in person. *It must be Barbara*, I thought. *Maybe Gemma's being fussy.*

"Hello?" I said into the receiver.

"Verity." It was Barbara, and she sounded odd. Stricken or something. My heart leaped nearly into my mouth.

"Is Gemma sick?" I asked quickly. "Should I come home?"

"No, it's not that." And then she sobbed. "She's gone! Oh, Verity, Gemma is gone!"

Chapter 1

Tuesday the twentieth of May started out as a day much like any other. I woke at around six thirty and spent a few minutes stretching under the sheets, a usual preliminary to putting my feet on the floor. And then, sitting up and swinging my legs over the side of the bed, I sent a message to my daughter, wherever she was, telling her I loved her and always would. Wishing her a happy day. Wishing her a good life.

I would send these messages to my daughter throughout the day. My daughter is never far from my mind. She lives with me, inside me, around me, always.

Always.

Then it was down to the kitchen to make coffee and eat breakfast. After breakfast, a shower and a mental note to add hair conditioner to the shopping list. Not coconut scented. David hates to smell like a coconut, and since he was nice enough to change the brand of hand soap he used for me, the least I could do was buy strawberry-scented conditioner. David doesn't mind smelling like artificial strawberries.

The day ahead included a quick stop at the good old-fashioned family-run pharmacy downtown here in Yorktide; another stop at the library to pick up a book they're holding for me, a study of the life of Joan of Arc I've been dying to read; and then on to my studio at the college, where I'd put the final touches on the syllabus for an art class I'm scheduled to teach this summer. Now that the spring semester is officially over there's no excuse not to be ready for the next round of students.

I was almost to the front door when the landline rang. I hesitated. Not many people call on that number, and most often it's someone with something to sell. But then I thought, *Marion—it might be my once-almost-mother-in-law,* and I hurried back into the kitchen, where there's an extension next to the microwave.

"Hello?" I said. Only then did I notice that the caller's number was not Marion's.

"Is this Verity Peterson?" It was a woman's voice, melodic, with a noticeable Spanish accent.

"Yes," I said. "Who is this?"

"My name is Soledad Valdes. I'm with the Protection of Minors Agency here in Arizona."

Fund-raising? *No,* I thought, government agencies—if she was calling from a government agency—don't raise money through cold-calling. And then . . .

"You found her?" I demanded. My skin suddenly felt all prickly, and for half a second I thought I was passing out. "Is this what this call is about?"

"I had hoped to break the good news to you gently," the woman said, a bit of a smile in her voice. "I know it must be a great shock."

A shock? Oh yes, it was a shock. It still is a shock.

"How?" I asked, leaning back against the counter for support. "How did you find her? Her father, is he with her?"

Clearly and succinctly, Soledad Valdes told me the circumstances of Alan and Gemma's discovery. A man named Jim Armstrong had been caught stealing a car and was arrested. When his fingerprints were run through the national database, they were found to match those of one Alan Burns, long suspected in connection with the abduction of his infant daughter. Criminal record of assault. History of restraining orders.

"It wasn't difficult after that," Soledad explained, "to put the pieces together."

"How is she?" I asked, both eager and afraid to hear the answer to my question. "Is she all right? Is she hurt?"

"She's not hurt. But she is confused and more than a little angry. She was told you were dead, for one, so learning that you're alive and well has been quite a shock."

"So, Alan, her father—"

"He's admitted he took her, yes. He's not denying anything. And it seems he told Marni—that's the name he gave her—it seems he told her from the start that he'd, well, that he'd rescued her from an abusive home."

I don't know why the words hurt so badly—I'd suspected as much from Alan—but they did. To have some of my worst suspicions confirmed.

"But physically?" I asked again, dreading the answer, feeling my hand tighten on the receiver. "Is she healthy?"

"She seems to be fine," Soledad said. "Even though she's furious with her father, she swears he treated her well. I've been in this business a long time, and I've learned to recognize a lie when I hear it. And kids lie for some very good reasons. But I'd say she's telling the truth. She's not an abused child."

Well, that was something for which to be grateful. Except that she'd been lied to from almost the first day of her life. Wasn't that abuse?

"Where is she?" I asked. "Where is my daughter?"

"She's under our care. She's with a very solid foster family until we can arrange for you to be reunited."

"I want my daughter," I said. "As soon as possible I want her here with me."

Soledad attempted to soothe my growing agitation with the promise that the bureaucratic wheels were in motion, but I wasn't satisfied. I'd waited for seventeen years, sometimes patiently, sometimes not so patiently. Now I felt that if I didn't have Gemma back home with me immediately, I would burst. I said as much.

"I assure you, Ms. Peterson," she went on, with a truly admirable degree of patience, "that we're working to get your daughter back home as soon as possible."

She promised to get in touch with me again when there was more to say, and ended the call with these words: "I'm so very happy for you, Ms. Peterson. So very happy."

So very happy.

Not long after Alan and Gemma went missing, I allowed myself to be coaxed into joining a support group for parents of missing or dead children. I was the only parent whose child had been kidnapped, and by her own father at that. The seventeen-year-old son of one man had run away, leaving a scathing note of blame for his unhappiness. This father swore endlessly that he had been guilty of nothing more heinous than mild punishments when his son had disobeyed a direct order. The twelve-year-old daughter of another man had died of brain cancer. Two sets of parents had lost children to car accidents; the daughter of one of the families had been driving illegally. The fifteen-year-old daughter of one woman had gone off with her twenty-year-old boyfriend. One young couple, about my age, in fact, was mourning their stillborn baby. We were a motley crew, united only in tears, anger, guilt, and bewilderment.

But it wasn't long before I realized I couldn't tolerate witnessing the pain of others. All it did was to reinforce my own pain. And that's what it felt like, a layering on of sorrow, a fastening on of grief, an exclusive club of misery, rather than a real way forward. I'm sure support groups help a lot of people. They wouldn't be in existence if they didn't. But it didn't work for me.

No one in the group encouraged me to stay. I believe no one there really cared about anyone else's pain but his or hers. Can you blame them?

What would anyone in that group say if they knew that after all these years I've been given back my lost child? Would anyone be happy for me, really, truly happy, as I believed Soledad Valdes was happy?

I abandoned my plans for the day, though I realized I had no idea what I was supposed to *do* while I waited for Soledad's next call.

Except to cry. The tears simply leaked from my eyes, and I let them come in a flood of great, great relief.

Chapter 2

We have our history, Marion Burns and I.

Marion is Alan's mother.

Marion is Gemma's grandmother.

After Alan disappeared with my daughter, and during the first nightmarish round of questioning by the police, it came out that Alan had what you might euphemistically call "a history." No fewer than three women in a town about two hours north of Yorktide had taken out restraining orders on Alan Burns, stalking being the reason for such measures, and about nine months before he met me, Alan was arrested for badly beating a man he suspected of being interested in his latest ex-girlfriend. The attack was unprovoked. Alan pled guilty, paid a hefty fine (funded by his mother), and the sentence was suspended.

The fact of Alan's disturbing behavior was bad enough, but what was worse—or so it seemed to me—was the fact that Marion, a woman who had almost become a surrogate mother figure to me, especially since my own mother had died when I was in my teens, had known all about her son's problems and yet had never told me. Needless to say, I was hurt and angry, and for several years I wanted nothing to do with Marion and her excuses for keeping me in ignorance.

Thinking back on those first years after Alan made off with

Gemma makes me unhappy for all sorts of reasons, not the least of which was my inability, or refusal, to allow Marion to mourn along with me. She, too, had lost loved ones, and she wanted to help me understand why she hadn't told me about her son's past. It hadn't been to hurt me. She had honestly thought I was a good influence on Alan, and that with me in his life, he would be able to turn things around. I knew she badly wanted my forgiveness. I knew because she told me so the few times I agreed to meet with her, but granting her forgiveness was impossible for me. I felt so very badly betrayed.

But things changed. I changed. It's not easy to live with anger. It wears you down. And the truth was that eventually I became aware that I missed Marion. I missed the times we used to spend together before Alan destroyed our family, the afternoons we would visit the mall or go to the movies or even just sit in her kitchen and drink tea with cream and sugar. And the bottom line was that Marion was a mother without her child. I was a mother without my child. Together, I thought, we might be stronger. Together we might better survive the grief.

This proved to be true.

I knew when Marion would be home. She's retired from her clerical job at the office of a local family physician and lives a very ordered life, with Bingo on Wednesdays at one thirty, church at ten o'clock Sundays, a trip to the grocery store just after breakfast on Mondays, and otherwise, mostly at home, tending her garden and reading historical romance novels. I was a little nervous about telling her the news—both the good and the bad of it. It would be a shock, and Marion isn't the strongest person. Briefly I considered driving over to her place to break the news in person, but at that moment, about an hour after the call from Arizona, I still felt too shaken to trust myself behind the wheel of a car.

Marion was home, as predicted. After she had told me all about the new bird food she was trying out and how the squirrels seemed not to like it and how happy she was that the finches and the sparrows and the chickadees were no longer bothered by the pesky rodents, she asked what was going on with me.

"Marion," I said. "I have something very important to tell you."

There followed a long moment of silence, and when I opened my mouth to continue, she spoke first.

"Is he dead?" she asked, her voice barely audible.

"No. He's in police custody."

"And the baby? Gemma?"

"Fine." My voice broke, and I fought down a fresh flood of tears. Tears of relief and of joy. "She's healthy. At least, that's what the woman from the child protection agency I spoke with told me. She's with a foster family at the moment."

"Thank God. But she'll come home, won't she? She has to come home!"

"Yes. She'll be coming home. But, Marion? It's going to be very, very difficult for her."

I knew Marion understood me. I didn't want her to meet Gemma right away, not until I had spent time alone with my daughter, not before I could assess the damage that had been done to her. As if I'm the expert!

"Yes," she said.

"We'll have to be very, very careful not to overwhelm her."

"You know best, Verity," Marion said, and now in her voice I heard once again the note of apology and submission that appeared every so often since our reconciliation.

You know best, Verity. Do I? I guess I'll have to know best, now that I'm finally getting the chance to be the mother I was meant to be.

"Is he well?" she asked then. "Was he hurt when they arrested him?"

I honestly don't know the answer to that question, but what I said was, "He's fine." Alan is, after all, Marion's son. I know she still loves him, in spite of everything. I know that for seventeen years she, like me, has been mired in worry about the fate of our children. I know that for seventeen years we've both been hoping beyond hope for Alan to decide he'd punished me long enough and that it was time to bring my daughter, Marion's granddaughter, back home.

"You'll let me know what happens?" Marion asked. "When Gemma is coming home? What's going to happen to Alan?"

"Of course," I promised. "Of course."

"It's a dream come true," she said then. "Isn't it?"

For some of us, I thought. *But not for Alan.*

And maybe not for Gemma, either.

Chapter 3

I mentioned earlier that I'm preparing to teach a class this summer, so, a bit more about who I am.

I'm an artist, a sculptor primarily, and for the past seven years or so I've also been teaching art classes at Yorktide Community College. Things in my career are going well, but getting to this point was tough.

At the time of the kidnapping I had a clerical job at the same company where Alan was employed, Rowland Electronics. When he wasn't on suspension. But when he ran off with our daughter, it was impossible for me to stay on there. I felt as if I were on display and that there was no escaping Alan's brooding presence around every corner, hovering above every cubicle. So I quit the job I'd only taken at Alan's insistence and took a job as a waitress at one of the popular seasonal restaurants that cater mainly to tourists. Fewer people to point at me, to recognize me as the woman whose ex-fiancé had stolen her baby. When that job ended for the winter months, I worked as a dog walker (I'm allergic to dogs, but being in the open air, it was tolerable); a stock girl at Hannaford, the local giant grocery store (easier to avoid conversations with locals; I would have earned more as a cashier, but that would have put me on display); and as an off-season housekeeper at one of the large resort hotels in Ogunquit. It was a hand-to-mouth existence at best, and there were months when I was hard-pressed to pay my rent or put gas in my car.

None of this entirely isolated me from public scrutiny, of course, but it allowed me to keep a relatively low profile for close to ten years. No friends, no social life. Self-willed isolation. Self-determined alienation. At one point, not long after the kidnapping, a friend from college days, someone I'd known at the time I'd first met Alan, contacted me. She'd moved away after graduation but of course knew all about what had happened to me. She wanted, she said, to reconnect. She wanted to know if she could help. But all I could remember were the arguments we used to have about Alan and his control over me.

"You say *controlling*," I'd argue. "I say *caring*."

"He's so unbelievably insecure," Marisa said once. "I don't know how you can stand it, all that whining he does, always following you around like a puppy. If I were you, I'd tell him to grow a pair."

"You don't know him," I'd replied defensively. "He's not insecure. He loves me. He doesn't *have* to follow me around, as you put it. He just wants to be with me. You don't know how wonderful it is to have someone always there for you, no questions asked."

Did I believe my own words? Yes, for a long time I did.

Marisa laughed. "Jared is there for me, thank you very much. But he has his own life too, and he lets me have mine."

That hit too close to home. "You're just jealous of what Alan and I have together," I snapped.

I'll never forget the look on Marisa's face then. She pitied me. She was worried about me. Also, she thought I was being a fool. "Jealous?" she said. "Are you kidding? I think it's pathetic the way he smothers you, and you let him do it. No offense, but where are his friends? And that jerk Rob doesn't count. He gives me the creeps. And why does Alan keep changing jobs?"

I broke things off with Marisa after that confrontation. And when she got in touch after the kidnapping, well, I was too embarrassed to allow a new relationship with her. I hadn't listened to Marisa back when it might have made a difference. Instead I'd allowed myself to get pregnant by that controlling, smothering man. And look what had happened.

Anyway, almost ten years after Gemma had disappeared from her crib in broad daylight, things began to change. I realized—and it was quite a shock—that I'd grown *bored* being all alone with my grief, that I'd allowed my world to narrow down to a ridiculously tiny place in which there was increasingly less room for air. Of course, I felt guilty about the boredom. Wasn't I supposed to keep the flame alive, devote every moment to the memory of my daughter and to the hope that one day she would come back to me?

Yes. But what if Gemma *did* come back to me? I'd be in no fit state to be a proper parent, barely making ends meet, without a friend I could turn to for help or even a reassuring smile.

It was tough, coming back to life. I struggled every step of the way to work up the courage to find myself a decent job— no, more than that, a career—that would allow me to provide for my daughter should a miracle happen and that would force me to really live this one life I'd been given, no matter how sad my circumstances.

So I interviewed for a teaching job at YCC. Now, that was a long shot. I'd never taught before, and though I'd returned to my art—my passion—a few years earlier, I had made no effort to have my drawings and sculptures placed in galleries or stores. In fact, I'd shown my work to no one. Who was there to care? Like I said, my profile was low enough at that point to be almost flat.

But luck was with me—or maybe the college was desperate to hire someone, and given my relative lack of experience, they could get me cheap—and I was given the teaching post and with it, a good studio where I could finally fully embrace my work with wood and clay and stone and show it once more to the world.

The hardest part of making this transition was learning how once again to be part of a working community—to make pleasant chitchat at faculty parties, to attend committee and departmental meetings and do more than just sit there, my mouth closed, and to befriend my colleagues. To care. I grew up a shy kid, and fought my way out of that trap in college, thanks in large part to the fellow art students with whom I came into contact. And then I met Alan, and over time, with his encouragement, I slid right back into my shell of isolation. Now it was time to break that shell again. Break it or go mad.

And I was able to do it with the excellent help of Annie Strawbridge, my dear friend and colleague at YCC, as well as her husband, Marc, and their daughter, Cathy. Both Marc and Cathy have become my friends too.

The main reason I took to Annie is that when we first met, at a faculty drinks party given at the start of my first fall semester, she was so up front and honest about the kidnapping. Most people are too afraid or embarrassed to say anything at all to me. Others can't help but bestow on me looks of great pity. Some can't resist blurting a completely pathetic word of sympathy on the order of *Oh my God, I'm so sorry! You must feel so terrible!*

Annie, however, put out her hand, and as we briefly shook, she said, "Look, I know what happened to your daughter. Well, of course I do; I'm a local. And I think it's the most awful thing that could ever happen to a parent. You have my sympathy. And now I'm not going to mention it again."

"But what if I want to talk about it?" I asked, surprising myself.

"Then talk. I'll listen."

We were fast friends after that.

Now, a day after the initial call from Soledad Valdes in Arizona, I was at Annie's house, grateful for her common sense, her loyalty, and her cinnamon buns. I can't tell you how many times I've sat at this kitchen table and shared a meal, feelings, troubles, and small joys.

"So the bum is finally behind bars," Annie said. "Good. There is some justice in this world after all."

"And he's not eligible for bail," I told her. "He's considered a flight risk."

"No wonder." Annie shook her head. "Not one word from the man in all the years since he fled. You'd think he might have wanted to taunt you, send you false tips as to his whereabouts, gloat."

"Alan's need for security was greater than any desire to further torment me. Anyway, he must have known he'd already committed the greatest crime he possibly could commit against me. There was no need to poke the wound."

"I think you're giving the man credit for more intelligence than he possesses."

"Maybe," I admitted. "But the fact is that for seventeen years he managed to avoid being found out. That takes some level of smarts."

"And a lot of luck. And luck always runs out, both the good and the bad."

"Alan's good luck certainly has. Unless some hotshot defense attorney manages to get him off with a slap on the wrist, proverbially speaking."

"Won't happen," Annie said firmly. "At least, I certainly hope it won't!"

Me too.

"You know, Annie," I said, reaching for a second cinnamon bun—why not?—"I'm afraid we'll never be done with Alan. Gemma and I. Though in my opinion he forfeited every single one of his rights to have a place in Gemma's life, he is still her father, and as long as he lives and even after he's dead, his story—the craziness and the kidnapping—will outlive him. We'll always be associated with the notorious Alan Burns."

"I think you're being a bit overdramatic, Verity."

"Am I?"

Annie shrugged. "Well, what do I know? I guess I'd be overdramatic if I were in your shoes. When is she coming home?"

"I'm not sure yet. Bureaucracy takes time, but I've been promised the wheels are turning. Annie?"

"Yes?"

"I'm scared out of my mind."

Annie reached across the table and took my hand. "I know you are. And I'm not going to tell you everything's going to be okay because I can't know that, and things might not be okay. But I do know you'll do your best."

"I will," I said. "My very best."

Chapter 4

And now about David of the strawberry-scented conditioner.

David, who's forty-six, is chair of the English department at Yorktide Community College. Before he came here to Maine, he was a big shot at the Michigan university where he'd earned tenure when he was just in his twenties. With two well-received books under his belt and a slew of articles in respected academic journals, it might seem an odd choice for him to walk away from what had become a bit of a cushy job to take on what is less of a purely academic and more of an administrative position at our little community college. But it was important for David to put a good deal of distance between him and his ex-wife, who had left him in a spectacular way for a colleague at the university. And David has no career-based ego issues. He strongly believes everyone deserves a good education and that it can be gotten just about anywhere, if both teacher and student are dedicated. YCC is lucky to have David Wildacre, and I don't say that just because he's my friend and lover.

David owns and lives in a beautifully restored carriage house on the property of a large Victorian house that's now the home of the local historical society. The carriage house is a post-and-beam structure with a picturesque cupola on the roof. The interior—one story with a loft sporting two large round windows—is open plan with the exception of the master bedroom and the bath-

room, each tucked away behind closed doors. The only down-
side of living in the carriage house is that visitors to the historical
society often assume it's part of the package, and more than once
David has been surprised to find a camera-wielding tourist in his
kitchen. He's learned to lock his doors.

I went over to David's last night, the night after the call from
Arizona that has changed my life in ways I can't even begin to
imagine.

"You won't be able to stay over at my place for a while," I
said, stroking his hair. David has lovely hair, thick and curly,
and though he says he always hated having to deal with curly
hair, and for years wore it closely shorn, I'm glad he's now decided to simply let it be. The fact that he's nicely built and has
the brightest blue eyes I've ever seen also doesn't hurt. Anyway, we were sitting side by side on the couch in the living
area. David had built a fire against the chilly evening and had
bought a bottle of my favorite red wine. He's a considerate
man. "And I won't be able to stay here. I'm sorry. It's just—"

David took my other hand and kissed it. "I know. It's no
problem. We'll find time to be alone. And we'll be talking.
You'll let me help you, won't you?"

I nodded but I didn't say yes. Frankly, I'm not sure what
kind of help anyone can give me at this point. I'm not sure of
what kind of help I'll need. I'm not sure of what kind of help
Gemma—Marni—will need. I began to feel panicked again,
and I guess it showed on my face.

"What?" David said. "What are you thinking?"

"Right now? I'm thinking I'm clueless about the future.
About my future with my daughter."

David nodded, and I began to ramble on.

"Did I tell you there was a time when I was convinced Alan
had managed to spirit Gemma out of the country, that they
were living in some remote coastal town in, I don't know, Por-
tugal or New Zealand?"

"Yes," he said. "But you can always tell me again."

"And there were other times when I was certain he'd abandoned her shortly after the abduction, just left her all on her own somewhere, Moses in the rushes, though unlike Moses's mother, I doubted that Alan cared if she was found by someone kind who would raise her as her own. There were times when I wondered if he'd killed Gemma and then himself, a murder suicide. The imagination runs wild when it has little fact, little real knowledge to go on."

"Now the fact of Gemma," David said, "can take the place of imagination. That should be a relief, even if things are tough for a while. When does she get here?"

"They've booked a flight into Portland, the day after tomorrow."

"That was a nice bit of luck, someone in child protection needing to fly east, being able to accompany Gemma."

"Yes," I said. "Though I wish I could magically swoop down on her right this minute and transport her home in the blink of an eye."

"Patience, Verity," David said. "Patience."

Oh, I know all about patience. Trust me.

Chapter 5

Last night—the night before Gemma was due to arrive, the last night of my seventeen-year-long vigil—was one of the most fraught of my life. My mind was and still is a jumble of questions and apprehensions, of expectations and fears, of hopes and, yes, of fantasies.

Once school starts in late August—or is it early September? I'll have to find out, now that I'm going to have a high-school student living with me. Anyway, once school starts, Gemma's days will be filled with classes and after-school activities and homework. She might want to go to the winter ball and the prom. I wondered how I would afford a formal dress for her. Then I remembered that the wife of the printmaking instructor at the college is a professional seamstress. Maybe I could work out a payment schedule with her, or we might exchange a dress for a piece of sculpture or a painting.

Point being that in a few months Gemma will be properly occupied, but the question of what to do with her until then—while we're getting to know each other—needs to be solved . . . and quickly. So, naturally, I began to panic. She's sixteen—well, technically she had turned seventeen in March; Soledad Valdes told me that Alan had given Gemma a phony birthday in August—way too old for childcare or a day camp. She isn't too young for a full-time job, but the thought of sending my daughter to work after the trauma of the past weeks prevented me from even glancing through the local papers for job ads. *This girl needs rest,* I thought. Rest and care and coddling. Of course, she could stay at home when I'm teaching at the college or when I'm at my studio there, working on pieces for my big gallery show in July. But what would she do here? Sleep. Read. Watch movies. Play video games. Sunbathe, providing she used sunblock. (Alan burns easily. Does Gemma?) She would be lonely, sad, angry, and, quite possibly, bored. It doesn't escape me that I'm going to have to—let's put it bluntly—sell myself to her as a person she wants to live with, not just until she turns eighteen, but for some years after that. I want her to like living with me and sharing my world. I want her to find her own new world to share with me. I want her to love me, a total stranger.

Of course, I turned to thoughts of Cathy Strawbridge and what she would be up to this summer. Annie had told me that Cathy had taken on another babysitting gig, which means that three days a week she'll be occupied from eight in the morning until four in the afternoon. There's also soccer. Cathy loves to play soccer, and there's always some sort of summer program that keeps her busy in the hours she isn't working or attending violin lessons. And Cathy has friends. I've met a few of them over the years, and I know that at this point in her life there are three girls in particular with whom she spends as much time as she can. They're nice girls, all from stable homes; all do well in school, and one of them, Becca, is said to be a math prodigy. Hildy is even more devoted to soccer than Cathy, and Melissa is the group's leading mall rat, though the girls, all fifteen, are too young to get themselves to the mall in South Portland or the ones in Kittery or Newington without an adult driver. Still, all this means that Cathy and her friends probably won't have any real time to devote to getting to know Gemma—or Marni, we'd still have to see about that—and even if they did, I can't count on their being interested in spending time with my daughter, a person I know very little about. What I do know—that Gemma and her father had lived a peripatetic lifestyle, moving from place to place every year or so, and often on the spur of the moment, and that my daughter had spent her formative years in the care of a criminal and troubled man—well, none of that bodes well for a smooth fit. I have no exact idea what experiences my daughter has accumulated in her years with Alan, but I feel pretty certain that those experiences will isolate her from Cathy and her posse, girls who have always lived safe, ordered, innocent, normal lives.

In the end, I had to content myself with putting together a list of activities that might interest Gemma—would she laugh at the idea of miniature golf?—and places she might like to visit with me when I had time off. We might go to the Ogunquit Museum of American Art (kind of a high entrance fee, but I might be able to wrangle some free tickets from someone at the college), to Portland for the shopping (assuming she likes to shop . . . and about that, as about so much else, I have no idea), to the Rachel Carson National Wildlife Refuge in Wells for long walks through the woods (does she have proper shoes for hiking? Is she allergic to pine trees?). Has she ever been to the top of a lighthouse? Has she ever been, however briefly, back to the East Coast after being spirited away by her father? I'm fairly certain Alan had never brought her anywhere near New England, but maybe he'd taken her on vacation to Disney World in Florida. Did he have that sort of money?

Here's another question: Has Gemma ever been to church? Would she want me to take her on Sundays? I could do that easily enough; though I haven't been to a church service in years, going to one each week would be a small sacrifice to make. Has she ever been to a zoo, or gone on a ski trip, or ridden on a roller coaster? *Oh Lord,* I thought, *does she have a pet, a dog or a cat or a bird, that she's being forced to leave behind?* Soledad Valdes hadn't mentioned a pet, but maybe she and her coworkers had simply overlooked this detail. And what about Gemma's medical records, and her school records? Where are they? I need them.

Sleep, when it came, was fitful, and when I woke this morning at five, an hour before the alarm was due to go off, I felt an immediate and almost overwhelming sense of fear that warred viciously with an immediate and almost overwhelming sense of excitement.

This, I thought, *even more so than the day of my daughter's birth, is the most important day of my life.*

Chapter 6

We were to meet in a private room at an airport hotel. This had been orchestrated by the child protection people, who had been looking after Gemma since her father's arrest.

While I waited alone in the nondescript room for her arrival, I found myself thinking about a man named Harold Mair.

Let me explain.

I'd been renting the house on Birch Lane, in which I currently live, from the owner, Mr. Mair, for almost a year at a very reasonable price when he died quite suddenly, and I thought, now the house will be sold, or his surviving relatives, whoever they may be, will raise the rent to a prohibitive amount and I'll be forced to move. I'd always known I'd have to leave the house at some point in time; I'd just hoped it would be at some point far in the future.

Imagine my surprise then when Harold Mair's will was read, and I learned he'd left the house to me. The mortgage had been paid off long ago, so getting the news of my unexpected windfall totally floored me. "But why?" I asked his lawyer. "I'm not family. He hardly knew me, not personally." The lawyer had simply shrugged. "I have no idea why," he said, and I swear I got the feeling he was lying, that Harold Mair had confided in him. "But I'd not look a gift horse in the mouth." Well, I certainly didn't, and I came to suspect that Harold Mair, a man who had lived his entire eighty years in Yorktide, had of course known of my daughter's kidnapping, and though he'd had the delicacy never to mention it to me, this childless, widowed man must have decided that to leave me his home was his way of offering comfort. I have no proof of his intentions, but that's what I believe. I would never have been able to afford to buy a lovely little house like this on my own. Mr. Mair was my very good guardian angel. Now I had a permanent home to give to my daughter, if someday she were to come home.

That someday is now.

I looked at my watch. Gemma and her guardian for the journey were due in minutes.

I wondered what I would see when my child walked into the room.

Gemma's hair would have changed color over the years, something the sketch artists I'd hired for my website devoted to the case had tried to take into consideration. At two months, Gemma's hair had been scanty and pale brown. Now it might be as dark as my own. Or maybe she was coloring her hair blue and purple and green. Women of all ages are doing that now.

How tall was Gemma? Did she have her father's aquiline nose? Did she have my habit of cocking my head to the left when thinking hard about a problem? Was my own mother, long gone, traceable in my daughter's smile or the shape of her hands? Gemma's eyes, too, would have changed color. They might be dark brown, like mine, or maybe they were blue-green, like Alan's. I never fully grasped the eye color dominance thing they teach you in high school biology.

I'd been wondering about all this for years, always supposing that my daughter was alive and growing into womanhood. But along with these speculations were also those horrifying, sick-making moments when I'd become convinced she was dead, at that very moment the victim of a gruesome murder. The lack of real, solid knowledge was torture. Whoever said ignorance is bliss is, well, ignorant.

I heard a voice in the hall. A woman's. A feeling akin to terror overcame me. I realized I was about to get what I had been wishing for so fervently for over seventeen years. And I wondered if I was ready for it.

Chapter 7

She stiffened in my arms. I released her immediately.

Mistake number one, I thought.

"Gemma," I said.

The girl, the young woman, my daughter, frowned. "My name is Marni."

"I know," I said. "I mean, I know that's the name your father gave you. But your legal name is Gemma. And it's what I've called you since the day you were born."

"You haven't seen me since I was a baby." Her tone was off-putting, her expression grim.

I was acutely aware of the representative from the child protection agency at my back, and I wondered if this reunion would be any easier if Gemma and I were alone, without a witness.

But on some level, I was terrified of being left alone with this angry young person before me.

"Yes, but that doesn't mean I haven't thought about you every single day," I said. "I'll try to remember to call you Marni, but it'll be hard. I'm sorry."

"I can't call you Mom. I won't."

"That's okay. I didn't expect you to." *But oh,* I thought, *how I hoped you would!*

She was dressed in a pair of jeans that were almost threadbare at the knees. A T-shirt with the words ABERCROMBIE & FITCH printed in faded letters. A pair of dirty sneakers. Her hair was scraped back into a ponytail. I noticed she had only two bags; one was a stained duffel bag, and the other one of those old hard-bodied suitcases, without wheels, and badly scuffed. I wondered how much she had left behind. But maybe all her worldly possessions were in those two bags.

"How was the flight?" I asked. I was beginning to feel a bit desperate. I wanted to say so many things, important things, but I knew this wasn't the time. Or was it? I felt very much in need of help. There's no standard script for this sort of thing, is there, meeting your own child seventeen years after she'd been kidnapped and led to believe you were dead?

Gemma shrugged.

"Did you get something to eat? It's almost noon. You must be hungry."

"I'm all right," she said.

I looked hard at this stranger standing before me, not quite meeting my eye, and tried to visualize the latest forensic portrait on the website I'd set up so many years ago. *Bring Gemma Home* it's called. There was some resemblance between the imagined portrait and the real person, but not much. Still, I wondered if I would have recognized Gemma as my own without prompting. Would my maternal instinct have been enough to pick her out of a crowd?

"You're staring at me."

"Oh, I'm sorry, I'm sorry," I said hurriedly. Mistake number two. The last thing I wanted to do was to make her feel uncomfortable, but I seemed to be doing just that. "It's just that I'm so happy to see you. I'm so happy you're here."

"I didn't ask to come," she said.

"I know."

"You should know that this wasn't my idea."

"Yes."

"They didn't give me a choice." Gemma shot a dark look at her travel companion. The woman—her name was Mallory

Smith—didn't react. I thought she was probably used to dealing with angry, sad kids.

But I'm not.

Gemma looked around the room then, at the ceiling, back to the door, at the windows. "So, what's next?" she said.

"Next," I said, barely able to keep the tremor out of my voice, "we go home."

Chapter 8

Verity went to the ladies' room.

The woman who'd come on the plane with me—Mallory—asked me if I was okay.

Really?

"Yeah," I said. A lie.

We look alike. Verity and me, I mean. Not totally alike but enough.

But I feel no connection to her at all. None. There was no big moment of *Wow, I know her.* I could have been handed over to a stranger, and it wouldn't have felt any different. It wouldn't have mattered.

These past few weeks have sucked, and I doubt things are going to stop sucking anytime soon.

I suppose I could have slipped away from my so-called guardian at the airport here or in Arizona, but it didn't even cross my mind, that's how—I guess you could say that's how *depressed* I feel. Literally depressed, like flattened. Maybe I'm sort of in shock. I mean, I wasn't always like this. When I first heard that Dad had been arrested and then when I was told he'd done what he did, stolen me, and then lied about it to me for years, I was furious, totally, absolutely, awesomely furious. I broke some plates and all our glasses, and I took a scissor and cut up his favorite T-shirt, the one from a Rolling Stones concert back in the eighties. I swear, I could have killed some-one. Probably him. They say most murders are committed by someone who knew the victim well, maybe even loved him. I understand that.

When she, Verity, came back to the room, my jailer smiled one of those fake sympathetic smiles. "We'll check in with you in a few days, okay?" she said brightly. "See how you're set-tling in."

I said, "Whatever."

Verity said, "I can't thank you enough for all you and your colleagues have done for my daughter."

I'm her daughter. But that doesn't mean she's got a right to me.

And as soon as I turn eighteen, I'm out of here.

When Mallory left the room, Verity and I were alone for the first time. It did not feel good.

"Here," Verity said, "let me carry one of those bags."

I shouldered my duffel bag and picked up Dad's old suit-case. "I'm fine," I said.

That was a lie, again.

But hey, I'm the daughter of a liar, so what do you expect?

Chapter 9

The ride to her house took about forty minutes. I checked the time on my phone. I don't have a watch.

I said nothing on the way because I didn't have anything to say. She said stuff like, "Is the air conditioning on high enough?" and "Do you need to stop at the store for anything before we get home?" Yes, the AC was high enough. No, I didn't need anything. Except to get back on a plane to Arizona.

I was born here, I thought. Maine. Not Rhode Island, where Dad had told me I was born.

My first thought when we pulled into the driveway of the house on Birch Lane was: *This is a lot nicer than anyplace Dad and I ever lived in.* My second thought was: *Don't be disloyal to Dad.*

"This is it," Verity said. "Where I live. My house."

I was struck by her choice of words. "You own it?" I asked.

"Yes. By a stroke of good fortune, actually." And she told me about how the old man who'd owned it before had left it to her in his will. I wondered if he'd been her sugar daddy—I mean, why else would some old guy who's not your grandfather or your uncle leave you an entire house? But I said nothing.

"We can bring the bags in later," she said. We got out of the car, and I followed her around to the front door. There were three kind of long low steps leading up to a porch that ran the entire length of the house. "It's called a bungalow," Verity said. "Or a Craftsman-style house. It was built in 1932."

And why, I thought, *would I care when it was built and what it was called?* Still, I had to admit it was kind of cool that she owned the place. Dad and I had never owned any of the houses or apartments we'd lived in. And Verity's car was in way better shape than ours. Well, the car that used to be ours. Not the one Dad stole—the one that was legitimately ours. It occurred to me then that I had no idea what had happened to the car. I don't think it's worth very much, but still, if someone we trusted could sell it for us, then Dad could get the money and use it to pay the lawyers. But then again, we don't know anyone we can trust. We never have. And I don't know if people in jail can "make" money. It's all so screwed up.

Anyway, Verity opened the front door, and we were immediately in the living room, no front hall. "I'll give you the tour," Verity said, and I thought she sounded unsure, like she might be worried I'd hate the place. And even if I did, so what? I'm stuck here.

"There's only one bathroom," she said. "Sorry about that. But I'm sure we can work out morning schedules once school starts."

I didn't say anything, but I thought, *Does she think I ever lived in a place with more than one bathroom?* And I can't tell you how disgusting some of the bathrooms were, tile permanently stained with who knows what, and rusty faucets that dripped all the freakin' time, and sometimes there was no shower, just a bathtub. Do you know how much time it takes to wash long hair when all you have is a bathtub?

I can't say I paid much attention to details, like what color the couch was or if there was stuff hanging on the walls. Like I said, I think I'm still a little flattened. She showed me through the kitchen, which was right off the living room and kind of long and narrow. Just behind it, a step down, was a sort of entry/exit area with sliding glass doors leading out onto a deck almost as big as the porch out front. The deck was covered with a retractable awning, and for the first time in days my mood lifted a bit and I had a seriously hard time not saying something like, *This is killer! I can't believe this is all now mine!* Well, mine and hers.

The bathroom was off the kitchen—no tub but a shower, super clean—and behind the bathroom was a tiny room Verity told me she used for storage. There were stacks of plastic bins, most of which, she said, contained winter clothing. "Winter gear takes up a lot of space," she said. I thought, *I wouldn't know*, but I said nothing. A smallish washing machine and dryer lived there too. *No more collecting quarters and lugging laundry to the local Laundromat,* I thought. Cool. And then I wondered if Verity would offer to do my laundry for me. Mothers do their kids' laundry, right?

From this storage area we walked into a decent-size room; I could see the living room just on the other side of the open door. "And this," she said, with a gesture like she was on one of those game shows and her job was to point out the stuff people might win, "this is your room."

I looked around the room. It was just a room. No big deal.

"You'll have plenty of privacy when the two doors are closed," she said. "And I didn't know how you might want to decorate it, so I just left what was here. I've been using it as a sort of study, but I'll pay the bills and stuff at the kitchen table from now on. The couch pulls out into a bed, but we'll get you a regular bed as soon as possible."

When I didn't say anything for some time, she said, "Unless you like the idea of a sleeper couch. Your friends could hang out in here more easily then. I mean, the friends you'll make."

I felt such a jumble of emotions right then, anger and sadness and a bizarre impulse to laugh until I puked. The friends I'll make. That implied that my future lay here, in Yorktide. That implied that people—at least some people—would want to get to know me. To like me.

"My bedroom's upstairs," she said then. "And there's a small room next to it I use as an at-home studio for preliminary sketches, things like that. The light's good. Do you want to see the upstairs now or maybe we should bring in your bags so you can get settled?"

She was being so nice. I didn't want her to be nice, then or now. It makes this whole starting-a-new-life thing that much harder for me to handle. Maybe that doesn't make sense to you, but it's how I feel. If she were nasty to me, if she made it clear she resented my being dumped on her and her neat little life in this cute little house, then there'd be something real I could fight against. And why do I feel I need something to fight against?

Because my father totally screwed up my life.

"I'll get my stuff now," I said, and I walked out of the room, through the living room, and out the front door.

Chapter 10

I was a nervous wreck, showing her the house, what is now her home. I want her to like the house, be happy in it, and I'm willing to make all sorts of changes—well, anything I can afford—if they help her to feel settled. I know so little about where she and Alan were living when he got arrested, just that it was a rental apartment. How big or how nicely furnished or how long they had been there—these were details Gemma would have to tell me. If she chose to tell me.

I told her we would eat at six. At five minutes after she appeared in the kitchen, and we sat across from each other at the old rectangular oak table I'd found at a flea market years ago. It had been sort of a wreck, but one good practical thing about being a creative person is that often you can see possibilities where others might see only a piece of garbage. You can resurrect things, give them new life. But only things, not people.

When I'd set out the food and we'd begun to eat, I found I couldn't stop talking. Nerves, I guess. "Our neighbors to the right," I said, "that's the house with the green door, are the Gallisons. They're a young couple with two-year-old twins, and they keep pretty much to themselves. I suspect they're probably too exhausted to socialize. And to the left are the Pascoes. They're an older couple—mid-seventies, I think—and are both very nice, though they're the old-fashioned sort of neighbor—always willing to lend a hand but sometimes a bit too nosey. Get either one of them chatting, and you'll be stuck for half an hour. But don't worry. I've asked them to give us some privacy while you get situated." I smiled. "I know Glenda is dying to bring over one of her famous chocolate layer cakes as a welcome."

If I had hoped for a smile in return or, for that matter, a word of thanks, I was disappointed. Gemma kept her head bowed toward her plate.

"Have you ever had lobster?" I asked.

"No."

Well, I thought, *one word is better than none.* "We'll get some lobsters this week. A few of the lobstermen sell to the locals at a reduced rate."

"I don't like fish," she said.

"All fish or just shellfish?"

"Fish."

I watched as she ate. She held the fork in her fist, not as you're supposed to hold a fork. Had Alan not taught her basic table skills? And she shoveled the food into her mouth, chewing vigorously, slurping from her glass of water (she'd asked if there was Pepsi; there was not) after every few mouthfuls. I restrained the impulse to comment or correct her. *Poor thing,* I thought. *She's eating as if this were going to be her last meal for days.* And then I wondered—strange thought!—if she were eating like a ruffian on purpose, to annoy me, to shock me. Alan had been brought up to be almost an obsessively neat, even delicate eater. How could he not have trained her otherwise?

There's just so much I don't know.

"I'm glad you like the chicken," I said. "You'll have to tell me about the foods you like to eat."

Gemma looked up at me for the first time then, but for the life of me I couldn't read her expression. "I like fried stuff," she said. "Dad used to get us McDonald's fries all the time."

It was the first time she had used the word *Dad* in my home—in our home—and it hit me hard. I responded carefully, without, I hoped, sounding critical of her father.

"Well, fried food isn't exactly healthy. It's okay some of the time, but—"

"You asked what I liked." This was said without looking back up at me.

"You're right," I said. "I did." *Tread lightly, lightly, lightly,* I told myself. "You know, earlier, when we got out of the car, I said that this was my house. What I should have said was that it's our house. I'm sorry."

Gemma shrugged and said, "Okay."

To say our first meal together was a success would be to lie. It was perilously close to a disaster. But what had I expected? This is going to be a long and challenging process, this learning how to be a family, and it's going to require patience.

"Do you want dessert?" I asked. "I usually don't keep sweets in the house, but I brought in some ice cream. I figured most people like ice cream."

"What flavor?" she asked.

"Chocolate with mint chips, and a pint of maple walnut. That's kind of a Maine thing."

Gemma shook her head. "That's okay," she said. "Can I go now?"

"Of course. Do you want to watch television? Or maybe I could show you my bedroom and my little studio upstairs." What I wanted was for us to spend time together; I didn't care if that meant sitting in awkward silence on the living room couch.

"I want to go to my room."

"Sure," I said around a lump in my throat. "You must be tired. And you must want to unpack."

She pushed her chair back, and it scraped harshly on the floor. I watched her leave the kitchen, suddenly exhausted myself, restraining the desire to reach out for her retreating figure, to beg her to stay there with me for a few minutes more. With some effort, I got up from the table and began to clean.

Again, that feeling of near desperation I'd experienced in the hotel room earlier returned and threatened to overwhelm me.

I couldn't afford to feel defeated so easily; it was way too early in our relationship. It was just that I'd had so much emotional energy invested in this reunion. God knows, I'd imagined it almost as often as I'd imagined getting a call from the police telling me that Gemma was dead. But you never know what the reality of the moment is going to be, no matter how many versions you've imagined.

I heard nothing at all from Gemma's room. I had a disturbing feeling the room was empty, even though I'd seen her go in and close the door behind her. But there was the back door, the one that led into the room where I keep the washing machine and dryer. . . . Walking as hurriedly but as softly as I could, I went over to that door and put my ear against it, and at that moment I flashed back to how, when Gemma was an infant, I used to listen intently every night for any change in her breathing, for the slightest movement, for a murmur of distress. Not through a closed door, of course. Gemma slept in a crib only a few feet from my bed.

Was that crying I heard now? The desire to rush in—assuming Gemma hadn't locked the door from the inside—was enormous, but I managed to conquer it and step away.

At eleven o'clock I went upstairs to my room, feeling almost too tired to sleep but unable to focus on the P. D. James novel I'd been enjoying.

I thought of calling David. He'd still be up and I knew he would be eager to know how things had gone, but I didn't feel ready to share anything about today with anyone. Honestly, I wasn't sure what words would come out of my mouth if I tried.

This is a dream come true.

This is a mistake.

No. Not that. Never that.

At long last my daughter was back home with me, the two of us sleeping under the same roof for the first time in seventeen years. Mother and child. I buried my face in my pillow and wept tears of joy.

Chapter 11

I lied to Verity earlier at dinner when I said I didn't like to eat fish. Honestly, I'm not sure I've ever *had* fish. Well, except for shrimp. We were at this chain restaurant once with some guy who worked with my father at the time and the guy's wife ordered shrimp with beer batter. She let me taste one and it was pretty good, but maybe it was the fried coating I liked. Anyway, Dad doesn't like fish, so we never have it at home. We never *had* it at home.

Why did I lie? Because I don't want to be happy here. Because I want things to be the way they used to be.

I didn't tell her, but the chicken thing she made was really good. And there were roasted red potatoes and green beans. I'm not a big vegetable fan, but the beans had some sliced nuts over them, and they were actually pretty tasty. Way better than the stuff in a can, which is what Dad and I mostly eat. I guess I should say, what we mostly ate. Past tense. Until some other time in the future . . .

She's so thin, I guess I expected her not to eat a lot, but she ate as much as I did, and I'm taller and bigger all around than she is. More like Dad. But her hair is so like mine, down to the widow's peak. It's kind of creepy to sit across the table from someone you have absolutely no memory of but who everyone says gave birth to you and is the reason for half of you being the way it is. Her eyes, too, are mine.

I should probably be saying my hair and my eyes are *hers*, not the other way around. She came first. Then me.

I wandered around the room for a while—my room—though there isn't much to explore. There's a small bookcase with only a few books in it, mostly novels but nothing I've ever heard of. I wondered if Verity had cleared it out so I could use the shelves for my stuff. Not that there's much of it. There's a small desk and chair. I opened the long shallow top drawer of the desk. It was empty; maybe she'd done that for me too. There's a dresser with three rows of drawers. I thought about unpacking my bags and putting my stuff away and then didn't. Somehow that would make this all too real—this place suddenly being my new home.

My new home and my "new" name. I know Verity would like it if I agreed to be called Gemma, the name I was legally given when I was born. And it still is my name in the eyes of the law, like I care about The Law, the entity that tossed my father in jail and sent me across the freakin' country to live with a total stranger Dad had always told me was pretty much the devil incarnate. That was his term, by the way, and the first time he used it, he had to explain to me that it meant the devil made flesh, the devil here on Earth. Pretty useful term, actually. I've met a whole bunch of devils incarnate in my life.

To be honest, I never much liked my name—Marni never felt right, like a pair of jeans that are baggy in the butt—but right now the last thing I feel like admitting to this woman calling herself my mother is that I like the name she gave me better than the one Dad gave me. So when she asks if I want to take back the name she gave me, I'll tell her I have no interest in calling myself Gemma, and if to other people I'm still Gemma, then that's their business and I simply won't reply to them. I know it must make her feel weird to call me a name my father gave me, the guy who in her eyes stole me from her before I even really knew who she was—my mother. But I don't really care about her feeling weird, do I? What matters is that *I* feel weird, weird and unhappy and resentful and depressed, and I have every right to feel all those things.

I didn't bother to open the bed in the couch—Verity had asked me if I wanted help with it, and I said no—I just lay down on it and folded my hands across my stomach. It's a habit. Sometimes I sleep all night like that. Dad once said I look like an Egyptian mummy when I'm asleep. I know that whenever I was sick, he used to watch me sleep, sitting for hours in a chair in a corner of my room, or on a plastic milk crate when we didn't have a chair to put in my bedroom. He's a worrier, my father. He's one of those protective sorts.

And I wondered what Dad was doing at that very moment, if he was scared of the future or if he was feeling brave about all the crap that was going to happen. The trial and all, whenever that would be. Maybe he was thinking of me, wondering how I was feeling. Maybe he was asleep. There was a time difference, though; it was two hours earlier in Arizona, but I don't know if the prison guards enforce a mandatory lights-out for the prisoners and if a prisoner gets punished for using a flashlight under the covers to read. Stupid thought. Why would a prisoner be allowed to have a flashlight he could use to smash in someone's skull?

"Dad," I whispered into the dark, not at all believing he could somehow hear me. "I love you."

Chapter 12

"Do you have any Froot Loops?"

I restrained a grimace. "Afraid not," I said. "But I do have Cheerios."

Gemma shrugged. I brought the cereal to the table and watched as she dumped three teaspoons of sugar into her bowl. Let me be clear. I'm not anti-sugar, but so far it seems to me that Alan hadn't done a very good job of teaching our daughter the basics of proper nutrition. That would be up to me now.

I'm nervous about how Gemma's going to react to her local celebrity. The community has been invested in the kidnapping since the very day it had taken place. Right from the start people, strangers and acquaintances, had brought me food, like they would bring food to a grieving widow, all of it meant to comfort and sustain the body if not also the spirit. Casseroles and breads still warm from the oven, and coffee cakes. People had voluntarily nailed signs to posts and distributed them throughout Yorktide and as far away as The Berwicks, signs asking: HAVE YOU SEEN BABY GEMMA? Local businesses had offered rewards for any information as to her whereabouts. One wealthy couple, since deceased, offered a ten-thousand-dollar reward for Gemma's return.

Now that she was finally back here with me, with us, that caring community had to be acknowledged, if also kept at bay.

I've given it a lot of thought, and I feel it's best to meet it head on, not to keep Gemma virtually hidden away. That might only fuel people's curiosity and, worse, it would make Gemma feel like a prisoner. Annie, too, thinks that immersion into the community might be the best way to proceed.

"I took today off work so I could show you around a bit," I said. "Yorktide has its charms. And we can drive into Ogunquit, too, maybe have lunch by the water."

"You're a teacher," she said bluntly. "I thought teachers have the summer off."

"I need the money," I said frankly. "My salary isn't huge, so I teach concentrated summer courses at the college. Some classes count toward a student's degree. Others are open to the general public, anyone who wants to make some art."

"You sell the stuff you make? Statues?"

"Sculptures, yes. If I'm lucky. But you can't count on being lucky."

Gemma didn't respond to that; she just got up and poured herself a cup of coffee from the pot by the sink.

"Do you want milk with that?" I asked. She shook her head and dumped two spoonfuls of sugar into the cup.

"So, I'm really already seventeen," she said, a statement, not a question.

"Yes. Since March twenty-sixth."

"I've always celebrated my birthday on August sixteenth. I'm supposed to be a Leo."

"Do you believe in astrology?" I asked.

"Not really. I had a Leo necklace once. It broke."

I'll buy her another one, I thought. *A good one that won't easily break.* And then I thought, *No. I'll buy her a necklace with the sign of Aries, her real birth sign. The ram.* And then I thought, *Slow down, Verity.*

"That scar on your chin," I said. "How did it happen?"

"Fell off my bike."

"A long time ago?"

"Yeah."

I wondered if the cut had been stitched. It probably hadn't been, to leave such a scar. I fought down a surge of anger, directed, of course, at Alan. "You'll probably be wanting a bike now, I imagine," I said.

"I don't really care."

"It's not terribly easy to get around without wheels of some sort," I explained, "unless you don't mind walking a few miles each way. There's a trolley service in summer, but it caters to the tourists, not the locals who don't live in the heart of town, going to and from the motels and resorts."

Gemma didn't answer. She reached again for the sugar bowl, and I bit back a comment on sugar intake.

After breakfast Gemma went back to her room for close to an hour. I don't know what she was doing in there. I wanted to knock on the door, ask if she would be ready to head out soon, but I didn't. *What do I do,* I wondered, *if she doesn't come out all day? Can I demand that she appear? Should I? Or should I just leave her alone? Let her set the pace?* I was in the midst of trying to answer these troubling questions when she emerged and said in a flat voice, "I'm ready."

First I took her through downtown Yorktide, where the town council had erected a massive banner across Main Street. It read: WELCOME HOME, GEMMA! in bright-pink letters. Gemma couldn't have missed it, but she said nothing. Neither did I.

From Yorktide I took her past beautiful farms and famous historic buildings; I showed her the grammar school and the high school; I pointed out a few of the more popular lobster pounds and the YMCA. Here and there we passed more handmade signs welcoming Gemma home, some on front lawns, others posted on storefronts. She said nothing at all about those, either, or to my running commentary, but she did seem to be looking at what passed before her eyes. *But what,* I thought, *is she really seeing?* We were sitting mere feet away from each other in the front seat of my car, but it felt to me as if we were miles and miles apart.

We were.

At noon I took her to Barnacle Billy's in Perkins Cove, though it's not a place where I can afford to eat frequently. But it is one of the most picturesque spots in Ogunquit, a lovely town, and if I was hoping to win her over with the sight of a beautifully created garden and well-maintained boats bobbing peacefully at their moorings, I think I can be excused.

"It's not really the season yet," I explained as we were led to a table for two on the patio. "We're lucky. After July fourth, it's near impossible to get a table in any of the restaurants without a reservation or a long wait."

Gemma didn't reply to this, just opened her menu and frowned at it. I suddenly realized I had little appetite, but in an effort to make this first day together as normal and drama free as possible, I decided I would have to eat. Families eat meals together. And we are a family, Gemma and I.

"Gemma, what would you like?" I said when our waitress arrived.

"Marni," she said. It wasn't the first time she'd corrected me since we'd met, but I thought that this time she didn't sound particularly upset.

Gemma ordered a cheeseburger, which came with French fries and a soda. I didn't press her to choose water instead. I ordered a spinach salad. Children learn by example. But Gemma is no longer a child, not entirely. At this point I have no idea if anything I say or do will have a positive impact on her continued growth into maturity. I have no idea if she'll simply choose to ignore me.

No one approached us while we ate our lunch, though I did have to shake my head in warning at one woman I vaguely recognized from around Yorktide who seemed on the brink of rushing over to us. If Gemma noticed the woman or my signal to her, she didn't say.

"Did you enjoy your meal?" I asked her when the waitress had taken our plates.

Gemma shrugged. "It was okay."

You know, you take what you can get in this life.

Chapter 13

I unpacked this morning after breakfast, before Verity took me on a tour of what she keeps calling "my new home." I'd never realized how little I own all to myself. I mean, Dad bought me everything, but it's mine because he gave it to me. And it all fit in those two old bags. Not that I'm complaining. I've got plenty. T-shirts, hoodies, two pairs of jeans. My sneakers, though they are kind of falling apart. I guess it's Verity's responsibility now to buy me a new pair. That makes me feel weird. I don't want to have to rely on her at all, let alone for something so personal like my clothes. Dad and I never had many books around the house, and when I had to leave the place we'd been living, I found only seven and took only two, a paperback copy of *To Kill a Mockingbird* that I got at a yard sale and a copy of *The Hobbit* a neighbor we had once threw away. I saw it sitting on top of his garbage can; it was a bit damp, but it dried out soon enough. I'm not one of those girly girls, so I've never accumulated makeup or jewelry or fuzzy toys. In fact, the only piece of jewelry I have is a mood ring that doesn't work anymore. I don't know why I don't just throw it out.

Anyway, it took about ten minutes to put all my stuff away, but I stayed in the room for about an hour. Just breathing. Just

being on my own. When I finally came out, Verity looked relieved, like she had expected me to hide from her all day. I'm
not pathetic. And I'm not afraid of her.

We drove around for a while, with Verity pointing out things
I guess were supposed to interest me—a farm stand she likes; a
really old cemetery; some local stores she says I'll get to know—
and I kind of cringed every time we passed a sign welcoming me
home, like this was ever really my home. At least nobody
waved at the car, which was something. I might have been
tempted to flip them the bird, because why not? I'll be in and
out of this place as fast as I possibly can.

Finally we had lunch at this restaurant in a place called
Perkins Cove—hey, I'm not going to pretend it wasn't pretty
much the nicest place I've ever eaten in—and after that, she
suggested we drive to the beach, which is, like, three minutes
from the Cove. I didn't argue. What was the alternative? Go
back to the house where I don't want to be living?

There were a bunch of bikes in the parking lot at the beach,
chained up to bike racks. I remembered Verity suggesting I get
a bike so I can get around on my own. But I don't want a bike
because I don't want to be part of this place. What's the point
of getting around if I'm only going to be here for a little while?

We walked down a slight decline to the sand, and for the
first time since getting out of the car, I really looked at what
was all around me.

"Have you ever been to a beach before?" Verity asked. "I
mean, the ocean, not a lakeside beach."

"No."

"I've never been to the desert. I'd like to visit the Southwest
one day."

I didn't respond, because I didn't have a voice, other than to
utter another one-word answer. Really. I was so totally stunned by
all that water! It's not like we don't have horizons and vistas in the
Southwest, but this was so completely different, I felt like I'd
landed on an alien planet. I felt totally terrified but also totally

impressed. You know how a lot of people overuse the word
awesome? Well, looking out at all that shimmering, rolling
water that looked like it went on forever, I thought: *This* is
what should be meant by awesome. I felt awestruck. At least, I
think that's what I felt. I do know that I'd never been affected
by any place so strongly before.

Verity suggested we walk along the shoreline. "You might
want to take off your sneakers," she said, kicking off her sandals. "The tide's coming in, and it can come in fast." So I took
them off—not because I was obeying her, but because wet
sneakers can get smelly—and kind of followed her down the
beach. What I mean is, I didn't walk right next to her, like
friends would do, but a few feet behind and to the left. I wondered if people would think we had just had a fight or something.

Anyway, every few feet Verity would bend down and pick
up a shell and either toss it into the water or put it in her bag.
I didn't ask her why she was collecting shells or why she rejected some and kept others. I was kind of curious, though.
And I wondered if after so many years living here, she was
blown away by how beautiful this all was—if she ever had
been—or if by now it was all just background.

As we walked along, the thought did cross my mind that if I
had a bike, I could probably come here to the beach and not
have to talk to anyone. It stretches for miles and miles—or for
what looks like miles and miles—and I bet it's easy to be alone
even when other people are sunning themselves or playing
Frisbee or whatever else people do here. (I saw a lot of people
reading, but I mean, if you have this truly awesome view to
look at, why would you want to stick your nose in a book?)

When we had walked for what seemed like an hour maybe,
Verity suggested we turn back. I could have stayed on that
beach all day and into the night, except I was getting hungry
again so I said, "Whatever." Of course it took close to another
hour to get back to the parking lot, and during that time neither of us spoke much, and I only said things like yeah or no in

response to Verity's few questions. "It's a beautiful afternoon, isn't it?" And, "Do you have a pair of sturdy sandals?"

I fell asleep on the ride back to Verity's house.

The minute I walked into the bungalow, I noticed that on every windowsill (well, at least on the first floor) there was a line of pure white seashells in descending size, large to small. (Or ascending, I suppose, depending on your point of view.) I wondered how long it had taken her to collect all the shells (there have to be way over a hundred), and then I thought maybe she bought most of them, or maybe they're fake. But somehow—and I really don't know how, because I don't know Verity at all—I don't see her as the type of person to buy a ready-made collection of anything. And then I thought about her picking up the shells earlier when we were at the beach. *So that's what she does for fun,* I thought.

What happens when she runs out of windowsills?

"Come upstairs," she said. "I'll show you my bedroom and studio space."

I followed her up the steep narrow stairs and into a smallish room. The bed fills almost the entire space. I've never slept in a bed that big. It must be a queen size or something. There's a dresser and a small table. On both of those there are framed pictures of a baby. An infant. Of me, I guess. The earliest photo that Dad had of me was my kindergarten class picture. I'm in the back row. I wonder if he has the picture, any pictures, with him in jail.

"This little lamb," Verity said, picking up a small plushy toy from the dresser. "It was yours. Alan left it behind for some reason."

Suddenly I felt really uncomfortable. I mean, she seems nice enough on the surface, but am I really supposed to feel all sympathetic for her, hanging on to this stupid little toy for seventeen years? I said nothing.

Verity pointed to a row of three smallish paintings on the wall over her bed. They were pictures of seashells, about three or four different kinds, not the kind on the windowsills. I think one of the shells is called a conch, but I'm not sure. "The paintings are mine," she said. "I'm not a painter primarily, but I do like to try my hand with oils on occasion, and more often with water-color."

So she collects and paints shells. One more bit of information that's probably useless to me in "my new home," but there it is.

"The studio," she said, "is across the hall."

The studio is tiny. It's crammed with stuff, but everything looks neat and orderly.

Dad is super neat. He likes everything in its place. That's something he says all the time: "Everything is best when it's in its place."

"Those sketches are preliminary studies for a new piece I'm contemplating," Verity was saying, pointing to some sheets of paper pinned to a board on an easel.

Still, I said nothing. What was I supposed to be saying? "Oh" and "That's nice" and "I see"?

"And that's it," she said. "Now you've seen the entire house. Well, except for the basement. It's unfinished. There's nothing down there but the boiler and a few old bits of furniture I keep saying I'm going to restore someday."

"Okay," I said then. "When do we eat?"

Chapter 14

I made something easy, pasta with pesto sauce, a salad, and bread. Gemma looked at the pesto with deep suspicion and then bent down and sniffed hard. Only then did she take a bite—after slicing the linguini into tiny pieces. She ate the entire plateful and had two pieces of bread, though no salad.

Vegetables are going to be an issue.

"Do you have any questions?" I asked when I had cleared the plates.

"About what?"

"Anything. About the town, for example? About the places we saw earlier?"

What I didn't say was, *About what really happened between your father and me all those years ago?* There will be time enough for that discussion. At least, I hope there will be.

Gemma shrugged. "No."

Neither of us spoke after that, and once again, directly after dinner, Gemma went off to her room and closed the door firmly behind her.

By that time I was exhausted. Bone-tired. I assumed Gemma was too.

I took my time cleaning up, though there wasn't that much to wash and put away. I suppose I hoped that Gemma—Marni—

might come back out of her room and want to talk. Or just to be with me.

The name thing is a problem. Try as I might to remember to call her Marni, I keep calling her Gemma. A habit of a lifetime is hard to break. And I really *should* be calling her by the only name she's ever known. Our names are so deeply a part of our identity and I suspect that my daughter's sense of her self—of the familiar face in the mirror—must be in a pretty precarious state right now. She doesn't need me always reinforcing the fact that she's been dumped smack in the middle of an identity crisis.

Later I went up to my room, closed the door, and called Annie. I was careful to keep my voice low.

"How's she doing?" Annie asked.

"I have no idea," I said. "She's not giving much away. Well, other than the obvious—she'd rather not be here."

"Of course she wouldn't. Can you blame her?"

"No."

"How are you holding up?"

"All right. Fine, I guess."

"Verity."

"Okay, not fine. Very glad she's here. Very aware she doesn't want to be. Very . . ." But I couldn't find any more words.

Annie said good night, and I crawled into my bed. As I'd suspected, sleep didn't come easily in spite of my great weariness. A barrage of memories filled my head, each clamoring for notice.

The one-year anniversary of Gemma's kidnapping. We'd made the front page of most of the local papers again. *Baby Gemma Still Missing. Brave Mom Hasn't Given Up Hope.*

The time I did give up hope, those months a few years later when I just couldn't muster the faith in a decent universe, in justice, in a happy ending for my daughter and me. The moment I felt that Gemma was dead. The moment I felt I couldn't go on. The terror that overtook me, and my subsequent fight to recover from despair.

The occasions when people would come up to me on the street, sure they had caught a glimpse of Alan in a neighboring town or that they had seen his face on television, at a ball game, one of a crowd, but certain it was him. More than once I lost my temper with these generally well-meaning people. "You should be telling this to the police, not harassing me with your silly ideas!"

On and on the memories came until some time after midnight I must have worn myself out. The next thing I remember, it was morning.

Day three of my new life.

Chapter 15

There are so many new things to freakin' process. New sites, new faces, even new tastes. Dinner was the first time I ever had pesto sauce. Usually I'm not a fan of green food—I mean, broccoli? Really?—but this smelled like garlic, which I love, and so I tried it and it was delicious. Not that I said anything about it to Verity.

Okay, so she's my mother, my biological parent. So what? What does that *mean*? What does that *matter*? She wasn't there for the first part of my life, so what gives her any rights over me?

She keeps calling me Gemma. And I keep correcting her. Honestly, right now, at this very moment, lying here on this couch in what is now supposed to be my room, I wonder if I even care. Gemma Elizabeth. That's what was put on my birth certificate. The real one. Not the false document Dad somehow managed to get. When you think about it, he's a pretty smart guy. Keeping our real identities a secret for all those years. Getting his hands on phony identification papers and whatever else he had to do to create Jim Armstrong and his daughter, Marni.

Too bad he didn't put all that talent into something less criminal.

What would it have been like if he hadn't run away with me?

That's way too big a question to ask, let alone to answer. And suddenly I felt really sick. Maybe I was having a panic attack, I don't know, but all of a sudden I felt like I might throw up and then sweat began to pop out on my forehead and then I think I might have made a sound, like a whimper.

But I got control of myself. I'm good at that, sometimes. I swallowed hard and thought about my breathing, and after about a minute I was okay.

Still, I wished I could call Dad. I can't remember when I last felt the need for my father's comforting arm around my shoulder, but I felt it then, bad.

And then I thought, *If I'm going to survive this sentence I've been handed, I'm going to have to get my shit together.* No panic attacks, no breaking down, no lowering my defenses.

I didn't think I'd be able to sleep, but I did.

I never dream.

Chapter 16

This morning I got a call from a representative of a local church. It's one I know of but not a lot about, other than that its members are Christian. The man who called was very nice, not at all pushy, but what he had in mind appalled me.

"We want," he said, "to give Gemma a welcome home party. We'll invite the entire community of Yorktide, not just our little congregation. We think we can manage to barter for use of the middle school auditorium. When one member of the community is lost, we're all lost. And when one member of the community is found, so are we all found."

It was a lovely, if misguided, offer, and I had to tread carefully in my rejection. In the end he was not to be entirely deterred and said, "Well, when Gemma has had time to get used to her new home. We'll speak again in the autumn."

I had no choice but to agree. Just the other day Annie and Marc had reminded me—as if I needed reminding, what with the banner across Main Street!—that the community (that strange and powerful thing) had been deeply invested in the story of Gemma's disappearance and that they would want to be a part of her return—for honest as well as for prurient reasons. "You'll have to acknowledge the well-wishers," Annie said. "As well as the vampires."

How true, I thought now. Ever since the story of Gemma's

having been found hit the national news sources, not to mention the local papers, I've been bombarded with messages of congratulations from people I know only vaguely, tangentially, like the chairman of the town council (I've attended maybe five meetings in the last five years), as well as from my colleagues at YCC and others I know on a practical, daily-life basis, like the woman who cuts my hair once every six weeks and the hygienist at the dentist's office who scolds me for not flossing properly and the guy who owns the car wash I visit only once a year. I've even gotten a call from a major newspaper in Boston, looking for "an exclusive." But our lives are not for sale.

I didn't tell Gemma about the proposed party or about the offer from the newspaper.

Later in the morning there were two separate deliveries of flowers, both from the most expensive florist in town. The first one, a bundle of seventeen white roses with a few ferns and some baby's breath for good measure, came from the local branch manager of my bank, and the other, a massive arrangement of purple and yellow irises, from the college. Both bouquets must have cost a small fortune.

"They're pretty," I said, wondering if I had a vase big enough to hold the roses.

"Too bad it's not candy." Gemma frowned down at the two tiny cards. " 'Welcome home,' " she read. " 'We never lost faith.' "

"As you saw yesterday," I said, "you're a bit of a celebrity. There's no avoiding it entirely, but I hope we can manage it."

I handed Gemma the letter I had composed after the call from the church representative this morning. It's a letter I'll ask the local papers to print, thanking everyone in Yorktide for their prayers and support all these years, and asking now for privacy. I hope it doesn't sound too much like one of those statements celebrities issue when they're getting divorced. Self-aggrandizing. Reminding people you exist and are important while at the same time asking them to forget those very things.

Gemma read it quickly and handed it back.

"Okay?" I asked, hoping for some comment, bad or good.

"Whatever."

"I guess I should show you the website. There's no point in not showing it to you before I shut it down for good."

Let me be clear. I don't want to give Gemma information overload, but I'd rather she learn truths from me than from a stranger.

What am I saying? To my daughter, I'm a stranger.

"What website?" she asked.

A spark of curiosity! I was thankful for it.

"A few years after your father took you," I explained, "I created a website devoted to the abduction case. It's called *Bring Gemma Home.*" Naturally enough.

I took a seat at the kitchen table, flipped open my laptop, and opened the website.

Gemma sat next to me, within two feet, but again it felt as if she were miles away. "But you weren't sure that my father had been the one to take me," she said. "Right?"

"Well, yes," I admitted. "The police could find no evidence, but everyone assumed Alan was guilty. I mean, the two of you going missing the same day . . . It seemed like more than a co-incidence."

What I didn't tell her then was that the reason I'd moved out of the apartment Alan and I had shared was because one night, in one of the frenzies that had begun to come over him since Gemma's birth, he accused me of holding her "all wrong" and tried to yank her out of my arms, and as I told you earlier, if I hadn't been able to catch her as his grip faltered, she would have fallen to the hardwood floor. She might have died. Re-calling that frightening moment, I never had any doubt at all that Alan was the abductor.

I snuck a look at Gemma. Her face was blank.

"Portraits aren't my strong suit," I said, "and I don't have the reconstructive forensic skills. So each year I commissioned a sketch from a freelance forensic artist of what you might look like in the present. And here," I said, pointing at the screen, "here's where people could send me any information that might surface, someone spotting a man and a child that could have been Alan and you. I'm told a missing persons case usually gets about six hundred to eight hundred tips. Your case got well over one thousand."

"What did you hope was going to happen?" she asked very quietly.

"For one, I hoped one day you might stumble across the website and see I was still searching for you. I know, it doesn't make much sense. Even if you had found the website, it might not have rung any bells if Alan had lied about your past. You'd have no reason to think you were the missing girl from York-tide once known as Gemma."

What I didn't say to her was that I often wondered if I was putting her at risk by maintaining the website. It had occurred to me that if Alan knew about it, he might retaliate by hurting Gemma. Still, I decided it was worth my effort. If Alan did lash out at Gemma, assuming he was still insanely possessive and thinking I was out to steal Gemma back (which, of course, I was), there was a chance that someone—a neighbor, a friend—might witness his bad behavior and intervene, ultimately bringing Gemma to safety. I know. Ridiculous. But I think I can be excused for grasping at straws.

"He told me that we had lived in Rhode Island," Gemma said suddenly. "The three of us, I mean."

And I knew from Soledad Valdes that he had also told Gemma that I was a crack addict and that I had tried to harm her, forcing Alan to flee. "We lived right here in Yorktide," I said. "When you were born, we had a small apartment on Front Street." I had been forced to move back to that apartment after the kidnapping and after Barbara, the friend with whom Gemma and I had been living, asked me to leave. My presence in her home was too upsetting for her. I hadn't stayed for long in that apartment on Front Street. Alan's remembered presence there was too upsetting for *me*.

"He told me that he had no family of his own," Gemma said then, still staring at the screen. "That both of his parents

were dead. When I turned fifteen, he told me that he had stum-
bled across the fact that my mother had died of an overdose
years before. He said now we were all alone in the world, with
only each other."

God damn him, I thought. "I'm sorry for all the lies."

"Not your fault."

I doubted she really believed that.

"I have to admit," I told her, "at one point I got pretty obsessed with the website. There were months when I checked it
every few minutes in the hopes that there was some new bit of
evidence. And when I wasn't able to check, like when I was
driving, I was thinking about checking."

"What changed?" Gemma asked.

I was embarrassed to admit this to her, but I went on. "What
changed was that one day when I was behind the wheel, my
mind totally on an e-mail someone had sent that morning with
what sounded like it might be a viable sighting, I almost
caused a serious accident. The details don't matter, but it jolted
me back into a more normal and reasonable state of mind."
And this near-disastrous event was one of the factors that had
led me to get my act together enough to apply for the job at
Yorktide Community College and thereby reenter the world.

Like I said, none of it was easy.

"Could I look at it alone?" she asked.

"Sure," I said, getting up from the kitchen table. "I've got
some work to do in my studio."

I went upstairs to my studio, with the intention of finishing
a few sketches, but I could do nothing but sit at my drawing
board and stare at nothing, wondering what Gemma was feeling as she read through the website, wondering what would
happen next.

Chapter 17

I sat staring at the screen of Verity's laptop for a long time, scrolling through page after page of the website, reading e-mails from people offering sympathy or what they thought might be clues as to where I was, clicking on links to what seemed like hundreds of newspaper articles about the kidnapping. I wondered if she'd kept a paper file of those articles too. And I read all of the statements she'd written, from the time the website first went up until . . . until the morning after she learned I was alive and well and living in Arizona.

My dream has come true. My child has been found. I offer my heartfelt thanks to everyone who has helped me to keep the flame of hope alive all these years. I'll keep this site updated for the next few days, but for the sake of my daughter's privacy, it will be shut down after that.

Most people would say that here was proof of my mother's love for me, of her desire for my safe return. But just because she wanted me back doesn't mean I wanted to come back. Verity is a stranger to me, in spite of the fact that she thinks she knows me. In spite of the fact that she thinks she's got a right to me.

As I scrolled through each page of this—this tribute—to me,

I wanted to shout, *I'm* not *missing! I never was missing! I was right there all the time, being me, with my father!* But then I thought—*Wait a minute, I* was *missing. I was missing to myself.*

And then it occurred to me, sitting there at Verity's kitchen table in Maine. Not once in my life did I suspect that my name, or Dad's for that matter, were false. Yeah, he'd told me he'd run off with me, but he'd also made it plain that my mother hadn't wanted me and that with no family on either side, there was no one to come looking for us. There was no one who cared. Stupid. Why didn't I put it all together long ago!

Looking at all those drawings of me-but-not-me, all based on a few not very good photographs taken of me as an infant, a gallery of Gemma Through the Ages . . . It gave me the creeps. Some drawings were pretty accurate, and some were way off the mark. And none of the images looked—alive. I mean, every single image looked to me like the portrait of a dead person. Flat. False. Or maybe not a dead person but a puppet or a doll. They gave me the chills. The people who make those missing person pictures like the ones Verity had commissioned aren't painting idealized portraits to hang in some museum. They're essentially making shit up, aren't they?

Dad wasn't one to take a lot of photos of us—now I know why—and we weren't on Facebook (he'd tried to stop me from getting an Instagram account, but I'd figured out how to get one without his knowing; you don't need the details), but I'd seen enough photos of myself in the early years of my life to know what I looked like in first and second and third grade. But those sketches. I don't know, it was like I was on display in some creepy museum, what's that place, that famous wax museum. All these strangers staring at imagined images of me . . . I felt kind of violated, even though I understand why Verity built the website.

I think I understand.

I exited the website and closed the laptop. Then I went back to my room.

Chapter 18

I lay awake for a long time last night, wondering how Gemma felt about all I'd told her, and about what she'd seen on the website. When I came back downstairs and into the kitchen to start dinner, my laptop was closed and she was out back, her arms on the rail of the deck, her head held toward the sky. I let her be and went about preparing two chicken breasts for the oven.

I didn't mention the website at dinner, and I didn't really know how to ask what she had thought about it without seeming to put pressure on her to tell me what a devoted mother I'd been for all those years. I did ask if there was anything she needed immediately for her room, like another lamp or lightweight blanket (it's not quite summer weather here yet and could continue to be cool through the end of the month), and she said that no, she was fine. Again she ate ravenously, and right after dinner she went to her room and I was faced with another lonely evening.

You know, before Gemma came home to me, I sometimes wondered if I'd be able to tell if an imposter showed up on my doorstep, someone pretending to be my daughter. Why anyone would do such a thing, I have no idea, but still, the weeks and months and years were so long and there was so much time to imagine. . . . I never believed for one second that those forensic sketches I commissioned were all that accurate. How could they be? The first image was based on the face of a two-month-old and two-month-olds all pretty much look alike. Really, how could anyone create the future from such a poor source? And even if the first artist had had a more fully formed, individual face from which to work, people might be a lot thinner or fatter than the artist imagined them to be. A broken nose might not have been mended. Hair might have been cut or dyed.

Now Gemma is home with me, even if she's calling herself Marni. I don't at all doubt that this young woman is my biological child. But what if the real Gemma died long ago, you might ask, and Alan snatched someone else's child as his own? Anything is possible in this crazy world, but I refuse to consider that scenario. Besides, the only way Gemma's biological connection to me could be finally proven would be through a DNA test, and even if I had the nerve (the cruelty?) to ask her to take one, I doubt she'd comply. And if she did agree, and if such a test should prove that Gemma was not really my child, what then? Would I throw her out? Or would I accept what had been given to me—someone I could take care of.

Though it might seem hard to believe, there were times over the long and lonely years when I felt that it might not be such a good thing if Gemma came home to me. It might, I thought, be too painful for us both, a relationship doomed to failure. There were times when I thought that if only I could know for *sure* that Gemma was well, I would be content to live without her. There were times, in the depths of despair or sheer exhaustion, I felt willing to let go of hope.

Hope. I wonder if Gemma feels at all hopeful about her life right now.

She won't tell me anything about the last time she saw Alan before she got on that plane to Portland. I know it took place in prison. Soledad Valdes told me that; I suppose she thought I should know. Anyway, this morning I made the mistake of asking Gemma—over a breakfast of pancakes and local bacon, prepared to whet her appetite for something more substantial than Froot Loops and hopefully to soften her mood—if she wanted to talk about the last time she spoke with her father face-to-face. She shut me down pretty quickly with a sharp no. I wasn't stupid enough to try again.

Whatever exactly happened at that last meeting, whatever exactly was said and whether there were tears of anger or sadness, whether there were slamming doors or desperate hugs, it can't have been a success. Gemma can't have left that prison building feeling positive about the future, uplifted, optimistic. She probably felt depressed, sad, and maybe even furious at what Fate (and her father?) had thrown at her—an uncertain future with a total stranger halfway across the country.

Me.

Chapter 19

Verity wants to know if I need to talk about the last time I saw Dad, before I was shipped off to stay with her. Is she crazy? What does *she* have to do with Dad and me? How can it make any difference to her what went on between us? How can her knowing what we said to each other change anything for me now?

Anyway, it was a disaster, that meeting. First off, let me tell you there's pretty much nothing that can prepare you to see your father—or your mother, I guess—in *jail*. I thought I'd be okay, that I could handle the whole thing without freaking out like some girly girl, but the minute the social worker woman driving the car pulled into the visitors' parking lot outside this big ugly building that looked like a fortress—like it's supposed to, I guess—my stomach fell into my sneakers and my heart started to race and it took every ounce of self-control I possessed not to fling myself out of the car and run off. Which is a good thing, because I'd probably have been mistaken for an escaped prisoner and been shot to death by an alert guard. Shit like that happens, I'm sure.

It was amazing how quickly the police found out Jim Armstrong, my father, was not really Jim Armstrong but Alan Burns. A man who had been on the run from the law for seventeen years. The wheels of justice might turn slowly, but when it comes to running fingerprints through a database, bingo, a match can turn up in a matter of seconds. At least, that's how it seemed to me.

Anyway, the social worker people had already told me about my abduction shortly after Dad's arrest. Would there ever have been a good way for anyone to tell me that my entire life was a lie? Would there ever have been a good time for me to hear it? No.

At first, I didn't believe them. Maybe, I thought, Dad had been hit over the head during the arrest and was suffering a concussion or some other type of brain injury that was making him talk gibberish and claim to be a deranged kidnapper when he wasn't that at all, just my sometimes stupid father. But the social worker people had the proof. My father had abducted me from my mother when I was just two months old. No doubt about it. And my mother, my birth mother, was alive and well and living in Maine.

Now, a few days later, I was finally going to see Dad face-to-face. My criminal, lying father. In a visitors' room in jail. No bail, as he's considered a flight risk.

I had questions. A lot of questions. And I wasn't going to make this conversation easy on him.

"Tell me this, Dad," I said, before I said hello or *Are you okay?* In fact, I never did say those things. "How can I be sent back to live with my mother if my mother is dead? You told me that she died when I was six."

"She isn't dead," he said. He looked awful, like an old man. "I was . . . mistaken."

Mistaken? I thought. How could you be mistaken about something like someone being dead? He was wrong, is what he was. But did that mean he had lied to me, or had someone told *him* a lie?

Don't let him off the hook, I told myself. *He screwed up your entire life. He's got to pay for it.*

"You told me she was a violent drug addict. If that was true, how could I be sent to live with someone dangerous like that?"

Dad said nothing. Silence.

"Were you lying?" I asked. Of course I knew he'd lied. But I wanted him to admit that to me.

More silence. Then, he cleared his throat and said, "I acted for the best."

I felt a wild rage overtaking me. "For whose best?" I shouted. If that was all he was going to say to justify his actions . . .

"Why'd you steal the car, Dad?" I pressed, leaning across the table where we were sitting. "Why'd you do something so stupid?" *I really have to know the answer to that*, I thought. *Because if he hadn't stolen it and gotten caught, none of this crap would be happening to me.*

He mumbled something about needing money, a sure thing, a guy had promised him it was all arranged.

In other words, bullshit.

This man sitting at the ugly metal table across from me, not meeting my eye, was not the man I had thought him to be all my life. But what had I thought him to be? Not a hero. Not a great man. Just my father.

All the questions I still had to ask him!

Had she, my mother, my normal, not-drug-addicted mother, ever tried to find me? Oh yes. There was a massive search, an intense manhunt. Every house within miles of Yorktide was searched from attic to basement and back again. Ponds were drained and rivers were dragged. There were volunteer search parties and official search-and-rescue teams, complete with dogs. Even the FBI made an appearance. (How did my father know all this? I wondered. Maybe he had followed the news somehow? Or maybe he was telling me a story again, creating a tale of what probably happened based on a TV show he'd seen.) People were questioned over and over again. But the police could find no hard evidence and no trace of my father and me, so after about a year the case was declared cold. Not closed, not solved, just—dead.

Had we ever come close to being found out? Yes, he told me. A few times. At least, he'd thought someone might be on to us.

It was what kept us moving, the *real* reason . . . A lot became clear to me then. Like the time we were living in the nicest place we'd ever lived, a really cool private house we were renting with a garden full of cacti of all kinds and a small swimming pool. We were happy there. And we still had months on our lease and the landlady had already told us she'd let us sign another one. So why did we suddenly leave, losing our first and last months' security deposit and probably doing something illegal by just walking away from a signed contract? Because Dad thought someone was on to us. I see that now, but then I believed his story that the landlady was upping the rent to a price we couldn't afford and it was "best to get out while we could." I know. It makes no sense. But I was a kid. A kid who for a long time kind of worshipped her father, the only family she had, and who believed every piece of crap that came out of his mouth.

"What is my mother's name?" I asked him. "You told me it was Sabrina. It's not, is it?"

"No. It's Verity."

I laughed. Verity. In other words, truth. How ironic.

"So Marni Armstrong isn't my real name, is it?" I asked, though by now I knew the truth about this, too. Thing is, I wanted to hear the truth from *him*, for once in my life. "The name she gave me when I was born."

"No. Gemma. That was your name. Gemma Elizabeth."

That is *my name,* I thought. Gemma. How freakin' weird.

"And your real name is Alan," I said. "Too bad. I kinda liked Jim."

He attempted a smile, if you can believe it.

"How old am I, really?" I asked.

"Only a few months older than you think you are. You were born in March. The twenty-sixth."

"What else did you lie about, Dad?"

But he would say no more. He just sat there, eyes shifting slowly from one side of the room to the other, never alighting on mine. *He's crazy,* I thought. *My father is a crazy person.*

"Why, Dad?" I persisted. "Why did you do it, if my mother wasn't trying to kill me, and she wasn't, was she? *Why!*"

The guard then asked me to leave. I mean, he told me I had to go. I was upsetting people, I guess. The social worker put her hand against my back and kind of guided me out of the room. I didn't look back.

Since that day I sometimes think it would have been better if I'd never learned the truth about the kidnapping. Ignorance is bliss, right? If Dad had to go to prison for stealing that car, then fine. I'd be there when he got out, pissed at him but also glad to have him back so we could pick up our life where we'd left off. The same old me, Marni Armstrong, not who I am now, a total stranger to myself. At least, that's the way it feels. A stranger with an entire history of what might have been dogging her every footstep.

But that could never have happened, the past remaining a secret, because my idiot father's fingerprints were on file from some silly offense when he was a teenager, and there was no way he could run away from *that* reality.

When I left the prison that day, I didn't care if I never saw my father again. Part of me still doesn't, but that part gets smaller every day, now that I'm thousands of miles away from him. I *do* want to see him again, and I worry it's going to be years before I'm able to. It's not cheap to fly almost all the way across the country, and I'm not sure if Verity would allow me to go even if I did have the money. And would the social worker people let me see him again? I just don't know. I try not to dwell on stuff like that. I try to stay calm and tell myself to be patient. Dad's lawyers will tell him what to do and say when he gets to court. He'll do and say what they tell him to, serve his time, and, if he focuses and has a little bit of luck, he'll get out early on good behavior. And then we can be together again.

That's what I want.

Chapter 20

"What did you bring me?"

I held up the white paper bag. "Sustenance in the form of a ham and cheese on rye, yellow mustard, one pickle."

David smiled. "She knows me so well."

I took the chair on the other side of David's desk. He might be head of the department, but his office is no bigger than that of the other department staff, which is to say it's tiny. And the disorder that reigns supreme within its four walls gives the impression that the room is an even tinier space.

David, you see, is the classic messy, absentminded, downright sloppy professor, from his threadbare cardigans to his wild uncombed hair to the reading glasses he's always losing. Often enough, he eventually finds the glasses on the top of his head or hanging around his neck. To be fair, this is not at all a studied presentation. He's just not a neat guy. But he's intelligent and kind and funny and loving, so frankly, it doesn't matter that in addition to being sloppy, he's also very handsome and well built. My priorities are in the right place, but I am a mere mortal after all.

Have I mentioned that David's academic specialty is mid- to late-nineteenth-century British fiction? The novels of everyone from George Gissing to George Eliot, from George Meredith to Anthony Trollope, from Elizabeth Gaskell to William Makepeace Thackeray are crammed onto shelves that are close to buckling under the weight. Of course, there's also a copy of *The Riverside Shakespeare,* and one of every other volume any self-respecting professor of literature must have, from Norton Anthologies, to *The OED,* from tomes by Harold Bloom to works by Dennis Donohue.

A small sculpture, an abstract bird in cherrywood I made for David a few years back, sits on top of a filing cabinet alongside an ancient coffee maker and a badly done bust of Mark Twain. At least, I think it's supposed to be Mark Twain. Some guy with a mustache anyway. David inherited the piece from the previous tenant of the office. I don't know why he hasn't stowed it away somewhere dark.

David cleared a space on his desk for our sandwiches and water bottles, and I spread out our lunch.

"You look tired," he said.

I took a bite of my sandwich—tuna salad—chewed, and swallowed before answering. "I am tired. David, there are so, so many questions I want to ask Gemma. Did her father take her to church? Did they have a Christmas tree each December? When was the last time she went to a dentist or a doctor? Alan didn't seem to keep records of such things, at least not as far as anyone can tell. What sort of books does she like to read, what sort of music does she like to listen to? So, so many questions." I laughed, but there was nothing amusing about the moment. "I feel I should just give her a questionnaire, get it all over with at once. What's your favorite color? On a scale of one to ten, rate your feelings about peanut butter and jelly."

David reached across his desk and took my hand in his. "Don't be impatient," he said. "You'll learn about her over time."

"But I want to know about her *now*," I protested, aware I must sound petulant and childish. "So I can be a good mother to her."

"You'll be a good mother by letting her take what time she needs to open up to you."

"Easier said than done!" I could hear that my voice had taken on a slight note of panic. "What if I miss a vital clue to her health or her happiness, all because I'm ignorant of almost everything about her? Then I'll have failed her as seriously as her father failed her."

"Verity." David's tone was commanding. "Take a deep breath. I know this is hard. I can't imagine *how* hard."

"Too hard," I said quickly. "That's how it feels at some moments. But I know I can't make this about me. It has to be about what's best for Gemma, even though I've been the one living with this empty, needy space inside me for seventeen years."

"Speaking of empty and needy, eat your lunch."

I did, finishing the sandwich quickly—I find myself to be very hungry these days—and wishing I'd bought a cupcake to go with it.

"Soledad Valdes called me," I said, sitting back in the very uncomfortable guest chair. "It wasn't a surprise. The woman who accompanied Gemma to Maine told me someone would be checking in with us."

"And?"

I shrugged. "And she was very nice, as always. She asked how things were going. I told her we were fine. She asked if I needed any help, someone to talk to, or if I thought Gemma would benefit by seeing a therapist."

"Reasonable questions."

"Yes. I told her no, we were doing fine on our own, but that I wouldn't hesitate to reach out if necessary."

"And would you? Just asking."

I was angry for about half a second, and then I wasn't. David knew about my not very successful experiences with professional therapists and support groups in the past. Of course he'd wonder if I'd reject that avenue of help.

"Yes," I said firmly, "I would reach out. Now that Gemma is in my care, everything has changed."

"Good," he said. "What else? Your face is all screwed up."

"Is it?" I rubbed my fingers along my eyebrows, as if to

smooth away the lines of tension. "It's just that sometimes I catch Gemma looking at me with what I'm sure is amused contempt."

"Verity," David said with mock sternness.

"No, David, I'm sure I'm not imagining it. And other times I wonder if she hates me, and then I think, she doesn't care enough to hate me. I'm beneath her notice."

"She does care about you," David said, "and about what you think of her. I know it. And she doesn't hate you."

I felt momentarily annoyed. "How can you be so certain?" I demanded. "You haven't even met her yet!"

"Because," David answered calmly, "I'm far more objective than you are. I'm more objective than you *can* be. You so want her to love you that you perceive any word or gesture—or look— short of abject adoration as hatred or, as you said, amused contempt."

I sighed. "Maybe you're right," I conceded.

"I know I'm right. You have to relax a bit, Verity. I know it's easy for me to say. I'm not the girl's long-lost mother. I'm not the one yearning for a relationship with her. But I worry about your happiness. You shouldn't make things harder on yourself than they need to be."

"I appreciate your concern, David. I do."

"Even if I sound like a fusspot?" he asked with mock solemnity.

I laughed. "A fusspot? Now that's a word I haven't heard in an age."

"My grandmother used it all the time. If someone wasn't a fusspot, she—it was usually a female who was at the point end of her verbal daggers—then she was a hussy or a skinflint."

"Yikes. One of those old-fashioned formidable grandmothers, was she?" I asked.

"She was old-fashioned even in her youth, from what I'm told. Right out of the Victorian age in terms of her code of behavior and morals. I don't know how she got that way. Neither does my mother. Mom was the last of six children and says she knows the least about Grandmother. Her siblings, my aunts and uncles, were never willing to talk about The Family—I'm using capitals there—to the younger generations. Too painful, maybe."

"And your mother? Is she as formidable as Grandmother?"

Now it was David's turn to laugh. "Not in the least. Mom— she just turned eighty, by the way—is the sweetest, most laid-back woman you'd ever want to meet. Not weak or silly or lacking in courage. Just—nice."

I thought about my own mother, about how she was much like David had described his, and how I still missed her. And suddenly I remembered a line from an episode of *Miss Marple,* one starring Geraldine McEwan as the elderly sleuth. A character is recalling the little girl she once cared for. "*Poor, motherless mite,*" she says and when I first heard those three words spoken with such feeling, I immediately associated them with my daughter, wherever she was. I associated those words with me.

I still haven't been able to watch that episode a second time.

"David?" I said then, not really expecting an answer but needing to ask the question. "Do you think I have a right to hate Alan? He made me a victim, but I chose him in the first place, so some of the responsibility has to be mine. But with Gemma, it's a different situation. She definitely has a right to hate him, I think. She's an entirely innocent victim. She didn't ask for Alan to be in her life." Or, I thought, for me.

"I don't know about anyone having a right to hate. Hate is ugly. It always seems to rebound on the hater. Certainly, there can be a motive to hate, but I'm not so sure it should be acted on."

I sighed and got up from the chair. "You're right," I said. "Hate is never the answer. Well, I should let you get back to work."

"And you want to get home and check on Gemma."

"Guilty as charged."

David came around the desk and gave me a kiss. I held on to him tightly. I do love this man.

While I drove home to Birch Lane, I thought more about

what David had said about hate, and I also thought about forgiveness. For years I've been wondering if I'll ever be able to forgive Alan for an act that was so ignoble, that had no purpose other than to cause me pain and deprive me of my child. Alan's stealing away Gemma was an entirely selfish act, one with absolutely no thought for the well-being of me or, more important, of our daughter. I don't care if Alan is officially diagnosed as mentally ill. Mental illness shouldn't be an excuse in a case like this. I posed no threat to Alan. I did nothing to hurt him. But for all of our relationship, he saw me as an object, as a possession, not as an independent, self-determining person. And for most of our relationship, I let him do that. So maybe it's me I can't forgive.

I've spent years wondering about that, too.

Chapter 21

I recognized the handwriting, of course. I'd known it all my life, that large, round, almost childishly deliberate hand. It was my father's. The Florida postmark further identified the card as being from Tom Peterson. He would have read the news of Gemma's return on my website. I'd always suspected he'd followed the progress of the case—or, the lack of progress—though he never mentioned as much in his annual birthday and Christmas cards to me.

For a split second I had the impulse to bury the card way down deep in the trash. But that would solve nothing.

I handed the card to my daughter. It was addressed to Gemma Peterson-Burns.

"Tom and Valerie Peterson," she read.

"My father and stepmother."

"What happened to your mother?"

"She died when I was a little younger than you are now. She had pancreatic cancer."

"Oh. Sorry." Gemma looked down at the unopened envelope.

"Thanks," I said. "It was pretty awful, actually. We were very close."

"What was her name?"

"Elizabeth. Everyone called her Betty."

"Is that why my middle name is Elizabeth?"

"Yes."

"Are you close to your father?"

"No." The word came out a little too harshly. "We fell out over something very important to me."

"But he keeps in touch," Gemma said now, looking up at me. "I mean, he's got your address."

"He sends the occasional card."

Gemma asked no more questions. She tore open the envelope and then opened the card. There was a rather amateur picture of a daisy on the outside. I wondered for a moment if Hallmark made a card to celebrate the safe return of a victim of an abduction, and almost laughed at the absurdity.

"Twenty bucks," Gemma said, extracting a bill.

"What does he say?"

" 'Dear Gemma. We are very glad you are home safe and sound. Love, Grandpa and Valerie.' "

Without comment, Gemma stuffed the money into the pocket of her jeans, put the card on the kitchen counter, and left the room.

I guess I should tell you I'm an only child, whether by chance or design I don't know, and now that Mom's gone, I never will. I was very close to her, as I'd told Gemma. My mother was a warm and loving person, ready with her affection, but in her efforts to keep me safe and happy, she rather sheltered me. I was shy by nature as a kid, and my mother's fussing about me only served to compound my social awkwardness.

My parents' marriage was perfectly functional, but as far as I could tell, not a passionate one. But what does a kid know? Tom Peterson was a good husband and father in terms of not straying and of providing food and shelter for his family. Betty Peterson cooked, cleaned, and generally made life pleasant for her husband.

It was only when I hit adolescence that my passion for art really emerged, and the desire to paint and sculpt and to show my work to others began to war with my shy and retiring temperament. Increasingly, I felt I had to know if I was any good or if I was deluding myself. Interestingly, it was my overprotective mother who really encouraged the pursuit of my artistic interests. One day when I was about fifteen, not long before the cancer killed her, my mother sat me down and said—I'll never forget her exact words—"I never followed my dreams. To be honest, I can't even remember what they once were. I want you to follow your dreams, Verity. I don't want you to live a disappointed life."

The unspoken part of that message being that she, Betty Peterson, had led a disappointed life.

My mother's death really shook me, but I remembered her words, and by the time I was in college, I was taking her advice about following my dreams by enrolling in classes in drawing and sculpting and metalworking, showing in student exhibitions, staying up until all hours to perfect a piece, and working odd jobs so I could buy materials without having to ask my father for money. He paid perfunctory attention to what he called my "hobby," so what support I found was from my teachers and fellow students. It would have been nice to have my father's active and enthusiastic encouragement. But I never really expected it, so I never really missed it. Or, I thought I didn't.

When I met Alan and we started to date—my first serious relationship—it was pretty obvious that my father considered Alan a godsend. After my mother's death and Dad's rapid remarriage to a woman with whom I could never bond because she was the opposite of my mother in every way I could see, he had little interest in being a hands-on emotionally supportive presence in my life. When Alan came on the scene, with his meticulous care of and concern for me, with his professed love, my father breathed a sigh of relief. I suppose that I did too.

I never told my father about the bad aspects of my relationship with Alan. There would have been no point. So when four years or so later Alan made off with my baby, my father was at a total loss as to how to respond to my grief. I would have appreciated a show of outrage, anything really other than what he said to me a few weeks after the abduction. "Are you sure you didn't do something to make him angry enough to run off?"

Then I was the one feeling the outrage. "You're saying it's my fault Alan stole my child, is that it?" I remember asking, my voice shrill.

"No, no, of course not," he protested. "It's just that—"

I didn't let him finish his sentence but demanded he leave the tiny apartment in which Alan and I had once lived together. And I haven't seen my father since.

Not that he didn't try to see me. For a while he would leave messages on my answering machine, and two or three times he slipped a card under my door, asking if we could meet for coffee, asking if I needed anything, even asking me once to come home. I never called him back, and I tore up the cards. Whenever I saw him in the grocery store or coming out of the post office, I would turn the other way. If he saw me those times, he didn't pursue me, and that also made me angry. I didn't want my father in my life, not after what he had said to me about it being my fault that Alan had stolen my daughter. But I *did* want my father in my life. Of course I did. I wanted the man who had taken me for ice cream the last day of every school year, the man who had mended my favorite doll when her plastic arm had fallen off, the man who had made me laugh until my sides hurt with his imitation of Daffy Duck.

But I just couldn't let him come back to me. I couldn't.

Then my father and his wife moved to Florida. Christmas and birthday cards continued to find their way to Maine, but any other attempts to get through to me trailed off over the years. Really, you couldn't blame the man for giving up; I had worn him down with a stubbornness I couldn't seem to control. Frankly, I wouldn't have been surprised if he had cut ties altogether.

And yet here he was, sending a welcome home card to my daughter. His granddaughter.

Chapter 22

I'm not a big fan of Verity (that's an understatement), but it's too bad her mom died. And cancer sucks. But is losing a mother to cancer worse than losing a mother to—to what? To a lifetime of lies? To basically never having a mother in the first place? I mean, to having one but not knowing you have one?

Shit. It's all so messed up.

You should know that the child protection people had petitioned the court to forbid contact between my dad and me, but because the court (does that mean a judge and a jury or just a judge?) determined that Dad hadn't been an abusive father—I mean, would an abusive father have insisted that his five-year-old kid wear not only a raincoat but rain boots and a rain hat and carry an umbrella for even the slightest bit of rain?—we were allowed to talk.

We were given a schedule. Once a week Dad can call me at an appointed time and for a limited amount of time. Our calls are going to be monitored by the people at the prison. That annoys me—I mean, do The Authorities really think we would be dumb enough to plan a breakout or something over the phone?

I have to admit, I was pretty nervous, waiting for the first call earlier today. I mean, I hadn't spoken to Dad since that disastrous day at the prison. At a minute after eleven the phone rang, and I snatched the receiver of the phone extension in my room.

"Dad?"

"Marni. I'm glad you're there."

The sound of his voice, so familiar, almost made me burst out crying. All the anger I'd felt toward him for what he did to us suddenly disappeared. "Of course I'm here, Dad," I said when I'd gotten control of my emotions. I didn't want to waste one minute of this call blubbering. "I wouldn't miss your call."

"How is it there?" he asked. His voice sounded anxious. I know he's concerned about me. "Are you all right?"

"I'm fine," I said. "It's fine. Don't worry about me." He has, I thought, enough to worry about already, like staying away from guys with knives hidden in their sleeves. Do prison uniforms ever have long sleeves? I wonder. Maybe they don't to prevent stuff like people hiding knives.

"What's she saying about me?" he asked then.

"Nothing," I said. "Nothing much." It was true. I'd expected Verity to start slinging abuse the minute she met me, but so far, anything she's said about Dad has been fairly neutral. Of course, she might be playing a game with me, lulling me into trusting her and then wham, she'll rip Dad a new one.

"Is she there? Is she listening in?"

"No, Dad. I'm in my room, and she's out back, doing something with her garden."

"Good." He actually breathed a sigh of relief. "How was the flight? Were you scared?"

I laughed. Good old Dad. "No," I said, "it was fine. I don't see why people are afraid of flying." I guess I didn't mention that the trip to Maine was the first time I'd been on an airplane. Dad and I had never had the money for real vacations. And Dad doesn't trust any vehicle that goes over fifty miles an hour, so trains were out too.

"Is it hot there?" he asked.

"Not as hot as back home." Again, I almost started crying.

I know we talked some more, but for the life of me, I can't remember what we said. Not much of anything, I guess, knowing that someone was listening to us. But I guess Dad forfeited his right to privacy when he did what he did. Forfeited my right to privacy too.

Finally he said: "I have to go now. The guard's here. . . ."

Suddenly I felt all panicky, like this was the last time I would ever hear my father's voice. "Dad?"

"Yes, Marni?"

"Be careful, okay?" What I didn't say was, *Don't piss people off the way you sometimes do*. My father can be difficult to get along with, though every time he gets into a stupid argument with someone and gets fired from a job or thrown out of a store because of it, he blames the other person.

"I will," he said. "Love you."

"Love you too."

And that was that.

I refused to cry. I wanted to, but I refused. I didn't want her coming in from the garden and hearing me through the flimsy doors of my bedroom. I didn't want her to witness anything real about Dad and me.

But I have one question I'd like to ask someone, anyone. How can you be furious with someone for having done something outrageously stupid and yet, at the same time, love him with your whole heart?

Chapter 23

The entire time Gemma was on the phone with her father, I felt sick to my stomach. God knows what I actually did to the poor plants, no doubt over or under watered them. I couldn't think about anything other than what they were saying to each other, if Alan was further poisoning Gemma's mind with false tales of my sins, if she was telling her father I was treating her badly. Would such rumors get back to Soledad Valdes? Would she and her colleagues investigate and, in spite of evidence to the contrary, take Gemma from me?

When I finally went inside after what I knew to be the allotted amount of time for Alan's call, Gemma was leaning against the kitchen sink, drinking a glass of Pepsi. (In a moment of weakness I had bought her a bottle. One battle at a time.)

"Are you okay?" I asked. I did my best not to stare at her as if for clues of what had transpired between her and Alan.

Gemma nodded.

"If you want to tell me anything, I'll just listen. I mean, I won't judge or comment; I'll just listen."

Gemma shook her head. "No," she said. "I'm fine."

I went to the fridge and took out a carton of grapefruit juice.

"Where are Dad's things?" Gemma asked suddenly.

I turned back to her. "What do you mean?"

"You know, the stuff he left behind."

It was not a question I had expected. "That was a long time ago."

"I know," Gemma said in a tone that suggested I was an idiot. "But where are they?"

"I'm afraid there's nothing left," I said, carefully pouring a glass of juice with a hand that was slightly trembling. It wasn't a lie. I had destroyed all vestiges of Alan, cutting him out of the pictures taken in the hospital at Gemma's birth, throwing out what clothes he'd left behind, tearing up and then burning the notes he had written to me in the early, good days of our relationship.

"How could you not have kept even one thing?" she demanded.

I have to walk carefully, I thought. Gemma loves her father, and I really don't believe there's any good to be had by going out of my way to reveal to her the depth of my anger with Alan.

"It was too painful," I said evasively.

"You were going to be married to the man. You couldn't have hated him all that much."

"We had broken up not long after you were born," I explained. "But you're right. I didn't hate him before he took you." *But after . . .*

"But you *made* him take me. He told me all about you."

He also told you I was dead. "I'm sure he did," I said evenly. "And I'm also sure that most of what he said was a lie."

"Why should he lie?" Gemma was practically shouting now.

"If he told you the truth, that I was a good person and a good mother, what excuse would he have had for taking you?"

Gemma slammed her empty glass on the counter. "You're trying to trick me," she said angrily. "I'm not stupid, you know!"

"I know you're not stupid," I said, my heart breaking for my daughter. "And I know the truth, as it comes out, is going to be hard to hear."

The whole truth, I thought, even revealed slowly, might be

too much for *anyone* to hear, let alone my and Alan's daughter. Maybe she never would learn it all, every last detail. There are some things I don't think she needs to know. Anyway, whatever I tell Gemma now might have been—or might soon be—contradicted by Alan, and at this moment in time she's far more likely to believe his version of the truth than mine.

"Do you want some lunch?" I asked my glowering daughter.

Without answering, she stormed out of the kitchen, and a moment later I heard both doors to her room slam shut.

Chapter 24

I have only one picture of my father—of us. Dad doesn't like his picture taken. I sometimes wondered if he was like the members of that tribe in a jungle somewhere—or is it the North Pole—who believe that a camera image steals your soul or something. I never asked him. (And now I know the truth about why he didn't want his image getting around.)

Anyway, he didn't even know this picture was being taken. We were hanging out in the teeny yard behind the last place we were renting. One of his temporary buddies from work (all his buddies were temporary) had come by with this huge bag of packaged chicken parts for us. He didn't say where he'd gotten them, but the truth was clear in the way he and Dad laughed and slapped each other's hands and clinked their beer bottles. The guy—his name was Stan—had stolen the chicken and who knows what else, and was playing Mr. Generosity by giving out packages to his friends. He brought his son along with him, a quiet, nervous kind of guy around my age, I guess, or maybe a bit older. He didn't go to my school, I know that much. He had a major camera slung around his neck and went around taking pictures of the cacti in the yard. At one point he took a candid picture of Dad and me, each taking a huge bite of a chicken leg (I forgot to say that Dad grilled the chicken immediately), and then another one of us sitting side by side in folding chairs and laughing. I didn't know he had taken the pictures and neither did Dad, because he would have been mad and demanded the kid delete them. Anyway, a few days later, when I got home from school, here was this guy—sorry, his name was Tim—waiting for me with an envelope inside of which were prints of the photos of me and my father. I remember saying thanks but then also, "What do you want for them?" and expecting the worst.

But Tim only blushed—can you believe it?—and said he wanted nothing, just for me to have them, and then he went off. I felt kind of bad for having suspected him of being a slime, but better safe than sorry. Anyway, I don't know what happened to the picture of Dad and me eating the stolen chicken. It must have gotten lost somehow when I was taken from the house after Dad's arrest. But the other one I have. I kept this one, the photo of us laughing, inside a folder filled with random stuff I'd saved over the years, like an article about the dinosaur bones some scientists had recently found in New Mexico, and old birthday cards from Dad. I knew he never went through the folder.

I threw the folder out before I left Arizona, all except the picture. Now it lives tucked into the frame of the mirror over the desk in my room.

Looking at it then, after Dad's phone call and the fight with Verity, I felt insanely confused.

Verity *has* to be at fault somehow; she has to have done something to drive Dad away, even if she wasn't a violent crack addict like Dad said she was.

She said she and Dad had broken up not long after I was born. What she meant was that she left him, and that was what must have made him so depressed that he . . . But wait. He told me she'd tried to hurt me, and *that's* what had made him take me away. Is it all true or only part of it or none of it?

Just this morning, before I got out of bed (the mattress is more comfortable than the couch cushions) it occurred to me that maybe I'm the one to blame for the mess that is my family. Maybe I'm the one to blame for my parents splitting up, which as far as I can tell—assuming Verity really wasn't ever a violent, abusive drug addict—led to my father's running off with me. Hang on, it might make sense. I mean, people have babies for all sorts of stupid reasons, right? So maybe Verity and Alan were trying to save their relationship by having a baby, but then when I came along they—she? he?—realized things were still screwed up and that my being there actually made things worse and . . .

And what? How does that explain Dad's running off with me? It doesn't. Nothing explains it.

I wish I had said yes to lunch. My stomach is growling. But there's no way I'm going to give her the satisfaction of going back out there so she can do something nice for me. No. Way.

Chapter 25

I stopped by Annie's house on my way back from doing chores in town. Gemma hadn't wanted to go along with me. When I'd said, "Are you sure?" for maybe the third time, she snapped at me. "What's wrong with your hearing? I said no."

Annie was home (both Cathy and Marc were out), and she invited me in for coffee. What I probably needed just then was a good stiff whiskey, but that wasn't going to happen. We sat at her kitchen table and immediately, in that warm and familiar environment, I felt a bit less hopeless than I had only moments before. Not exactly hopeful, but less hopeless.

Annie brought a cup of excellent coffee to the table (she and Marc recently splurged on a genuine espresso machine), and I took a grateful sip.

"How about a cookie with that?" Annie asked. "Cookies always make a dark day brighter."

True, but I shook my head. "No, thanks," I said. "The coffee's enough." There was, after all, a slurp of maple syrup in it, Marc's secret ingredient.

Annie sat across from me with a coffee of her own. "So," she said. "Talk to me."

For a moment I wasn't sure how or where to begin, but then the words came spilling out. "Gemma is a stranger to me," I said, "a complete stranger. And I'm a stranger to her. There's no obligation for her to like me, let alone love me. I believe that. And yet, I feel under an obligation to love her. And I do love her. I always have, from before she was born. But . . ."

"But what?" Annie asked. "You don't *like* her?"

I sighed, maybe a bit too dramatically. "It's an awful thing to say, knowing what she's been through, the odd, uncertain life she's lived with Alan. But no, I don't much like her."

If Annie was shocked by my admission, she hid it well. "She's making it hard for you to like her," she said matter-of-factly. "It sounds like she's constructed quite an impregnable system of defense. But that might change. It's hard to resist the impulse toward connection with another human being. It's hard to ignore that need for too long without reaching out, even tentatively."

"I hope you're right. Look, Annie, don't get me wrong. I'm not sorry she's back home. Not at all. It's just that sometimes—most times—I wish it weren't so difficult."

Annie rolled her eyes. "If wishes were horses . . ."

"She seems so hard," I said then. "So fierce. I wonder if she cries. Most teenage girls cry fairly easily, don't they, or is that just a cliché? I know I cried all the time, and not just when my mother died. I wonder when was the last time something touched Gemma deeply enough to make her cry."

"Hearing about her father's arrest," Annie suggested. "That might have done it. Of course, maybe what she mostly felt then was anger. Anyway, why is it so important to you that Gemma be able to cry?"

I laughed. "Because then we'll have something in common. A vulnerable heart."

"Isn't it time Gemma met us?" Annie asked.

"You don't think it's too soon?"

"What I think isn't important. But since you asked, no. I told you before, I think the sooner you try to normalize the situation for Marni—Gemma, whoever—by introducing her to your friends and getting her familiar with the way things work in Yorktide, the sooner she'll feel comfortable putting down some roots. Maybe."

"You're right," I said. "How about I bring her here to your house? Sometimes I wonder if she's feeling claustrophobic at my house. I mean, our house. A change of scene might be helpful."

Annie shrugged. "Sure. Why don't we say after dinner some night this week? You can let me know. We won't make it a big deal, just a quick visit. One step at a time."

I thanked Annie for the coffee, the invitation, and the talk, and headed back home, unsure of what I would find. Gemma disgruntled. Gemma depressed.

Gemma gone.

Chapter 26

Gemma wasn't gone. She was on the deck out back, and the awning was completely retracted.

"Did you put on sunblock?" I asked before even saying hello. It was midday, and the sun was strong.

Gemma didn't bother to turn around. "Dad doesn't make me wear sunblock," she said. "I never burn. "

Remembering her annoyance with me that morning, I said nothing else and went back into the house. And I thought about how protective Alan had been of me and of our unborn child throughout my pregnancy. Protective and obsessed. He orchestrated every day of those nine months, and I let him.

He came with me to every doctor appointment. "You might not understand something the doctor or nurse tells you," he'd say, as if I were simpleminded. "Or you might forget to tell me what was said when you get home. It's better I be there."

I remember how the nurses and other staff would tell me how lucky I was to have such an interested and concerned partner. "He'll make such a doting daddy," they would say, to which I would smile and nod.

He monitored my diet. He decided what I could have and how much of it and when I should have it. He kept a log of how many hours I slept each day and made a mark on his checklist when I took my prenatal vitamins. For those nine months we were rarely apart for more than an hour. By then we were working for the same company, so it was easy for him to keep an eye on me. "You have an enormous responsibility, Verity," he would tell me day after day after day, as if I could ever forget. "You're carrying our child. It's vital that you not do anything stupid or careless. Everything I'm doing I'm doing for the good of our child."

How could I argue and not sound ungrateful or callous?

And how to reconcile the man who let his daughter go without protection from the sun with that overly protective father-to-be?

Gemma came inside then and made for the fridge.

"I'd like you to meet my friend Annie," I said. "And her husband, Marc, and their daughter, Cathy. Cathy's a little younger than you are."

"Whatever."

"Annie teaches math at YCC, and Marc's an accountant."

No response. Gemma went on staring into the open fridge for a moment and then let the door slam shut.

I began to feel a bit desperate. I pointed to her left ankle; her skintight jeans were short enough for the tattoo of a heart with what looked like an arrow through it to be seen, if only partly. "I see you have a tattoo."

"Yeah."

"When did you get it?" I asked.

"A few years ago. Why?"

"Just curious. I've never had the nerve to get a tattoo."

"It's no big deal. It hurts while it's being done, but you get over it."

"It's the risk of infection that always stopped me."

"I've got another one. Here." Gemma twisted around and lifted her T-shirt to show me the image of a heart with wings.

Oh God, I thought. Not a tramp stamp. If that's antifeminist, and it probably is, then go ahead and point the finger at me. Not all artists are wild spirits free from archaic prejudices.

"Dad knew someone who knew someone who does inking," she said. "We got a deal."

Still, I thought, it must have cost money that might have been better spent on some decent clothing for my daughter, or more nourishing food than McDonald's French fries. Or a tube of sunblock! But I said nothing.

"Are you also afraid of piercings?" she asked in a slightly taunting tone.

"Not afraid, no," I said honestly. "Just not a fan, except for the standard ear piercing."

"Everyone I know back home has tattoos or piercings. Except Dad."

That statement startled me. Not the first part, the second. The thing is, Alan does have a tattoo, but in a place where a daughter wouldn't know about it. He got it before we met. It's the image of an anchor, and until this moment I'd forgotten about it totally. I remembered now asking him why he'd chosen an anchor, and all he'd done was shrug. I wondered why Alan had lied to Gemma about it. Or maybe she had just assumed. The topic wasn't worth pursuing.

I decided to take a chance and ask a question that might produce a volatile answer. "The people back home," I said, wincing a bit as I spoke that last word. "Do you miss them? Do you miss your friends?" The reason I asked is that as far as I could tell, Gemma wasn't in communication with anyone from her life in Arizona, except Alan, that is. I hadn't once seen her texting, but of course that didn't mean she wasn't spending hours each night in touch with her girlfriends. And had there been a boyfriend?

"No," Gemma said, and there was an unmistakable note of finality in that word.

I chose to believe her. At least, I chose not to pry. To admit she did indeed miss someone might, in her eyes, make her seem vulnerable to me, even weak.

"I thought we'd have pork chops for dinner," I said. "Okay?"

Gemma half laughed. "Whatever," she said, and left the kitchen.

Chapter 27

Last night we went to Verity's friends' house after dinner. Annie and Marc Strawbridge. (I know I'm going to call them The Strawberries. I can feel it.) And their daughter, Cathy. I wasn't looking forward to it at all—why should I have been? I don't *want* to get to know a whole bunch of people here. I want to just . . . get through. And leave as soon as I can.

Anyway, it was okay. The Strawberries (see?) have a nice house, a lot bigger than Verity's (wait, I wonder if she's going to make a will and leave the house to me; parents do that, don't they, leave stuff to their kids?), even though there are only three of them. We hung out in the basement. It's partially finished. There's a carpet on the floor and what Annie called a bar-sized pool table (the felt's not in great shape; I used to go to this bar with Dad for a while, and they had really good pool tables; Dad still lost every game he ever played, though), and an old arcade-style game machine, the kind Dad told me he used to like to play. This one was Space Invaders. We'd already had dinner, like I said, but Annie (I guess it was her; maybe Cathy helped her) had put out cheese and crackers and a big bunch of green grapes and a bottle of wine and some sodas. Verity has a freak-out about soda, like it's a dangerous drug or something. I mean, Dad drinks soda all day long, and he's fine, and not even diet soda. Huh. I wonder if he gets soda in jail.

I'll ask him next time we talk, but if the answer is no, I'll feel bad about it. I mean, the guy didn't kill anyone. If he wants soda, he should get it.

Anyway, it was just us girls, as Annie said. Marc was fixing something in the second-floor bathroom. Annie poured Verity a glass of wine, but she hardly touched it. I took a Pepsi. Cathy had a Diet Coke.

At first I felt like I was on an interview or something, that these friends of Verity were going to ask me a bunch of questions and then, depending on how I answered, judge me. Okay, Verity, she can stay, or nope, send her back. She failed the test. She's not one of us. We don't like her.

Like I really care what anyone thinks of me! Still, it took about half an hour for me to relax enough to realize that Annie and Cathy weren't coming across as judgmental and that they were actually okay.

I have to say that Annie's kind of strange looking. I don't know how to describe it. At first you think, wow, she's actually kind of ugly. I mean, her features are kind of all over the place, if you know what I mean: her nose too big, her mouth too small, her eyes too far apart. But the oddest thing is that after a minute, after you say to yourself, whoa, she's kind of ugly, you find yourself saying, wow, she's actually kind of beautiful. I admit that I like Annie, and not only because she said hello without trying to touch me—unlike Cathy, who almost smothered me with a hug and who smells way too flowery. What *is* that perfume she douses herself with? I'll tell you one thing. There's no way Cathy Strawberry has a tattoo!

Anyway, Annie also called me Marni and didn't slip once. Well, neither did Cathy. I guess it's easier for them to remember who I am—who I was for all that time with Dad—than it is for Verity.

Physically, Cathy takes after her father, and I know this because he came down to the basement at one point. He didn't stop, just waved his hand, said, "Hey, welcome," and went to the dark, unfinished part of the basement where Cathy said he

keeps his tools. Anyway, they're both tall and broad shouldered. Cathy went on about how she loves playing soccer. I
wonder if being tall and broad helps. I have no idea. When she
asked me if I liked to play soccer, I laughed. "God, no," I said.

"Have you ever tried?" she asked. "Because if you haven't,
I bet you'd love it."

"No," I said. "I haven't tried and I wouldn't love it."

That was the end of the talk about soccer.

Annie mentioned she'd gone to the most recent town meeting and that some local guy was petitioning the Board of Se-
lectmen for permission to build a second home on his property
for his son and the son's new wife. The problem was that the
site was officially too small for another house, and there was
some issue about the existing septic system not being able to
handle the job of two residences. It all sounded pretty stupid
to me, but Cathy had a pretty strong opinion about it—she
thought the guy should be refused because his elderly neighbors had been harassed by the son when he was younger and
they didn't want him living next door any longer—and what
was kind of interesting was that her opinion was the opposite
of her mother's, who thought the guy should be allowed to
build as long as he upgraded the septic system and promised to
keep his delinquent son in line. They argued about it for a few
minutes, Cathy pointing out that Annie's solution wasn't really
a solution because it didn't deal with the fact of the plot being
too small, but without getting nasty. I couldn't help but wonder if Annie and Cathy were typical of mothers and teenage
daughters. I mean, if I had lived with Verity all my life and not
alone with Dad, would she and I be close enough to argue but
not be stupid about it?

It doesn't matter. And I seriously doubt there'll ever be a
time when Verity and I are close.

Then, somehow, the conversation turned to movies. Annie
asked if I'd seen the latest Avengers movie. I said I hadn't.

And then I thought about all the times Dad and I would go

to the movies together. We tried to go on discount days and at times when tickets were half price, like ten o'clock in the morning on a Wednesday, but sometimes we so badly wanted to see a particular movie that we'd go on a Saturday afternoon and pay full price. We'd sneak in snacks, too, which you're not supposed to do, but have you seen how ridiculously expensive movie snacks are? We like action movies best, like anything from the old days with Bruce Willis in it and *The Terminator*, but I also got into those Lord of the Rings movies, and The Hunger Games, though Dad got seriously freaked by the whole idea behind The Hunger Games. He said it was because he's a parent, and nothing is worse for a parent than the idea of losing a child.

Thinking about all those movie dates—that's what Dad and I called them—was not a good idea, because suddenly I felt like an alien again, seriously out of place. What was I doing in this basement in Yorktide, Maine, with these people I hadn't asked to know, these people I didn't want to know, thousands of miles away from my father?

I felt a moment of panic, like I was going to explode, and I squeezed the edge of the chair cushion with both hands.

Maybe Verity sensed something was going wrong with me— well, of course she didn't; she doesn't know anything about me! Don't be stupid, Marni. Anyway, for whatever reason, Verity got up from the couch at that moment and said we had to leave.

On the drive home she said, "I hope you enjoyed meeting them. Annie's been a good friend to me through the years."

"It was okay," I said.

When we got back to the house, I went straight to my room and closed the door.

It's hard to be tough all the time. It's hard pretending.

Is pretending just lying by another name?

Just before I fell asleep, I thought: How weird. Dad told me nothing is worse for a parent than losing a child. And Verity lost her child because of Dad.

Chapter 28

I lay awake for a long time last night after we'd come home from the Strawbridges' house, going over the little gathering. On the whole I'd say things went all right. At least, when I asked Gemma on the drive home if she'd enjoyed meeting Annie, Marc, and Cathy, she hadn't given me a flat no for an answer. What she said was: "It was okay."

She went straight to her room when we got to the house.

I say things went well "on the whole," because at one point I suddenly thought I could feel something dangerous emanating from Gemma. Fear? Anger? Both? I don't think I imagined it, but maybe I did. Her hands were gripping the seat cushion, but that might have meant nothing. Anyway, I decided it was a good time to go home.

Maybe something one of us said upset her in some way. It's so hard to know. Every new experience is going to bring with it unforeseen consequences, maybe trigger a painful memory, or maybe recall a sweet one that in turn might cause sorrow and a sense of loss.

I don't foresee any great friendship springing up between Gemma and Cathy. Seeing them side by side, I felt that the differences between them appeared extreme. At least, they did to me. I wonder if Annie got the same impression.

Cathy gave me a big hug as we were leaving and whispered,

"Keep the faith." I have to say, though it seems a terrible thing to admit at this point, but there have been times through the years when I've almost regarded Cathy as a daughter. Not Gemma's replacement, but a daughter of sorts nonetheless. And there have been times when I hoped that if Gemma and I were ever reunited, I would find that she was like Cathy in being warm and affectionate and, well, pleasant.

Don't misunderstand me. I can't help but feel I'm betraying Gemma by comparing her to Cathy, and I'm trying very hard *not* to compare her, but it's difficult not to let the differences take center stage. What I've got to do is give Gemma time to show me who she really is, past the anger and resentment. Or, maybe I should say I need to give her time to become the person she will become, living here with me. Something like that.

I finally got to sleep, and when I came down to the kitchen this morning, Gemma was already there. She had started the coffee. After breakfast, she asked if she could use my laptop for a while. I told her she could, and she took it to her room. She's been there ever since.

A little while ago I saw Mrs. Pascoe peering at our house through the curtain in her kitchen window. I suppose I should introduce her to Gemma. After all, we are neighbors, and she is a nice enough woman. But like Annie said, one step at a time.

Chapter 29

I took Gemma to my studio at the college today. My work is so integral a part of me, of who I am in the world, that of course I hoped my daughter would appreciate it, at least a little bit. At least, that she would appreciate the fact that the work means so much to me.

I was disappointed.

She looked around the studio, with no obvious sign of interest.

"This is where I make my sculptures," I told her. "It's also where I teach. Over here is where my various modeling tools are stored, calipers and smoothing ribs and clay shapers. Casting materials are stored in the next cabinet to the left. Those are armature stands in the corner, and that's my trusty torch wheeler, not something you want to mess around with, given the propane in that tank."

There was no reply to any of this.

"These days," I went on, "I'm working mostly in wood, but I haven't given up clay or bronze." I pointed out a poster with the words—well, a few of them—of Sir Francis Bacon. "This is one of the truest things I know," I told her. I read the words aloud: " 'There is no excellent beauty that hath not some strangeness in the proportion.' "

Gemma still didn't comment. I wondered if she'd ever heard of Sir Francis Bacon.

I continued the tour of the studio, and while Gemma dutifully followed me, I had no idea if she was paying attention to what I was saying and to the things I was pointing out, like the new supply of walnut and mahogany that had arrived only the week before and the carefully laid-out selection of gouges and mallets I kept a close eye on, as I do all my tools. When the tour was finished, I turned to her and said, "Well? What do you think?"

She shrugged. "I don't have much use for art," she said. "Any use, I guess. I mean, what good is it? What does it do for anyone?"

It was such a ridiculously ignorant question, I wondered for a moment if she was joking. And then I realized she was quite serious. "That's a pretty big question," I said, hiding my shock, "with a lot of very big answers."

"Like?" she challenged.

"Like art brings beauty into our lives, for one. For another, art can challenge us to think differently about all sorts of things. It can change our lazy assumptions into thoughtful opinions. It can make us aware of the world around us, of different cultures."

Gemma yawned. "Whatever."

I hid my disappointment as best I could—and, it must be admitted, my annoyance; had Alan never scolded her for being rude?—and we left the studio not long after that.

On the way home, we stopped at the bakery in town for a loaf of whole wheat bread. I'm pretty sure Gemma's never had whole wheat bread in her life. Maybe that's an unfair assumption to make, that Alan never fed her anything healthier than McDonald's fries and squishy chemically compacted white bread.

When we came back out to the sidewalk, bread in tow, I spotted a familiar face. "See that woman over at the gas station across the street?" I said to Gemma. "The one wearing the orange T-shirt?"

"Yeah. What about her?"

"That's Amanda Jones. She would have been your third-grade teacher."

"But she wasn't," Gemma snapped. "Why do you always go on about what would have been? It's seriously annoying."

Was it? Had I been going on? How could I explain to my daughter that in some ways what would have been—what should have been—was more important to me than what really had happened? All the special moments that were stolen from me: Gemma's first missing tooth; her first day of school; her graduation from grammar school. I was even deprived of the opportunity to care for her when she was sick with a cold or with chicken pox. An act as simple but as meaningful as trimming my little girl's hair had been denied me. I needed to think about what would have been—even if it drove me a little mad.

"I'm sorry," I said.

Gemma shrugged. "Whatever."

I guess I'm just going to have to get used to the shrugs and the whatevers. "So," I asked, when we'd gotten back into the car. "What was the name of your third-grade teacher? The one who really was, not the one who might have been."

"I don't remember," she said. "No, wait, I do. That was the time we moved in the middle of the school year. One of the times. We ended up in a different county or something, so I had to transfer. I don't remember the name of the first teacher I had, but the second one was Ms. Butler. We called her Ms. Butt. She had a huge ass."

I was angry. If I had raised Gemma, you can be sure she would not have been making fun of a teacher, especially at such a young age, and using such crude language. But I said nothing. How could I? Life with my daughter reminds me of the proverbial walking on eggshells. No matter how carefully you tread, shells are going to break and your feet are going to get cut. Better to suffer in silence and keep the criticisms to yourself, especially when you suspect the criticisms will only invite anger.

Chapter 30

Nature versus nurture. Which is the more important and influential in the end? It's an unanswerable question, in my opinion. Well, in everyone's opinion, I guess.

But it's a question that's been obsessing me ever since I took Gemma to visit my studio this morning. Ever since she's been back home with me, really. Face it. Except for those first weeks of Gemma's life, Alan has been the one in charge of the nurturing part. He's been the one in charge of the social training, the daily instruction, the forming of habits, and the gathering of opinions.

To a large extent, Gemma is Alan's product, just as all children are to a large extent the product of their parents' style of upbringing.

But I so want to find connections between Gemma and me! And I so want to find the Gemma who isn't tainted by Alan's peculiarities, even if that Gemma has, in the end, little to do with her mother.

What I don't want is for her to see my desperation to relate, to connect. I don't want her to despise me.

Gemma likes Gala apples. I don't know if she realized that the apples I brought home from the farmers' market the other day were Gala, but I watched as she devoured one after another of them (glad she was eating fruit and not candy) and saw that that was one small thing we have in common. A liking for Gala apples.

Then again, Gemma has "no use for art." And to a great extent, art—the making of it and the appreciation of it—is what defines me.

But there are the physical similarities that unite us, undeniable to anyone who really looks at us. The thick dark hair with the widow's peak. The large dark eyes. And Annie's pointed out that we cross our legs the same way. I never gave any thought to anyone crossing her legs in a way that is distinctive, but Annie swears she saw what she saw. Strangers see the resemblance too. The other day a clerk in the shoe department of Macy's, in the mall in South Portland (Gemma badly needed new footwear, and I've learned the hard way that it's more practical in the end to invest in a decent brand up front), asked, "What size sandal does your daughter wear?" He might have recognized us from the papers, but somehow I don't think that was what was going on, because his affect was polite but impersonal. Then, when we stopped into the Apple store, also in the mall, a place I'd been only once before and that was a few years back, one of the employees, someone I'd certainly never met before, said, "We're a bit backed up at the moment, but someone will be with you and your daughter shortly." Again, I didn't get the feeling we were being recognized as local celebrities. But who knows, maybe we were.

I don't know how Gemma feels about these incidents—well, yes, I do; she hates them; the eye rolling is one indication—but I love them, I hold them in my mind like one holds a precious gem in the palm of one's hand (not that I've ever held a precious gem), carefully, almost reverently. Our bodies and our faces, if nothing else, proclaim us family.

Does my daughter really have no sense of beauty? Has Alan never taken her to a museum or to a gallery or even to a run-of-the-mill arts and crafts fair? Or is this attitude of supreme indifference largely an act? (It hadn't seemed like an act in my

studio, that's for sure.) It's an attitude Gemma displays to almost everything I introduce to her, to almost everything I offer
her. The shrug. The whatever.

I know there are all sorts of reasons, and good ones at that,
why we haven't really begun to bond. But still, it hurts.

It hurts a lot.

Chapter 31

We were in town this morning. Verity had to coax me to come along—I think she's worried I'm going to do something stupid if I stay home alone, like accidentally set the house on fire or purposely set myself on fire—and by the time I agreed to come along, I was seriously annoyed with her. But at least she stopped bugging me.

We had just come out of the convenience store when this man about Dad's age coming into the store stopped right in front of us, and I swear, the look on his face made me think, *Oh crap, this guy is going to faint.*

Verity must have had the same thought, because she took the guy's arm and gently moved us all out of the doorway.

"Gemma," she said quietly. "This is Bill Morrison. He was one of the lead detectives on your—on the abduction case."

The man, who looked a little bit more alive now, put out his hand. I don't like touching people a lot, but I took it. I swear I felt it tremble, though it was a big, strong-looking hand.

"Retired now," he said. "I can't tell you how good it is to meet you. Of course I'd heard you'd come back to us. And I have to admit, I had to restrain the urge to go running over to your mother's house to be sure it was real. To be sure you were real."

I felt kind of embarrassed and awkward. Being the center of

attention isn't for me, but there was something really sincere about this guy so I smiled a bit and said, "Thanks." And then, suddenly, he started to cry. Not loud bawling, but real tears.

"I'm sorry," he said, wiping his cheeks with the back of his hand. "It's just that I've been carrying around this awful guilt all these years about not finding you. My own daughter was just about a year old at the time of the kidnapping. I guess you could say I took the case very personally."

I really was tongue-tied now. I tried to smile at him again, and I hope I did smile and not grimace by accident. Verity, I noticed then, was also crying. Crying was the last thing I felt like doing. I guess by then I was feeling kind of numb and confused.

The guy went off then, after shaking Verity's hand and wishing us well.

"He was so good to me," she said as we watched him go into the convenience store. "They all were, after I was cleared of suspicion."

That took me by surprise. "The police suspected you? But why? You weren't the one who disappeared. Dad was."

Verity sighed. "It was thought I might have killed you, and Alan. I might have conspired with Alan to take you and then plan to join you both later on. Though why I should do such a thing was always a mystery to me. The point is, the police are thorough. As they should be."

"Not thorough enough that they found us," I said, and then I wished I hadn't.

"No. Not thorough enough."

On the drive home I thought about how Cathy Strawberry has it so easy. Two parents right there. No complications like detectives and manhunts and a father in jail. And a dual identity. And a mother who was a suspect in a mysterious disappearance.

Here's something. Meeting that guy, the former detective, makes it all so real. I mean, sure, it's a fact that my father ran off with me—I'd have to be stupid to deny that when he himself admits it—but what I mean is, meeting the detective makes what happened to *Verity* much more real to me.

I snuck a look at her profile. She frowns a bit when she's driving. I guess she's concentrating. (I remembered how she told me she'd almost caused a bad accident that time because she wasn't focused on the road but on thoughts about my website.) Anyway, I can't help but think that if I allow myself to actually *like* Verity, I'll be being disloyal to Dad. I mean, he might be flawed, but he's still the guy who made me pancakes every Saturday morning and put a Band-Aid on my knee when I fell off my bike (the times when I had one). Actually, now that I think about it, Dad's kind of squeamish, so it was usually me who put the Band-Aid on while Dad cringed and said things like, "Please, please be all right"—but at least he cared. And he was the one who was *there*, and that should matter for something.

Then again, he was the one who was there because he abducted me from Verity. See? He didn't give her a choice. Too freakin' complicated.

I wonder if Dad ever realized Verity would be under suspicion of foul play. He must have. Maybe he didn't care. Well, of course he didn't care. He hated her. To hate somebody so much that you would . . .

You know what? I'm sick of thinking about it.

Chapter 32

Alan's mother called me this morning, as is her habit. Once a week, usually on a Tuesday, she calls me on my landline. If I'm not there to take the call, she leaves a message on voice mail, and I call her back that same day. It's our little routine.

"When can I meet her?" Marion asked after the preliminaries. "You will let me meet her?"

The need in her voice was touching. Once, I might have found it pathetic. But that was when I was furious with Marion for deceiving me about Alan's past. Now all I feel for her is sympathy.

"Of course you'll meet her," I said. "She's your granddaughter. How about you come over this Thursday afternoon, around three?"

Marion breathed what must have been a sigh of relief. "Thank you," she said. "Thank you so much."

After the call, I had a momentary twinge of misgiving. Things aren't exactly going swimmingly with Gemma and me. Maybe I should have postponed the meeting with her grandmother, given Gemma more time to adjust to her new life. Then again, how could meeting Marion cause any more damage than meeting the Strawbridges or Bill Morrison or the guy behind the counter at the convenience store? As long as Marion doesn't start going on about how wonderful Alan was—like she'd done with me in the old days, before things got so bad between her son and me. A doting mother's glossy view of her less than glossy son.

And I certainly am not going to tell Gemma that her grandmother kept her son's bad behavior and criminal past a secret from me. I doubt Marion would ever reveal such a thing either. She was ashamed of what she did to me, I know that, keeping me in ignorance while Alan became increasingly controlling and even abusive.

When I learned soon after the abduction that Marion had withheld Alan's past from me, all the while encouraging our relationship and pretending to be my friend, I lost it. I opened my mouth and screamed at Marion. I told her I never wanted to see her again. I told her to go to hell. And then I stormed off. Really, thinking back on that scene now, I'm mortified I behaved so badly. But at the time it seemed justified.

She tried to contact me after that awful encounter, even going so far as to wait for me outside work (shades of Alan's stalking days?), but I'm ashamed to say I ignored her pleas for reconciliation. Once I even yanked my arm out of her grasp when she grabbed ahold of me, tears streaming down her face.

It took a few years before I could bring myself to reach out again to her. And it wasn't because Yorktide is a small town and avoiding her was difficult, almost a chore, and it wasn't because in the end, getting along with a person is often a lot easier than not getting along. It was because I'd come to realize that in some ways Marion was also one of Alan's victims. I know I should have been able to see that from the start, but I hadn't been able to. Or maybe I'd been unwilling to embrace her as a fellow victim. But better late than never, right?

Is that always true? Will it prove to be better for Gemma that she was reunited with me, her mother? Or will it prove that meeting me, especially in these circumstances, is the worst thing that could have happened to her?

I don't know.

Chapter 33

"There's someone else who wants to meet you."

Great, I thought. Some gawking local yokel wants to see The Little Kidnapped Girl up close and personal. The detective guy, nice as he was, had already freaked me out. But I said nothing. It was bad enough, being stared at whenever Verity and I were in the grocery store or stopped at the gas station or even going through a tollbooth. I'm not kidding. Yesterday afternoon, when Verity couldn't find her E-ZPass thingy and we had to stop to pay the toll in cash somewhere in Kennebunk, I think, the lady in the booth practically fell out of it in her excitement at recognizing us. "You're the woman," she cried, pointing a long bony finger at us. "And you're the girl!" Verity didn't answer the woman and sped out of the booth and though she said nothing about the incident, I could see by how tight her hands were on the steering wheel that she was upset.

"It's your grandmother," Verity went on, when I didn't reply. "Your father's mother. Remember, I told you her name is Marion."

The woman I was told had been dead for twenty years. Like my mother was dead. I shrugged. "Whatever."

"You don't have to meet her, at least, not yet. If you want more time—"

"I said it's okay." I kind of yelled the words, but Verity didn't seem to care. Is she really that *good?* I know I've provoked her in the past weeks, but not once has she been rude back to me. Something's got to snap at some point.

"Good," she said. "I mean, I've told her to come over this Thursday at three, all right? She's been so eager to see you since you've been . . . Since you've been back."

Oh right, I thought. She knew me once. As much as you can *know* an infant. And of course, I have no recollection of her.

"So, are you guys close?" I asked, not that I really cared.

Verity didn't answer right away. Finally she said, "We once were very close. And then we were estranged. But we've become friends of a sort again. Allies, almost."

"Allies against my father?" I snapped. Again, Verity ignored my tone.

"No. I mean allies in loss. We've tried to help each other over the years."

"Why were you guys estranged? What happened?" This time, I did care about the answer.

But Verity just shook her head. "It doesn't matter now," she said. "It's in the past. Look, I really should be getting to my studio at the college. There's still so much to do before my show in July."

She looked at me then with an expression of concern. "Are you sure you don't want to come with me?"

"I'll be fine here."

"You have my cell phone number, right? Just call me if you need anything."

What? I thought. *Like a ticket back to Arizona?*

Finally she left, and I went out to the back deck and flopped onto one of the plastic lounge chairs. (There's no way I'm going to hang out on the front porch and be a public attraction.) I'd wanted her to go, I'd wanted to be left alone for a while, away from her suffocating concern, but it's odd. Almost as soon as I heard her car drive away, I realized I was lonely. But I wasn't sure and I'm still not sure what I felt lonely for.

Chapter 34

"I'll get it." Verity went to open the front door, and I waited in the kitchen. She had laid out milk and sugar for coffee, and there was a plate of oatmeal raisin cookies she had baked that morning. I snatched one before my mother and my grandmother got to the kitchen. Fortification or something. Not that I was nervous.

I don't know what I expected Marion to look like—I think I probably had no expectations, actually—but I was still kind of surprised. Here was this tiny little woman, not skinny like Verity, in fact, a bit fat, but not even five feet tall and with features that came straight from a rubber baby doll. Not literally. I mean, her face was soft and small, and her eyes are either way too big for her head or she keeps them wide open like that on purpose. I didn't want to stare at her to find out, but really, she has, I don't know, this air of defeat about her, like she'd long ago given up trying to fight back at life, or maybe like she'd never even known how to fight back. Anyway, she was wearing what reminded me of a leisure suit from the seventies, not as bad as that, but a matching, pale-blue short-sleeved jacket and pants, and she was clutching an enormous fabric patchwork bag to her chest. It struck me that she was using the bag as a sort of shield against what she thought was going to be a difficult meeting, and suddenly I wished I had a sort of shield too.

"Gemma," Verity said. "This is your grandmother."

"It's Marni," I said. "Hi."

Marion took a small step forward, and for one horrible second I thought she might want to hug or kiss me. But she stopped, and I saw her eyes had gone all watery.

"I can hardly believe it's you," she said.

Something possessed me to be a bit of a jerk. "Believe it," I said with obviously false brightness. "It's me. Marni Armstrong, in the flesh."

Marion was clearly flustered, so Verity led her to the table and sat her across from me. Did she think if she sat Marion next to me I'd scratch her or something? Marion and I sat there in silence while Verity chattered about the weather or something as insipid—I wasn't really listening—and brought a pot of coffee to the table. I like coffee. I've been drinking it since I was about ten. When Marion saw me pour a cup for myself, she smiled.

"Your father always loved coffee," she said. "Does he . . . Does he still?"

I nodded. "Dad doesn't look like you."

"No. He takes after his father. Two peas in a pod. Look." Marion began to rummage through that huge bag of hers, and finally she extracted a small leather wallet-type thing, inside of which were old snapshots. She extracted one from the pile and handed it to me. "That's Albert, when he was about your father's age now."

I studied the photo of a man who could have been Dad's double. It was weird, seeing my father's father, my grandfather. I handed the picture back to Marion. "Thanks," I said, reaching again for the coffeepot.

"I hope you like it here, Gemma," Marion said now. "Sorry. Marni. I mean, I hope you like it here in Maine. It must be very different from what you're used to. Not that I know much about Arizona, places like that. I've never traveled, you see. Not farther than Connecticut."

"Yeah," I said. "It's different."

Marion looked disappointed that I wasn't chattering on. I knew I wasn't making it easy for this woman who was my grandmother. You're supposed to respect your grandparents. And this woman looked so—insignificant. Like if you closed your eyes for thirty seconds and then reopened them, she'd be gone as if she'd never been there. I looked quickly to Verity and saw she was frowning. Only slightly, but still. And then I felt kind of bad for Marion, Dad's mother. It couldn't have been easy for her, knowing—suspecting—that your only child had stolen your only grandchild, and now he was sitting in a jail cell somewhere, alone and possibly the victim of seriously violent criminal types with nicknames like Killer or Blood 'n' Guts.

"I'll adjust," I said. "Being close to the ocean is nice, I guess." Especially, I thought, since I'd never seen it in real life before. And because I almost passed out at how amazing and beautiful it is.

Marion's face lit up. "Your father used to love going to the beach when he was a boy. He used to build the most beautiful sand castles. Intricate, they were. I don't know how he managed it. And nobody taught him, either."

Verity raised her eyebrows. "I never knew that," she said. "He never mentioned it."

I said nothing. So my father had loved the beach. I loved the beach. And I was wrestling with the image of my father as a child, a little boy kneeling by the water, constructing a sand castle. I'd never thought he had much imagination, not the adult I know. Where had it gone? I wondered if he ever thought of those times, when he was small. I wondered if he ever missed those days before everything got all complicated. Before he messed things up.

Marion asked me a bunch more questions about Dad and about me. Did I have a recent picture of him? I went into my room and brought back my one photo of Dad and me. Marion looked at it for a long time before asking her next questions. Was he in good health? I shrugged and said, "I guess so. He never goes to doctors." Did I enjoy school? "It's all right," I said.

"I do okay." Did I like art, like my talented mother? I shook my head. "No."

It went on like that for a while, with Verity sitting silently except for when she asked us if we wanted more coffee. Marion said no and I said yes. Finally, after about an hour (which seemed like six hours), Marion got up to leave.

"I hope I'll see you again soon," she said. She sounded almost wistful and unsure, as if I might really refuse to see her. Well, I hadn't been particularly warm and fuzzy toward her, had I? But was I supposed to be?

"Sure," I said.

Verity walked Marion to the door, and I stayed sitting at the kitchen table. A few minutes later Verity was back.

"It's been hard on her," she said quietly. I think it was meant as a reproach.

"Yeah. She's . . ." But I didn't know what I wanted to say.

Verity began to gather the cups, the milk, and the sugar. "Hamburgers for dinner, okay?"

I nodded and went off to my room, suddenly feeling like I might start to cry. I lay down on the couch and stared up at the white ceiling. It could have been worse, I suppose. And it was only as bad as it was because of my lousy attitude.

My hands were shaking from all the coffee.

Chapter 35

Alan building sand castles. Now there was a thought. During the four years of our relationship, all he'd ever done was at best ignore and at worst insult my creative work. What had happened to him from the time he was that little boy playing with sand and broken shells and the time he was the young man I was planning to marry?

Well, there's no point in wasting any time on that sort of speculation. The fact is that I don't really care about Alan's transformation from a state of innocence to a state of . . . well, whatever state he's been in for all his adult life.

There were some sticky moments, but overall the meeting between Gemma and Marion went all right. I would have liked there to have been a Hallmark reunion—Gemma and Marion falling into each other's arms—but those don't come very often in life and possibly never when there's been something as bizarre as the return of a kidnap victim who, until a few weeks ago, had no idea she'd been kidnapped.

And I really do have to find the right way to suggest to Gemma that she not drink so much coffee. Four cups in the space of an hour seems extreme. But maybe she'd drunk so much because she was nervous. Not that coffee was the thing to calm anyone down. At least I hadn't caught her sneaking the vodka.

At dinner Gemma announced she wasn't prepared to call

Marion Grandma. *Of course not,* I thought, *not when you can't even bring yourself to call me Mom.*

"I'm sure she'll understand," I said, not at all sure she would.

"Was Dad nice to her?" Gemma asked, poking at her broccoli—her hamburger was already half eaten—and not meeting my eye.

What a question! Was it nice of a child to encourage his mother to conceal his troubled past from someone—in this case, me—who might very well become a victim in the present? But here I was, also concealing Alan's troubled past from our daughter. At least, I thought, she's out of his clutches. For now.

"He was dutiful," I said. "He visited her once a week and brought flowers on her birthday and Mother's Day. That sort of thing."

Gemma nodded and pushed a piece of broccoli around the rim of her plate. "It's true he's an only child?"

"Yes. And so am I. I'm afraid you have no aunts or uncles or cousins."

Can you guess what Gemma did? That's right. She shrugged and said, "Whatever."

Chapter 36

I was on the back deck, lying on the plastic lounge chair I'd claimed as my own, my eyes closed and a glass of iced tea on a small table close-by, when suddenly this chipper voice broke through my thoughts. I was thinking about how I haven't had pizza in a long time. And I bet if I told Verity I wanted pizza for dinner, she'd run right out and bring back two extra-large ones with every topping I'd requested.

"Hi, Marni!" the voice said. I opened my eyes to see Cathy Strawberry standing at the foot of my lounge. She was wearing a Pepto-Bismol pink T-shirt and white jeans. I would never wear pink or white.

"How did you get here?" I asked. "Do you have a car?" That would be cool, I thought. I mean, I don't really like Cathy all that much—even though she does remember to call me by my real name, by which I mean the name I know myself by— but I could pretend enough if she were willing to drive us around.

"Bike," she said. "I'm only fifteen, remember? I don't have my license."

So much for that. "What do you want?" I asked.

Cathy shrugged and plopped onto the lounge chair next to mine. "Nothing. Just to say hi."

"Well, hi."

Neither of us said anything else for a while, which was fine by me. And then, out of the blue, Cathy said: "You don't seem very happy here."

I laughed. "Not happy? I'm miserable." That was an exaggeration—sort of—but sometimes I just can't help myself. Maybe I should go into acting someday.

"Oh," she said. "I'm sorry. You're not going to—"

"What? Are you worried I'm going to jump off a bridge or something?"

"No, of course not!" she cried. "I was going to say you're not going to run away, are you?"

"I said I was miserable, not stupid. So I stick it out here until I turn eighteen, if Verity can continue to pretend she loves me, and then I'll be on my way." I laughed again. "She'll probably even pay me to take off. Call it my inheritance or something."

Cathy looked extremely uncomfortable. "She *does* love you. She's not pretending."

And I wondered if Verity had been talking about me, about our relationship, to Cathy. That bothered me. My life belongs to me, not to these strangers. "Whatever. Anyone in this dopey little town ever run away?"

"Not that I know of. Well, there's this one girl in town who ran away from somewhere in Vermont a few years back, but she and her father are living here together now."

"A happy ending?"

"They do happen," Cathy said, and it was clear she really believes that.

"I knew two people who took off." Hmm, I thought. Why am I telling her this? "One was a guy I sort of hung out with for a while. He wasn't a friend or anything, just sort of always there. Anyway, he tried to kill himself a few times, but it never worked out. He was such a loser. I mean, how hard is it to kill yourself?"

"Maybe he didn't really want to die," Cathy said. "Maybe

it was a cry for help. We had a course about depression and bullying and suicide in middle school. I think it's pretty common, not succeeding in a suicide attempt."

Does she really believe you can learn about that stuff in school? "Well," I said, "whatever happened, one day he left. No note, just cleared out some of his stuff from his stepmother's house—his father had died—and left."

"If he didn't leave a note, how did anyone know for sure he'd run away?" Cathy asked. "How did they know he hadn't finally succeeded in killing himself?"

It wasn't an unreasonable question. "They knew he'd run off," I told her, "because people had seen him leaving town. After about two or three months the police tracked him down in Albuquerque. He was living in some squalid apartment with a bunch of other kids who'd run away from home. And he was working as a male hooker."

Cathy's hand shot to her mouth. "That's awful!" she cried. "The poor boy! What happened to him then?"

"The police hauled him home to his stepmother. A few weeks later he was dead. Seems he finally figured out how to kill himself after all. I guess those other kids he was living with in that dump taught him a few tricks other than how to get paid for sex."

Cathy sat back in her lounge.

"You look shocked," I said.

"I am," she admitted. "You know stuff like that happens, but . . . I've never actually met anyone who knew someone . . ."

"You wanna know what happened to the other person I knew who took off? Her name was Gerri."

"No. I don't."

"Why not?" I asked, and I could feel the evil jerk part of me stirring. I had an overwhelming desire to antagonize her. "It might do you some good."

"What kind of good would it do me?" Cathy demanded, with more force than I'd expected. "And I can't help those people you knew, can I?"

"Your life is so cushy here," I went on. "So insulated. What gives you the right to ignore the crappy lives other people are forced to live?"

"I'm not ignoring them!" Cathy protested. "My mom and I volunteer at the food bank in town. And we shop at the store that gives all its proceeds to the day shelter at the Baptist church. It's just that your telling me about those people you knew—the *way* you're telling it—doesn't serve any other purpose than . . . than to hurt me. You're trying to make me feel bad about my life."

I wondered: So that I could feel better about mine? That didn't seem right. I said nothing.

Cathy got up now from the lounge. "One more thing. If that guy was such a loser, the one who ran away and then committed suicide, why did you hang out with him in the first place?"

Cathy didn't wait for a reply, which was good because I didn't have one ready. She just walked off and left me feeling suddenly deflated and like the jerk that I am.

I'll tell you, Cathy Strawberry might be a lot of things, but she's obviously not a jerk. Not with the sort of relationship she has with her mother. Not if the two of them really do stuff together like volunteer at the food bank. (I didn't even know Yorktide had a food bank or people who needed it.) *Someone who's a jerk probably isn't capable of a good relationship with anyone*, I thought, *let alone with her mother.*

The sun was hurting my eyes. I put my hands over them.

His name was Kirk. That guy who finally killed himself. He wasn't really a loser. Actually, he was kind of nice. He could be funny. I felt bad when I heard he was dead.

Chapter 37

"I met your mother," I said into the phone. "My grandmother."

It was the second scheduled call from Dad. Verity was in her little studio upstairs. Every so often I could hear one of the wooden floorboards creak over my head.

"Oh," he said, and he sounded wary. "How is she?"

"Happy you're alive. Not so much that you're in jail."

"Yeah." That was followed by a nervous laugh.

"Dad? You never called her after . . . after we left Maine? She was probably really worried."

"I know," he said. "I felt bad about that. But I had no choice."

There's always a choice, I thought. He could have sent postcards, something. All you had to do was look at Marion and know she would never have told the police where they could find her son. Even if it had meant keeping Verity in the dark. I'm not the most sensitive person around, but even I can read someone like Marion Burns pretty clearly.

"So," I said, thinking I'd better change the subject before I got really annoyed, "how do you spend the time? I mean, does the day drag?"

"Sometimes. But there's the meals and time for exercise. That passes the time."

"Dad? Why did you tell me your parents were dead?" So

much for changing the subject. "Okay, I know your *father* really is dead but—"

"Because then you might have wanted to meet your grand-mother. And that wasn't possible."

True. I might have wanted to meet her. But he could have chosen to tell me that Marion was as violent a drug addict loser as Verity. Was one lie better, more effective than the other? Both lies had kept me from my family. None of it makes any sense to me. Sometimes I wonder if it ever will.

"Marion showed me a picture of your father. And she told me that you used to like building sand castles when you were a kid."

"What else did she say about me?" he asked, and now there was a distinct note of alarm in his voice.

"Nothing," I said. "Not much."

I thought I heard him sigh. "Good. Okay."

I wanted to ask him if he was sorry for what he did, but I didn't know where to begin. Sorry for abducting me? Sorry for lying to me about practically everything, including my own name? Sorry for hurting Verity and Marion? Sorry for stealing a car? And something else held me back from asking the question, and that was the answer he might give. No. Not sorry.

Luckily, the guard cut off the call after Dad and I had exchanged a few more banalities. I felt suddenly exhausted and wanted nothing more than to take a nap. But when I tried to relax and close my eyes and let sleep come, it wouldn't. I got up and went to find Verity.

Chapter 38

"Why did you leave my father?" I demanded. Verity was still in her studio upstairs. She whipped around from her drawing board and put her hand over her heart.

"You startled me," she said with a small smile. "I was so focused . . ."

Focused on trying to hear my conversation with Dad through the floor vent? I wondered.

"The short answer? I left for the sake of your safety and your future."

I laughed. "Didn't it ever occur to you that it might have been better to *stay* for my safety and future? Dad wasn't a bad man. He didn't hit you, you told me so. He didn't mistreat me, right? So why couldn't you have just stuck it out? Then he wouldn't have been forced to do what he did. It's your fault, really, that he took me away. You gave him no choice. He was afraid he'd never see me again if he let you take me."

Verity put down the pencil she had still been holding. When she spoke, her voice trembled a bit. "I did consider staying in the relationship," she said. "Of course I did. I weighed all the options, pros and cons, and in the end . . . I know I did what I thought was best."

I snickered. "Yeah, well, obviously, what you thought was wrong."

Then Verity finally lost her temper. Just a bit. "I don't owe you an explanation of my thoughts and behavior," she said. "I'm your mother. Please try to have some respect for me."

"You're only my mother in name," I shot back.

Verity went pale. "More than just in name," she said, "whether you like that fact or not. And you should understand that, and if you can't make yourself understand, then you should at least accept that I always did what I thought was best for you, without demanding to know every painful detail of my thought process."

Well, I thought, *at least she can stand up for herself.* And then I turned and stomped—literally—out of her studio and down the stairs, back to my room. Where, of course, I slammed the door behind me.

I can be very predictable.

Chapter 39

I felt bad I had lost my temper with Gemma. I felt bad I had played the pity card. Poor me. But it was bound to happen at some point. Still, that's no consolation.

It's become a pattern. Alan calls Gemma. And then Gemma challenges or attacks me. I suppose it's not a surprise that his calls have such a powerful aftershock. At the very least they must emphasize the enormous difference between what was and what is.

And she must have so many questions! I know I still do, though I doubt I would ever get any coherent answers from Alan. Once, I thought I would welcome the chance to confront him face-to-face, to demand an explanation, an apology. But now, when the dream has come true—Alan located and in the process of being punished, Gemma home safely with me—now the last thing I want to do is speak with him, even via phone or letter. I don't want to hear what he has to say. In some ways, I no longer care.

Gemma assumed that her father had never mistreated her. But how to explain the time he grabbed her out of my arms and she came very close to falling to the hard wooden floor? He'd taken a big risk for no apparent reason—for no good reason, just his own warped vision of his world. It was something I could never tell Gemma. It was the turning point, the moment when I knew I had to leave and take my baby with me.

How to describe the mingled feelings of relief and loss, of sadness and euphoria I experienced those first days away from Alan? The situation at Barbara's wasn't ideal. Gemma and I were in a small interior room without a window (it's illegal to use a room without a window as a bedroom, but I didn't know that then), and I worried that if Gemma woke at night and made a fuss, Barbara's sleep would be disturbed and she would regret her decision to let us stay. And Barbara had two dogs, mixed breeds, both with long, shaggy fur, and though I love animals as much as the next person, as I said earlier, I'm very allergic to many of them. But Barbara was letting me stay with her in exchange only for my cleaning up after Gemma and myself and doing our laundry, so I wasn't going to complain about sneezing fits.

When after a few days it seemed that Alan was handling my defection with an unexpected degree of maturity—no midnight hang-ups, no hate mail, no dead animals left on Barbara's doorstep—I suggested we meet on neutral ground, a public place, just us two. The first meeting went well. When I saw him walk into the diner I'd chosen as our meeting place, I had to fight back the tears. I had loved this man so much and for so long. I had given him so much of myself. I had given him a child.

After that we met for coffee a few more times. And when at one point he asked if he could see Gemma, in my presence, in a public place, I said yes and took her with me when we went to the diner and to the park on my afternoon off. Alan didn't demand more visits with his daughter—of course he didn't, not when he was planning all along to steal her for himself!—and for the first time in years I saw some of the sweet, charming Alan from the early days, the man who had seemed to be taking care of me because he loved me, not because he needed to control me.

I allowed myself to be lulled into a state of less than hypervigilance.

And I've been paying for it ever since.

Chapter 40

There was another thing that was bound to happen. I'm sure we both knew it would someday.

Mirelle Turner is a fixture in Yorktide, a woman in her mid-sixties now who lives in a lovely cottage out on Cherry Hill Lane. In all my years in Yorktide I've never known her to hold a job; how she paid for that charming little house was anyone's guess, as there was no other outward evidence of a healthy private source of income. The woman dressed in clothing she must have kept from the seventies, and there were times when standing behind her on line at the convenience store was an odiferous experience. A literal filthy-rich eccentric? Maybe.

I best knew her as a particularly ridiculous woman, the sort who regularly offends almost everyone with whom she speaks by saying the one thing most likely to cause pain. I don't think she's entirely conscious of the effect she has on others. I think she's just very stupid. Fortunately for mankind, she never procreated, at least, not as far as I know.

Now she rushed toward us, waving her hand madly as if we could possibly miss her. There was no way we could avoid a confrontation without being downright rude, turning away, and hurrying off, an incident she would embroider and circulate throughout the town of Yorktide by nightfall. I felt my grip on the strap of my handbag tighten.

"I'm so glad I caught you!" Mirelle cried, putting her right hand on Gemma's arm and her left hand on mine. Instinctively, rude or not, we both stepped out of her grasp. She turned her attention to Gemma. "I've been just dying to know. What was it like, finding out you'd been kidnapped?"

"Who the hell are you?" Gemma snapped, and I opened my mouth to intervene. But before I could, Gemma said: "And what kind of a fucked-up question is that?"

I winced. Mirelle Turner's eyes grew to the size of the proverbial saucers, and for once in her life she seemed to be without something idiotic to say. In sync, Gemma and I walked around her, leaving her stock-still in the middle of the sidewalk. I know because I couldn't resist looking over my shoulder once we were at the corner.

"I told you about your unfortunate status as a local celebrity," I said quietly as we waited for the light to turn green. I could feel the anger emanating from my daughter. "I'm sorry you had to experience it in that particularly obnoxious way. If it's any consolation, Mirelle Turner's got a reputation as, well, as being a very stupid woman."

"I know just what that woman is thinking right now," Gemma said bitterly as we stepped into the street. "She's thinking, what happened to that sweet little baby girl? That helpless little victim we've all been so worried about. How did she get to be such a bitch? The little victim is supposed to be all grateful and humble. And she's also probably wondering if I was sexually abused or if I was used in a bunch of bizarre rituals with chicken blood and I don't know, ceremonial knives or something."

I couldn't argue with Gemma's assessment. "Yes," I said. "You're probably right. But as I said, she's a stupid woman." Which is not to say that some people in town didn't listen to her rattling and rantings and inane remarks. No doubt the tale of Gemma's less than gracious response to Mirelle's insensitive question would circulate rapidly. At that moment I didn't care one bit. I still don't.

Of course I'd considered the possibility of taking Gemma away from Yorktide, but for several reasons I'd decided it wasn't a good idea. Most obviously, I'd have to sell my house and give up my job, and who knew if I'd ever be able to afford to buy us a house of our own and get a good enough job to keep us in medical insurance and buy the other necessities. But more important, Gemma has spent her entire life on the run—even if she hadn't quite known it—and I just don't think running away again is the answer for her. I knew from the moment she came home to me that I would have to trust the good people of Yorktide to give Gemma the time and space she needs to settle into a steady life among them. And so far, with the exception of Mirelle Turner, people have responded well to my requests for privacy, even that guy from the church who wanted to give Gemma a party.

"Come on," I said. "Let's go home."

I was acutely aware of how that last word—*home*—hung in the air between us.

Chapter 41

Annie and Cathy came over for an hour or two this afternoon. The four of us were on the back deck—the awning fully extended against the sun, which even in Maine can burn skin to a crisp—drinking iced tea and talking about nothing and everything. Well, Gemma was drinking iced coffee and not saying much other than the occasional yes or no. I wish I knew exactly what she's thinking when she goes all quiet. Was she always this way? Or is this new behavior, brought about by the discovery that she isn't the person she thought she was?

"Look!" Cathy cried, pointing toward the Gallisons' house. "The twins!"

"What are their names again?" Annie asked. "I am so bad with names."

"Molly and Michael Gallison. The parents are Peter and Grace." I waved at Grace, who waved back.

"Oh my God, they are so cute, I can't stand it." Cathy turned to Gemma then. "Don't you just love little kids?"

Gemma shrugged. "Not really. I mean, why?"

Well, I thought, *at least she's using her words.*

"Just because they're so cute!"

"I've never really been around little kids," Gemma said. "A girl I knew once had a half brother who was ten years younger.

She always got stuck babysitting him when her mother wanted to party. Which was, like, all the time."

My hand tightened around my glass. What sort of people had my daughter grown up among? Of course, there's nothing I can do about her past now except try to make things better for her future.

Cathy sighed. "I can't wait to have kids of my own."

"Not before you've finished college and have a good job," Annie said.

"Duh, of course!"

"I'm not ever having kids," Gemma said. "They take up all your time."

Except, I thought, *when they're stolen from you, and all you dream about is getting them back and never letting them out of your sight ever.*

"Do you ever think about that nursery song, the one that starts with 'Rock-a-bye, baby, on the tree top'?" Annie said. "I mean, how is that supposed to comfort anyone, let alone a child? The bough breaking, the cradle falling to the ground, the impact probably crushing the baby to death."

"Mom, you're so weird! It's just a song."

Annie gave Gemma and me a conspiratorial look. "This is the respect I get. I cook, I clean, I put up with a bunch of kids who want to be anywhere else but math class, and what do I get? I get called weird by my own daughter."

Cathy jumped up from her chair—the adults had the lounges—and bent down to give her mother a hug. "And one for you too," she said, coming over to me.

And the moment Cathy put her arms around me, I was intensely aware of the contrast my daughter and I present to Annie and Cathy.

Cathy went back to her chair, and while she and Annie talked about what they were going to get Marc for his birthday and Gemma sat silently, thinking whatever it was she was thinking, I thought about how I want nothing more than to hug my prickly daughter and not have her stiffen in my arms. She tolerates it when I touch her arm when I want to point something out to her when we're in the car or walking in town. But anything more than that would be unwelcome. You don't have to be particularly sensitive to see her resistance to touch in the way she holds herself, the way she folds her arms across her chest even when she's sitting alone, halfway across a room from the nearest person. And the look on her face . . . Maybe that's why when I first introduced Gemma to Annie, Annie made no attempt to touch her. She saw. Cathy, not insensitive but with the exuberance of youth, flung her arms around Gemma, who stood, her own arms at her sides, her lips a thin line of—was it really anger? Maybe it was fear. I don't know.

I was brought back to the moment by the piercing wail of one of the children next door.

"Uh-oh, Molly fell," Cathy announced. "Poor little thing! I'm sure her mommy will kiss it and make it all better."

Gemma got up from her chair. "I'm going inside."

Chapter 42

It was probably rude of me to just get up and walk away from everyone like that, but jeez, Cathy going on about the kids next door was driving me crazy. It had brought back this memory I'd thought was long gone. I wish it really were gone.

Thing is, I don't know how I can remember something that must have happened when I was in, like, first grade or maybe even kindergarten. I could have made it up, I suppose, but why would I? Or it could be something I saw happen to someone else or maybe on TV, and later on my brain made me think it was a memory of something that had happened to me. I'm not a neurosurgeon or a psychiatrist, so I don't know.

Anyway, this is what happened or didn't. Dad and I were in a grocery store, and he was looking at the big table of bananas. I wandered away a bit, not far (I was very attached to Dad in those early days), and was looking at the apples or pears or something when this woman came up to me and said, "You have such beautiful hair." Then she reached out to touch my hair, and I just stood there, kind of stunned, I guess. Then the woman said, "But your mommy should have brushed it better this morning. Look, there's a big tangle."

And suddenly in my memory Dad was there, and he was furious. "Don't touch my daughter!" he yelled, and the woman scurried off, probably afraid he was going to hit her.

And that's it. But when Cathy was going on about Molly and Michael, I remembered the incident. And I also remembered that when Dad asked what the woman had said to me, all I said was, "You have nice hair." I didn't tell him the mommy part. I thought it would make him feel bad, that he wasn't my mommy and that he had done something wrong by not brushing my hair enough.

See? Wasn't I too young to make that judgment and to have those feelings or insights? So maybe the incident never happened.

Funny about the hair, though. It seems I got my hair, thick and dark and straight, from Verity.

Mommy.

Anyway, I don't believe in maternal instinct. I mean, come on. Take a look around. How many women with kids even really wanted them in the first place? How many times do you see a woman yank her kid's arm when he's being stubborn and won't walk as fast as she wants him to, or yell at her kid when he won't stop crying? I've seen that sort of thing a lot, and you can't tell me those women are really glad they had kids.

Maybe I'm a selfish person but the idea of always having to sacrifice for someone else who probably doesn't even appreciate what you're doing sounds ridiculous. I want stuff for me.

Besides, who says I'm qualified to be a decent parent? Isn't it like an extreme act of ego to think you're smart enough to have a kid and not screw him up entirely? There should be a test or something to determine who's allowed to have kids and who isn't.

Would Dad have failed that test?

I bet there were times when Verity was glad I wasn't around, pestering her and using up her time and her money. Now that I'm back, she pretty much has to pretend she's glad, at least until next year when I'm eighteen and she doesn't have to care any longer.

But there was the website.

All right. I'm being a jerk for some reason. Maybe I'm cold.

Not entirely. I mean, I feel stuff. But maybe not as much as most people. Normal people. Maybe I was born this way, or maybe something happened early on to make me—hard. But what? Dad was always good to me, and he obviously loves me.

But he was lying to me all along. Do you think it's possible I sensed that at the bottom of our life together, there was this massive lie, and that's what made me not give a shit about stuff I probably should have given a shit about?

Sometimes lately I feel like I'm driving myself crazy, thinking too much. But there's so much to think about.

Like how Cathy Strawberry is one of those touchy-feely types. I bet she's like that with people she's not super close to, like just an acquaintance at school. Some people are like that; they have no boundaries, and they don't respect the boundaries of other people. Either way, it's obvious Cathy considers Verity close, maybe even a friend, because she's always touching her or saying something just to her—telling secrets?—when other people are around. And Verity doesn't seem to mind it one bit. I know she must be thinking, *Why isn't my daughter more like my friend's daughter?* and frankly, it pisses me off. Why can't people just accept me for me?

Dad's an affectionate guy. At least with me he is. Was. He was always hugging me or trying to. He couldn't pass me on the way out of the kitchen without laying a hand briefly on my shoulder or kissing the top of my head. I often got the feeling he had to touch me to make really sure I was actually there, that I was his. Now, don't get me wrong. There was never, ever anything at all gross about Dad's touching me. I think he'd die before ever even thinking of being sexual with me. But he's a touchy-feely parent. That's actually nice when you're little. It's comforting, reassuring. But when you're not so little, believe me, it gets seriously annoying. And he'd be all huggy and kissy in front of what few kids I ever had to our apartment or house or wherever it was we were living. It was embarrassing. I know it was only his way of showing he loved me, especially when he wasn't able to do things like buy us a house of our own or a car less than fifteen years old that wasn't about to disintegrate from all the rust. With Verity, I have no desire to be close, physically or emotionally. That first time we met, at the hotel by the airport, I'd tolerated the quick hug. Barely. She got the message, releasing me as if I were on fire. Now she doesn't make many attempts.

Still, now that there's no one to put a hand on my shoulder, I sometimes feel . . . What? Lonely? Bereft? Kind of like I don't really exist. Maybe if we had a dog or a cat, it wouldn't be so bad, but Verity's allergic so that's the end of that. (Dad had always said we couldn't afford a cat or a dog and we probably couldn't, but I finally decided that the real reason he didn't bring home a pet for me was that he figured it would steal my attention away from him. Crazy but true.) There's always a guy, of course. I mean, I don't know anyone here yet, and I don't see how I'm going to get to know anyone other than the people Verity wants me to meet unless I walk the freakin' three miles to town and back, with everyone staring at me and wondering who I'm going to curse out next. I can't wait to get a car of my own. But in the meantime, if I can manage to meet someone, I could at least have sex. And that always makes you feel—at least for a few minutes—like you exist. Like you're *there*.

I wonder what Verity would think if she knew I've been having sex since I was fourteen. I wonder what Cathy would think. Not that I'm going to tell either one of them anytime soon. My life is really nobody's business but my own. It used to be Dad's business too, but now . . . now he's forfeited the right to be part of my life, hasn't he? Or has he?

Almost a week to go before his next call.

Chapter 43

This morning Verity took me to see the high school where I'll be enrolling in the fall. It was a warm and sunny morning, but even with not a cloud in the sky and French toast for breakfast (she used this bread called challah, which I'd never heard of before; it was pretty good), I couldn't work up any enthusiasm for the venture. I mean, school is school, right? From the outside Yorktide Memorial High School (that's its official name, but Verity said people usually just say Yorktide High) looks pretty much like a lot of the schools I went to—square and boring. Like a prison. I have to admit that the inside is a lot nicer than most of the schools I went to. All of the schools, actually.

The woman who guided us around the place, Aida Collins, is a Spanish teacher there. Verity said she knows her through Aida's husband, who works at the college in administration. Aida—she told me I could call her that and not Ms. Collins—has this chipper personality and she looks like one of the characters from that hilarious cartoon show *Bob's Burgers*. I mean, she has no chin! I can't imagine how I'm going to keep a straight face if I wind up in her class this fall.

Verity introduced me as her daughter, Gemma Peterson-Burns. I didn't bother to correct her. I could go on calling myself Marni for the rest of my life if I wanted to—I don't care much about the Armstrong—and I could go on asking people to call me Marni, but I guess I have to accept that for now my legal, official name is Gemma Peterson-Burns. A hyphenated last name. It makes me sound like I'm British or something, and rich. I don't care about being British, but that last part's not too bad.

Anyway, Aida led us through science labs, regular classrooms, the gym, the library, the auditorium, and the cafeteria, all the while going on about academic standing and good results of standardized tests and the percentage of graduates who go on to college and a bunch of other stuff that didn't interest me in the least. Verity seemed to be paying attention, as she said things like, "Oh, really?" and "That's impressive." Then Aida Collins took us outside and showed us the playing fields.

"There's a girls' soccer team and track and lacrosse," she said. "Football games are held every Friday night and are a big social event for the school. Most everyone comes out to cheer our boys on. When there's an away game, we rent a bus for those students who can't get a ride from a parent."

"That sounds like fun," Verity said, looking to me to agree with her.

"I'm not into sports," I said flatly. That's not a lie.

Aida went on brightly, as if I hadn't spoken. "You'll be given a laptop, of course, which you'll return at the end of the school year. It's only for use for homework and research, but most people have a personal computer at home for other purposes."

"Yes," Verity said. "We've got one."

We've, I thought. *Now Verity and I are a we?*

"I know it's hard to transfer schools," Aida was saying then. "We have a wonderful staff of counselors to help our students adjust to all sorts of challenges."

"Transferring isn't hard for me," I said bluntly. "I do it all the time." *Well*, I thought, *I used to do it all the time.* Who knows how long I'll be at this school; it's possible I'll be here until I graduate.

Verity looked uncomfortable, and neither of them said anything more. We said good-bye to Aida Collins after that. Neither of us spoke on the drive home, though once, Verity pointed out a very tall old man walking an enormous white fluffy dog. "That's Tarquin," she said. "The dog, I mean. Isn't he beautiful?"

Tarquin was beautiful, but I just grunted and went back to my thoughts. I was trying to figure out how many different schools I'd attended over the years and was coming in at around twelve to fourteen.

The thing is, I'm naturally smart, so it wasn't really hard for me to catch up with the rest of the class if they had gotten ahead of where we'd been at my old school. And more than once, I was way ahead of my new class, sometimes because I'd already read on and looked up a bunch of information on whatever topic we were studying because I was so unbelievably bored by the way the teacher kept us creeping along at the pace of the dumbest kid in the class.

I'm not only smart, I'm tough by nature too—or maybe that came with living with someone like my father; I mean, did I instinctively know he wasn't the strongest or smartest father around and so I learned to rely a lot on my own strengths and intelligence? Anyway, by tough I don't mean that I would pick fights or look for trouble; just that when someone picked a fight with me or trouble came my way no matter how hard I'd tried to avoid it, well, pretty much I could handle things. Like in almost every single new school I went to, there was someone in my grade—usually a girl—who wanted to make me suffer for being new and who tried to bully me into submission or, at least, make my life uncomfortable if not unbearable.

I remember this one chick who had it in for me from the moment she first saw me. Her name was Megan, though everyone called her Mo, and she was the female version of the classic bully from old movies, big and kind of stupid looking but mean enough that no one would dare to make fun of her for being either fat or dumb. And unlike what most girl bullies are supposed to be like—cunning and doing a lot of damage behind a person's back—she was right out there with her attitude. I hadn't been at that school long, maybe a month, when one day as I was leaving the building after detention (it was no big deal—I hadn't done some homework), Mo suddenly blocked my path. There was a girl on either side of her, but really, Mo was so big, she didn't need the backup. She said, "I don't think you want to go this way," and she grinned like she'd said something smart or funny. I said nothing and turned around to walk back inside the building and leave through another door—I'm not stupid enough to take on a fight I can't win—and boom, she shoved me and I fell to the rough pavement, landing on my knees and my palms but mostly on my chin.

All I felt at that moment of impact was sheer rage. But somehow—being tough—I controlled my fury and got up, half expecting to be knocked down again. "Gonna tell on me?" she taunted when I turned back around to face her. "Gonna report me?" "No," I said, wiping blood and grit from my chin. And then I turned my back on her again and walked through the door I'd come out from.

Whether she respected me after that, I had no idea and I didn't care; all that mattered was, she never bothered me again. When I got home, Dad saw my face and turned as pale as a sheet of paper in a notebook. I helped him to sit in our one old armchair that we had for a while and got him to put his head between his knees until he felt more normal. I told him I was fine and that I'd tripped and fallen. An accident was all it was. I still have the scar, by the way. It's the one Verity asked about; I lied to her about how I got it. I don't want to give her any ammunition against Dad. She has enough already. Anyway, maybe the cut should have been stitched. Dad didn't suggest it at the time and I wasn't eager to go running off to the hospital, so I just let the cut mend on its own.

Can you imagine what Cathy Strawberry would have done if she had been the one knocked down by that chick? Gone running to the principal and her parents and maybe even to the police and made a big stink of it all and made it worse for herself in the end because who would respect her? What kids, I mean. I know that's what you're "supposed" to do—tell an adult if someone's bullying you—but come on. If I had told an adult what had really happened, I wouldn't have been able to go anywhere in that crappy little town without being taunted and knocked around. My life would have been hell.

I didn't like to always have to defend my right to be there among all those kids who'd been together since forever. It was exhausting. I just wanted to get through the day and get out of the building and get home to Dad—or, sometimes better, to an empty apartment where I could do as I liked.

But also in every school there would emerge a few other kids like me—or maybe not especially like me personality wise, but kids who were also sort of outcasts (like that guy Kirk I'd told Cathy about)—and we'd somehow find one another, drift toward one another, and hang out after school, pool what little money we had for soda or beer or cigarettes, and just go sit somewhere, like, it seems to me now, the stereotypical teen outsiders we were. No one shared big confidences, and mostly we were quiet—smoking, thinking, listening to music—and when we weren't quiet, we'd be laughing over something stupid one of our teachers had said or something lame one of our supposedly popular classmates had done. We were all sort of friends, but no one was invited to anyone's house and we never went anywhere other than the park, if there was one, or the steps down to a parking garage to just hang around. We were a sort of club or gang, exclusive, but not because we thought we were better than the other kids. No, we were not under any illusion that other kids were dying to get in tight with us. What we wanted was to be left alone. And largely, we were. Which suited me fine, or I always used to think so.

And the bottom line is that not once did I try to reconnect with one of my "gang" after moving to a new town or school district. And not once did any of them try to connect with me, not even via text. None of us really cared all that much about one another, I guess. Maybe we felt we couldn't afford to care.

In case you're wondering, no one from my last school made a big deal of Dad's arrest. I mean, the local papers showed more interest in me than any of my so-called friends from school. Even the neighbor who had said hi to us all the time and who had once baked a cake for us (I have no idea why) didn't try to see me after I was taken "into care." I know because I asked the woman I was sent to stay with if anyone had wanted to see me, and she told me no. She was okay, by which I mean, she left me alone. Her husband gave me the creeps, but he worked double shifts at the convenience store in town, and anyway, I was only with them for less than two weeks. Which was good, because I absolutely loathed the other girl living there. She chewed with her mouth open. How the hell do you do that, anyway? It's disgusting. I mean, I know I don't have the best table manners, but still.

At dinner tonight Verity asked me what I thought of the high school. It was a silly question, because I thought I'd made my feelings pretty clear.

"It was a school," I said, biting into an ear of corn. It was my third; corn on the cob is probably the best thing about being here in Maine. Anyway, I knew I was being rude, but I wasn't in the mood to fake excitement over a language lab and the stupid football team.

"It's got a good reputation," she went on. "Did you hear what Aida Collins was saying about the foreign language department being among the top ranked in the entire state?"

I shrugged and wiped a trickle of butter from my chin with the back of my hand. "It doesn't matter. There's nowhere else to go, right?"

I saw Verity's hand tighten on her water glass. "There are other schools, private ones, but I can't afford them."

"See? So what does it matter how good or bad Yorktide Memorial High School is?"

Really, I thought, watching as Verity got up abruptly from the table and began to clear the dishes, *I can be such a jerk.*

Chapter 44

All those years my daughter was scuttling around from town to town, house to apartment, school to school—I was told what little I knew by Soledad Valdes and the tidbits Gemma let slip here and there—I was hunkered down here in Yorktide, afraid to leave the place where I'd last seen Gemma, held fast by some superstition that if I just sat still and waited long enough, Gemma would find her way back home.

It can't have been easy on Gemma, living the kind of life she'd lived, changing schools so often, leaving friends behind—assuming she'd had time to make any friends, and assuming Alan, with his overprotective, stifling ways, had let her—but she hasn't complained to me about it, either because she really wasn't bothered too much by all the upheavals in her life or she just doesn't want to admit to me, of all people, that she was bothered. I'm still the enemy. I might always be the enemy, as unfair as that is—but does fairness have a place in this family dynamic? In this world? Was it fair that Gemma was a victim of kidnapping? No. Was it fair that I was left for seventeen years to suffer agonies of not knowing the fate of my only child? No.

I hope she likes the high school. I hope she makes friends there and does well in her classes. I hope so many good things for her. But I'm afraid good things won't happen unless she lets them. They often don't.

And what others think is a good thing for you sometimes just isn't.

At one point a therapist I was seeing—briefly, as it turned out—suggested I have another child. Aside from the near impossible to bear financial strain that would have meant, I was repulsed by the idea of trying to replace my child, and I said so. The therapist, a woman with two kids of her own, pointed out that having another baby wouldn't be replacing Gemma; it would be augmenting my life, helping my heart to heal. "When you are actively loving someone," she said, "when you're caring for them, there's less time for grief and obsession with what's gone. You have a lot of love to give, Verity."

"Do I?" I replied. "I feel empty inside." And I did feel empty. And for a long time I also felt I didn't deserve to be happy, that I didn't deserve to do something for myself that might bring joy. Besides, what if I did have a baby and found that I was unable to love her? What then? I'd have destroyed yet another life because there's no way a child who is not really loved can be happy or successful. The whole idea was insupportable, and I stopped seeing that therapist shortly afterward. What did she know about grief, I thought, other than what the textbooks had told her? Had *she* had her child stolen from her?

In retrospect, of course, I realized my attitude had been immature. Every human being knows grief; it comes to us all in time, and most human beings have a healthy degree of empathy, too, so that they can feel another's pain to some degree, even if they haven't suffered the same wrongs. And in my more rational moments, I can readily admit that you really shouldn't try to quantify grief. To some, losing a friend is as devastating as losing a child; to some, losing a beloved pet qualifies as the worst pain they've ever had to endure. You have to have respect for the grief of others. At least, you should try to. Sometimes, that's not an easy thing.

I decided I needed to see David. I needed someone to hug me, to reassure me that things would be all right. To lie to me if necessary, tell me things were going to be all right.

Fighting down the guilty feeling that I was abandoning my daughter, I told Gemma I was going out on an errand.

"I'll be back within the hour," I said, hoping she wouldn't ask where it was I was going.

And she said: "Whatever."

Chapter 45

Cathy decided to show up at the house again. Dad hated when people would do that, just ring our bell or knock on the door, though not many people ever did. He would jump like a scalded cat (that's a gross expression—sorry I used it) and shoot me a look of fear or suspicion. It used to make me laugh sometimes. Now I know what he was expecting.

"You're here," I said, meaning to be ironic or dry or something, but Cathy just smiled and said, "Yup."

We went out to the deck, and I flopped down on my lounge. I thought that maybe I should ask her if she wanted something to drink—it was pretty hot—but then I thought, if she wants something, she could get it herself. I'm not a servant.

"So, what's going on?" she asked, leaning against the deck's wooden railing.

"Nothing."

Cathy Strawberry was undeterred. "My mom told me you checked out the high school."

"Yeah."

"You'll like it there."

I frowned. "You can't possibly know that."

Cathy shrugged. "Well, no, but what I mean is that it's a good school. We've got a no tolerance for bullying policy, and we've gone two entire years without one incident. I think that's pretty impressive."

I shrugged. I'm not worried about bullying. I'm worried about being stared at or worse, treated specially. The Little Kidnapped Girl.

"You're blocking my view," I said.

"Oh." Cathy left the railing and sat in the other lounge. "Sorry." And then she sighed.

"What?" I asked, against my better judgment.

"It's nothing, really. Except that my father's being totally unreasonable about this trip to Boston I want to go on. It would be me and one of my friends and her cousin. Anyway, Hildy's cousin is eighteen and she'd be driving, and the plan is to go to a concert—you know the band Lash Out?—and stay overnight in a motel and come back the next day."

"And?" I said. "What's the problem?"

"The problem is that my father won't let me go. He says I'm too young and that Sheila—that's Hildy's cousin—is also too young to be 'in charge' of two fifteen-year-olds. Can you believe it? I mean, I'm a totally responsible person, and the concert tickets are only eighty dollars. We'd split the cost of the motel bill three ways, so that wouldn't cost too much. Anyway, he's being totally stubborn about it and—"

I kind of lost it then. "God," I said angrily, "you have no idea how good you have it, do you? I can't believe you're complaining about not going on some stupid road trip. At least you *have* a father at home to give a crap. My father's in jail right now, remember? Prison. And he's probably not going to get out anytime soon."

"He's in prison," Cathy replied blandly, unfazed by my outburst, "because he broke the law."

"He's in prison because he got caught." The moment the words were out of my mouth, I knew how ridiculous my "argument" was. "Anyway," I added quickly, "it still stinks."

But Cathy was having none of it. I have to say she's tougher than she looks. "He had to have known the risk he was taking when he stole that car," she said, "especially after what he did to you and your mom. I can't feel sorry for him; I just can't. But I do feel sorry for you."

And then it happened, that all too familiar surge of pure anger. "You're a self-righteous little bitch!" I cried. "I don't need your pity!"

Cathy, still unmoved or pretending to be, just sighed. "Then what *do* you need? What do you want? It's exhausting being around you sometimes, Marni."

"Nobody's forcing you to stick around," I snapped.

"You're right. I'm going home."

I wasn't sorry to see her go. She had probably only come over because Verity asked her to. It's no secret Verity is very concerned with making me feel welcome here in Yorktide, and that means begging her friends to pretend to have an interest in me. And what makes Verity think I have any interest in *them*?

I know I can be combustible. That's a more acceptable way of saying I can be an ass. Where my father would sulk and act in a passive-aggressive way (hey, I love the man, but over time my eyes opened), where he would wheedle and whine, I would fling harsh words, slam doors, storm off. People are never left in any doubt as to my feelings. This is partly a good and partly a bad thing. You could say I'm an honest person, if brutally so. And you could also say I should grow up and learn some self-control. Both opinions would be justified. It's just that since my father's arrest, I've been having a really, really hard time keeping my temper in check and considering anybody's feelings but my own. Justifiable, I think. At least, understandable. But not always fun for the people around me. Problem is, I don't much care.

Still, thinking about it now, I don't feel I was entirely justified in lashing out at Cathy. No one chooses the people they grow up with. No one chooses to be born, for that matter. It's just an accident of luck—good luck or rotten luck—that you get the parents or the guardians you get. If you get any at all.

Cathy doesn't deserve to be punished just because she lucked out with two totally normal, average, mildly annoying, kind of boring parents.

When Verity came home from her studio around five o'clock, she asked if I'd spent time with Cathy today. Of course she had probably arranged our little get-together, so she knew we would have seen each other, and now I wondered if Cathy had gone home and told her mother about our fight and if Annie had called Verity to complain about my behavior. The less said, I figured, the better.

"Yeah," I said. "She came over for a while."

"Did you have a good time?"

"It was okay. We don't have a lot in common."

Verity sighed and I thought, *Wow, she looks genuinely sad about that, like it's somehow her fault Cathy's from Venus and I'm from Mars.* "I'm sorry," she said. "I know it's stupid to assume that just because two people are the same sex and the same age, they're going to enjoy each other's company. I think that's only a guarantee with toddlers."

I didn't know what to think. Maybe Cathy hadn't complained about me. Maybe she had and Verity didn't think my bad attitude was a big deal. "It's all right," I said. "It doesn't matter."

"Still, I wish I knew someone—"

"It doesn't matter," I repeated. "I can find my own friends." *If I want to*, I added silently. *And I'm not sure I do.*

Chapter 46

Gemma and I were in downtown Yorktide this afternoon. With more tourists than locals on the sidewalks now, we can enjoy at least a degree of anonymity. We were only greeted once, and that by Matilda Gascoyne, outside the bakery. Somewhere in her sixties, Matilda was dressed as she always is, in a pair of jeans, T-shirt, plaid shirt worn over it with the sleeves rolled up, her long gray hair in a braid down her back.

"Verity," she said, "hello."

"Matilda, how are you?"

"Can't complain," she said with a brisk shake of her head. "Busy as usual now summer's here and the tourists are so kindly bringing their money to spend at the restaurant."

Then I introduced Matilda to my daughter, though of course Matilda knew who she was.

"It's so good to see you here, Gemma," she said, with not a trace of sickly sweet sympathy in her voice. The Gascoynes don't do sickly sweet anything. "I do hope you're adjusting to life in Yorktide. Things might seem a little dull at the moment, but just wait until the Fourth of July. Then the place will be hopping!"

Gemma managed a smile that seemed genuine enough.

"Well, must be off. Al's short staffed at the restaurant today, so I'm lending a hand."

When she was out of earshot, Gemma said: "She was okay. Not like that other one."

"Matilda Gascoyne is lovely. She's from one of the old families in town. Five, six generations of the Gascoynes have lived here, and I suspect they will until the end of time."

"What was that about a restaurant?" Gemma asked.

"She and her husband own The Friendly Lobsterman, as well as a fish market. One of their sons also has a lobster boat. And like a lot of families around here with a good deal of land, they grow most of their own vegetables and keep some chickens for the eggs."

"So they're farmers?"

"Yes."

"Are they rich?"

"Interesting question," I said. "I suspect they struggle as we all do. But I'd say they live a very good life." I wondered if Gemma understood what I meant by that. I didn't want to insult her by asking.

We got into the car, and when we'd driven only a few yards, Gemma asked: "How did it happen? I mean, where were you when Dad took me?"

The question had come out of the blue—well, for me it had. Clearly, something had turned Gemma's mind to the past that is never gone and haunts us both.

"I was at work," I said, eyes on the road. "You were at home with Barbara. She was the colleague you and I were living with at the time, just until I could find an affordable place on my own. She went out back to hang some laundry on the line. She was only gone a few minutes and when she got back, your crib was empty. She called me immediately."

"Where's she now?" Gemma asked.

"She moved away not long after that. She was devastated by it all, the police questioning her, the publicity. She felt guilty. She felt scared, too, in retrospect. She kept thinking about what Alan might have done to her if she'd caught him in the act. In the end, she just couldn't take living here any longer."

"Does she know I'm back?"

"Yes. She sent me an e-mail. Needless to say, she's thrilled. And she apologized for having abandoned me after the kidnapping. That was her word, *abandoned,* but really, all she was doing was saving her own sanity. See, shortly after you went missing, she asked me to move out. My being in her house was driving her mad. I went back for a while to the apartment I'd shared with Alan on Front Street. But not for long."

"Would she come back, do you think, now that it's all over?"

"No. She's not ever coming back to Yorktide. She's made a life elsewhere."

"Why didn't you ever leave?" Gemma asked.

I shook my head. "I know it sounds crazy, but I guess I thought it would be easier for you to find me if I stayed put. And over time I made a life for myself here, against all odds. Now I don't want to leave."

"Did Dad have any friends here?"

That was another unexpected question.

"Not really," I said. "There was one guy, Rob. They'd known each other in high school, I think." What I didn't say was that Rob was one of those people who couldn't hold a job for more than a few weeks without getting fired for stealing from petty cash or forgetting to show up at all.

"Did he know Dad was going to leave town with me?"

"He swore not. He thought—"

"What?"

"He thought that what Alan did was wrong. He was angry with Alan. And he did offer to do what he could for me." But what with being an alcoholic, that wasn't ever going to be much.

"Is he still around? Do you see him?"

"He died in a drunk-driving accident years ago. Sad to say, his death didn't come as a big surprise to anyone who knew him. He was always reckless."

Gemma grunted. "I wonder why he was friends with Dad

then," she said. "He's the most cautious person I've ever known. He won't cross a street on the green light without looking both ways, like, three times."

Cautious, I thought, *or obsessive.* But I said nothing.

"Not that he'll be crossing any streets for a while."

I glanced at Gemma, and she gave me a half smile. "Well," she said, "he won't, will he?"

Chapter 47

I'd known about Annie and Marc's twentieth-anniversary party for months, but it seemed that suddenly it was upon us and I realized Gemma had nothing decent to wear to it. So we went shopping. It was a fairly hellish experience. She has no interest in style whatsoever, and while style doesn't matter all that much to those of us who live in snow boots and mufflers for six months a year, I wanted my daughter to look presentable. I wanted the other people at the party—all locals, from what I had gathered—to look at her and think, *She's doing well.* As if clothing ever really tells the truth about a person's emotional well-being. Clothing is so often a convenient form of disguise.

But it was all about my vanity. A mother's vanity.

"If you feel uncomfortable," I told Gemma on the ride to the house on Maple Street, "just let me know, and we'll leave."

"I'll be fine," she said. It was one of her usual answers, one that managed to minimize if not avoid the potential magnitude of what was to come.

The party was in full swing when we got to the house, and as soon as we entered, I thought, *I don't want to be here.*

It hit me like the proverbial ton of bricks, this feeling of serious discomfort. I'd never felt my difference so strongly as I did in that moment, standing just inside the front door, the absence of a husband (though that was my doing; David had made it plain that he would marry me the moment I said yes), but more than that, the fact that I'd brought a child into this world with a man not worth his weight in gravel. If I had been thinking clearly, if I had had a strong sense of self-esteem, say what you will, I would never have made such a poor choice as Alan Burns. By the time I was smart and brave enough to get out, it was too late. I'd sealed my daughter's fate.

Anyway, my reaction to being at the party took me by surprise. Annie and Marc are my closest friends. I should have felt glad and even honored to be part of this celebration, not focusing on my own insecurities.

"I'm going to find the food," Gemma said, and she went off on her own through the crowded room. I saw people notice her—nod to their companions, even discreetly point—but Gemma, if she noticed the attention, pretended not to. Then she was lost to sight.

Annie joined me then and handed me a glass of wine. She was wearing a pair of tan dress slacks, pleated down the front, and a silk blouse. It was the most dressed up outfit I'd ever seen her wear. She has even less interest in style than my daughter seems to. I wondered if Cathy had taken her in hand, as I had taken Gemma.

"You seem like you're having a terrible time," she said, looking at me keenly. "Are you?"

"No, no, of course not!" I lied. "Just a bit of a headache. Sorry. I promise not to spoil the party."

"Good, because it's costing us a pretty penny. Since when has a sheet cake cost as much as a good cut of beef?"

"Still, twenty years is something to celebrate."

"I know." Annie's eyes scanned the crowded living room. "Where's Gemma?"

"I don't know. Mingling? Well, that's doubtful. Maybe she's with Cathy."

"Remember, smile. Or take an aspirin."

Annie slid off through the crowd, and almost immediately a woman approached me, hand outstretched.

"Amanda Kelly," she said.

"Verity Peterson." I took her hand briefly. I felt as if I were being accosted by a politician on election day. She had that fixed smile and the direct eye contact that pins you in place.

"Yes," she said. "I know. Is your daughter here tonight?"

"Yes. Somewhere." *And,* I thought, *the last thing I want to happen is for this person, whoever she is, to go chasing after her.*

But the woman stayed put. "I hope she's adjusting all right," she said. "I can't imagine how hard it must be." Then Amanda Kelly cocked an eyebrow at me. "Are you a woman of faith?" she asked.

Faith in what, I wondered. Fate? Luck? God? Really, it's an impertinent question, isn't it? Chances are that the person asking the question *is* a person of faith, and if you answer no, you're going to hear an admonition or a sermon or possibly even an outright criticism. When I didn't reply—because I was thinking all this—the woman went on.

"Because if you are," she said, with a firm nod of her head, "then your faith will see you through."

She went off after that—hopefully not to track down my daughter—and I was left to puzzle out the odd encounter. Who was she? I wondered. She seemed to think I'd recognize her name. An old friend of Annie's? That didn't seem likely. Probably the wife of one of Marc's important clients, the kind of client he felt obliged to invite to a party like this.

I realized I was frowning. I realized I'd finished my wine.

I went to the drinks table to get another glass.

Chapter 48

I was afraid I would stick out at the Strawberries' party—it's bad enough, being who I am—but it turned out Verity knew what she was doing when she picked out clothes for me when we went shopping the other day. I didn't look so different from the other girls at the party; most of them were also wearing jeans and sandals. Verity had told me the party wasn't going to be fancy, but I was still worried. She was more dressed up than I was—most of the older women were, and a few men were wearing ties—but at least no one was wearing tuxedos or gowns.

Anyway, let me just say now that the Strawberries are so freakin' normal. Well, maybe they're not normal. I mean, they're, like, out of a storybook. Three times I saw them in a group hug. Three times in, like, half an hour! And as far as I could tell, they weren't posing for a picture.

But they had put out a lot of food, and there were these delicious pigs in a blanket. I ate, like, six of them before it occurred to me that maybe I should leave some for other people. But then I took one more. I mean, they probably had more in the kitchen.

Verity told me that most of the guests were people from the college and people Marc knew through his work as an accountant. I guess a lot of people become friends with their accountants, because the entire first floor was packed. Dad never had an accountant. There was never enough money to account for.

In fact, it occurred to me then that I don't remember him ever paying taxes, but he must have. Or was he living so under the official radar that he somehow managed to evade the long arm of the government? Another thing I could ask him during our next call but probably won't.

Cathy suddenly appeared at my side, a guy in tow. She was wearing a sleeveless pink-and-white-checked dress that came to her knees. It reminded me of those red-and-white-checked tablecloths people use at picnics. I noticed she was a bit taller than the guy. He was wearing jeans and a polo shirt. I think that's what you call them, with the short sleeves and the collar and an animal stitched on the pocket.

"This is Jason," Cathy said brightly. "My boyfriend. And this is Marni."

Jason mumbled something, and I said, "Hey."

"Isn't it a great party?" Cathy said. "I'm *so* glad so many people were able to come. Oh, the Simmonses just came in! I have to go say hello."

She darted off, leaving me alone with her boyfriend.

And suddenly I had a funny idea. Not funny ha-ha. Funny perverse.

"Jason, right?" I said, moving closer to him, like I was going to whisper something in his ear. Then I ran a finger along the bare skin of his arm. He didn't move away. In fact, he shifted a little closer to me so that for a second our hips touched.

"Want to get out of here for a while?" I whispered. His eyes were now slightly hazed over. I know that look. His breath was coming a bit faster.

"What's going on?" a shrill female voice demanded. It was Cathy.

Jason, whose face now turned bright red, went running off without a word of apology or explanation to his girlfriend. I mean, what could he say?

"I'm sorry," I said quickly to Cathy. "It was just a joke." Not a joke, really. But I *had* wanted to shake things up.

"A joke?" Cathy laughed and shook her head. "What sort of joke is coming on to your friend's boyfriend?"

Did she really consider us friends? That was weird. And it made me feel kind of bad.

"Look," I said. "I don't even think he's attractive."

"That's nice! So you flirted with him, why? To make me jealous?"

Nice going, Marni. "I don't know, all right," I whispered fiercely. "God, why are you making such a big deal out of nothing?"

"It's something to me. And you had to do it at my parents' party!"

Cathy stomped off before I could come up with another stupid answer. I saw her walk right past Jason without a glance, even though he reached out for her. Poor guy. He looked pretty miserable.

I thought about finding Verity and telling her what I'd done (so she wouldn't hear it from someone else who might put a really bad spin on it), and I wondered if Cathy would go running to Annie or if anyone else had seen me flirting with Jason. I wondered if word would get around this stupid town that The Little Kidnapped Girl was a whore. A whore with a foul mouth. In the end, I said nothing to anyone.

I don't know why she would be, but I think Verity was as miserable at the party as I was because it was she who suggested we leave right after the cake was brought out, this big sheet cake with chocolate icing and candles in the shape of the numbers two and zero. As we drove away from the house, I could hear a burst of loud laughter and someone turned up the music and it looked like the party would go on for a while.

"Did you have a good time?" she asked when we were on the main road.

"Yeah," I said. "You?"

"Yeah."

I think we both knew we were lying.

Chapter 49

Something odd happened this afternoon.

I went with Verity to her studio at the college, more out of boredom than any real interest in watching her work. Like I said, I've never had any use for art. Not long after we got there, Verity got a text from a colleague in another studio, asking her if she could come over and help her stretch a canvas (whatever that means). So Verity went off, and I was left alone in her studio. It's a big room with windows that go from a few inches above the floor to a few inches below the ceiling. Artists need a lot of light, I guess. The other times I'd been there, I hadn't really paid much attention to all the stuff in the room, but for some reason, today I did. There are three or four (now I can't remember) easels and two long tables with benches on either side of them, and a jumble of all sorts of stuff on top, like paintbrushes and some kind of knives and chisels and hammers. There are a bunch of stands around the room—I guess that's what you'd call them; it's clear you can adjust their heights—on top of which are unfinished sculptures. I'm guessing they're unfinished, because some just look like lumps of clay or pieces of wood that have been chiseled or chopped away in places. Other pieces look like they might almost be done, like one of a bird, though kind of an abstract bird, in some sort of wood. There's also a gigantic bookcase (actually,

I remember now that Verity told me she'd made it) stuffed with books about art, some sitting horizontally on top of the ones standing vertically. I remember the title of one book being *Terracotta—The Technique of Fired Clay Sculpture*, by someone named something Malmstrom. Another was *The Care of Bronze Sculpture*, by a guy named Patrick Kipper. There was one with the words *El Greco* on the spine, but I don't know who that is. Maybe an artist, or maybe the author. There was another book on The Impressionists, and even I know who they are.

I looked again at that poster Verity had pointed out to me the first time I'd been at the studio. *There is no excellent beauty that hath not some strangeness in the proportion. I'll have to think about that,* I thought. I remembered my first impression of Annie, how I'd thought she was ugly, but how after a few minutes I'd changed my mind and realized she was beautiful. Was that what this guy Bacon was talking about?

Imagine going through life with your name being bacon?

The last thing that caught my eye was an old-fashioned folding table (Dad and I had one we'd picked up at a garage sale) on top of which there was a blue ceramic vase with some flowers— they looked like wild flowers—and next to it was an arrangement of fruit (I think they were wax, because none of the pieces were at all brown, and it was pretty hot in the studio): a pear and an apple and a small nectarine or something. And there was also a crumpled green cotton napkin.

Obviously, some of Verity's students had been drawing the flowers and the fruit. There were a bunch of sketches pinned to a board behind the folding table. Looking up at them, I suddenly thought, *I could do better than that,* which was a weird thing to think, because I hadn't done anything remotely artistic since I had some coloring books when I was a kid. There was an open sketchbook on one of the long tables, and two chipped mugs crammed with all sorts of pencils and pens. I reached for one of the pencils—don't ask me what kind it was, because I didn't notice—and I looked at the flowers and the fruit and I just started to draw what I saw.

It was like I was in a dream or something. It was just happening, and I felt like I was watching it happen at the same time I was making it happen. It was weird. When I realized I had pretty much finished drawing the stuff on the table, I flipped to a new page and started again. And like the first time, my hand just kept moving.

Suddenly I was aware of voices in the hall, two or maybe three people and one of them was definitely Verity. Quickly, I tore the pages I'd used out of the sketchbook, and without really thinking, I crammed them under a pile of magazines, stuffed the pencil back into the mug, and scurried into the center of the room.

Verity came through the door then. "Sorry it took so long," she said. "I hope you weren't bored, waiting for me."

I felt guilty, though I didn't really know why. "No," I said. "I'm fine."

"Good. I need to do about an hour's work, and then I thought we'd grab an early dinner at The Friendly Lobsterman, if that's okay with you."

I felt the familiar irritation come over me. I wish she would stop always asking if things were okay with me. *Just make a decision*, I thought. *Tell me what we're going to do.* But all I said was, "Sure."

Chapter 50

I'll be introducing four new pieces at the gallery show in July, rather, four parts of one larger piece. I've called the work *The Four Seasons*, and as the title so clearly indicates, each individual piece represents a conception of a particular season. It's taken me the better part of a year to complete the work, to perfect *Winter*, *Spring*, *Summer*, and *Fall* as separate but related works. I'm also planning on showing several sketches of each season in process. I chose the sketches carefully for visual interest, and for all four pieces, I wrote up a short statement of intent and purpose and a description of the path from initial idea, through changing iterations, to final form. I framed the sketches in rough wooden frames to match the wood used for each season—walnut for *Winter*, butternut for *Spring*, cherry for *Summer*, and white pine for *Fall*. For some people, preliminary sketches and the studies that come before a work is finished are themselves works of art. Process is as important as the final product. And, let's be practical, for those who want to collect art but have a limited budget, this sort of thing is far more affordable than the final pieces.

Anyway, I don't mind telling you that I'm anxious about Gemma's being at the opening of my show. I want her to be proud of me, even if she can't find an interest in what I do. I want her to know I am a responsible, reasonably successful person on whom she can rely. And I want to impress her too, no matter how silly that sounds. I want her to know I have some reputation as an artist. I want her to realize that people who do care about art take me seriously.

Alan didn't care about art. And he never took my work seriously. He never took *me* seriously. But that's typical of emotionally controlling and possessive men.

Let me explain.

In the early days of our relationship, Alan pretended to be supportive of my art (but of course at the time I thought he was sincere), even if he admitted to not understanding it. "I think it's great," he'd say about a particular piece. I'd ask him what exactly about the piece made him say it was great. He'd shrug. "The whole thing, I guess." It didn't matter to me that he was no art critic. It only mattered that he paid me a compliment.

But over time he took more and more to belittling my achievements, specifically, my sculpture in clay and stone and wood, denigrating the work that meant the most to me. I can't tell you how often he opined that playing around with wet clay and chipping away at blocks of stone was all well and good, but I was meant for better things. At least, a more steady choice of jobs.

"Like what?" I would ask every time he brought up the subject of My Life.

"Like pretty much anything," Alan would reply. "Why don't you change your major and get a degree in accounting?"

And every time I would say, "Alan, it's too late for that. Besides, I hate doing math. I'm no good at it, and it doesn't interest me."

And round and round it would go. To be fair, money was tight in our household, what with me still in school and Alan not making very much money. And even when I'd graduated, we still sometimes had trouble making the rent. I was working part-time as a waitress while devoting the majority of my days to my art, creating new pieces, learning new techniques and perfecting the ones I'd already learned, submitting pieces to local gallery shows. There were times, I admit, when I felt demoralized and wondered if in pursuing a life in art I was being willfully naïve or selfish. I'd remember what my mother had told me about following my dream and feel bolstered for a moment or two, but then I would think of my father's none too subtle hints about "settling down" and getting a "proper job," and always there was Alan's not so subtle pressure. It became more difficult with each passing day to sustain enthusiasm for what had once been so important to me.

There were more than just economic reasons behind Alan's pressuring me to quit art. He didn't like me going off to the tiny part of town where artists congregated to work; he began to follow me to my studio and wait outside, sometimes for hours, for me to leave. He didn't try to hide, either—just parked his beat-up old car across the street and sat. He began to show up unexpectedly at my lunch dates and to invite himself along to gatherings of fellow artists, where he'd be a dark, negative presence in the room. Later he would criticize my friends for being lazy and morally suspect and lacking civility. "Not one person had the decency to ask what I do for a living," he would complain. I never did, but I should have replied that *he* never asked one question about anyone's work, either. Instead I would soothe his petulance and say stupid things like, "You know how artists are," no matter that I was insulting myself as much as I was insulting my friends.

But Alan persisted in his subtle and not so subtle methods of undermining my commitment to the thing I most loved, and finally, worn down, tired of being broke, and without another emotional resource but for Marion, who, as Alan's devoted mother, always echoed his opinions and sentiments, I put away or sold most of my materials and canceled the lease on the tiny studio I had been renting. Alan praised my wisdom and told me he knew I would now also put aside the dubious characters—especially the men—I had once worked among.

As luck—really?—would have it, there was an opening for a deadly boring clerical job at Rowland Electronics, the company for which Alan was currently working. I applied and got the job immediately; frankly, I was way overqualified, and as a result, not very good at the work. But in Alan's opinion, the situation was ideal. He could keep an eye on me at all times and hey, we could even commute together, which, he announced, was cost saving and efficient. Who could argue?

I'll probably never tell any of this to Gemma, definitely not at this point in our relationship. For one thing, I don't want to sound accusatory. For another, I'm not proud of behaving the way I did with Alan, of pretty much handing over my independence and abandoning my interests. If he's to blame for manipulating me, then I'm to blame for allowing it. But maybe neither of us is to blame, assuming we were hardwired to play out the relationship as we did. But no. I can't let either of us off the hook that easily.

I just remembered something. I wish I hadn't.

At one point a few years after Gemma's abduction, I decided it might be a good idea to see a therapist again—this was a year or so after the therapist who suggested I have another child as a way to heal the pain of Gemma's loss. There had been a similar case to Gemma's in the national news, but unlike in Gemma's case, the stolen baby had been found within days of being taken. He was in the hospital for observation, doing well, though a little dehydrated. His mother was hysterical with joy. His father, the abductor, had been arrested, along with his female accomplice.

I was happy for the mother and child. But their happy ending only highlighted my own state of uncertainty.

At our second session, the therapist told me that after seven years (it varies from state to state, but it's seven years here in Maine), a person could have another person declared legally dead. "And?" I asked. Seriously, I had no idea where he was going with this bit of information. "And," he said, "having

Alan and your daughter declared legally dead might help bring some closure. After all, the odds of them being found alive are pretty small. Infinitesimal, really."

I remember a sort of fury rushing through me then, fogging any clear thought. When my mind returned a moment later, I realized that having Alan declared legally dead was the last thing I wanted, because as long as he was presumed guilty of child abduction and was, therefore, a fugitive from justice, there was in my mind every reason to hope he was alive and would someday be caught and prosecuted and sentenced.

And as for Gemma . . . "Screw the odds!" I shouted at the therapist. "What happens if my daughter does come home to me someday only to find I've had her declared dead? What in God's good name will she think of me, that I cared so little, that I gave up hope!"

The therapist (obviously an idiot) tried to calm me down with some words I was too furious to register, but I was already half out the door. And I never paid the bill. That was the first and only time in my life I made such a stand.

Seriously, maybe now I've exorcised that awful memory once and for all. I certainly hope so.

Because there's still work to be done if I'm to be ready for the opening.

Chapter 51

I went with Verity to her studio at the college again. If she wondered why I was along for the ride, she didn't say. I know she likes us to spend time together because she's always the one asking me to do stuff with her. Maybe she doesn't care why I go along as long as I do.

When we got to the studio, I sat at one of the long tables and looked through some of Verity's books about art while she worked. Let me tell you, some of those books weigh a ton, and you should see how much they cost. I'd never seen books like them, not the inside of them, I mean. They're full of pictures of paintings and sculptures and buildings, both really old ones like European cathedrals and ones from the last century, like some by this American guy named Frank Lloyd Wright. It was kind of like watching the Travel Channel in some ways, flipping through those books. And kind of like being in history class but a lot more interesting. Occasionally I looked up and watched Verity as she stood at one of the easels, paintbrush in hand and a pencil behind one ear. I'm pretty sure she didn't notice I was watching. She seemed so focused. She looked so on another planet at one point I thought she probably wouldn't even hear the fire alarm if it went off. And it occurred to me that I'd never seen Dad concentrate so hard on anything. Ever. Maybe that's why he always loses at cards.

I wonder if he plays cards in prison. What does he have to bet with?

"Look at the time," Verity said suddenly, glancing at her watch, and grabbing a rag to wipe the paintbrush. "I've got a meeting with the department head, but I should be back in about half an hour."

"Okay," I said.

Verity nodded toward the book opened in front of me. "Rodin," she said. "Interesting?"

I shrugged, still pretending that art bored the life out of me. "He's okay."

Verity sort of smiled and left the room. When she had gone, I peered into all four corners of the ceiling. There was no obvious sign of a security camera, though I know security is an issue. Verity keeps the room locked when she isn't there; she'd explained that the stone and wood and clay she uses in her sculptures isn't cheap and that she can't afford to lose a piece to a thief. And, she said, there were always those strange people who think that vandalizing art is a way to make some sort of statement.

"Like what?" I'd asked.

"Don't ask me," she'd said. "I'm not one of that crazy bunch."

Anyway, with Verity out of the room and as far as I could tell no security guard watching me via cameras, I was good to go. I had no idea if I was about to steal school property or if Verity had paid for the sketchbook on her own, not that I'd feel any better about stealing from her than I would from the college. Stealing was Dad's thing, not mine. Stealing people and things.

There's a tall metal cabinet against one wall. I'd seen inside before, and I knew it was where Verity stored supplies. I opened the door of the cabinet and grabbed a sketchbook from the top of a stack of about ten and stuffed it into my bag. I don't always carry the bag (I'd bought it with the twenty dollars Tom had sent me) so I hoped Verity wouldn't suddenly ask me why

I was carrying it now. I wasn't entirely sure I could keep the guilt off my face. But even if she caught me with the sketchbook, I was pretty sure she wouldn't be angry. She would be Verity, which means she would probably apologize to me for some bizarre reason and assure me that all I had to do if I wanted something was to ask. She's annoying that way.

As promised, Verity was back about half an hour later. "Ready to go?" she asked. "I'm too tired to work more today. Maybe I'll do some at home after a nap."

"Yeah," I said. "Sure."

I was glad when we drove away from the campus. Away from the scene of the crime. So, you're asking: Why steal a sketchbook? Why not just buy one? How much could it cost? The thing is, I'm so high profile in this town that all I need to do is walk into a bakery and order a coffee and the entire population of Yorktide would know exactly how many sugars I put into my coffee in about two minutes flat. (Two, by the way, sometimes three.) I just don't want people—strangers—gabbing about how The Little Kidnapped Girl bought a sketchbook. *Just like her mom!* people would say. *See? It's the mother's influence that counts!* Or some silly stuff like that.

Anyway, there was no need to steal a pencil. Pencils are easy enough to come by at home, and unlike a sketchbook, a few missing pencils won't be noticed as easily. Verity keeps stacks of all sorts of pencils around the house. I just chose a few—one dark soft lead, one hard light lead, one thick charcoal—and brought them to my room. Pencils can also be used for writing, I'm told. Or they were, back in the old days. Only kidding. Of course I know they can be used for writing. Dad is a mechanical pencil freak, the cheap yellow plastic kind that cracks really easily. He was always bringing them home from whatever office he was working in at the time. I mean, he was always stealing them.

I feel kind of ridiculous hiding the sketchbook—it's not like I'm doing anything illegal—but I just don't want Verity or anyone, really, knowing what I'm doing. Don't ask me why, exactly. Maybe—and this is just a guess—maybe I need something entirely my own, something private. Since being shipped to Maine to live with Verity, I feel so . . . exposed. (I can't forget that idiot Mirelle Turner.) I feel so out of control of any aspect of my own life. Back home with Dad, I knew what was what. I knew how and where to carve out my own life in spite of—well, because of—his overprotectiveness. But here . . . it's different. I feel so powerless. And keeping a secret can give you some power. At least, it can give you the illusion that you have power over the person you're keeping the secret from. I wonder: Did keeping my real identity from me all those years give Dad a sense of power over me? I don't really want to go there.

I also don't want to think too much about the fact that I find myself both resenting and being okay with the fact that maybe I've inherited what artistic interest (I won't say talent) I have from Verity, someone who's still such a stranger to me.

My mother.

Chapter 52

I let the phone ring three times before I answered it. I'm not totally sure why. I mean, I knew it was Dad calling, and I wanted to talk to him. I want to know some *real* things about my father, from before the moment he snatched me from my crib and his life of deception began. (Although for all I knew, he'd been living a bunch of lies since the day he first could talk.) I wanted to ask him if he had liked growing up around Yorktide. If he remembered the Nubble Light. Verity's taken me there; it's pretty famous, she said. I wanted to ask him if he remembered the name of his favorite lobster pound from when he was a boy; maybe, I thought, I'd suggest to Verity we go— if it's still around—but I wouldn't tell her why. Not that she would refuse to take me. She's so freakin' nice to me.

But I haven't asked Dad any of those things. I'm not totally sure why not, except that part of me expects I'll only hear more lies, and even if Dad did tell me the truth and answer honestly, how would I know?

So we talked about boring day-to-day stuff. Well, maybe not boring for him. Maybe day-to-day is fraught with terror for my father. If it is, he's not saying. I feel like I have less and less to say to him each time we talk. And he either has less and less to say to me, or he's protecting me from the ugliness of his life behind bars. Whatever the case, it's depressing, and I got off the phone pretty quickly. He didn't protest.

I took out the sketchbook and one of the pencils I'd cadged and began to doodle. I say doodle and not draw because while my hand moved, my mind was a million miles away; I wasn't copying something I saw right in front of me like I had been that first day in Verity's studio.

And I wondered. How did my father keep all those secrets for all those years? It's hard keeping secrets, even the ones you have to keep because if they're found out, they could hurt you, get you into trouble. I wonder if there were times when he wanted to tell someone what he had done, the truth about who he was and who I was. When he was drunk, which wasn't often, but I wonder if then, sitting at some dive bar next to one of his buddies—I wouldn't call them friends, and he never did either—I wonder if he was seriously tempted to come clean and relieve himself of the burden he was carrying. He had to have felt the burden of what he'd done all those years ago, even if he didn't actually feel guilty for stealing me away from my mother, who, it turned out, wasn't a violent drug addict bent on putting out her cigarettes on her baby daughter's arm. I mean, my mother has never smoked in her entire life. That's what she tells me, and I believe her, because from what I can see, she's not a liar. Annoying sometimes, but not a liar.

Anyway, I wonder what he's telling himself now? Himself and other people, his cellmate and the guys he sits with in the cafeteria, about what happened seventeen years ago. (Do you have to sit with the same people all the time? Or is it like on *Orange Is the New Black* and high school, people get into cliques?) Is he telling his version of the truth about what he'd done and the good reasons he'd had for doing it? That he was saving his daughter's life by taking her away from her abusive mother? Would anyone really *believe* him or would everyone nod and think, *This guy's a nut*? Probably they would think he's a nut. A sane person doesn't drop off the face of the earth with a two-month-old infant he believes is in physical danger.

A sane person goes to the police or a family member or a friend, *someone* . . .

How did he keep it all a secret from *me*? I mean, my origins, my real origins. Didn't he ever feel that he owed me the truth about who I really was, at least let me have my real name? How dare he keep me in ignorance all those years, my entire life! And just to cover his own tracks. Still, I really don't believe that holding the truth from me made him feel any sense of power over me; he's not that kind of person. The kind of power he wants over people isn't a strutting power. It's something meaner. It comes from his own deep sense of weakness and need. I learned that much over the years!

I wonder if it ever occurred to him that if I ever discovered the truth—that he stole me from a perfectly good mother—that I'd hate him. I wonder if he was ever scared of losing me that way. I wonder if instead he thought I loved him so unconditionally, I'd stick with him no matter what insane crap came into the light.

I wonder if he ever truly loved me. Ever truly loved anyone. I wonder if he knows how. Because possession isn't proof of love. It just isn't.

The experts (like I really know; I read this online somewhere once) say that a father's relationship with his daughter—how he treats her, if he loves and respects her or if he ignores and disrespects her, if he nourishes her ambitions and interests or if he thwarts them, if he tells her she's beautiful or that she's too fat or has too big a nose—all this matters very, very much to the sort of woman the girl's going to become. Not so much the mother. The father. So where, I wonder, does this leave me? Because although my father professes to love me—and I've always believed he did, that he does still, while he's rotting away in a prison cell—he's so totally screwed up my life that it's hard to reconcile the two. How can you love someone and basically force her to live a lie of your own devising? I mean, where's the logic in that? But maybe for people like my father, logic has very little to do with love or with anything else in life. People like my father. Screwed up. A liar. So entirely self-centered that he simply can't see beyond his own whacky needs.

I looked down at the sketchbook and almost laughed out loud at what I had drawn. Weird, grotesque clown faces. Dad is afraid of clowns.

Then there was a knock on the door. I stashed the sketchbook and pencil under the couch and opened the door to find Verity. Of course. Who else would it be?

"You okay?" she asked.

It was what she usually asks after a phone call from Dad. Never *What did he say?* though I know she must be curious.

"I've been worse," I said. "And better."

"Any interest in going to that new ice cream place out on Rosehip Highway?"

If she was trying to bribe me with food, it was working. "Yeah," I said. "Let me just run to the bathroom first." That's where we keep the aspirin, and I could feel a real splitter coming on.

Chapter 53

It was the first time a phone call from Alan hadn't sent Gemma after me like a particularly hungry cat after a particularly fat mouse. I was happy about that, being spared an attack. On the other hand, I wondered what had been different about this call from her father to have made her less hostile to me. Had he disappointed her in some way? Was she beginning to realize the magnitude of Alan's failure?

While we were eating our ice cream cones on a bench at the top of the beach, Gemma brought up the subject of a bicycle.

"I thought about what you said, about not being able to get around too easily without wheels. So I guess I should have a bike after all."

"Sure," I said. I was happy she had asked me for something; it was the first time since she moved in with me that she'd asked for anything. She hadn't even asked for the real bed I'd offered. It makes me feel good to be able to give her something she wants, specifically something that will help her to gain some independence in her new world.

The cost could be a problem, but I feel sure we can find something at a yard sale or through the local papers. And Marc is an avid cyclist. Maybe he can check the bike over before we buy it and then help fit the seat to accommodate Gemma's height.

A memory came to me then, and I hesitated, unsure if I

should share it with Gemma. It didn't hold particularly bad vibes for me, but who knew what it might trigger for my daughter. But then I went ahead.

"Your father and I had a tandem bike for a while," I said. "A bicycle built for two."

Gemma grunted. "I didn't know he could ride a bike. But I guess everyone can at some point in their lives."

"We had some fun with it—this was about six months into the relationship—but then it was stolen, and we couldn't afford to buy a new one. Remember, I was in college then."

"And Dad never made any real money, did he?"

I answered carefully but honestly. "No," I said. "I don't think he did."

"Did he ever play sports? I mean, other than cards and pool. He likes to gamble but only with pennies."

I frowned at my half-eaten ice cream. "Now that you mention it, I don't think he did. We'd have to check with Marion about the years before I met him, but I don't recall his ever mentioning being on a team. He liked NASCAR though."

Gemma laughed. "Tell me about it! How boring is it to watch cars go around and around a track, over and over again! It's only good when someone crashes. Well, you know what I mean."

"I used to watch races with him, at a bar he liked. I was bored out of my mind."

"Then why'd you go?" Gemma asked.

"He liked me to be there with him. And for a long time, I liked to be there too."

This last admission was met with silence. I wondered all sorts of things, only one of which was: Does Gemma believe me, that I wanted to be at the bar with him? After a time she said: "That's what people in relationships are supposed to do, right? Do stuff that makes the other one happy."

"Until it gets out of hand or abusive or until the stuff becomes something that does you harm."

"Or until you fall out of love."

"Or stop loving someone," I said. "There's a difference."

"I wouldn't know. I've never been in love."

"You will someday." I winced. "Sorry. I used to hate when adults would say that sort of thing to me, like they really know the future."

"Yeah. I hate it too. Adults don't really know much more than kids, do they?"

"Some do," I said. "I'd like to think I've learned a few lessons over the years. But it's true there's always more to figure out. Growing up never ends in some ways."

"It sounds tiring."

I laughed. "It is!"

"By the way," Gemma said, wiping her hands on a paper napkin, ice cream cone gone. "What are we having for dinner?"

Chapter 54

My new bike is pretty cool. It's a Tyler, which isn't a big famous brand, but I don't care about that as long as it works. Yeah, I know I said I didn't want a bike, but I figured, what the hell? While I'm here, I might as well have my own transportation so I don't have to rely on Verity for everything. I don't want her to think I really need her or anything. What I need is independence.

What I also need is to be forgiven, something kind of new to me. No, let's be honest. Something entirely new to me.

I leaned the bike against the Strawberries' house and knocked on the front door. The Strawberries have one of those old-fashioned knockers. It's in the shape of an anchor, I guess because they live close to the water. (We all do here in southern Maine.) Anyway, I can't be sure, but I thought I saw a curtain in the living room twitch, as if someone was deciding whether or not to open the door, based on who was out there. A Jehovah's Witness? Don't answer, though I have to say I've met a few, and they've all been very nice. A guy with a big cardboard check from the lottery? Answer. I was about to knock again when the door opened and there stood Cathy. Before she could say something like, *I hate you; get out of here,* I said:

"I want to apologize again for what I did at your parents' party. It was stupid, and I'm really sorry."

Cathy half smiled and shrugged. "It's okay," she said. "I forgive you. Come in."

I followed her inside and to the kitchen. Why does everyone always end up in the kitchen? I'm not complaining. It's where the food is kept.

"Just like that," I said. "You forgive me?"

She shrugged again and opened the fridge. "Yeah. Anyway, I've been thinking about it. Jason should have just walked away when you pretended to flirt with him. I'm thinking I should break up with him."

"Don't break up with him just because I was a jerk!"

"I'm not." Cathy took a pitcher of lemonade from the fridge and two glasses from a cabinet over the sink. "My mom made some awesome granola bars," she said. "Do you want one?"

I'm not a fan of health food, or, as Dad calls it, "nuts and bolts," but I said sure. Sometimes granola bars have chocolate in them.

Cathy put a sealed plastic container on the bar top, along with the lemonade and glasses. I peered through the wall of the container. I was pretty certain I saw chocolate chips. But I waited for Cathy to open the container and offer me a bar. I mean, I'm not a total cretin.

"A few friends are coming over tomorrow night to hang out," she said then. "Just girls. Why don't you come?"

It's kind of the last thing I want to do, hang out with Cathy's friends, but right then I felt that if our truce was going to hold, I should probably say yes. So I said, "Okay."

"Good. You'll like my friends. I've known Hildy, Becca, and Melissa since I was a toddler."

To hell with the truce. Instant regret for agreeing to join them. Talk about being an outsider. But before I could voice some lame excuse for backing out of the invitation, Cathy was babbling on. I should be nice and not say she was babbling.

"Do you know there are families in Yorktide and Ogunquit and Wells that have lived here for generations? Hundreds of years, in the same houses, on the same land. That's pretty amazing, isn't it? I mean, to grow up with such a sense of belonging to a place. To have roots."

Honestly, I'd never thought about it—not even when that Matilda Gascoyne, from one of the old families, had said hi to Verity and me in town—and I said as much. By the way, there were chocolate chips and what I think were dried cranberries or cherries in the granola bars. They were amazing.

"Well," Cathy said, "think about it now. Think about how you'd probably feel sort of special, knowing that someone way back in say the early 1800s looked out of her bedroom window, which is now your bedroom window, and saw pretty much exactly what you're seeing right now, in the twenty-first century. The same trees, the same ocean, even some of the same houses. It kind of blows my mind. I wish I had that sort of connection to the past. I think I'd feel sort of indestructible somehow, like a part of me would always be in the *present*, even the present a hundred years from now. People would always know that Cathy Strawbridge was a person. I'd be alive in memory."

Boy, I thought, *is this chick a romantic.* But I thought about what she'd said. I thought about the way people in Yorktide stare at me, how they think they know all about me, The Little Kidnapped Girl, and I thought, living in the same town where your parents and grandparents and great-grandparents lived and died must be the most claustrophobic thing ever. You could never be yourself, could you? You'd always be so-and-so's child, grandchild, great-grandchild. Everything you did or said would be compared to everything your ancestors did or said, and you'd be judged accordingly. There would always be someone else's reputation, good or bad, to exceed or to live down.

"I think it sounds really suffocating," I said. What I didn't add was that I was probably the last person to have any real understanding of the benefits there might be to sticking around the old family homestead for any length of time. Not with my past, never staying in one town or apartment for more than a year.

I went home soon after that and after thanking Cathy for the snacks. I think she was disappointed with my failure to share her excitement about, I don't know, family history or whatever. When I got home, I turned on the TV in the living room, and even though there's, like, a million things to watch at any given time, I couldn't find one show or movie I wanted to watch. So I turned it off, and I thought about my life with Dad.

For a long time I didn't have a sense that we were running from something, Dad and I, when we moved to a new apartment in a new neighborhood, or even the time when I was very little, maybe second grade, when we moved from New Mexico to Arizona. Well, the reason I was oblivious that time was because I was really young, maybe seven or eight. But the other times after that, no, I guess I mostly just accepted Dad's vague explanations, which could range from, *It's time to skedaddle* (said with a smile and a wink), to the more prosaic explanations like, *The landlord is raising the rent, and we can't afford to pay more than we're already paying.* I heard that sort of explanation often enough, that someone was basically persecuting us, so at some point along the line, I can't remember when exactly, I decided there was something iffy about Dad's claiming we were the victims of yet another—let's call it conspiracy. Or, more specifically, that *he* was the victim. When I finally stopped to think about it, I realized that every single time he left a job—either because he quit or because he was fired—it was because his boss was a jerk, his coworkers were idiots, he was too smart for the job and his colleagues were jealous. On and on and on.

But like I said, it never really occurred to me that behind or at the bottom of all the moving around was a big dark secret that, if found out, could stop me and Dad from being a family. I see now that Dad worried that the longer we stayed in one place—or he stayed in one job—the better the chance someone might recognize him from the Wanted posters (where do people put those things, besides the post office?) or he might make a verbal slip and accidentally reveal that he wasn't who he said he was, Jim Armstrong, with a daughter named Marni. Now, that's not to say maybe Dad wasn't legitimately fired a few times—he could be a real whiner at home and with his passing acquaintance buddies, so why not also on the job?—but mostly it must have suited him to be let go.

Anyway, whenever Dad made the announcement that we were moving to a new apartment and sometimes a new town, there was the hurried packing of our stuff into pillowcases, an old sleeping bag he had gotten somewhere, a few battered old-fashioned suitcases (the kind without wheels, like the one I brought with me to Maine), and what cardboard boxes he could coax from the local grocery store's loading guys. We didn't have very much, so it never took very long to get ready to leave, which we invariably did crammed in someone else's car if ours was "acting up" at the moment (which it often was; maybe Dad had no money for gas that week) and once, in a flatbed pickup truck Dad rented from a guy who lived next door, and on we went with our clothes; some books (mostly mine); a toaster oven that always burnt the toast and whatever else we tried to cook in it because something was wrong with the wiring; two small cacti we had for a while, until we forgot them during one move; and a random collection of what I now see as crap but that for a long time as a child I saw as treasures—an aqua-colored plastic vase; a picture showing the desert at sunset (torn from a magazine and taped onto a piece of stiff cardboard); a small ceramic statue of a coyote in a slinking posture. None of those so-called treasures exist any longer. They got lost or badly broken along the way, but I still sometimes think of them, especially the slinking coyote, the visual opposite of that old cartoon character Wile E. Coyote from the Bugs Bunny programs. My coyote was magical, like the coyote often is in Native American legends, sometimes a hero, sometimes an antihero, and sometimes a comic trickster.

Sometimes, he's all three at once. Crafty, intelligent, stealthy. That was my coyote. He was the closest thing I ever had to a pet, I guess. Or a real friend. Wow, that sounds pathetic. Forget I said that.

I turned the TV back on and found something to watch after all. Some cartoon show about wrestling.

Chapter 55

"I hope Gemma will have a good time with Cathy's friends."

Annie sat down across from me at my kitchen table. Even though the coffee at my place isn't half as good as it is at hers, out of fairness I do have to be the host sometimes. "You sound worried," she said.

"I am," I admitted. "Frankly, I'm surprised she accepted Cathy's invitation."

"Because they haven't really been talking since the anniversary party, you mean."

I frowned. "What was that about, anyway?"

"I don't know, exactly. Cathy won't tell me. I assumed they argued about something."

"I didn't even know that anything had happened. I just thought . . ." I shrugged. "I don't know what I thought. Well, I guess I put it down to the fact that they're two very different young women."

Annie laughed. "They're like night and day! And I don't think it's only because of how they each grew up. But maybe it is. Who can say?"

Ah, yes, I thought. *There's the old nature versus nurture theme again.*

"She asked me about the day she was taken," I said.

Annie looked surprised. "Really? And what did you tell her?"

"I kept it simple, by which I mean I left out the violent shaking and the vomiting that followed the phone call from Barbara and the fact that when we were at Barbara's house later that afternoon, two police officers had to restrain me."

"Christ, why restrain you? You never told me that!"

"They thought I was going to harm myself," I said, at this distance of seventeen years feeling none of the shame I'd felt for a long time after. "I don't remember it too clearly, but supposedly I was sort of ranting on about it being all my fault, Gemma's being missing. Supposedly, I started to scratch my face."

Annie sighed and put a hand on mine. "Poor you. Okay, so if you left out the ugly details, what did you tell Gemma?"

"I told her I'd been at the office when Barbara called. I told her that Barbara left Yorktide soon afterward because she couldn't stand the memories. Gemma also asked if her father had had friends, and I told her about Rob. Oh, and she asked why I didn't leave town too."

"How did she take it all?" Annie asked.

"Calmly. I guess she needed to know." And then I smiled.

"What?"

"She mentioned Alan's love of NASCAR to me one day and how she thinks it's lame, and I told her how I'd spend hours at a local pub with him, watching the cars go around that stupid track over and over again, just because he liked my being there with him. And then we talked a bit about being in love. And about falling out of love."

"Verity, this sounds like fantastic progress! You're actually getting more than one-word answers! And you're talking about things that matter. You must feel so relieved."

I did. I do. Still . . .

"At least once a day," I told Annie, "I find myself apologizing to Gemma for something, even stuff I can't possibly be blamed for. I'm sorry your room isn't bigger. Not that she's ever complained about it. I'm sorry we're out of the milk you like. Which is full fat, by the way. I'm sorry it's raining today and you can't go out on your bike. I'm sure I'm driving her nuts. What I re-ally should be saying is, *I'm sorry all this has happened to you. You're innocent in all this.*"

Annie leaned forward. "As are you, Verity," she said in that forceful way she has that can make you believe almost any-thing she's saying. Almost. "Don't ever forget that."

But the thing is, I do forget that, all the time.

"I'll try not to," I said. "Now, how about another cup of coffee?"

Annie grimaced. "No offense, but no thanks."

Chapter 56

This morning, when I was going through the pile of magazines on the living room coffee table, looking for something good, like a copy of *People* (no luck; I don't think Verity likes celebrity gossip, though I get a kick out of it), I found the card Verity's father had sent me not long after I came to live with her. I have no idea how it got there. Anyway, I'd spent the twenty dollars he sent me on that bag, but I'd never written back to him. Now I decided I would send him a note or something. At least I could thank him for the money. I probably should have done it before. For all I know, the guy's on a fixed income and twenty dollars means a lot to him. I mean, he's probably retired. I know Marion is retired. So far she hasn't given me any money, not that I'm looking for her to.

You know, Dad always used to say that money is the root of all evil. I think having that attitude was for him a way to justify the fact that he never had any money. I doubt that anyone with a decent amount of money in the bank thinks it's evil.

Anyway, I wrote a thank-you note to Verity's father, and then I thought: *Why do I feel sort of antsy?* And then I thought: *Because I'm nervous about going to Cathy's house to hang out with her friends.* I've never had my own group of girlfriends, not the sort that had parties at one another's houses and told one another secrets and had pillow fights while wearing their pajamas. (Do real girls really do that, or is that totally male fantasy? It's gotta be male fantasy.) I never even went to a sleepover when I was a kid. Dad wouldn't let me. He'd say he didn't know the parents well enough to trust them. Now I know the truth. He didn't know the parents—anyone—well enough because we were in hiding and he didn't want to know anyone closely in case they somehow figured out who we really were. So I was kept home while other kids were having fun staying up all night and gorging on ice cream and pizza. Whatever.

I needed to clear my head.

I told Verity I was going out on my bike for a while, and she told me to be careful, like parents are supposed to do. Like Dad always did, even if I was only going to the corner and back. Anyway, I headed to the post office in town to mail the note to Tom. It was the first time I went into the heart of Yorktide on my own, without what protection Verity could offer, which wasn't much, though she did her best to fend off idiots who wanted to stare at me, say stupid things to me, or worse, take a picture of me, The Little Kidnapped Girl. I didn't get off my bike and go inside the post office, though, just stuck the envelope in the mailbox outside the building and headed back to the house. Still, I felt kind of good that I'd made the trip on my own (mostly just focusing on traffic and not getting myself run over by moronic drivers and avoiding hitting the tourists who for some reason tend to wander out into the middle of the street).

When I was coming up our driveway, I saw that neighbor Verity had told me about, Mr. Pascoe, at his front door, bent over and looking closely at the doorknob. Then I saw he was actually peering at the lock and jiggling a key in it. I hadn't met either Mr. or Mrs. Pascoe yet, though a few times I'd seen one or both of them peeking out a slit in the curtains in what I think might be their kitchen. From there they can see our kitchen and the back deck. I was tempted just to go inside and ignore the old man—Verity had warned me that the Pascoes liked to talk endlessly and that they could be nosey—but he looked kind of pathetic all bent over, and a better instinct made me go over to him after I'd parked my bike.

"Can I help?" I said.

I must have startled him—maybe he has bad hearing and hadn't heard me coming—because he turned around quickly and dropped the key. I bent over and picked it up.

"Darn thing won't turn," he said. He seemed genuinely flustered, whether because of dropping the stupid key or meeting me in this way.

"Let me try," I said.

Mr. Pascoe stepped aside, and I inserted his key into the lock. It was a bit stiff. "I think maybe the lock should be oiled," I said, continuing to jiggle the key. And then I got the key to turn, and I pushed open the door.

You'd have thought I handed the guy a check for a million bucks or something, the way he smiled at me. "How can I ever thank you?" he said.

I was embarrassed. I shrugged. "It was nothing. Maybe you should try a spare key. See if that works any better."

I began to turn to head back to my house—Verity's house—when he said, "It's so nice to finally meet you. My wife and I are so glad you're all right."

I felt . . . I felt touched. This guy and his wife were strangers, and yet they were glad I was okay. See, I believed the old man. Against all my worst instincts.

And am I all right? Am I really okay?

I smiled. "Thanks," I said, and hurried back home.

Chapter 57

"I hope you have a good time."

I didn't look at Verity. I couldn't because I didn't want her to see any evidence on my face of the near panic I was feeling.

"Thanks," I said, getting out of the car. *You can do this*, I told myself. *You've done much scarier things.*

Had I really?

Verity pulled away from the Strawberries' house, and I rang the doorbell. Annie opened it, and I felt glad it was her and not Cathy. I still needed a bit of time before joining those girls.

"Follow the sound of the shrieking," Annie said in a tone that made me feel like a conspirator, like we both knew this was hard for me. But maybe I was imagining that.

There wasn't really shrieking, but there was laughter. I went downstairs to the basement, where I found Cathy and three other girls sitting where Verity and I had sat the first time I'd been to the house.

"Marni!" Cathy jumped up and rushed over to me, and I tensed, knowing she was going to throw her arms around me. But she didn't; she just took me by the arm and led me over to the others. I resisted the urge to yank my arm away. Finally she let go.

"Everyone," she said. "This is Marni, my new friend."

The three girls said things like "hi" and "hey" and I sank into the one empty chair with a weak smile. "Hi," I said.

"Help yourself," Cathy said, pointing to the low table on which were bowls of chips, dips, and what I found out were mozzarella sticks. They were kind of cold by then but still good. And there was soda.

"Since Marni's new to the group," Cathy said, "let's everyone tell her about who we are, and then she can tell us all about her."

It sounded like a horrible idea to me, especially that last part. What could I possibly say about myself without dragging into it the fact that I was kidnapped by my father, who's now in jail? (Not that everyone doesn't already know.) I mean, most days I feel like a total stranger to myself, so how am I supposed to describe that stranger to anyone else? But before I could make a dash for the stairs, the girl sitting to my right began.

"I'll go first," she said. "My name is Hildy, and the biggest thing you need to know is that I'm totally into soccer."

Cathy laughed. "She's obsessed!"

No surprise there, I thought. Hildy looks like one of those super-healthy people, who probably runs five miles each day before breakfast and lifts weights before and after lunch. Seriously, I bet that girl can bench-press five hundred pounds or something. (I don't really know anything about bench-pressing. I just know the expression.)

"I am! So is my dad. I get it from him. Anyway, I'm hoping to get a scholarship to help pay for college. And then, well, if I'm not good enough to play professionally somewhere, I'll become a coach. Oh, and I have twin brothers who are nine. Mostly they're okay, but sometimes I want to strangle them."

"That's the beauty of being an only child," Cathy noted, and I thought, *What is?* Sometimes I think I'd *like* to have a sibling around to strangle!

The girl to Hildy's right was next. "I'm Becca, and I'm the

math nerd," she said, and she sounded proud about it. "I'm not saying I'm a genius or anything—"

"Yes, she is!" That was Hildy. "She goes to math camp every summer."

Math camp, I thought. *What's that about?* I mean, I'm okay in math, but I don't *like* it. I just do it in class and walk away. Anyway, she doesn't look like the old stereotype of a nerd. I mean, she wasn't wearing thick glasses, though maybe she was wearing contacts, and she didn't have bad skin or teeth. In fact, she kind of reminded me of this nun who taught at a Catholic school I had to go to once, only for about a semester. And no, not the old stereotype of a nun, all in black and wielding a stick for beating kids. I really liked Sister Martha. She had this gentleness about her, this sort of otherworldly, thoughtful thing going on, and the weird thing was that kids listened to her. Even though she spoke softly and was about ninety pounds soaking wet, everyone respected her. Maybe, I thought, Sister Martha was into math too, the kind that deals with theories of the universe.

"I go to math camp so I can *learn,*" Becca insisted. "I know I'll be a math major in college. After that, I have no idea. There are so many directions in which I can go. Maybe I'll do the full academic thing, get my PhD and teach and publish articles and write books."

"Her mother's an engineer," Cathy added. "That's where she gets it."

Becca turned to me. "My dad's the stay-at-home parent. I'm the youngest of four. I don't know what he's going to do with himself when I go off to college!"

"What did he do before?" I asked. I don't know why I was interested.

"Believe it or not, he was an executive at an ad firm in Boston, making a ton of money. But when my oldest sister came along, he chucked it all. Mom had no problem with that. She makes good money, and they both really liked the idea of a parent being at home. Anyway, I guess he could do some freelance ad work if he wanted to," Becca went on. "But maybe he'll finally go on those long cycling trips he's been talking about for years."

One thing's for sure, I thought, smiling vaguely at her, *my father won't be going on any long trips, cycling or otherwise, not for a very long time.*

"Your turn, Melissa," Cathy announced.

Melissa is super tall (it was easy to see that, even though she was sitting down), maybe almost six feet, and is seriously pretty in the kind of way that almost makes you uncomfortable. Well, makes *me* uncomfortable. Like, her looks are too good to be true or something. Anyway, she told me she wanted to go to FIT. "That's the Fashion Institute of Technology," she explained, before I could ask. The look on my face must have told her I didn't know what she was talking about. *And no surprise there, either,* I thought. Melissa could easily make a living as a model if she wanted to.

"It's in New York," she went on. "But if I can't get into FIT, or if Mom and Dad can't afford it, I'll go to a regular college with a good art program. Either way, I'm going to work in fashion. I want to design, but I also really like to write. I'm starting up a style blog, but I haven't come up with a really catchy name for it yet. The competition is fierce. There are soooo many style bloggers out there, but if you're good enough, you can make a lot of money at it."

These girls, I thought, *are exhausting me.* They all have so much ambition and drive. How does that happen? Where do ambition and drive come from? Do they come from a sense of security? If you can trust someone older to be handling the day-to-day stuff for you—like paying the rent or the mortgage and making sure you have plenty to eat and not dragging you around from lousy apartment to lousier rental house, from substandard school to a school with metal detectors at each entrance—maybe then you have the luxury of dreaming and planning and actually envisioning your future. I wouldn't know.

"Cathy," Becca said. "Last but not least."

"Well," Cathy began briskly, "I'm definitely hoping I can

get a soccer scholarship, not that I'm as good as you, Hildy. Still, any money will help, especially if I want to go somewhere other than YCC." Cathy turned to me then. "Because my mom works there, I can get a tuition discount. You can too, Marni. But I think eventually I want to study early childhood development, which means I'll need at least a master's to get a good job." Cathy laughed. "I'm gonna be in debt till I'm fifty!"

"What are you into, Gemma?" Becca asked. "I mean, Marni. Sorry."

The question kind of embarrassed me. I mean, I like certain things, but I've never been *into* things. I guess we never had the money for me to get involved in a hobby. Hobbies cost money, don't they? You have to buy equipment, like, I don't know, a loom if you're into weaving. And to collect things, like china dolls or old coins, must cost a lot. But maybe not having money is an excuse. *Maybe,* I thought, *I'm just lazy and dull.*

When I didn't answer immediately, Melissa said, "What's your passion? What do you absolutely have to do or else you'll go mad?"

I was about to say, *Nothing,* when I thought about my drawing. But was that really a passion? I don't know. Besides, my being "into" drawing isn't something I want anyone to know right now. Maybe ever—who knows? The whole conversation was making me uneasy.

Finally I shrugged and said, "I haven't found my passion yet," in as I-couldn't-care-less a way as I could manage.

"Nothing inspires you?" That was Melissa again.

I thought of making a joke of some sort, but I couldn't think of what sort, so I just shook my head.

"So, what are you going to study in college?" Hildy asked. "I don't think you have to declare a major until your junior year, but I'm not sure about that."

College? It wasn't something I'd ever given any thought to. Honestly. I mean, I know I'm smart. I don't know how smart I *really* am, because I don't feel I've ever been around any seri-

ously smart people, so I can't compare. (Actually, Verity and
Annie are probably the two smartest people I've ever known.
There's no point in denying it.) The idea of *learning* sounds
good. But Dad never said anything to me about my going to
college. Once, a long time ago, he told me he'd dropped out
before finishing his degree because he didn't need the degree to
get work. It wasn't until about two years ago, during one of
those times when our cash was seriously low and we were eating Ramen noodles every night for about a week, that I began
to think Dad's dropping out of college might not have been
such a smart thing to do. Of course, I said nothing.

"Oh," I finally said, again pretending a nonchalance I didn't
at all feel. "I'll figure out something. Maybe I'm one of those
late bloomers."

There was an awkward silence after that, and I knew every
single one of those girls was thinking the same thing. That I
was lost. That because I'd come from a "disadvantaged home"
(I'd seen that phrase recently online), I'd been deprived of direction. That no one had been around to inspire or encourage
me. And the really awful part was that they were right. Dad
was a good father to a certain point. And after that, he just
couldn't cut it.

I don't like to be pitied. I was on the verge of saying something I'd probably regret—like, *Why are you people even pretending to give a shit about me?*—when Hildy suddenly said
brightly, "Enough talk about the future. I want to know about
something happening now." She turned to Cathy and asked,
"So, are you going to ditch Jason like you said you were?"

My stomach dropped. This was a nightmare! I had no idea
if Cathy had told her friends about what had happened at her
parents' anniversary party. But Cathy shot me a quick smile
and said, "Yeah. I'm tired of him. And he was beginning to
push me to do stuff I'm so not going to do yet."

"You mean, have sex?" The words were out of my mouth
before I could stop them.

Cathy looked mildly disconcerted. "Yes," she said.

"But sex is no big deal." *Stop talking,* I told myself.

"Then why do it?" Becca demanded. "I thought sex was *supposed* to be a big deal."

"I don't know," I said. "You have sex because it's fun, that's why."

Hildy frowned. "Snowboarding is fun too, but it's not always good for you. You could break a leg if you're not careful."

"So," Melissa said. "You've had sex?"

"Yeah. A few times." That was a lie. It was a lot more than a few times, though honestly, not in the past few months.

No one responded to that. And I was aware I was presenting myself as, I don't know, colder, less feeling than I actually am. The truth is that I never enjoyed sex as much as I said I did. It was just a clichéd way of rebelling, I suppose, although I don't really know what I was rebelling against; pretty much every kid I knew was having sex. It was the norm. I guess sex was more a way of, I don't know, easing loneliness. Not that it always worked, and when it did work, it wasn't for very long.

You'll have guessed by now that I've never actually had a real boyfriend, someone who I cared about and who cared about me.

Not that I wouldn't want a boyfriend someday, someone who really loves me, someone I can trust. If that's even possible.

"Anyway," Melissa said forcefully, "the point is that no one, male or female, should be forced to do what they don't want to do. There has to be consent, and not only because someone feels pressured to say yes."

"You're right," I said, hoping to make up a bit for the trouble I seemed to be causing without all that much desire to cause it. "It should always be a choice."

Things kind of wound down after that conversation, and at ten o'clock on the nose Hildy's mother came by to take Hildy, Becca, and Melissa home. She seemed surprised to see me with the group and asked if I needed a ride home. Before I could reply—Verity had told me to call her, and I really didn't want to be stuck in a car with three girls who I suspected didn't like me all that much—Cathy said, "That's okay, Mrs. Leonard. My mom's taking Marni home."

Annie did drive me back to Birch Lane. (It's too dangerous to ride a bike at night around here. It's so dark, and the roads are very twisty.) Cathy came with us, and I thanked them both when I got out of the car. Still, I'm pretty sure I won't be getting any more invitations to hang out with Cathy's friends.

That's okay.

Chapter 58

I was really tired, but I just couldn't fall asleep. I kept replaying the time at Cathy's, remembering every word and every laugh and every time I felt like an alien. At least none of Cathy's friends had asked me any stupid questions about how it felt finding out your name wasn't really your name or meeting your mother for the first time at seventeen. Either Cathy had told them not to be idiots or they're smart or sensitive enough to keep their mouths shut.

Smart. Sensitive. Those girls are just so totally unlike the kids I used to hang out with, they're almost a separate species. Seriously, I'd bet any money I had that not one of those girls has done anything more exciting or dangerous or against the law than crossing the street when the light is blinking or drinking milk that expired the day before. The guys in their crowd are probably just as bad—by which I mean good—but the only one I've met is Jason, Cathy's soon to be ex-boyfriend, and there was a look in his eyes when I was coming on to him that made me think maybe he's at least *thought about* doing something he'd have to keep a secret from his parents. There's no way anyone could expect me to be friends with that group, assuming they'd want to be friends with me, and I'm pretty sure that after tonight, they don't. I make them uncomfortable. I'm good at that, making people uncomfortable, though sometimes—and I'd never admit this out loud—I don't know why I do it, set out to rub people the wrong way. Yeah, I like to be left alone mostly, but that can't be the whole reason, can it? I mean, it's a bit aggressive of me, isn't it, to assume it's okay to make a perfectly nice person feel bad.

But it's not hard to see that with Cathy and her friends, there is a lot of caring going on, if sometimes in a way that makes me, personally, nauseous, all that girly-girly *oh my God, no way!* squealing sort of bonding. Maybe those friendships won't last much after high school, or maybe some of them will last a lifetime. Who knows? The point is, I guess, that in the here and now those girls—and maybe even some of the guys—really care about what happens to one another. They've got someone to turn to if they're having a crappy day or whatever. They've got people to have fun with. Even I have to admit that's probably a good thing.

I wonder if Cathy is going to tell her mother I've had sex. Annie will tell Verity, I'm sure of that. Oh well. I don't know why it should be a secret.

The first time I had sex was when I was only fourteen. I know. Now it seems insane, but then . . . Anyway, it was pretty awful, as you might imagine, totally all about him, and I only did it because I'd had an insane crush on this guy for months, and when he finally noticed I was alive, I was so blown away by the attention he started to pay me that I lost what was left of my mind. Of course, once we'd done it—in the backseat of his car; how clichéd—he never bothered with me again.

You'd think I'd have learned my lesson. I mean, I felt like such a complete loser; I swear it was the only time I've ever been seriously depressed in my life. You'd think I'd have waited around until someone who really liked me for me and not for what he could get came around, but how do you tell if a guy's decent? I mean, they're all full of lies, and even though I was always pretty street-smart, as the saying goes, I was still a kid. You know crap at fourteen and not much more at fifteen or sixteen, and I had no one older I could turn to for advice. I certainly wasn't going to talk to Dad about guys. He probably would have dropped dead of a heart attack if I even mentioned the word *dating,* let alone *sex.* I'd learned the facts of life the way every other kid I knew had—from older kids. Needless to say, the information we got was bad all around.

Anyway, after making another stupid decision, this time with a guy who swore he was into me and who even gave me a silver bracelet (which wasn't silver after all) but who turned out to have a girlfriend who found out about his affair with me—if you can call five minutes on a bench behind the high school one night an affair—and who then threatened to cut me if I didn't back off, I finally got the message. All guys, at least the ones I was likely to meet, were untrustworthy. That's a nice way of saying they were shits, so if I wanted to have sex for whatever reason, and I did, sort of, then I was going to have to drop any expectations I was stupid enough to have had in the first place and just focus on getting out of it what I wanted.

Momentary connection. Temporary attention. Oblivion for about thirty seconds. Whatever. No complications, at least of the emotional kind.

But back to tonight. It's not that I had a bad time at Cathy's. No one was openly nasty. It's just that it was pretty obvious I'm an outsider. Then again, I've always felt like an outsider, even when I was hanging out with the other outsiders!

I wonder if I'll ever feel like I belong.

A lot of the kids I knew from school—from all the schools I went to over the years—got in trouble by doing stupid things, like stealing from the convenience store or spray painting private homes or knocking over every garbage can in a neighborhood on collection day. But I wasn't stupid. I never stole. I never skipped school. Well, only once or twice. (I'm smart. Missing a few days here and there—without Dad knowing, of course—made no difference. I always got an A. And here's the kind of schools I went to. No one ever called Dad to ask where I was, was I home sick, had I been run over by a truck or something. No one ever bothered to care.)

Anyway, about stealing, a few times over the years I wondered where we'd gotten the money for the flat-screen TV (not a very big one) or for the brand-new microwave Dad brought home once. But I never asked. I decided I didn't want to know. The fact was that we always needed money or something that it could buy. I figured Dad did what he had to do, and as long as he didn't get caught, well . . . And if he did get caught, it would be easier for me to lie to the police the less I knew.

Like I said before, stealing was one thing I wasn't stupid enough to do, but I did make some stupid decisions about other things, only some maybe weren't that stupid, I guess. I mean, nothing bad ever happened to me because I smoked dope for the first time when I was thirteen and had my first beer at twelve. And both were easy for me to take or leave because I'm not an addict like my mother was. I mean, like I was told she was. Anyway, getting high is fun. That's all. And you can't have fun all the time, right? That's just common sense. So it was all under control, and I was always careful.

I wasn't always so careful with sex. (Here I am, talking about sex again!) That's where I made more than a stupid decision. I made a seriously *bad* decision. I was careless. The condom was old, and I didn't even recognize the brand. I mean, the package was *dirty*. The guy, who was actually sort of a buddy of mine, must have had it in his pocket or whatever for years. I should have known there was a chance the condom was defective but okay, I'd had a few beers and let's face it, booze doesn't go well with good decision making. When my period was a day late, I freaked out. When it was two days late, I really freaked out. There was no way I could go to Dad and tell him I might be pregnant. No. Way. As far as he knew, I was still his innocent little girl. And yeah, I was a bit afraid of what he might do. Not to me but to my buddy (not that I would have told Dad his name). Honestly? I was a bit afraid of what Dad might do to himself.

Think about it: I was fifteen and very likely facing a life of raising a kid on my own with only my father for help. Not good. The kid would have been doomed from the start.

I had no girlfriends I could talk to; though I knew of some girls at school who had been pregnant, I wasn't at all close to them, and I wasn't about to go advertising my situation to strangers. So I told my buddy (note I'm not calling him a friend), and he was no help, not that I'd really thought he would be. First, he denied a baby could be his. When I asked him why, was he sterile, and if so how did he know, had he been tested? Of course he had no answer. Then he told me he had no money, so I'd better not bother to ask for any. Then he said he knew someone who knew someone who'd had an abortion without her parents knowing and that was what I should do. Nice advice. Very helpful. "Maybe," he said finally, his face brightening, "maybe you'll, you know, lose it."

In the end, I was lucky. My period showed up a few days later, and I was spared having to make what totally would have been the most difficult decision of my life.

Lesson learned. I was insanely careful after that. Not careful enough to stop having sex, but careful enough to keep beer out of the equation and to provide the condoms myself.

I probably shouldn't have told Cathy and the others I've had sex. I mean, not that I'm ashamed or anything. That's so old-fashioned and totally antifeminist, and I'm a feminist. But it's also not like I want people to think I'm bragging about it. It's not something to brag about. It's not like it takes any skill!

And all the *activities* Cathy and her friends are involved in!

Most of the schools I went to had no real money for afterschool programs like soccer and orchestra, though most schools were able to afford some sort of crappy little band. Which was fine by me, because sports bore the life out of me, as you know; I have no interest in learning how to play an instrument; and I've always liked, ever since I was little, to be alone or, at least, not supervised by some annoying adult. And supervising me was something my father was always doing. Trying to control me, being overprotective, breathing down my neck. I had enough of that sort of thing at home, so I learned early on how to escape by blocking him out (that's a nice way of saying *ignoring him*) and by walking away (that's another way of saying *sneaking away*).

Sneaking away, sometimes at night, when Dad was asleep.

Compared to Cathy and her friends, I'm wild and crazy, I guess, but I don't really see myself as a risk taker. I mean, I've taken risks (I'm not talking about sex here), but mostly because I was forced to. Like, there was the time—a few times, actually—when Dad forgot to pick me up after school when I had to stay late for detention, and I lied to another kid's mom about him waiting just around the corner and then I walked home alone in the dark along some pretty empty roads where there was no place to hide if some creep pulled up alongside me in his car.

Okay, I bet you're saying, so if your father was such a control freak, so overly possessive of you and always so concerned for your safety, how could he possibly forget to pick you up from school? And how could he have neglected to take me to the dentist a few years in a row, which he did neglect to do, not that I like going to the dentist but parents are supposed to make you do the stuff that's good for you even if you put up a stink. The answer to those questions is that I really don't know.

I mean, I can't really explain my father, not even now, except to say that somehow this weird and annoying obsession with my safety existed right alongside this weird and only sometimes annoying habit of almost forgetting I was even in the room. To be honest, as time went on and I turned twelve and then thirteen, I preferred the times he got all broody and preoccupied because it allowed me *space*. I could be on my own and do what I liked until suddenly, and it was like someone had snapped two fingers in his head, he'd remember I was there in his life and freak out about every little detail of my day. Who did I talk to between classes? How many potato chips had I eaten at lunch? (I mean, have you ever known anyone who counted potato chips? Unless they're anorexic or something and then it's just sad.) Did anyone suspicious follow me home? I remember thinking: *What? Is he for real? Who the hell would want to follow me home?* Okay, a psycho stalker might trail a teenage girl, but every time Dad asked that question, I got the impression he meant someone—official. Someone wearing a suit and driving a fancy car. Someone wearing those so not discreet earphones.

Now I know I was right.

Like I said, seriously annoying stuff but nothing worse than that. He never once hit me. He tried to punish me a few times that I remember—no video games for a week, stuff like that—but he was never able to go through with it. I think he was afraid I wouldn't love him anymore, but seriously, where would I have gone if I suddenly decided I didn't love my father? Could he really have been worried I'd leave him?

The times I'd fight back and tell him to leave me alone, he'd get all sad looking, and sometimes his eyes would get wet. (I started to wonder if he could cry on command, if it was an act.) Once or twice he raised his voice with me, saying things like, *I'm the parent* and *I know best*, but his bark was way worse than his bite and I'd just stand firm, and the next thing you know, he was apologizing to me like crazy and telling me how much he loved me and asking me if I wanted to go out to my favorite place for dinner (if we had the money) and almost groveling.

In the year before our life together completely fell apart, I'd come to see it all—Dad's behavior, I mean—as pretty pathetic, but I didn't take any pleasure in that. I felt bad about thinking my father was pathetic. I know a lot of people probably think I'm cold, but I'm not. "You're all I've got," he'd say. "You're the only one who loves and understands me." And at those moments I hated not him but my mother for putting me in this position by being a violent drug addict. Which, of course, she seems not to have been at all . . .

Anyway, the point is that it's a seriously heavy burden to bear, meaning so much to someone, especially when you're only a kid and he's an adult and should be able to stand on his own two feet.

And not get caught stealing a freakin' car.

Chapter 59

"Did you like that movie we watched last night?"

"Yeah."

"Benedict Cumberbatch is such a good actor, isn't he?"

"Yeah."

"And it's horrifying to think that so few years ago gay people were considered sick."

"I know."

I restrained a sigh and focused on keeping the car on the road. Sometimes Gemma is so frustratingly uncommunicative. For example, when Gemma had come back from her solo trip into town the other day, I'd asked her how it went. She'd shrugged. "Fine. Why shouldn't it have?" We both knew why it might not have been "fine," but I didn't pursue the matter; it only would have sounded as if I wanted an argument. And I'd had no idea she'd helped Mr. Pascoe with the lock on his front door. Mrs. Pascoe told me when I ran into her in the grocery store. "Bert said she was so nice," she gushed. "Just a lovely young woman!" I suspected that one or the other of the Pascoes was exaggerating for my benefit, but that's okay. Still, I wondered why Gemma hadn't told me about the incident.

I didn't get much out of her about the get-together at Cathy's house, either, other than it was "okay" and the onion dip was good. And it seems Annie didn't get much out of

Cathy, either, at least, nothing she felt should be passed on to me. I don't mean to say I'm spying on my daughter. It's just that any little bit of information about her I can glean from other sources is welcome.

"We're here," I said unnecessarily as I pulled the car into a spot outside The Grey Gull. It's a family-style restaurant overlooking the ocean at York Beach. "I hope we can get a table upstairs. The view's better."

We did get a table upstairs, and Gemma went off to the ladies' room. While she was there our waitress came to the table to pour water and take a drink order. I asked her to come back when Gemma had returned.

Gemma rejoined me a few minutes later. "I drank, like, a gallon of seltzer before we left the house," she explained, settling in the chair across from me. I'd let her have the seat with the better view of the water. "I think I'm getting addicted to it."

Better than soda, I thought. My plan was working!

"The waitress came to take a drink order," I told her. "I didn't know what you wanted—though now I'm guessing seltzer?—so I told her to come back."

Gemma laughed. "Dad would have just decided he knew what I wanted and ordered it."

Gemma, too? *My God,* I thought. What other experiences do we have in common, and how can I find out what they might be without sounding as if I'm digging for dirt on Alan?

"Really?" I said casually.

"Yeah. He did it all the time, not that we went out a lot. But whenever we did, he'd order for me even if I was sitting right there with my mouth open to tell the waiter or the counter guy what I wanted. It drove me nuts."

"What did you do?"

"I'd tell the waiter what I really wanted. And if I'd, like, gone to the bathroom and Dad had ordered for me while I was away and something I didn't want showed up, I wouldn't eat it. I mean, he's a super-controlling person. I think he means it to be caring somehow, but it can really get on your nerves."

And then I decided to take a risk.

"He would do the same thing with me," I said. "Only, when I'd protest, he'd give me this look like I was a moody child and say something like, 'Now don't be silly. Of course you want a hamburger.' After a while I just started giving in and ate what he'd ordered for me because the times when I'd argue, he'd look hurt, like I had rejected him. At least, I thought he looked hurt." Maybe, I thought, Alan had been faking it as part of his plan of manipulation. But was he smart enough to devise a plan?

Gemma shook her head. "But didn't it make you insane?"

"Not at first," I admitted. "But yes, after a while."

"Wow. It's weird, him acting the same way with us . . ."

"Not so weird," I said. "Alan is Alan. People rarely change all that drastically. At least, in my experience they don't."

The waitress returned then, and we ordered our drinks (Gemma had a soda; you can't win all the time) and dinner. When the waitress had gone, Gemma said: "He took the house keys with him to work once. I mean, he took my set."

"Why?" I asked. *Oh boy*, I thought. I was right. People really don't change.

"He said he'd heard there was some child molester running loose. But he was wrong. I mean, there was a child molester running loose, but he was three or four towns away, and the police had found him the night before." Gemma looked at me closely. "Did he ever do that sort of thing to you?"

I sighed, though I hadn't meant to. "Yes," I said. "There was a big thunderstorm once, long before I had you. It was my day off work, but I needed some cash and I wanted to return a book to the library. When I went to leave the apartment, I couldn't find the keys. So I called him at his office to see if he'd noticed them before he left for work. Sometimes I was careless with them. He told me he'd taken my keys because he didn't want me out in bad weather. I told him I needed cash to pay back our neighbor who'd lent me ten dollars the day before. He said he had my bank card and would get the money for me."

"Shit. What did you do?"

I shrugged. "I stayed home. And I stewed. What did you do?"

Gemma laughed, as if I'd asked a stupid question. Maybe I had. "I left the apartment unlocked!" she said. "I wasn't about to be anyone's prisoner. Besides, we had nothing much to steal."

"You stood up for yourself. I didn't. Not for a long time."

"Dad never frightened me."

And there was the difference. Alan *had* frightened me. Not always, but after a time.

How self-sufficient she is, I thought. I'm impressed by my own daughter.

I decided then to share some of the nice things Alan had done for me early on. It can't hurt to be fair, can it? "Your father was very sweet when we first met."

"Really?" she asked, a distinctly dubious note in her voice. "How did you guys meet anyway?"

"On line for coffee. It was one of those fancy overpriced coffee shops that seem to attract the very people who really shouldn't be spending their money on specialty drinks. Students, for one, like I was. Anyway, when it came time for me to pay, I realized I didn't have my wallet. The guy behind me— your father—said he'd pay for me. I turned around and—well, that was it. I was immediately attracted to him. Nothing like that had ever happened to me before. Nothing so romantic."

"So what happened then?" Gemma asked. I thought she sounded genuinely interested.

"We took our coffees to a table in a corner and sat there for almost two hours, talking. Eventually I had to go to a class, and he asked if he could walk me there. I said okay, and then he asked for my phone number. The rest was pretty much history."

"Was he your first?"

It wasn't a question I'd been expecting, but I supposed there was no point in lying. "Well," I said, feeling more than a little embarrassed, "yeah, as a matter of fact."

"And you were nineteen? That's kind of old."

"Everyone's different," I said, thinking about the fact that Gemma and I hadn't yet talked about sex and birth control and STDs. We would have to, and soon.

"Why couldn't you remember those good things about Dad later, when things got weird?" she asked suddenly.

"I did remember them. But remembering made the present worse. You can't live on the fumes of what used to be, not for very long. It's what's happening now, in the present, that makes us happy or sad. And it's the present that sets the tone for the future."

Our dinner arrived then, and as usual Gemma ate as if this were her last meal. All conversation about anything more important than the food ceased. It wasn't until we were in the car and on our way home to Birch Lane that I said: "You asked me if Alan was my first."

"And you want to know if I've had sex. Yes. I have."

"Oh. All right."

"And yes, I know about protection."

"Okay."

"Anyway, I'm not really interested in getting involved with anyone right now, so there's nothing to talk about."

"Okay. But if you need anything at some point . . ."

"Yeah."

The uncommunicative Gemma was back.

Chapter 60

I rode my bike, the Tyler, to the beach yesterday afternoon. With Marc's advice, we bought it from a bike repair guy who has his own business out of his garage. Marc's bought bikes and parts from him before, so we knew we could trust him. It cost eighty bucks, and though Marc said there was no charge for the minor adjustments he made to the bike before I could comfortably ride it, I wonder if Verity gave him something anyway. In my experience, not a lot in this world comes without a price. Anyway, I took my sketchbook and a few pencils in an old set of panniers Marc had passed on to me. For free.

When I got to the beach, I found a relatively private spot to myself about halfway to the Wells town line, and sat on a log that had been worn smooth by exposure to the sea. It seemed weird to me at first that there'd be a tree trunk on the beach, but Verity says they often wash up; sometimes a tree on the coast of an island is torn down in a storm and falls into the water and sometimes, the tree trunk isn't a tree trunk at all anymore but a mast from a boat that's come apart. Other weird stuff washes up too, Verity said, though so far I've only seen mounds of stinky seaweed and some battered lobster traps. (It's illegal to take them, as they belong to the fishermen and have identification on them. All those people who display old lobster traps on their front lawns are probably breaking the law.)

Anyway, I sat down on the log, got out my sketchbook and a pencil, and thought about what Verity had said about the past, present, and future. It was true. If you were going to live a normal life, you had to let go of the way things used to be. I mean, you had to stop expecting things to be the way they were.

I think I'm coming to understand that. Even if Dad gets out of jail tomorrow—that would be a miracle and probably a serious miscarriage of justice!—we could never have our old life back.

Still, I want to remember that old life. At least, I don't want to forget it. And life here with Verity isn't as awful as I was afraid it was going to be, which makes keeping memories of the old life alive more difficult.

Here's another thing. As close as Dad and I were—as close as we *are*—we never really talked about the sorts of things Verity and I talk about, like Life with a capital *L* and even, briefly, sex. I don't think it's because we're father and daughter and some topics are supposed to be off-limits, if you're like from the dark ages. I don't know why it is. Does Dad even *think* about the big stuff? He must. Doesn't everybody at least sometimes? Maybe Life overwhelms him too easily so he can't risk spending too much time and energy trying to figure it all out. If that's the case, maybe he *should* be spending the time trying to think things through.

But what do I know?

After all that thinking, I got down to some serious sketching, by which I mean I concentrated on looking closely at the other end of the log on which I was sitting. There were the remains of some roots, and they were sticking up and out like skeleton fingers or something else equally as creepy. I also made a fairly decent detailed drawing of a big clamshell that was sticking half out of the sand. There's a lot going on with seashells, all these lines and ridges and subtle colors. I can see why Verity likes to collect them and to paint them.

Then, as I sat there sketching, something occurred to me. I don't know why. Well, yes, I do. It probably had something to do with my realizing that I want to remember my past. I turned to a new page of the sketchbook, and without making a concentrated effort to see Dad's face in my mind's eye, I just started to draw. I'd never tried anything like that in the short time I've been sketching, drawing something from memory, especially not something so . . . so intimate and subjective as a human face. The face of someone I love.

It was a disaster. I got as far as sort of outlining the shape of the head and the eyes, nose, and mouth when I stopped. Not only did the unfinished image on the page look nothing at all like the image of my father in my head, it hardly looked like a human face at all.

Maybe I'm just not ready to tackle that kind of a project.

Or maybe I've already started to forget.

Chapter 61

"She wrote back to my father."

Annie and I were sitting at her kitchen table, cups of coffee before us.

"So?" she said. "Didn't you say he sent her a card and a twenty-dollar bill? Maybe she just thanked him for it."

"I know, but I just didn't think she would contact him. I told her we aren't close."

"That doesn't mean *she* can't be close to her grandfather."

"I know," I said. "He wrote her back. I saw the envelope this morning when the mail was delivered. That's when she told me she'd written to him."

"Why does this bother you?" Annie asked. "I think I'm missing something."

"I never understood why my father remarried so soon after my mother's death." I hadn't planned on saying that. But there it was, an old hurt revealed.

"Common wisdom has it that people—men, in particular—remarry soon after they're widowed because they enjoyed being married. In a way, it's a compliment to the first spouse."

I frowned. "I'm not sure I buy that. And to get remarried to a woman so totally unlike my mother!"

"Is that what this is about?"

"What?" I know I sounded defensive.

"Your being upset that Gemma is in touch with your father. Are you still angry with him for having moved on with his life? Doesn't he deserve to be happy?"

I didn't answer right away. I felt embarrassed. Was I really so immature? "I told you what he said to me after Alan took Gemma," I said then, pointedly not answering Annie's question. "He asked if I'd done something to make Alan angry enough to steal my child."

Annie sighed. "Come on, Verity," she said. "The man was probably at a loss. I mean, how often is the average person witness to the kidnapping of someone close to him? I can't really believe he meant anything by it. He was probably just trying to figure it all out, as were you."

I thought about that. It made some sense. But I wasn't—I'm not—ready to reverse my position regarding my father.

"It's been how many years since your mother died?" Annie asked then. "Over twenty, right? Let it go, Verity. At least, let your daughter have a relationship with her grandfather if she wants to. Who knows? Gemma might be the one to heal the rift between you and Tom."

My first thought was to doubt that Gemma might affect any such thing, but then again, miracles do happen. Gemma had come home. She was no longer in the grip of her crazy father. And that led me to exclaim:

"How could Alan have allowed her to get multiple tattoos—let alone one tattoo!—when she's only a kid? Worse, she said she got the first one when she was fourteen!"

"Are you certain Gemma's father knew about the inking?" Annie asked.

"She says he took her to a friend of a friend who did both for a discount. Isn't that illegal, getting a child marked with a needle and ink?"

"If it isn't, it should be. But then again, I'm squeamish. And curious. I've seen the heart on her ankle. Pierced by an arrow, no less. What's the other one she's got?"

I winced. "It's a tramp stamp. Right above her butt. A pair of wings with a heart between them."

"Ow. Well, at least it isn't a skull or a nasty word. And tattoos can be removed, if you want them to be. And I'm not sure we should be using that term, tramp stamp. Women need to respect the choices of other women. Stick together and all that."

"Sorry," I said. "You're right. Anyway, I doubt Gemma's going to want her tattoos removed. She'll probably be accumulating more ink before too long. Not that I'll give her permission, but that won't stand in her way."

"Don't make assumptions. You might ask her not to get another tattoo until she's eighteen. She might say okay."

"Or she might run right out and get some particularly sensitive part of her body pierced."

"Is she really that reactionary? That perverse?"

I sighed. "I don't know. It seems as if she is, at least with me. But not all the time. I'm being grumpy. I should give Gemma the benefit of the doubt. And the space and time she needs to come to terms with the sense of dislocation and loss she must be feeling."

"It couldn't hurt to try."

And I am trying. Honestly. I'm trying all the time.

"Do you know," I told Annie, "that when Gemma first came home to me, she was so down, so closed off, I was afraid she'd try to commit suicide. So many teens do."

"Gemma's not the type," Annie stated with certainty.

"I know that now. At least, I think I do. Anyway, is there really a *type* to commit suicide? Isn't it entirely possible that almost every person at some terribly low point in his or her life could be tempted to end it all?"

Annie thought about that for a moment. Finally she said: "Tempted, yes. But to actually go through with it? No, I don't think that the majority of people would make that choice. For some it would be because of religious reasons. For others, fear of what might be an even worse existence after life on earth. Some people might just decide that the prospect of a good cup of coffee in the morning was enough to live for."

"Or, in Gemma's case, a good cup of coffee accompanied by a chocolate doughnut."

Annie laughed. "The girl does have a sweet tooth!"

Chapter 62

Verity had pressed me into going with her to watch the Independence Day parade this morning. I've never been into parades. Well, that's not really true. What I should say is that Dad didn't like to go where there were crowds of people. He never said why. Now I wonder if it was something to do with feeling exposed, like someone in the press of people would sense his massive guilt, assuming he felt any, and he wouldn't be able to run away. Whatever the reason, I didn't grow up going to parades, big or small.

"It should be fine," Verity said, and I know what she meant. I've been here over a month already, and except for that one stupid woman who accosted us that time, Mirelle what's her name, no one else has been trouble. Everyone at the parade would probably be too busy cheering on the marching bands and the floats to pay attention to The Little Kidnapped Girl.

So we went. It was okay. The marching band sounded a bit off to me, but maybe that's because I'm not big on that kind of music. The float Verity had helped make for the local veterinarians was cool. She had built a huge version of one of those carpeted towers that cats like, and on every level or perch there were papier-mâché models of all sorts of cats. Around the base of the tower there were papier-mâché models of dogs and even a few real dogs, on leashes of course.

Around eleven we went to the beach. The Strawberries came too, and Marion. Marion was wearing a matching top and capri pants, white with orange stripes. For some reason she looked to me like a soda can, though I don't think I've ever actually seen an orange-and-white-striped soda can. She had this rickety old folding chair that wasn't even a real beach chair (not that I'm an expert on beach chairs already, but everyone knows an indoor folding chair when they see one!) and a bag that was one of those recycled things supermarkets are always trying to get people to reuse. I wondered if she was poor, or maybe she just didn't go to the beach very often. So there she was, sitting in her chair, her hands folded on her lap (probably because the chair had no arms) and her feet together, with what looked like a really old thermos leaning against one leg of the chair. Anyway, I suddenly had this overwhelming feeling of pity for her, and it annoyed me. Why, I thought, did she have to sit there, looking all tiny and vulnerable and forlorn? But then she gave me this big happy smile and I thought, *Stop reading into things! She's just an old woman enjoying an afternoon at the beach. Just because she's your grandmother . . .*

"Marni!" It was Cathy. She was wearing a sort of wet suit but with short sleeves and legs. It was for body surfing, she said. I don't know about you, but I'm not going into the water above my ankles. I mean, the ocean is beautiful, but it's big and powerful and I don't swim and I've seen now how waves can knock a person down and how sometimes it seems like forever before they can get up. If that means I'm a coward, fine. Hey, Dad's a coward. I'm just a chip off the old block.

"Are you wearing your bathing suit?" she asked, eyeing my jean shorts and T-shirt.

"Don't have one," I said. "Swimming is not really my thing." That isn't entirely true. I like pools, but the ocean is too intimidating.

Cathy seemed to be giving that some thought. Finally she said: "It must be kind of weird to be living on the East Coast after growing up in the Southwest."

"It is weird," I said. And then I was off and running. "Arizona and New Mexico are so amazing. The desert is the best. It's way more exciting than the ocean." I was lying through my teeth, as that old saying goes, probably a skill I picked up from my father without even knowing it. And I was totally aware I was being defensive. I mean, I *love* the ocean. How many times have I already been down here at the beach on my own since getting my bike? A lot. So what was I doing?

"I bet you've been to the Grand Canyon a few times," Cathy said, oblivious to or ignoring my perverse mood. "My parents took me two summers ago. It was awesome. The colors of the rocks when the sun was setting on them were amazing. I'd never seen reds like that in my life, except in pictures. And I'd never really imagined that there were pine trees in the Southwest!"

I wouldn't know about the reds, I thought. I've never been to the Grand Canyon. Dad and I hadn't ever really gone on what you could call a vacation. I think it was mostly because of the money. I mean, we didn't have any to spare. I suppose we could have borrowed some camping equipment from someone—lots of people out where I grew up go camping pretty regularly—and we could have set up a tent on the rim of the canyon and cooked our own meals over a small fire, and that wouldn't have cost a lot. We knew families who did just that. But we, my dad and I, never did. The fact that we never really *did* anything fun or interesting had never really bothered me; at least, I hadn't let it bother me. But now, with Cathy looking all smug and content—or my thinking that she looked all smug and content—I felt angry. Why hadn't I gotten to go anyplace more than twenty miles from wherever we were calling home at any given time?

I shrugged. "Yeah, the Grand Canyon's okay," I said. "But the second and third time you see it, you're like, okay, I get it." Liar.

"Really?" Cathy's eyes had gone wide. "I don't think it would ever fail to amaze me. Look who's over by that purple umbrella!

It's Vera, from school. Wait, you don't know her yet. Be right back."

And Cathy was off, loping along the sand like the soccer player she is. I wonder if I should go to one of her games, you know, just to be nice.

That's an odd thought.

And here's another odd thought. It dawned on me that this was the first "family event" I'd ever attended, even if "family" means just Verity, Marion, and me. Of course Dad is family too, but it's different now with three generations together in one place. I thought, too, of Verity's father, my grandfather, and of how in his note to me he asked me to say hi to Verity for him. So I did tell her Tom said hi, but she didn't say anything and then kind of turned away from me. I wondered what she was feeling.

Maybe I'll ask her.

I spotted a shell I thought might fit one of the few gaps in Verity's collections, and stuck it into my pocket. I'd give it to her later. Right now she was talking to Marion, sitting cross-legged on a blanket, her hands on her knees. She looked really young, and I realized she *is* really young. And Marion isn't really old, either, not by today's standards. They could be around for a long time. My mother and my grandmother.

I turned away and thought about last year and what Dad and I did on the Fourth of July. We were living in a trailer park—it wasn't as gross as it sounds; this one was actually pretty nice—and the people in the trailers on either side of ours got together and we had a barbeque. Someone had an old grill; one of the legs was gone, so it was kind of propped up on one side with an old metal pole, but the grill part worked fine. Someone else brought sparklers, and I was glad there was nothing bigger or more dangerous than that. A guy we knew in the town we'd lived in the year before got seriously burned on the Fourth because he was stupid or drunk enough to be all impatient and peer into the metal garbage can into which he'd stuffed some fireworks. I remember the first time I saw him after the accident, and I'm embarrassed to admit I felt kind of sick to my stomach when I saw what was left of his hands and what the fire had done to his face.

"Marni!" It was Marc. "Any interest in helping me with the hot dogs?"

Another memory flashed at me then, of Dad at the grill, refusing to allow me anywhere near it because he was afraid I would get burned. For about a second I thought I was going to cry, but I got control of myself and went to join Marc.

Chapter 63

I was pretty wiped out, not having gotten to bed until almost two that morning. See, I'd gotten a call from the local veterinarians, a really nice couple I know from around Yorktide, at close to eight the previous night. A fire had totally destroyed the float they'd built for the parade this morning and what with me being a sculptor—in other words, I can wield a hammer and use a blowtorch and a chainsaw without somebody losing a vital body part—Jack and Hugh wondered if I could help them put together a new float. "Not elaborate," Jack had assured me. "Just something we can be proud of."

Not exactly a small task, but the guys are really nice people, so I packed up some plywood I keep in the basement, made a stop at my studio at the college for some tools, and headed out to the gorgeous old farmhouse Jack and Hugh call home.

I think people liked the float. At least, there was a lot of cheering from the crowd. Then again, maybe people were just happy to see the dogs for adoption Jack and Hugh are boarding, riding along with the papier-mâché models of dogs and cats. (Luckily, the models were in storage elsewhere when the float itself caught flame.)

Anyway, tired or not, I was happy to be right where I was, spending the day with the people who mean the most to me. Well, all but for David.

"Hey."

I turned to see Gemma coming toward me across the sand.
I'd pretty much browbeaten her into putting on sunblock before we left the house. "Trust me," I'd said. "Even if you don't
usually burn, you can burn at the beach. Something about the
reflection off the water." Honestly, I'm not sure that's true, but
it convinced Gemma to slather on the lotion.

"I know a lot of people find seagulls annoying," I said,
nodding toward a group of five birds dipping their beaks into
the wet sand at the water's edge. "I mean, they do have a harsh
cry and they can be pests when you're trying to eat, but I like
them. I think they're beautiful, actually."

Gemma nodded. "Some of them are huge. Especially the
white-and-gray ones. They look, like, two feet tall."

I laughed. "One time I was at Jackie's Too, in Perkins Cove,
sitting at one of the tables in the open, and a gigantic seagull
swooped down and took a French fry right out of my hand. I
can laugh now, but I was terrified then."

"They're scavengers, aren't they? I mean, they have to eat
whatever they can find, right?"

"Right," I said. "So it's hard to be mad at a creature who's
simply being what he's supposed to be."

Gemma had no reply for this, and suddenly I was seized
with the desire to reveal to her something I'd never revealed to
anyone, not even to Annie and David. I had no idea how she
would react to this revelation, but I felt bold. Maybe it was the
exhaustion, pulling down my caution and defenses.

"You know," I said, "every year on your birthday I come
down to the shore just at dawn. I bring with me a little bottle
in which I've put a note, wishing you well and asking the universe to send you home safely. And I toss the bottle into the
sea." Now, I thought, there was no need for me to perform this
ritual ever again.

Gemma didn't say anything for a long few minutes, and I
began to regret having shared. Then she said, "Is it cold here in
March?"

Her response didn't really surprise me. I hadn't expected her to throw her arms around me or kiss me on the cheek and tell me what a wonderful mother I was. "It's always cold before the sun has been up for a few hours," I said. "And yeah, it's not unheard of for us to get snow as late as April."

"I wonder if anyone's ever found one of the bottles."

"We'll never know. It's not like I put my name and address on the notes."

Gemma smiled a bit at that. "Do you go in?" she asked. "I mean, into the ocean?"

"Not above my knees," I said. "At least, not when there are big waves. I'm not a good enough swimmer."

Gemma nodded and then she went off. I watched her go up to Marion, sitting in state in her folding chair, and crouch down at her side. I wondered what Gemma was saying to her. I saw Marion smile and then actually laugh. Marion doesn't laugh often.

I turned back to look out over the water, at the kids splashing around in the shallow water and at the intrepid surfers farther out. I say intrepid not because the waves were so big—they weren't—but because the water is still so cold. David told me he tried surfing once, on a long-ago trip to California. It didn't go well. I wished he could have been there at Ogunquit Beach with us, but his mother is sick, not terribly but enough that he felt a visit to Michigan was warranted. I do want him to meet Gemma, and I had thought that maybe a group setting like this would be ideal. There'd be no pressure on either of them to spend too much time one on one.

"Hey." It was Annie. "Penny for your thoughts."

"I'm thinking about David," I told her. "And Gemma. I've been thinking about all the reasons why I haven't introduced them to each other yet."

"Are you afraid she's going to see David as a threat to her relationship with her father?"

I shrugged. "I don't know. How am I supposed to know anything about how she'll feel and react to things? It's not like we're the average divorced family, where Mom brings home her new fiancé and the kid automatically hates him on sight because he's not her father. Gemma was *abducted*. Her father's in *jail*. Maybe she'd actually welcome another, more normal adult male in her life."

"Exactly. You just don't know what she'll feel. And the only way you're going to know if Gemma will like David and David will like Gemma is to introduce them."

"I know. I had been hoping he could be here today, but . . ."

Marc's voice reached us from the grill station. "Burgers and dogs and corn on the cob, everyone!"

I realized I was starved. I wondered if anyone had brought the ingredients to make s'mores. Gemma, I thought, would like that.

Chapter 64

Verity had made spaghetti carbonara for dinner. You know that stupid old sexist saying, "The way to a man's heart is through his stomach"? Well, it's true in my case. The way to my *female* heart is through my stomach, only I never knew it until now. I mean, I've always loved to eat, but it was more to fill a hole than because I actually enjoyed what I was eating, like I do now. Do you know that carbonara sauce has some sort of bacon in it? How amazing is that?

"So, what new and exciting thing happened at work today?" I asked when Verity had taken her seat. She always sits in the same place, in the chair closest to the fridge. When I first came here, I used to sit wherever, but now I always sit in the chair directly across from her.

"Nothing all that new," she said, "but something kind of exciting."

"What?"

"I was tidying up the studio, and I came across these two sketches. They must have been done a few weeks ago when we were running that first summer drawing class for adults. I recognized the still life."

I kind of choked a bit on my pasta. My sketches. "So," I said when I'd finally swallowed, "what's so exciting about finding some old sketches?"

"What's so exciting is that they're really good, but the thing is, I don't quite recognize them as being from the hand of one of the adult summer students. Or any of the regular art students, for that matter. I asked around a bit in the department, but no one seems to know anything about them. And the hand is distinctive enough that if any of us had seen other work by this person, we'd remember."

I had a distinctive hand? The sketches were really good? "So, what did you do with them?" I asked casually, pretending less interest than I actually felt.

"I put them aside in a folder. I certainly wouldn't throw them away; they're far too good and show so much promise. I just hope that the artist comes back for them. I might have a prodigy on my hands, if I can persuade him—or her—to take a class. Julia Einstein gives the basic drawing classes, and she does do some private classes if she thinks the person's got real talent and the dedication to develop it."

Talent and *dedication*. I'd never thought those words would be used in relation to me. Ever. "What if the person who did the sketches isn't a student at the college?"

Verity shrugged. "I don't see why that should matter one way or the other. But I do wonder how someone not associated with the college could be in my studio. . . . Anyway, it's a mystery for the moment."

We went on to talk about other stuff, like how little rain we'd had since summer started (I hadn't noticed of course; East Coast weather is new to me) and how it would affect crop production (a serious thing). Later, when Verity had gone to bed and I had gone to my room, I really gave this question a thought: Why did I leave the sketches behind? Why hadn't I stuffed them into my pocket? Okay, I had heard Verity coming along the hall and I didn't want to be caught messing around with someone else's stuff, so maybe I panicked a bit. But maybe my subconscious mind had *wanted* Verity to find the sketches. I mean, who knows what goes on in the mind! Maybe a part of me realized that the sketches were good, though I don't know *how* I would have known. I mean, I'm no judge of art. Right? The only time I was ever in a museum was on a class trip in fifth grade, I think. We went to a small museum of Native American art. It's funny how clearly I can remember that day and all the things I saw, like the kachina dolls of the Zuni and the Hopi tribes, the painted pots and woven baskets, the intricately carved Navajo silver jewelry. I remember I thought it was all really cool, but no one told us how anything was made or why it was supposed to be "art." I also remember there was this chunk of polished turquoise in the gift shop and I really wanted it, but I had no money for souvenirs. And no, I didn't for one minute consider stealing it. A small hand-printed cardboard sign by the stone said that turquoise is the stone of health, happiness, and good fortune. I think about that stone a lot.

And I thought again about what Verity told me at the Fourth of July party, how every year on my real birthday in March she goes down to the beach and sort of performs that ritual. Of course I hadn't said anything to her about how I felt hearing that. Like how for half a second I thought, "yeah, right" and then in the next half a second I believed her and wanted to cry. And I thought about the conversation I had with Marion afterward. It was nothing important like what Verity had told me about the birthday messages, but I had kind of enjoyed it anyway. I hadn't known Marion had once been a Boggle champion. Okay, only the champion of the county, but still.

What's up with all these tears?

Chapter 65

I was stuffing dirty clothes into the washing machine, thinking that maybe I should suggest to Gemma that she do some of our laundry, help out a little around the house, when she appeared.

"Here," she said. She was holding out a white seashell. "I found this when we were all at the beach on the Fourth. I kind of forgot about it. I think it might work for your collection in the bathroom."

"Thank you," I said, taking the offered seashell. "I think it's the perfect size." I purposely didn't make a big deal out of the gift, but let me tell you, I deeply appreciate it.

"Did I tell you Tom said hi in his note?" Gemma asked.

I poured liquid laundry detergent into its little well and started the machine before answering. "Yes. You did."

"Oh, okay. I couldn't remember. What did he do for a job?"

We went into the kitchen, Gemma right on my heels.

"He worked for the local power company. He was a line-man for a while and then, when he got older, he drove the trucks rather than climb the poles."

"Did he go to college?" she asked.

"No."

"Did your mother work? I mean, did she have a career?"

"No," I told her. "She was a stay-at-home mom. She did

some volunteer work at my grammar school, PTA stuff I think. And she had a friend who lived on the next block. They spent a fair amount of time together, until the woman had to move away because her husband's job got transferred. On the whole, my mother lived a pretty quiet life."

I had surprised myself by saying so much, especially since Gemma hadn't asked for all that. But maybe Gemma needed to know her family's past, to place herself somewhere in the family history. It wasn't much of a heritage the Petersons or the Burnses had to offer, but it was hers.

Gemma dug into the front pocket of her jeans. "When you said volunteer work, that reminded me. You got a call earlier. Sorry I forgot to mention it. Here, I wrote down the message. Someone from Pine Hill Residence for the Elderly."

I took the slip of paper Gemma handed me. The message was from another person on the committee to have a signalized crossing where there currently isn't one.

I explained this to Gemma. "The Pine Hill bus takes residents into Yorktide each afternoon so they can shop or simply meet a friend. But closer to the home there's a cute little café where a lot of the residents like to go. The problem is, they have to cross a busy road at their own risk in order to get there. So a bunch of us locals have formed a committee to petition the town council to have a push-button activated stoplight installed."

"Why do you need a committee?" Gemma asked. "What's the big deal about there being a stoplight?"

"Some people—and I won't name names—who use that road frequently don't want to have to stop to let a person cross the road."

Gemma laughed. "So they'd rather run down some harmless old person on his way to get a cup of coffee?"

"You and I see that sort of attitude as selfish. The opponents of the stoplight would argue they're protecting their right to get where they're going without delay."

"That's so totally ridiculous!"

"Yeah, well, that's the way it is."

"Do you know anyone who lives there?" Gemma asked. "At the home?"

"No," I said, "but that doesn't matter. These people have been part of the community their entire lives. Just because they live in an assisted living residence doesn't mean they don't matter and doesn't mean they don't want to remain involved in the social life of the town. Everyone needs to feel, well, needed and necessary."

"So, there's nothing personal in it for you?" Gemma asked, not belligerently.

"To be honest," I said, "it does feel good to do good. So in that sense, yeah, I get some personal satisfaction from offering my time and energy. But in a practical sense, no, there's nothing personal in it for me, if by that you mean money or public adulation."

Gemma nodded and then she said, "Cool."

Huh, I thought. Did I just gain a small victory in my quest to get my daughter to like me? Maybe even to admire me?

Maybe. But I'm not letting it go to my head. The quest is far from over.

Chapter 66

"Do you remember Verity's father?" I asked Dad. Until then we'd been talking about the usual, by which I mean, nothing much. They were getting mac 'n' cheese for dinner. He loves mac 'n' cheese.

There was a moment of silence before he answered. "Why are you asking that?"

"Because I'm in touch with him. He seems okay."

"I wish you wouldn't . . ."

"Wouldn't what, Dad?" I pressed. I hate when people don't finish what they start to say.

"He's telling you lies about me."

"He doesn't mention you at all."

Dad snorted. "Figures. He never had any use for me, that arrogant bas—"

"Dad. Stop." *What the hell?* I thought. First he doesn't want anyone to talk about him, and then he's pissed when they don't? Frankly, I couldn't get off the phone fast enough, though I felt a little bad about cutting the call short. Usually it's the guard who says when we have to stop talking. "I've got to go," I said. "There's someone at the door. We're expecting a package so . . ."

Did he buy my lame excuse? Who knows? Only when I'd hung up did I realize I'd referred to Verity and me as "we."

I flopped down on the couch in my room, and here's what I thought about: life with Dad. Everyone wonders how much kids know about what goes on in their parents' private lives. The answer is a lot but not everything. Sometimes too much. Sometimes not enough. In other words, it depends, I think, on a bunch of factors, like how attuned the kid is to emotional nuances and how good the parents are at hiding shit (faking smiles when what they really want to do is throw insults and maybe plates at each other), and very important, I think, how much the kid *wants* to know what's really going on. Kids, I think, the emotionally smart ones, anyway, sense when they've gotten a handle on about all that they can tolerate knowing, and then they look the other way. At least, that's how it was with me. In retrospect, I mean. I think I must have known that something *else* was wrong or odd or just not right about my father and me, other than our wandering existence and Dad's not ever keeping a job for long, and his refusing to have the news stations on in the house (though I knew he pored over the papers at the grocery store and in neighbors' apartments and spent way too many hours reading headlines on the Internet), and the ghost of my evil mother hovering over us, someone I was told never, ever to mention to anyone, ever, though I was given no reason for my required silence. I *must* have known at some point—and I must have chosen not to look any further. Dad was fooling me. He was lying about something, maybe about a lot of things, and for a time that made me mad, and I wanted to confront him and demand to know what was really going on with us. But I didn't. I kept my mouth shut, and I looked the other way until I no longer could do either. And that was because Dad had gotten himself arrested for stealing that car. And it wasn't even a great car, at that. I mean, if your father is going to screw up your life and his by breaking into and then driving away with someone else's car, the least he could do is make it a Jaguar or a Mercedes or something. But no, Dad chose a fifteen-year-old Subaru, probably the most boring car you'll ever see on the road.

Verity knocked (even though the door was open). I got up from the couch.

"The lamb," she said, stepping inside.

She meant my baby toy. It was sitting on top of the desk. "I didn't think you'd mind if I kept it in here," I said a bit defensively. "You said it once belonged to me."

She smiled. "It still belongs to you."

"I saw it again when I put that sweater I borrowed back in your room yesterday." I picked up the lamb and wiggled its tiny tail. "It's funny, but growing up I never had stuffed toys. I don't remember ever wanting them. I kind of liked action figures."

Verity laughed. "I was insane for stuffed toys. I still have one of my old teddy bears and a rabbit that was once big and pink and fluffy. Now, I'm sorry to say, he's entirely bald."

"What's his name?" I asked, kind of surprised I wanted to know.

Verity laughed again. "Bunny, of course."

When she had gone—again without asking what Dad and I had talked about—I thought about the conversation we'd had about her campaign to get a stoplight installed by the old people's home and how Dad had never ever gotten involved in any cause or club or anything other than his job at the moment. Now I know why. It's because he's the most self-centered, selfish person in the world. All he cares about is himself, and yet I don't think he's a very happy person. Anyway, he never got involved with doing good deeds for anyone else, because he didn't want to be found out as a kidnapper. All that's ever mattered to him are his own weird needs.

How does a person get like that?

I hope it doesn't happen to me.

Chapter 67

We left the house at five thirty. The opening didn't start until six and the ride to the YCC campus only takes about ten minutes, but I wanted to be there a bit early. Everything had been installed and I'd been at the YCC gallery only that morning, but a final check would help calm my nerves. At least, I hoped it would.

I glanced at Gemma, beside me in the front seat, and remembered how when she'd first come to live with me, only weeks ago, I'd felt miles and miles apart from her, even when we were sitting side by side. I don't feel that now. Things are changing.

There's the plush lamb, for one. I'm so pleased Gemma wants the little lamb. It seems to me there's a softness emerging, a vulnerability making itself known, not all the time but here and there. Not that I want my daughter to become a quivering mass of uncontrolled emotion! But I think it would be healthy for her to let down some of the defenses she was forced to erect over the years.

"There'll be food, right?" Gemma asked.

I smiled. I'd never known someone who likes to eat with as much gusto as my daughter. "Yes," I told her. Just a note: We'd already eaten dinner.

Gemma nodded. "Good."

Though I'd determined not to ask Gemma to change if she chose to wear her ratty old jeans that are way too tight for decency, I was glad when she came out of her room wearing the new jeans I'd bought her for Annie and Marc's party and a boho style top we'd gotten at JCPenney. As for me, I'd put on a taupe linen dress I hadn't worn since last summer and my only pair of sandals with heels. I don't have much in the way of what might be called important jewelry, but I wore what I have—my mother's simple gold wedding band on my right hand; small gold hoops I'd gotten from my father when I'd turned eighteen (I've always suspected that his wife chose them for him, as he was a notoriously bad gift giver); and a sterling silver bangle I'd bought myself with my first paycheck from Yorktide Community College. Overall, a very conservative look. There's some big money in a few of the towns adjacent to Yorktide, and I expected, rightly as it turned out, that most of the older well-heeled men and women who came to the show would be dressed quite spiffily in expensive, well-cut dresses and suits, and adorned simply with heirloom pearls and diamonds. And while on the whole they were an educated and liberal bunch, accepting of people who inhabited a different lifestyle, I thought it wouldn't hurt if I appeared—here's that word again!—presentable. And respectable. Not that the artist's personal appearance would affect the sale of a piece to someone intent on owning it, but it never hurts to show a bit of reciprocal respect for the buyer. Boy, am I my mother's daughter! Not wanting to give offense or make waves!

"Do you like these things?" Gemma asked when we were almost at the college.

"Openings? They're okay. I've gotten used to them, mostly. I'm not really a party person, but when my work is the stuff on display, then it all feels like a business event. I mean, basically the point of an opening is to make an eventual sale."

"You're trying to impress people."

"With the work, yes, I guess so. I mean, I want people to like my work."

"So you can make money off it."

The statement wasn't spoken with contempt. I got the feeling Gemma was trying to figure something out. "I need the money, Gemma. But honestly, I'd be sculpting even if I didn't need the money, if I were filthy rich. I sculpt because I have to. Any real artist feels that way. There's no choice about having to pick up a pencil or a knife. Or, for that matter, a power tool."

Gemma had no reply to that.

"I'll have to talk to people," I explained then. "People might have questions about the work, and I'll probably know almost everyone there, at least by sight."

Gemma shrugged. "I can take care of myself."

I know you can, I thought. *But why should you have to?*

"Do you want to stay with me? Or do you want to hang out on your own?"

"I'm okay. You should do what you have to do."

"All right. But if at any time you feel—"

"Verity. I'll be fine."

I shut up after that.

A few minutes later Gemma and I stood in the entrance to the gallery, which is on the ground floor of the building that houses my studio as well as all the other rooms used for various art classes, including dance and theater. "What do you think?" I asked. Gemma had been to the space before, but she hadn't yet seen the installation of my work. "Those four pieces there are the new ones. *Winter, Spring, Summer,* and *Fall. The Four Seasons.*"

She didn't answer right away, just looked around the exhibition from left to right and back again, and I felt my stomach drop. I know she's not into art, but like I said, I want her to be proud of me. Am I being pathetic?

"It's cool," she said finally. "And it's all yours? The drawings, too?"

"Yes," I said, with a feeling of great relief. "It's all mine."

"How long did it take you to make everything?"

"I've been working on the new sculptures for over a year."

Gemma turned to me then and smiled. "You really like to work, don't you?"

"Yes," I said. "I do. I more than like it. I love it."

"Verity?"

The director of the gallery was at my shoulder, and as I turned to greet him, I was aware of Gemma moving off into the room.

"The show looks great," he said. "Congratulations." Though American, Harry Carlyle got his graduate degrees at Oxford and had lived for some years after that in London. I've always wondered how he got to Maine but haven't wanted to ask. After all, I know all too well the value of privacy and how raw one can feel when privacy is ripped away.

"Thanks so much for all you've done," I told him sincerely. "For all the opportunities you've given me over the years."

Harry smiled. "My pleasure. And now, time to open the doors to the public."

Things were a bit of a blur after that, as people began to arrive in a steady flow. Still, I was able to keep an eye on Gemma as she moved through the growing crowd. She managed, I thought, to project a sense of aloofness, apartness, and I wondered if she was consciously trying to keep people from approaching her. But then I saw her smile in answer to a smile and nod from a middle-aged couple I vaguely recognized, and I felt somewhat assured. Of course I'd been worried she might feel overwhelmed, too much on display, but thankfully this crowd was smart enough to leave her alone and focus on what they were supposed to focus on.

The art. And the food and wine. I spotted at least twelve YCC art students stuffing themselves with shrimp and slices of veggies. Students, particularly art students, are smart when it comes to getting a free meal.

As I'd told Gemma, I knew most of the people, some only by sight, some more closely. There were, for example, Freddie Ross and Sheila Simon. Freddie, who's in her early eighties I think, only just retired from her law practice. Sheila's a photographer and a pretty good one at that. We have our work in a few of the same galleries here, most notably The Luna Gallery, owned by a woman named Anna Ross, as well as at The Winslett Gallery in Ogunquit, the BlowFish Gallery in Kennebunkport, and a gallery as far north as Portland. Freddie and Sheila have been together for over fifty years, a real feat in this day and age of disposable commitments.

The women came over to me now, Sheila impeccable as always in a black linen dress and bolero jacket, a magnificent silver pendant around her neck, and Freddie in a more casual outfit of chinos and blue Oxford blouse.

"How's she doing?" Freddie asked quietly. There was no need to name names.

"All right," I replied. "As well as can be expected, I suppose. Whatever that means."

"Time. The great healer. Just be patient."

Sheila shook her head. "Easier said than done, Freddie."

After the women had wandered off, I spotted the Higgins girls: Poppy, with her husband, Jon Gascoyne, son of Matilda Gascoyne, who had been so good about greeting Gemma in town a few weeks back; Daisy, who's about Gemma's age, I think; and Violet, a few years younger. The girls lost both of their parents within three years of each other. Sad. But money helps. I don't mean to be unsympathetic. But Annabelle and Oliver Higgins had been able to leave their children comfortably well off, with a big house fully paid for and a sound portfolio of investments. I know all this the way everyone in Yorktide knows the business of everyone else. Osmosis.

Sophie Stueben and her father, Dan, who had recently taken over Freddie's practice, came in then. With them was Allie Swift. All were friends with the Higginses. It wasn't long before Dan and Allie joined Poppy and Jon and Daisy, and Sophie and Violet drifted off on their own. I hoped Gemma would get to talk to the girls, especially to Sophie, whose own life story to date has been fairly traumatic. At one point I saw the girls moving toward Gemma, where she stood looking at one of the framed preliminary sketches, but Gemma suddenly walked rapidly across the room and seemed deeply interested once again in the food table. I don't know if the girls had had any intention of introducing themselves to Gemma—of course someone would have told them she was The Little Kidnapped Girl, as Gemma puts it—but Gemma must have thought so.

I checked my watch and looked toward the door and, as if summoned, David strode into the gallery. "Sorry I'm late," he said, reaching for my hand and giving it a squeeze. "The roof guy didn't show up until almost six. Is she here?"

I gave a slight nod in Gemma's direction. "I'll introduce you. But, David? I still don't think it's the right time to tell her that we're—"

David smiled down at me. "I'm your colleague and your friend. That's all she needs to know for now."

"Thank you. I know it's been tough . . . our not being together. . . ."

"I'm not a randy teen, Verity. I'm a randy closing-in-on-fifty-year-old. I can wait for the girl I love."

I smiled, though I still felt nervous about David's meeting Gemma, even as just a colleague and friend. I finished off my glass of wine, and together we made our way through the crowd—many of whom were now laughing and talking more loudly than they had at the start of the party—toward Gemma. She greeted us with a smile.

"A good turnout," David said, as I seemed to have lost my voice for a moment.

"Yes. Gemma, I'd like to introduce you to David Wildacre. He's the head of the English department at the college. And he's a friend."

David stuck out his hand, and for half a second I was terrified Gemma wouldn't respond, but to my amazement, she did, shaking his hand briefly. "Hi," she said.

None of us seemed to have anything more to add until David,

with one artfully raised eyebrow, said to Gemma, "So, what do you think of your mother's work? Or is that an unfair question?"

His words surprised me, but Gemma laughed. "Totally unfair. I plead the fifth."

David grinned. "I'm starved," he said suddenly. "I didn't get dinner. I'm going to grab the last of those mini quiche things. See you later."

And he was gone.

"He's a very good teacher," I said, flailing again. "His students like him."

Before Gemma could say anything at all, my arm was being grasped by one of those extremely well-dressed women I mentioned earlier, who led me away to meet a "very respectable collector." I mouthed a *sorry* over my shoulder to Gemma, who actually smiled back.

Chapter 68

There was only fifteen minutes left of the opening and people had begun to wander out, but there were still some who hung around, talking and laughing loudly and gesticulating wildly. I'd never been to this sort of a party before, and I realized I kind of liked it, even though in general I don't like parties. I don't know why exactly I liked it. Maybe it's because there were so many different sorts of people, from babies in those sacks you strap on your chest or your back to people who looked old enough to be my great-grandparents. Maybe it's because the music was kind of weird but in a good way. Interesting. And the food didn't suck.

There was a photographer there from the local paper, as well as from the *Portland Press Herald*. And a lot of people wanted selfies with Verity. It seems she's a bit of a local celebrity. Well, I guess for more than one reason. Artist and mother of the kidnapped baby.

I felt proud of her. Is that weird? I still feel proud of her. I know it's unfair to compare Verity to Dad, and it's something I do all too often these days, with Verity more and more winning out over Dad. But it's hard not to compare. It's hard not to see that Verity is successful. Okay, she's not rich, but look at all those people who showed up to see her work, and there was that guy who even bought a piece.

I probably shouldn't have said that about her sculpting just for the money. I would never have admitted it to Verity, but I was pretty nervous before the opening. I mean, I had this image in my head of everyone staring at me, whispering behind their hands, pointing. I mean, that hadn't happened at the Strawberries' party or at the Fourth of July parade, but that didn't mean it couldn't happen here. I'd told Verity I could take care of myself, but I wondered what I might do if someone said something stupid to me. I knew I shouldn't embarrass Verity on her big night, in front of all her friends and colleagues, but I wasn't entirely sure I wouldn't. I actually wished that the Strawberries had been able to come. At least I could tag along with them, which might keep people from trying to talk to me, but Marc's old uncle had died, and they had gone to New Hampshire for the funeral. Bad timing for me. Marion never goes to openings, because she tends to get panic attacks in small crowded spaces. Not that she would have been much help even if she weren't prone to panic attacks. Like I said, she has this air of, like . . . weakness around her. Like she could really easily just, I don't know, blow away or something.

Anyway, the whole thing wasn't at all as bad as I thought it might be. Most people spent a fair amount of time actually looking at Verity's work, and I found that pretty cool. A lot of people sort of smiled and nodded at me as they strolled from work to work but didn't stop to talk, for which I was grateful. One old lady did come up to me before I could scuttle away. She grasped my hand and I winced; she was only about eighty pounds, but her grip was like a vise's. She was wearing a billowy black dress that came down to the floor, and around her neck there were about five necklaces made, I think, of big chunks of wood painted in red, blue, purple, and green. I stood there, captive, having no idea what she wanted with me. When she'd stopped staring, she said, "I simply *adore* your earrings! Where did you get them?" I almost laughed in relief; I thought she had been going to ask me about my "time in captivity." I put my other hand to my ear to help me remember what earrings

I'd put on. "A friend gave them to me," I said. *A friend*. Cathy had given them to me; she'd said they'd never really looked right on her.

"Well, they suit you very nicely!" The old lady released her grip and moved off. I watched as she joined a group of three middle-aged women, each dressed more wildly bohemian than the other, in colorful caftans and oddly shaped hats, and I wondered if she had any idea who I was, the infamous Little Kidnapped Girl, or if she truly didn't know—or care?—that I was Verity Peterson's daughter. But that question was less interesting to me than the fact that I had spontaneously called Cathy a friend.

Verity didn't say, but I got the feeling she and that guy David she introduced me to are together. Maybe they're not in a relationship, but I bet they have sex. For one, he was the only person there she went out of her way to introduce to me. So, he's important to her, at least, more important than anyone else at the opening. Well, she's got pretty good taste. He's not bad looking at all, though he's way too old for me. And he has a sense of humor, which is always helpful. Dad laughs at obvious jokes, but he doesn't have a sense of humor, if you know what I mean. He can't make witty comments or get most sarcasm. Sometimes he asks me to explain a remark that had made me laugh, and let me tell you, there's nothing to kill humor, to make something suddenly unfunny, like having to explain it.

Anyway, as things continued to wind down and the last people in the gallery began to leave and the catering people began to clear away the plastic glasses and the last of the food, I got this idea. All night long I'd seen people shake Verity's hand or kiss her cheek or give her a hug. She seemed to like it. I mean, she didn't look uncomfortable or anything. It seemed like she'd been smiling since we got to the gallery. And like I said before, Verity isn't a faker.

So my idea was that I should give her a hug too. In congratulations. It probably wouldn't kill me, and Verity would appreciate it. I mean, pretty much everyone else in the place had hugged her or kissed her cheek, men and women. Why should I be the only one not to? It's not like Verity hasn't been good to me since I came to live with her. I'd be stupid to deny that she treats me well, even when I'm being ungrateful. So, what's a hug going to cost me?

I decided I'd do it.

"You made a sale," I said when we were finally alone. We were standing right outside the door to the gallery. The night was clear (you could see lots of stars) and warm, and I realized I was enjoying breathing it in.

I'd never enjoyed breathing before! I mean, it's so basic. Who even notices they're breathing?

"Yeah," Verity said. "Not the new work but one of my better pieces nonetheless."

"A lot of people turned up."

Verity shrugged. "Maybe it was the free food. Some people will show up anywhere for mini quiches."

"Nah. It was your work." And then I did it, before I could lose the determination. I won't say nerve. I put my arms around her, patted her back, said, "Congratulations," and stepped away. The look on her face almost made me laugh, though not meanly. She looked like she was going to burst out laughing and crying at the same time. For a split second I prayed she wouldn't do either—I so didn't want a big emotional scene—but she got control of herself, smiled a reasonable smile, and said, "Thanks. I'm glad you were here." I nodded, and we both started to walk through the parking lot toward the car. We didn't say much on the way home, and when we got into the house, I suddenly felt completely wiped out and said I was going to bed.

"It's been a big evening," Verity said as I turned to leave the kitchen.

"Yeah," I said. "It has."

Chapter 69

The opening was an unqualified success. That's not bragging; that's just being honest. The turnout was good. The meeting between David and Gemma, though brief, went well. I got to see and say hi to some very nice people I hadn't run into in ages.

But the best moment of the entire night, far better than making a fairly big sale, the money from which will help pay for a new dishwasher, as ours is dying a slow and painful death, was the fact that Gemma hugged me. It was brief and awkward, but it happened. It was at the end of the evening, when the two of us had just left the building. For some reason we both paused for a moment before walking on to the parking lot. And then she did it. I can't tell you how good I feel. I know, I know, it's only one battle won, not the entire war but . . . Come to think of it, maybe I should give up on the conflict imagery. Think more positively.

After breakfast this morning Gemma went to take a shower. I had just begun to put dishes in the dishwasher (hoping it would work), when the phone rang. I didn't recognize the number, though I did recognize the area code as one from Massachusetts. I picked up the receiver.

"Hello?"

"Hi, Verity. I bet you can't guess who this is."

The voice wasn't even vaguely familiar. It was, however, annoying. It had that overly bright, strident quality that immediately turns me off. For a moment I assumed the voice belonged to someone trying to sell me something I didn't want.

"No," I said. "I can't guess."

"Hold on to your hat. It's Ellen Burns-Cassidy. Alan's cousin!"

Who? I thought. And then came a very small recollection of having once or twice heard Marion mention her name. But that was a long time ago. That was a world away.

"Oh," I said, my hand tightening on the receiver. I don't know why I suddenly felt so anxious, but I did.

"I know, I know, it's been an age," she rushed on. "I'm so sorry Richard and I haven't been in touch, but time really does seem to fly by, doesn't it, and I know you've probably been busy too and—"

I blocked out whatever words came next and thought, *Busy? Yeah, I've been busy. I've been busy grieving my missing daughter.* As if Ellen had read my thoughts, she now said, and I heard her say it: "Richard and I are simply dying to see you and to meet our long-lost Gemma."

"I'm not sure that's possible," I replied as politely as I could, which probably wasn't very politely. I felt a sick combination of disbelief and outrage. I'd never even met this woman—she'd never once shown any interest in me or in my baby, and according to Marion, had written Alan off before I'd even met him—and now she was claiming rights to "*our* long-lost Gemma"?

"Sure it is," she said briskly. "How silly, I didn't mention that we rented a house on Katahdin Way for the rest of the summer so we could get to know Gemma. And to see you, of course."

I said nothing.

"We're having a few people over on Saturday about four," Ellen went on. "Nothing fancy, no need to pull the diamonds out of the safe! We'd love it if you and Gemma could join us."

"What people?" I asked. You know my policy about not exposing Gemma to a gang of gaping strangers. The opening had been risk enough. And diamonds? Really? For those of us who can't afford a decent diamond, that's not even remotely amusing.

"Just a few dear old friends of ours up from Massachusetts for a week," Ellen explained. "Not staying with us, of course. They're staying at The Starfish. Anyway, just a burgers-and-salad sort of affair. Do say yes."

"I'll have to get back to you," I said, casting an eye in the direction of the bathroom. The shower had been turned off. Gemma would be out soon.

"Please do say yes, Verity. You can call me at this number."

I got off the phone somehow—I don't really recall saying good-bye—leaned against the dishwasher, and put my head in my hands. After the emotional high of the night before, this call served to throw me into a mood of confusion, even despair.

You can control this, I told myself. *You're the one in charge.*

But I couldn't really believe that. I still can't quite believe it.

"You okay?"

I dropped my hands and looked up to see Gemma, wrapped in my old bathrobe, toweling her hair.

"Yeah," I said, managing to smile. At least, I think I managed a smile and not a grimace.

"We're almost out of shampoo," she said. "I'll put it on the list."

She turned and went off to her room.

My daughter, wearing my bathrobe, sharing my home, using my shampoo.

Gemma, I thought, *is mine. And it's going to stay that way.*

Chapter 70

In the afternoon while Gemma was out on her bike, I drove over to see Annie. If anyone could help me think clearly about the sudden emergence of Ellen Burns-Cassidy and my fiercely negative response to it, it was Annie. And David, of course, but he was at a one-day conference down in Boston. I'd have to wait until evening to talk to him.

But before I introduced my dilemma, I told Annie about Gemma giving me a hug.

"Bravo!" she cried. "Or is it brava? Either way, that's great progress."

"I know. I felt elated."

Annie regarded me closely. "You don't look elated. What's wrong?"

I told her about the call from Alan's cousin. "She wants to meet us," I said then. "At a party this Saturday. They've rented a house locally."

"The problem being?"

"I don't want Gemma to meet her. *I* don't want to meet her. Alan's family wrote him off when he was barely out of his teens. All but his mother, of course. And she's been trouble enough. But at least she's a known quantity. I have some control over her regarding Gemma."

"You're wondering about this cousin's motives in wanting to reconnect?"

"She was never connected in the first place! She didn't even acknowledge Gemma's birth. So why now? Maybe she wants in on the celebrity."

"Or maybe she really cares. Just saying."

"It's a possibility," I admitted grudgingly. "Anyway, I'm not sure I have the right to keep family from Gemma. Or to keep Gemma from family."

"Well," Annie said, "keep in mind that just because someone is family doesn't necessarily mean they're of more value than someone who isn't. Then again, I do understand your hesitation. Especially in Gemma's situation, knowing she belongs to a family larger than just a few people, knowing she exists in a context of blood relations, might be terribly important for her. It probably explains why she's corresponding with Tom. Her grandfather. She needs to connect."

Right, I thought. *I have to be consistent. I can't—I shouldn't— pick and choose with whom my daughter can have a relationship.* I wasn't thrilled she was getting along with my father, but that was my problem, not Gemma's. And as for Ellen Burns-Cassidy . . .

"I spoke to Marion right after I got off the phone with Ellen," I said.

"And?"

"And I asked her opinion of Ellen. I asked her to be honest."

Annie frowned. "Always a crapshoot with that one, from what you've told me."

"Yes, but this time I think she told the truth. She said Ellen is self-serving and always has been. She said it was the worst she could say about her."

"I'd say that's bad enough. Still, how much harm can it do to meet with the woman just once? You won't send Gemma alone. You'll be right there to intervene if she proves to be a wack job."

Annie was probably right, I decided. But I wanted to prolong the experience of Gemma and me and our new closeness for just a while longer before the intrusion of so-called well-meaning strangers.

"Still, I think I'll wait a day or two before I tell Gemma about Ellen's call."

Annie smiled. "I understand," she said.

And I know she does.

Chapter 71

I rode my bike to Cathy's house this afternoon. Like I said, it's not like we have much in common or anything, but she's okay, and if she can tolerate me, then I can tolerate her. Plus, there's always a chance Annie will be around, and I like her.

Annie wasn't there. She had been—and so had Verity, it turns out—but both were gone.

The Strawberries have a really nice backyard—not that ours isn't nice too—but theirs has something called a gazebo. It was built by the guy who owned the house before them. It's really just for sitting in, but I like it. Cathy was in the gazebo, and she wasn't alone. On the bench next to her—the bench, by the way, goes all around the inside of the gazebo, which is round—was one of those car seat carrying criblike things. I don't know what you call it exactly. And in it was a baby.

"His name is Thomas," she told me. "He's four months old."

I sat on the other side of the baby and looked down at him. He was asleep, his tiny fists on his tiny arms held up against either side of his head. And for the first time it struck me just how totally helpless and totally vulnerable a baby is. I mean, they can't do *anything* for themselves. Nothing.

I was even younger than Thomas when I was taken. I suddenly felt a sense of outrage. How *dare* Alan do such a violent, insane thing to an infant, and it doesn't matter one bit that the infant was his own daughter. I could have gotten sick so easily. I could have died! It took a lot of effort to get past that moment of outrage. If Cathy noticed my clenched fists, she didn't say anything.

"Mr. and Mrs. Collins tried for years to have this baby," Cathy told me. "They're beyond thrilled. Look, can you watch him for a minute? I'll run in and get us something to drink. Plus Thomas is going to wake up soon, and he'll want his bottle."

Cathy dashed off to the house, and I wondered then, not for the first time, if I was an accident or if Verity and Dad had wanted a baby, "tried for" one, as Cathy had put it. What a strange way to talk about having sex; *trying* sounds like effort and purpose, and shouldn't sex just be fun? But what do I know?

Looking down at Thomas in his car seat thingy I thought: *How must Verity have felt when suddenly I wasn't there?*

How could Alan have done that to her?

Very, very gently I touched Thomas's cheek with the tip of my finger. It was so smooth. His nose was so tiny.

Cathy reappeared a few minutes later with one of those wicker trays with handles. On it were two glasses with lemonade and a baby's bottle with milk, I guess.

"Mrs. Collins expresses her milk ahead of time," Cathy said, putting the tray on the small table in the center of the gazebo and handing me a glass.

Was I breastfed? I'd never thought about it. If I was, what did Verity do when I was suddenly gone? And how had Alan known what to feed me? I felt the anger building in me again, and I took a swig of cold lemonade.

"Is it too hot out here for the baby?" I asked. Then I wondered if I'd sounded like I was criticizing Cathy.

"No. See, he's dressed lightly. If it were, like, ninety degrees, we'd be inside with the AC turned on!"

"Oh." *Had Alan ever let me get overheated?* I wondered. Had I ever been sick enough when I was a baby that he had to rush me to the emergency room? Wait, I thought. He probably would have been too scared to show up at the ER with an infant and no mother, with the police looking for him!

"You're frowning," Cathy said. "Penny for your thoughts?"

"I'm not thinking anything," I said.

"You know," Cathy said, a few minutes later, "Verity always takes me back-to-school shopping. My mom hates to shop. And let's face it, she has no style!"

I felt a twinge of what could only be called jealousy, and it surprised me. How, I wondered, would Cathy feel if I hung out with *her* mother? But maybe she wouldn't care. Maybe it was normal for people my age to spend time with someone else's parents. How would I know what was normal and what was weird?

"This year, I guess the three of us will be going shopping together."

I didn't say anything. What was I supposed to say?

Cathy gave me a look then, one of those steady, kind of serious I'm-here-to-help looks. "If you're okay with that."

"Why wouldn't I be?" I snapped. I took another swig of lemonade. Not a perfect bad-temper diffuser, but it was all I had to hand. "Maybe I'll go back-to-school shopping with Annie."

That made Cathy laugh, though honestly, I'm not sure what I intended by saying that, about going shopping with her mother. If I'd wanted to make Cathy jealous, I'd failed.

Both of us watched Thomas for a while without talking. It's amazing how interesting it is to watch a baby sleep. I mean, nothing much happens, but I felt almost mesmerized. Maybe it was because it was my first time hanging around with a baby. A novelty. But I don't think that was it, not entirely.

"You know," Cathy said after a while, "I was thinking about Verity and David last night. I don't know why they haven't gotten married already. I mean, they've been together for a few years, and it's clear they're in love. So what's stopping them?"

I guess the look on my face revealed my ignorance, because then Cathy squealed: "Oh my God, I thought you knew! Didn't you meet him at the opening?"

"Yeah," I said. "And of course I know they're together."

She probably didn't believe me, but I can't help that.

I felt—I feel—kind of left out. I don't need to be protected from stuff. Still, I'm not really mad at Verity. I can guess why she hasn't told me about David yet.

Thomas kind of wiggled in his sleep then. He stretched his fingers, too, and then put both hands on the sides of his head, like he was thinking hard about something. (How do babies think?) Seriously cute.

"So," I asked, changing the subject but maybe not enough. "Did you dump Jason?"

"He's history." Cathy laughed, but it wasn't a happy laugh. "He's already got another girlfriend, if you can believe it."

I could easily believe it. Jason is a teenage guy. One big bag of raging hormones. "You were smart to get rid of him," I said. "Obviously, he's only out for sex."

And then I thought: *Cathy is way smarter than I've ever been, at least regarding guys.*

Thomas woke up then, and Cathy lost all interest in hanging out with me—that's probably what makes her a popular babysitter—so I left. When I got back to the house, the neighbors with the twins—I think Verity said their last name is Gallison—were walking up their front drive. Each parent held a kid and a few bags of groceries. As I got off my bike, one of the bags slipped from the mother's grasp and fell onto the pavement. I didn't think twice but called out, "I'll get it!" And then I dashed over to their front yard.

As I picked up the bag, I finally did think twice. Now I'd have to introduce myself. But the idea didn't bother me the way it would have a few weeks ago. I even knew what name I was going to use. I mean, why not?

"Hi," I said. "I'm Gemma."

"I'm Grace, and this is my husband, Peter. And this," Mrs. Gallison said, tickling the cheek of the kid she was holding on her hip, "is Molly."

"And that's Michael," I said. "Verity told me their names."

Grace and Peter look a lot younger up close than they do from across the yard. In fact, they look closer to my age than to Verity's. And they already have two kids. Yikes. I thought about what I'd told Cathy a while ago, that I wasn't ever going to have kids. And then I thought of cute baby Thomas. I suppose I should never say never. Right? Because all sorts of weird shit happens in life.

We began to walk toward the door of the house. I was still carrying the one grocery bag. "I hope there aren't any eggs in here," I said.

Peter laughed. "I'm just glad it wasn't the beer."

At the front door Grace put Molly down on her fat little legs and took the grocery bag from me. "Thanks," she said. "Feel free to drop by. I'm here all day every day with these two monsters. Frankly, I could use a break!"

She smiled as she said it, and I thought, *Well, maybe I will stop by someday.*

But I didn't make any promises.

Chapter 72

"I met the neighbors today," Gemma said. "I mean, the Gallisons."

"Oh?" I turned from the sink. Gemma was in her usual seat at the kitchen table.

"Yeah. Grace told me I could stop by sometime. She said she could use a break from the kids."

"Grace and Peter got married right out of high school," I told Gemma. "Not something I would ordinarily recommend, but in their case it seems to be working."

Gemma shook her head. "I can't imagine settling down with someone before I'm, like, forty."

"Lovestruck, I guess."

"Why didn't you tell me you're seeing David?"

I felt my stomach drop.

"How do you know?" I asked.

"Cathy told me when I was at her house this afternoon. She thought I already knew. I pretended I did so I wouldn't look like an idiot."

"I'm sorry. Really."

"Why doesn't he ever come over?" Gemma asked. "Why don't you ever spend the night at his place?"

I sat with her at the table. "I just thought that with all the new things you had to adjust to, the last thing you needed was some strange man padding around the kitchen in his robe and slippers. Well, you know what I mean. And I didn't want to be running off and leaving you alone at night. I still don't." I took a deep breath and went on. "By the way, David doesn't wear slippers. He wears a disgusting old pair of Crocs. Anyway, I was planning on telling you about David very soon. I guess I wanted you to meet him first without any, I don't know, preconceptions."

"I'm not a baby, you know. I don't need to be protected."

Of course you do, I thought. "I'm sorry," I said. "You're right."

"I mean, Dad dated women."

"Oh?" Oddly, I'd never considered that possibility.

"There was this one woman I remember most of all. Her name was Patty. She was very nice to me, not in an annoying way like she was trying to bribe me to like her. Kids can always tell when an adult is being phony."

True, I thought. "So, what happened?"

Gemma shrugged. "I don't really know. One day she came to the place where we were living while Dad was at work or something and packed up some stuff she'd left there and said good-bye. And then she said to me something like, 'All little birds must learn to fly away.' "

"What do you think she was telling you?"

Gemma seemed to consider the question. "I had no idea at the time. I mean, I was, like, eight or something. But now . . ." Gemma shook her head. "It doesn't matter."

I thought I knew what might have happened. Alan's possessiveness had driven Patty away. And Patty had been telling Gemma, my daughter, that one day she, too, would need to flee. But if Gemma hadn't already, she would someday figure that out for herself.

"So . . . what do you think of David?" I asked.

"He seems cool. He's funny. And he's good-looking. So, how long have you guys been together?"

"It's hard to say," I admitted. "We were friends first, and then things just sort of developed. About three years all in all."

"Cathy said she thought you'd be married by now."

"Cathy's a romantic. Which is not to say David and I haven't talked about it. But there's no rush." Especially, I thought, now, with Gemma so recently home with me. We need to be alone together. At least, I need to be alone with her.

Since we were being so open about things—so open and without anger—I thought it might be a good moment to tell her about Alan's cousin. I had vowed to keep my reservations about Ellen Burns-Cassidy entirely under wraps, so I chose my words carefully.

"A cousin of your father called me the other day. Her name is Ellen. Seems she and her husband, Richard, have rented a house in Yorktide for the rest of the summer. She says she'd like to see you."

Gemma shrugged. "Yeah," she said. "Okay."

The ready acceptance of this idea surprised me. "She never met you before your father . . . In fact, I never met her. She and Alan weren't close. Alan wasn't close to anyone in his family but his mother."

"You think she's another voyeur?"

I don't know why I was surprised Gemma should ask that question. My daughter is a very intelligent young woman. And a suspicious one. "Honestly," I said, "I don't know." Though I did know, at least I suspected, that given what Marion had told me about Ellen's character, she hoped to get something more out of meeting her long-lost relative besides a warm and fuzzy feeling. But I will not share my suspicions with Gemma.

"Whatever," she said now. "I can handle it."

And at that moment, thinking about all Gemma's been through since the spring, I believed she could indeed handle meeting Alan's cousin. Besides, I thought, we were so much closer now than we'd been at the start of the summer. Together, I thought, we could handle whatever Cousin Ellen threw at us.

"They've invited us to a party on Saturday around four. We'll see them once," I said, "be good doobies, then we don't have to see them again."

"We don't have to get dressed up, do we?" Gemma asked. "It was cool at your opening that people wore whatever they wanted to wear. I mean, did you see those ladies dressed like gypsies in a movie? And the guy in the red velvet suit? I don't know how he didn't sweat to death, but he looked like a celebrity or a rock star from the seventies."

I didn't tell Gemma I'd been a bit worried about what sort of appearance she would make at the opening. The daughter of the artist, all eyes upon her. "No," I said. "We don't have to dress up. Ellen stressed it was a casual thing."

Gemma grinned. "But no sweat pants, right?"

I grinned back. "Right."

Chapter 73

I was waiting for the scheduled call from Alan, but unlike what I used to feel when I first got here to Maine, which was eagerness to hear his voice and maybe even to hear some good news, like how charges were being reduced or something, now I kind of half wished something would prevent him from making the call. Not something horrible, like he'd been hurt in a fight or something, just maybe that there was a problem with the phone lines. Talking to him has really become difficult for me. Sometimes I just want to slam the phone down the second he says hello, which I could do, given that I talk to him on an old-fashioned landline phone with a separate receiver. Sometimes I want to scream, *How could you have deprived me of my own name, my own identity?* and then slam the phone down. And sometimes, well, sometimes I just want to cry, just break down and let him hear me sob.

Not that it would change anything.

I didn't let on to Verity, but I actually am interested in meeting Ellen. I mean, she's another flesh and blood relative of Dad. I'm curious. It's not that I really believe seeing his cousin is going to magically help me better understand my father and why he did what he did. But getting to know Marion a bit has been kind of illuminating. Anyway, I wasn't sure I'd tell Dad about his cousin popping up in Yorktide. I figured I'd see how the conversation went. He can be so . . . touchy.

Precisely on time, the phone rang.

"Hey, Dad," I said.

"I've been thinking."

No greeting. *Not*, I thought, *a good sign*. And thinking? Always a dangerous thing with Dad. "About what?" I asked, half dreading the answer.

"I'm thinking I'm not going to accept a plea bargain."

"Dad," I snapped. "Don't be crazy. You *have* to take it."

"I don't have to do anything," he said with that familiar note of petulance. "Besides, I know best."

It was hard, but I controlled my annoyance and my anger. "No, Dad," I said, "you don't. Your lawyers know best."

There was a long moment of silence, and I wondered if he'd heard what I'd said. And then he laughed harshly. "I know what's happening," he said. "She's been trying to turn you against me, hasn't she? That's why you can't see that I know how to handle things!"

Now I was seriously annoyed. "She has not been doing any such thing!" I took a deep breath before going on. "Look, Dad, just promise me you'll take the plea bargain. The less time you have to spend in jail, the better. Right? Don't you want to get out and see me again?"

There was another long moment of silence before he said, in a tone of false conciliation, "Sure I do. All right, I'll reconsider. I have to go now."

And that was that, the call cut short. I don't really believe he'll reconsider taking a plea bargain, but miracles do happen. Or it's said they do. Anyway, I felt as if I had been talking to a dim-witted, whiny child. And I was glad I hadn't told him about his cousin Ellen getting in touch with me. He'd probably see some conspiracy there, too. Anyway, since the time I told Dad I'd met his mother, he hasn't once asked about her, so how much can he really care about any of his family?

You know, not once since I've been living here with Verity has she ever bad-mouthed my father, though there must be times when she wants to. Well, maybe she's bad-mouthed him to Annie or to David, and if she has, I can't help that, it's a free country, but at least she's had the—the what? The decency?—not to do it in front of me.

But I wonder if Dad deserves such consideration.

Chapter 74

David had offered to be my plus one at Ellen and Richard's party, even though he hadn't exactly been invited. "You might need the backup," he'd said. "At least, you might welcome it."

But I didn't want to drag him into what might turn out to be a family debacle. And there was the fact that Gemma had only met David once. He was almost as new to her as Ellen and Richard would be, and that would be of little or no comfort to her.

The house Ellen and Richard had rented was one of those McMansions, a cookie-cutter house chosen from a brochure and customized here and there to distinguish it from the otherwise identical houses to the left and the right. It seemed to hulk over us as we pulled into the circular drive, like some oddly ineffectual monster, relying on its size alone to intimidate.

"It's huge," Gemma said.

"It's ugly," I said. "What I mean is, it's not my taste in architecture."

"I wonder if their house back wherever they live is this big."

"I have no idea." And I had no interest in finding out.

I parked next to a new-model Mercedes. Every single one of the other cars drawn up in front of the house was newer and way more expensive than my trusty Honda CRV. And did I mention they were shinier? Gemma didn't comment on the vehicles, and I hoped she wasn't the sort to care about owning a car as a status symbol, because that's something we just can't afford to do. On second thought, I seriously doubt Gemma cares at all about things like social status and one-upping the neighbors. But is that a positive lesson Alan taught her or a result of her not ever realizing or believing it's within the reach of most people to improve their lots in life?

A woman appeared at the top of the massive set of stairs leading up to the house, and waved. Gemma and I glanced at each other a bit warily and began the climb.

"Verity?" the woman said when Gemma and I had reached the top stair and found ourselves on a palatial paved stone veranda. "Of course it must be you! And Gemma. Or should I say Marni?"

"Gemma's okay," my daughter said.

I startled a bit when I heard my daughter use her birth name, but wisely, I didn't comment.

Ellen smiled. "Welcome! We're so glad you could make it."

I could see absolutely no family resemblance to Alan, though admittedly my visual memory of him isn't perfect in spite of the old images of him on my now defunct website and the more recent photo in Gemma's room—a photo I avoid looking at. I guessed her to be in her mid-forties, but who knows these days? If she's wealthy enough for Botox treatments and laser therapy and all that, she might be closer to fifty. Her hair is blond and clearly done at a salon; that much I can always tell for sure. She was tastefully dressed in a very crisp white blouse with the collar turned up, and a pale-pink silk scarf tied around her neck, navy slacks, and a pair of taupe-colored espadrilles. On her left hand she wore a substantial diamond solitaire (she'd told me not to break out the diamonds, but . . .) set in what I thought must be platinum, and a plain matching band. Her other jewelry was yellow gold, eighteen-carat for all I know, and quite frankly, beautiful. Italian design, I'd say, reflecting centuries of fine art and craftsmanship. Her bearing was dignified but not stuffy.

Ellen led us around the side of the house to an extension of the veranda. It was all I could do not to gasp. There was a large in-ground pool; two tables set for six and shaded by umbrellas; several well-padded lounge chairs; and an outdoor kitchen, complete with grill, sink, fridge, and bar. Modulated laughter came from the small groups of guests gathered at the bar and poolside. The air smelled strongly of roses; I guessed there was a rose garden around another side of the house, no small feat in this climate.

"Richard!" Ellen called, waving to a tall slim man standing not far away, by a massive potted rosemary bush. He turned to us. Along with his wife, Richard might have stepped out of the pages of *Town & Country*. Pressed chinos, a blue Oxford shirt, navy blazer, and a pair of broken-in brown leather loafers, sans socks. His wedding ring, I noticed, matched Ellen's simple band. On his left wrist I caught a glimpse of a large, heavy-looking watch. Rolex? Tag Heuer? Whatever it was, I was pretty sure it wasn't a good old Timex. I realized I had no idea what he—and she?—did for a living, and I thought it would be interesting to know. Was it good manners, I wondered (and still do) to ask the host and hostess how they could afford their largesse? I kept my curiosity to myself.

Richard smiled, giving us the full force of his perfectly straight white teeth. "Finally," he said. "We've been so eager to meet you both."

I noticed neither Ellen nor Richard had extended a hand for us to shake, and I wondered why. Is shaking someone's hand a no-no in these days of the renewed fear of infectious diseases? Or had I missed the memo prescribing the latest social mores of the upper crust? You can see my attitude toward my hosts was not the most open.

After a few minutes of mindless chitchat (there I go again), Richard took Gemma off to show her around the house. "Wait until you see the billiard room," he said as they walked toward a door that led into an obviously state-of-the-art kitchen.

"Is Marion coming?" I asked Ellen when I could no longer see my daughter. It occurred to me that I should have offered

Marion a ride to the party; though she's perfectly capable of driving herself, she would probably be nervous meeting this long-lost relative of her late husband once again. She might have appreciated the companionship.

Ellen grimaced. "God, no. I'd rather she didn't even know we're in town! No, I didn't want her to spoil the party. She's always been such a drip. No wonder her son turned out the way he did. Alan didn't stand a chance with either of those two as parents."

"So you feel sorry for him?" I asked, knowing I really should have kept my mouth shut.

"Not in the least," Ellen said stoutly. "He's not insane. He's still responsible for his actions. No, Alan got what he deserved, in my opinion."

And your opinion is all that counts, I thought. What I said was: "Please keep in mind, Ellen, that for better or worse Alan is Gemma's father, and he did take decent care of her for seventeen years. She loves him. I don't think she'd welcome your bad-mouthing him."

Ellen put a manicured hand to her heart, nails of medium length and painted a pale shell-pink. "Of course not," she said in an unnecessary whisper, "don't worry about that. I'm the soul of discretion."

I doubted that, but there was no point in prolonging the conversation. In any case, a newly arrived guest caught Ellen's attention, and she went off to offer greetings. I helped myself to a cold shrimp and asked the bartender (yes, there was a bartender at this casual affair) for a white wine. It was very good. Probably a vintage I can't afford. I could feel resentment and something else—fear?—come over me with every passing moment, and I really did try to keep it at bay. *For Gemma's sake*, I thought. *Keep an open mind for Gemma's sake.* These people might turn out to be of some good in her life. A positive influence. Help with college tuition? But only if they offered and only if there were no strings.

I used to be debilitatingly shy, but that was way back in the old days, and now I have no problem introducing myself to a group of strangers, if one by one. I soon found myself in a conversation about lawn fertilizer of all things with a man who boasted that he was eighty-five with the constitution of a sixty-five-year-old. He did look extremely fit and was still handsome in a debonair sort of way, and for a split second I wondered if he was flirting with me. I saw no wedding ring, but that means nothing, and at his age he might easily be a widower. The thought amused me until he began to get a bit too touchy-feely for my taste—nothing gross, just enough to make his intentions clear—and with apologies and excuses, I moved off to look for my daughter. Richard must have finished showing off the glories of this suburban castle, and no doubt Gemma was either bored stiff or sick to her stomach with the show of wealth for wealth's sake.

But when I found her back on the side veranda by the pool, she was reclining in one of the lounges, a plate of food on her lap.

"This burger is the best I've ever had," she said, smiling up at me. "And check out that carrot salad. I never knew you could make carrots taste so good. There's pineapple in it."

"I could make it for you at home," I said quickly, aware that I felt in fierce competition with these people with the palatial veranda and the best burgers ever.

"Cool. Thanks."

It was another small victory, but still a victory.

Chapter 75

Ellen and I were alone in the kitchen. She had asked me to come inside for a "private chat." That sounded ominous, like something the evil stepmother says in one of those old fairy tales when what she really means is she's going to tell you she's throwing you out of the house and disinheriting you, but I went with her, hoping that when I could go back to the veranda, there would be more burgers ready. I'm not a pig or anything. Just that they were so good, definitely not from some ordinary old cow.

Anyway, I watched while Ellen poured a glass of wine and took a sip of it. I tried to spot any resemblance to Dad, but I couldn't see anything. Not that it matters.

"Do you want a glass?" she asked, as if the idea had suddenly occurred to her. "It's very good."

"No, thanks." I'm not a wine person, though I've had a few glasses in the past. And I wondered what Verity would say if she knew Ellen had offered me alcohol.

Ellen raised one perfectly arched eyebrow. "What does your father have to say about his cousin looking you up?" she asked.

I shrugged. "Nothing. I haven't told him."

"Probably a good thing. We were never close, Alan and my part of the family."

"Why not?" I asked.

Ellen sighed and looked all fake sympathetic. Well, maybe she really was feeling sympathetic. "Let's just say none of us could relate to the path Alan chose for himself."

In other words, I thought, Ellen and "her" part of the family—whatever that meant—decided early on that Dad was a loser.

"Do you like it here?" Ellen asked then. "I mean, living in Yorktide. It's a pretty small town."

I shrugged. "I've mostly lived in small towns," I said. "It doesn't matter to me."

"Small towns are fine," Ellen said, "when there's a big city a short drive away."

"I thought Marion might be here," I said.

Ellen finished her wine before saying: "When I said that my part of the family was never close to Alan, I should have added that we were never close to his parents, either."

I don't know what prompted me to say this, but I said, "Marion's okay. She's nice. Verity kind of looks out for her."

"Does she? How good-hearted of her."

Something in the way Ellen said those words made me think what she really thought was what I used to think. That Verity was nuts for being nice to the mother of the man who'd pretty much ruined her life.

A woman, one of the guests, gestured to Ellen from the door then, and Ellen went off to join her. I wandered back to the veranda. I don't really know what to make of Ellen. She seems so different from Verity and Annie. From anyone I've ever known, really. Not intimidating or nasty, just—foreign. Richard is easier for me to feel comfortable with for some reason. I don't know why. Maybe because I didn't feel so scrutinized, like I did with Ellen. She didn't actually stare at me or look me up and down. Still, I felt she was watching me very, very closely. The Little Kidnapped Girl, local celeb. Maybe she was looking for a sign of my father's criminal tendencies.

Verity told me that Ellen and Richard don't have kids. I wonder why. They can certainly afford them. Maybe they don't like kids much, like me. Well, that's not true. I don't dislike kids; it's that I've never really been around them. The Gallisons' twins are pretty cute, now that I've seen them up close. I could spend some time with them, I guess. Grace did invite me over. Anyway, asking someone why they don't have kids is one of the rudest things you can ask someone, so unless Ellen decides to tell Verity or me why she doesn't, we won't know.

Not that it matters.

But maybe I'll ask Verity why she didn't have another baby after I was taken. I think I might have a right to ask her. She is, after all, my mother.

Speaking of kids, I was the only one at the party. In fact, I think I was the only one under, like, thirty-five. That was fine. Like I said, I don't have a lot in common with the average teenager you find around here. At least, the ones I've met and, granted, that's not a lot. Anyway, not one of the guests paid me more attention than to say hello or nod and smile as they passed. That was fine by me. Maybe they didn't know who I was. Or maybe they did, and Ellen and Richard had asked them to pretend I was just some nobody.

This group was pretty much the opposite of the people Dad and I hung out with—used to hang out with—not that we were ever all that social, like I said. And you didn't have to be a rocket scientist to see that the biggest difference between Ellen and Richard's friends and our old crowd was money. They have it; we didn't. We don't. Dad and me. And money, or the lack of it, means so much. I mean, if you have money, you can afford to get your teeth fixed. Do you know how many people I used to know who were missing teeth? I mean the front ones, the ones everyone sees. From what I could tell—and there was a lot of smiling and laughing going on at this party—nobody was missing any teeth.

I wonder how much money Verity actually has in the bank. I wonder how much her house is worth.

I like Verity's house. If I lived in a house as big as the one Ellen and Richard are renting, I'd probably only get lost.

I spotted Verity then, over by the pool, standing alone, and I went to join her. *I'll skip another burger,* I thought, *and suggest we just go home.*

Chapter 76

"Well, that wasn't too bad, was it?" I said with false bright-ness. In my opinion, we had stayed far too long, and I was eager to be back home in our lovely little bungalow. "We've done our duty."

"No, it was okay. Actually, I'd see them again."

"Really?" The word came out overloud.

Gemma shrugged. "Yeah. I mean, why not? And that pool is pretty sweet. Not that I'm a great swimmer, but I could sit in one of those lounges all day and look at it."

I felt inordinately disappointed by Gemma's words. I'd been hoping she had seen Ellen and Richard to be as bogus and stuck-up as I had. In fact, I'd been almost sure she would share my opinion.

"So, you liked Ellen and Richard?" I asked, hoping I had jumped to a wrong conclusion and that it was only the pool Gemma had liked. It really is a lovely pool, like something you'd find at a Mediterranean villa.

"They seem okay," she said. "I mean, they're different from anyone else I know. Why? You don't like them?"

I shrugged. "I'm not sure," I lied. I was sure. I didn't like ei-ther of them one bit.

"He gave me money, you know."

My hands tightened on the wheel. I was furious. "No, I didn't know. How much?"

"Fifty bucks. Cash, too."

"And you took it." I tried to keep any trace of bitterness out of my voice.

Gemma laughed. "Well, yeah. I mean, he said he and Ellen felt bad about never having bothered to see me when I was born, and they figured they owed me at least one birthday gift, considering all the birthdays they missed."

Well, that was clever, I thought. "He should have asked me if it was okay," I said.

"Why?" Gemma asked reasonably. "Why isn't it okay that I accept a birthday present from a relative?"

That stung, but I kept my mouth shut for the moment. Gemma, after all, was just a kid, a kid who probably hadn't ever had a wad of cash handed to her. Of course she would take the money, especially if she thought there were no strings attached. I thought about the twenty dollars my father had sent to Gemma shortly after she'd come home to me. Tom's money hadn't bothered me because I wasn't in the least afraid that he was out to steal my daughter away from me. Ellen and Richard, though, were unknown quantities, their motives equally unknown to me.

"What are you going to do with the money?" I asked. I wasn't stupid enough to suggest she put it in the bank account I'd opened in her name and into which I channeled what small sums I could spare from the weekly housekeeping budget, a budget that had been heavily stretched since Gemma moved in.

"I don't know," she said. "I'll think of something."

I have a strong feeling that Ellen enjoys playing the role of Lady Bountiful, condescending to offer assistance to the less fortunate in her path. I wonder if she makes a habit of rescuing strays, everything from dogs to down-on-their-luck relatives. Maybe Gemma is only the latest in a long line of those favored with Ellen's attention. And how long, I wonder, will that attention last? Some people are notorious for picking up and then abandoning good causes, leaving those temporarily in the limelight in a worse condition than they had ever been before the do-gooder had shown up.

Don't I have a right to be cynical and suspicious? Especially when it's on the part of my daughter?

Chapter 77

I have to admit that for about half a second I thought it was slightly creepy for some older man I'd never met before, who isn't even related to me by blood, to hand me two twenties and a ten. But Richard sounded sincere enough and he didn't touch me or anything, and Ellen came into the kitchen just then and she, too, said how bad they felt about not "being there" for me all these years—though how they could have been there for me when no one knew where I was, I don't know!—and that from now on they wanted to be part of my life.

I'm not dense enough to miss the signs from Verity that she's not happy about Ellen and Richard suddenly showing up. For one, she hardly said a word when we got back home from the party yesterday. I mean, all those years I was missing and she was alone, knowing nothing about what had happened to me, and not once did either Ellen or Richard call or write or send *her* gifts of cash. They never cared about her, or about my father from what I can tell, so why now decide to care about me?

That's the thing. I don't think Ellen and Richard *care* about me at all. And I don't care about that. I don't know what they want with me, but as long as they keep having us over to that enormous house with the pool and outdoor kitchen and as long as they want to keep making up for all the birthdays they missed, hey, I'll play nice.

Verity was at her studio at the college, so I took my sketch-book to the backyard and set about trying to draw the big pine tree (I really should find out what sort of pine it is), but it was rough going. I just couldn't seem to get the shape right without winding up with a sketch of a triangle. Too many images of artificial Christmas trees in my head, maybe. I know I should probably be taking lessons from someone who actually knows what she's doing. Some people teach themselves stuff like drawing or how to play the guitar, but they're probably geniuses or something. I wonder how much drawing lessons cost. I wonder if Verity would want to teach me.

Ellen and Richard, I thought, probably have enough money for drawing lessons. They probably have enough money to buy a few of Verity's biggest and most expensive sculptures. I wondered if there was a way to . . .

No. That's just not me, asking for a handout. If they want to give me—us—money or whatever, then fine. But asking is somehow—wrong. And I know Verity feels the same way. I think she might even be insulted if Ellen decided to buy one of her works. She'd suspect it was more of an act of charity than anything to do with artistic appreciation. She might be right, but in my opinion, she'd be crazy not to sell and take the money!

I heard the sound of a squeaky hinge and looked up to see Grace coming out the back door of her house, twins in tow. The Gallisons have one of those chunky plastic swing sets and a sandbox and a jungle gym in their yard, and the kids dashed right for them. Well, toddlers don't really dash. They kind of waddle, and when they fall down, it's more like their legs just buckle. Luckily, they don't have far to fall. Anyway, I got up from my seat and, leaving the sketchbook behind, went over to say hi to the neighbors.

Chapter 78

David was right on time. I thought: Alan is almost never on time. I opened the door to find him holding a bottle of wine in one hand and a bouquet of flowers in the other.

"Hi, Marni," he said. "These are for you. I hope you're not allergic."

I shook my head. "No allergies," I said. "And you can call me Gemma." Frankly? I'm tired of clinging to that old name, the one I never liked all that much anyway. That's why I introduced myself to the Gallisons as Gemma and why I told Ellen and Richard to call me Gemma. Now, let's see if I can get Cathy to switch over.

David came inside and followed me to the kitchen. "Something smells great," he said. "What's on the menu?"

Verity smiled at us both. I wondered if she and David were going to kiss, and when they didn't, I wondered if it was because of me. *Really,* I thought, *all this old-fashioned discretion has got to stop.*

"Bo ssäm," Verity said. "It's a Korean version of pulled pork."

David put the bottle of wine he'd brought onto the counter and got the corkscrew from its place in the silverware drawer. Of course he's been to Verity's house before and maybe a lot of times. I went in search of a vase in the living room and couldn't find the one Verity uses most often. I couldn't remember where she kept it and, thinking of David, who probably knew exactly where it was, I felt a little bit like a third wheel for about half a minute, but then I remembered where the vase was stored (behind some art books in the bookcase), and it was all right.

We sat down to dinner, Verity and I in our usual seats across from each other, and David between us.

"I hear you met your father's cousin on Saturday," David said to me.

"I told David they'd swooped into town," Verity explained. Swooped?

"Yeah," I said. "They're renting a house for the rest of the summer."

"Nice house?"

"Big. I counted four bathrooms. There could be more."

"Kind of excessive for two people," Verity said.

David shrugged. "Unless they plan on having a lot of overnight guests."

Verity said nothing to that and the conversation—what there had been of it—about Ellen and Richard was over.

The food was great, as usual. I don't know where Verity learned to cook, but I'm thinking I should get off my lazy butt and maybe start paying attention to what she does in the kitchen. If I'm going to wind up living with Dad again someday, I'm going to have to take over the cooking, because I'm not going back to eating the boring stuff out of a can that he makes.

And someday I'll be living on my own. I should probably learn to cook for myself, too.

"Do you have kids?" I asked David, in my usual abrupt way.

David finished chewing a mouthful of kimchi (it's *so* hot!) and said, "Nope."

Note that I did not ask him why he didn't have kids. "Verity says you were married before."

"I was. And she dumped me for one of my colleagues. Let me tell you, it was not a good experience."

"Ow. Do you hate her now?"

"Gemma . . ."

"No, it's okay," David told Verity. "No, I don't hate her. I'm not a big fan of hate. Too tiring. It'll be fine if I never see or hear from her again, though. And since we didn't have kids, there's really no reason she should contact me or vice versa."

And I thought about how Dad and Verity were always going to be tied together in some way because of me. And for the first time I wondered if Verity resented me for that. I think that if I were in her situation, I might resent the kid who kept me bound to a wacko. But then I thought: *No. Verity's not the type. She's nicer than I am.*

For dessert we had ice cream with fresh blueberries, and by eight thirty David had gone. He said he had an early morning appointment with his chiropractor. It was on the tip of my tongue to suggest that Verity spend the night at his place because it would be fine by me and they must be going crazy not being together, but I kept my mouth shut.

I like David. He doesn't bullshit the way so many people do. I can see why he likes Verity. She doesn't bullshit either. At least, not as far as I can tell, and believe me, I've been looking for evidence. I spent the first seventeen years of my life living with a liar and a cheat and a thief. I have no intention of letting myself be fooled again.

When Verity came back from walking David to his car, I offered to help clean up, which is not something I usually do. Well, it's not something I've *ever* done.

"Thanks," she said. "I'd appreciate that."

I didn't want to get into a big touchy-feely discussion about her and David, but I figured I had to say something, so I said, "He can really eat."

Verity laughed. "Then you two should get along."

I laughed too and stuck a plate in the dishwasher. "Yeah."

Chapter 79

I walked David out to his car after dinner last night.

"Well?" I said when we'd reached the curb.

"She's very smart. She's also very blunt. That could be a good thing or a bad thing, depending on your mood."

I smiled. "Tell me about it. Anyway, I think it went well."

"So do I. Let's hope Gemma thinks so too."

"She didn't correct you when you called her Gemma."

"She told me to call her Gemma. When she met me at the door."

I remembered then how she'd told Ellen and Richard they could call her by her birth name, and I thought it a positive sign she was finally beginning to adjust to this new life here in Yorktide with me.

David kissed me then, and I wondered if Gemma was watching from the living room window.

At breakfast this morning—English muffins, cereal, juice, and coffee—Gemma asked me why I didn't have another kid after she had been gone for a few years. (That was her word, *kid*, not *baby* or *child*.) She really does have a way of asking the most difficult questions in the most unnerving manner and at the most unlikely of times.

Well, I thought, we had been talking about kids at dinner

last night with David. It was a natural transition, I suppose. But how, exactly, to explain?

"It would have felt like a betrayal of you," I said after a moment's thought.

"But how?" she asked, not belligerently. "I might never have even known. If Dad hadn't gotten caught stealing that car, I probably would never have met you."

"It's complicated," I admitted. "But I don't regret my decision." That's the truth.

"Okay," she said, "then why didn't you ever get married? I mean, before you met David."

"I didn't want to get married." That is also the truth. "I didn't want to get close to anyone for a long time, male or female. I didn't want any attachments at all. I . . . I felt so guilty and sad about what had happened to you, I felt I didn't deserve a normal life, let alone a happy one. I'm not looking for pity," I added hastily. "That's just the way it was."

"But you got past that."

"I pretty much had to, yeah. For my own sake, but also because I always thought that someday we might be reunited and if I were a basket case . . ."

"I get it."

Gemma went to the bathroom. I was reaching for the coffeepot when the phone rang.

It was Ellen.

"Verity," she said, "I'd like to take Gemma out for a day. Do some shopping, have lunch, get to know each other a bit."

I was glad Ellen was asking my permission—sort of—even if I wasn't happy about her getting in touch with us again so soon. "I'll let you talk to her," I said.

I handed the phone to Gemma, now back at the table. "It's for you."

I went about pouring a second cup of coffee, pretending not to care about what was being said on the other end of the line.

Ha. I cared. After a moment Gemma said, "Sure. Okay," and then, "Bye."

"Ellen asked if I wanted to hang out tomorrow," she said. "I told her okay. I mean, we don't have any plans, do we?"

I was happy she'd asked that, and then I suppressed the jealousy that could, I knew, ruin this relationship my daughter and I were building. "No," I said. "No plans."

Gemma reached for another piece of toast. "This bread is really good," she said. "What kind is it?"

Maybe, I thought, *she really does care more about the bread than about her father's wealthy cousin.* "Seven grain," I said.

"Really?" Gemma eyed the piece of toast in her hand. "I always thought this health stuff sucked." And then she took a very large bite.

Chapter 80

Ellen took me for lunch at a pretty fancy place called M.C. Perkins Cove. When I saw the inside of the restaurant, I suggested maybe we could go to The Friendly Lobsterman or a clam shack, but she said she'd already made a reservation and that I would like this place. She was right about that. The view of the ocean is perfect, and the food was fantastic. And no one even looked at me weird because I wasn't dressed up. Actually, some people were in shorts, though not cutoffs, so I guess I didn't really stand out in my jeans. Ellen was wearing pretty much the same thing she'd worn at her party—I wonder if it was like a uniform for her—and this time she was carrying a bag that had what looked like two letter Cs kind of linked. "Chanel," she told me when she caught me looking at it, trying to figure out if it meant something.

I think it's probably a real Chanel. (I've heard about knock-offs. A guy Dad knew once sold knock-off Gucci stuff on a street corner in Albuquerque, until he got caught.) If it is, it probably cost, like, thousands of dollars. Why would anyone spend that on a bag?

When we had been served, Ellen asked a few questions about Dad and my life with him, like what towns we had lived in ("a bunch") and if I had ever had music lessons (no) and if he had ever gotten me a tutor ("I never needed one") and if I had ever thought about college ("a bit"). She didn't ask anything really personal, like if I missed Dad or how I felt about what he'd done. I'm not sure I would have answered questions like that. I mean, I'm still not sharing a whole lot with Verity.

At one point Ellen said, "Alan showed some promise when he was very young, you know."

"Promise of what?"

Ellen sort of smiled sadly. "Promise of being normal."

I didn't know what to say to that. I mean, I can't argue that my father *is* normal, can I?

Sitting across from Ellen as she sipped a second glass of Prosecco (what is that? It's bubbly like champagne, but if it were champagne, it would be called champagne), for some reason I thought about what Verity had told me about why she didn't have another baby after I was taken away. That it would somehow be a betrayal of me. And she was always so sensitive to what might upset me, from meeting Marion for the first time, to not bothering me about what Dad and I talked about, to knowing the truth about her relationship with David. Was it betraying Verity for me to be sitting here, having lunch with Dad's cousin? The idea made me uncomfortable, and I pushed it away.

"I have a little something for you," Ellen said suddenly. She reached into her bag, took out a smallish box, and handed it to me. There was a red ribbon tied around the box.

"But you already gave me the money," I blurted.

"That was different," she said. "Go ahead—open it."

I did. It was an iPhone.

"But I have a phone," I told her.

"This one is the latest model. You don't have that, do you?"

"No," I admitted.

"You'll need one."

Why? I thought. *Why will I need one, really?*

"Thanks," I said. I put the phone back in the box and stowed it in my bag. My twenty-dollar bag I'd bought with the money from Verity's father.

After lunch, we walked down to the water, and Ellen asked if I'd ever walked along Marginal Way, the path up on the cliffs to our left. I told her I hadn't. Not yet. She told me I should, it's beautiful, and then she told me she had a surprise.

I half laughed. "Another one?"

"Richard saw you out on your bike the other day."

"Yeah," I said. "Until I get a license, it's the best way to get around."

"He said it was an old machine."

"Not too old. Anyway, our friend Marc checked it out before we bought it. It's in perfect shape."

Ellen still looked doubtful. "Well, Richard and I would feel better if we knew you were riding something high-end, something safer and better made."

I immediately felt kind of insulted, like did she really think Verity would give me a piece of crap to ride or that I would be so stupid as to get on a bike that was falling apart?

I controlled my temper. It took some effort. Maybe she was sincere. What do I really know about her, after all? I should try not to be so judgmental.

"Really," I said, "that's okay. I like my bike."

"Now, Gemma, it's a done deal."

I didn't know what to say without being a total jerk, so I kept my mouth shut and squinted out at the ocean. Suddenly Ellen said: "Thank you for letting us do these things for you. You know we don't have children of our own. It's been . . ." She looked away then, toward the other side of the cove where the boats were moored, and gave a small sigh. "It's been difficult at times." Then she turned back to me and, for the first time, touched me. Just her hand on my arm, briefly. "You're really the one helping us. You're really our gift."

After that, we got back into her black Lexus GX SUV and drove to a bike shop in Kennebunk, where there was a Trek bike waiting for us. A guy from the store asked me to get on it and he made some adjustments and then I got off the bike and he put it on the rack on top of Ellen's car. "I have the same model," Ellen said, smiling. "Maybe we could ride together one day."

"Maybe," I said. "Sure."

Verity was out when I got home after a few more stops with Ellen—she wanted to browse some shops in Kennebunkport; in one of them she bought a vase that cost two hundred bucks—but she'd left a message on the kitchen table saying she'd be home by about five. To make us dinner, of course. There must be some days when she's not in the mood to cook a full meal, but since I've been living with her, she's done it every night, except for the few times we've gone out.

I went into my room then and lay down on the couch. Though I'd done nothing more strenuous than get in and out of Ellen's car, I felt exhausted. And kind of confused.

Like I said, I don't really need a new phone or a new bike. My old ones are perfectly fine. I don't really *need* anything. But I have to admit, I like getting stuff. I mean, it's a bit of a novelty for someone like me, who only got a gift on her birthday (her false one!) and Christmas, and who periodically went through what Dad liked to call "belt-tightening phases," which he tried to present to me as a sort of adventure or challenge. *Let's see if we can get through two weeks with no candy or cookies,* or *Pasta is a basic food, Marni. It's just bread in disguise. Let's see if we can eat spaghetti for dinner every night this week. In ancient times people pretty much survived on bread.*

I'm not sure I ever believed *that,* but a kid doesn't argue with the person putting food on the table, even if the food was limited or boring. Well, maybe a spoiled kid argues, but not someone like me. Until I was about twelve and the truth began to dawn on me—that Dad's "fun" belt-tightening periods were really about his not having enough money to feed us properly—I kind of enjoyed doing without. I mean, at least Dad and I were doing it together. It was us against the world.

It's pretty clear that Verity won't be happy about Ellen and Richard showering me with stuff I didn't ask for (even if they say I'm the one doing them the favor, and I'm not really sure I believe that). And I can guess why, though of course she wouldn't say. There's her pride, of course, and she's afraid I'll like them better than I like her—and I do like her—because they've got more money. It's kind of insulting actually, that she or anyone at all who knows me would think I give a shit about money, but I see why she would feel insecure. After all she went through when I was with Dad, not knowing if I was alive or dead . . . shit, even being questioned by the police in the beginning! Of course she doesn't want some rich cousin coming in and trying to buy me away from her. But I'm not going anywhere. Verity's going to have to figure that out and believe it.

I mean, I'm not going anywhere until Dad is released. Someday.

Chapter 81

When Gemma told me about the iPhone and the bike, I thought my blood pressure was going to soar high enough to send me into cardiac arrest.

The gifts are extravagant, and it was presumptuous of Ellen (does Richard know about the phone and the bike?) to provide for my daughter items I'd already provided for her. Okay, Gemma had come with the phone, but I was paying for it now. She's my daughter, and I support her.

To be fair, Gemma didn't seem particularly excited about either gift. And this morning after breakfast, she went out for a ride on the bike I'd bought her. And when I was dusting, I found the new phone, still in its box, on a bookshelf in the living room.

I thought about telling her—asking her, I mean—to return the gifts, but I couldn't bring myself to do it. I still can't. I don't want to deprive Gemma of attention or of the sort of things I can't afford, especially when from what I can tell, she's had so little in the way of extras in her life, but I can't shake the feeling Ellen is trying to buy my daughter's affections. David agrees with me, as does Annie, but they're prejudiced in my favor, so maybe we're all being overly suspicious. Can anyone blame us?

But neither David nor Annie is as worried as I am about possible fallout.

"They'll be gone in a few weeks," David reminded me when we spoke last night on the phone. "There's nothing to worry about."

"Yes, there is," I insisted. "What kind of damage are Ellen and Richard going to leave in their wake? They'll have raised her expectations too high for me to meet."

"Verity," David said in that terribly patient way he has, "don't insult your daughter. Okay, I hardly know her, but she doesn't strike me as someone obsessed with money."

No, I thought, *she doesn't, but money can corrupt. It can screw up even the most down-to-earth person if it comes at the right time and in the right quantity.*

Huh. Ever since Ellen's comment about breaking the diamonds out of the safe, a memory has been niggling at me.

When Alan proposed to me a few weeks after I'd told him I was pregnant, it was with a fairly substantial, brilliant-cut diamond solitaire on a yellow gold band. Before discovering I was pregnant, I'd been unhappy in the relationship and had vaguely considered leaving Alan, but when I saw how happy he was to be starting a family, I'd convinced myself everything would be okay between us. So I accepted his proposal. My father was thrilled, as was Marion. Thinking back on it, I see that Marion also expressed a sort of relief. "Everything will be okay now," she said, and at the time I didn't question her. I suppose I thought she meant that now the baby would be legitimate. Marion is old-fashioned that way. Now I know she believed that by marrying Alan, I could further take him in hand and keep him out of too much trouble.

Anyway, I wondered how Alan could have afforded the ring. His mother and his one friend, Rob, had no money to spare, and I wondered if Alan had taken a bank loan. I hoped he hadn't. How long would it take him to pay it back? He didn't make much money, and he was bad at saving what he did make—though he had used the argument of financial security when pressuring me to give up my art.

I figured the ring might be a fake, or at least, that the stone was a CZ or maybe even a white topaz, though I knew little about identifying stones. And if it was fake, or even partly so, there was no way I was going to call him on it and hurt his overly sensitive feelings. After all, it was the thought that counted, and with a baby on the way, it was smart of him not to spend money on something not strictly necessary.

When I eventually broke the engagement, not long before Alan ran off with our daughter, I tried to return the ring, but he insisted I keep it. "I know you'll come back to me," he said, tears in his eyes. "I know you'll see the truth, that I'm the one man who will ever love you entirely." I admit to a moment of panic at that point. I thought: *What if he's right? What if Alan is as good as it's going to get for me?* But somehow I summoned the courage to take Gemma and move out. I put the ring back into its box and tucked it into a corner of a dresser drawer in the room I occupied at Barbara's place.

About six months after Alan took off, I badly needed cash. With the rent to pay (Alan had always paid at least a part of it) and having lost time at work due to depression and an ulcer that had come out of nowhere and kept me in bed for almost two weeks—let alone the doctor bills that my measly insurance wouldn't cover—selling the ring seemed the obvious solution. I took the loathed thing to the family-owned jewelry store in downtown Yorktide to see what they might do for me. Imagine my shock when Mr. Nettles recognized the ring as one that had been stolen from a friend's jewelry store in Ogunquit the previous year. He couldn't be 100 percent sure, he said, and suggested I take the ring to the police. I did. And there was a record of the theft and a full description of the ring. Later the rightful owner claimed it. And yes, the stone was indeed a real and a very good diamond.

No one suspected me of dirty dealing. By then, with Alan and Gemma long gone, and Alan's criminal past public knowledge, all anyone felt for me was pity.

One thing's for sure. I'll never tell Gemma the ring saga. My one brush with important jewelry, and it turned out to be someone else's stolen property.

Chapter 82

I invited Marion for lunch yesterday. Gemma and I hadn't seen her since the Fourth of July festivities, and I was feeling a little guilty about that. I made Marion's favorite lunch—a tuna melt with Swiss cheese and tomato on white bread (she would accept a cheap squishy bread, but I would not and so used a good loaf of toasting white)—bought a bag of cookies from Bread and Roses in Ogunquit, and set the table on the back deck with china plates and real glasses and cotton napkins. On her own initiative, Gemma picked a handful of daisies and a few stalks of Queen Anne's lace from the garden and arranged the simple, delicate flowers artfully in a small vase at the center of the table. She has an eye after all, I noticed, and I wondered if she had constructed flower arrangements before. Alan certainly wouldn't have taught her how to.

Marion arrived promptly at noon—she's a person who eats breakfast at six, lunch at noon, and dinner at five every day she can possibly manage it. Being retired now, this means almost every day of every week. I could tell immediately something was on her mind.

We sat at the table, and I served the hot sandwiches and lemonade. Gemma, as was usual, scarfed down her food in moments, but Marion, always a slow and deliberate eater, was even more so this afternoon.

"Is the sandwich okay?" I asked, knowing the food wasn't the issue.

Marion raised a ghost of a smile. "Fine, Verity. Thank you."

I resisted encouraging a confidence. Asking Marion to share what was bothering her could and often did result in a very long litany of minor ailments, a good many of which, I suspect, are imaginary. Well, real enough to Marion. It turned out, there was no need for me to encourage Marion to speak.

"Alan's cousin hasn't called me since she and her husband have been in town," she said with a sigh.

Gemma said nothing. What could she say? And the last thing I wanted was to make excuses for Ellen's social snobbery.

"Since they've been here in Yorktide," Marion went on. "Well, there have been so many memories."

That's when I began to get really nervous. The last thing I wanted was for Marion to start strolling down memory lane and reveal secrets I didn't want Gemma to know, not now, maybe never. But short of being rude, I didn't know how to stop her.

"Did you know, Gemma," she went on, "that Alan's father, Albert, died when Alan was only just nineteen? It was a terrible loss for the both of us."

"But you still wear your wedding ring," Gemma said. "Unless you got married again?"

"Oh no. Albert was the only one for me."

"Sorry. I mean, that was a long time ago. You must have been lonely a lot."

I smiled at my daughter. She was revealing herself to be a far more perceptive person than I'd thought at first.

Marion went inexorably on. "Since shortly after our marriage," she said, her voice a bit shaky, "Albert was intermittently institutionalized for mental exhaustion. That was the term we used."

"Who's 'we'?" Gemma asked. "The doctors?"

Marion didn't quite answer her question. "I never told Alan

what was wrong with his father," she went on, fiddling with the napkin in her lap and not meeting Gemma's eyes or mine. "I never told him where exactly his father was going when he went away. I told him that Daddy had a weak constitution and sometimes needed complete rest."

"And he believed that?" Gemma asked, her tone harsh now and suspicious. My entire body was tense.

"He did believe that," Marion said forcefully. "At least, he never questioned me, not even after his father's death. By then, I saw no reason to tell him the truth. And the rest of the family, well, they never had much use for Albert, so no one saw the point in interfering with my decision. But sometimes I think that maybe they should have. . . ."

"What do you mean?" Gemma demanded.

"Marion, I don't think—"

Marion ignored me and leaned forward across the table, finally looking her granddaughter in the eye. I don't think I'd ever seen her so intent and sure of her purpose. "No," she said. "I think Gemma should know. There was some trouble with Alan and a few girlfriends before he met your mother."

I didn't know why Marion was telling this to Gemma, unless it was to relieve a burden of guilt. And if that were the case, then Marion was acting selfishly. Again.

"What kind of trouble?" Gemma shot me a look, and I felt my heart sink.

"Nothing physical. Just—"

"Stalking," I said when Marion seemed not able to go on. "There were restraining orders. Alan didn't take rejection lightly. He couldn't let go."

Gemma said nothing for a few minutes. Neither did Marion nor I. And then Gemma spoke. "You know how the police realized Jim Armstrong was Alan Burns, don't you?" she said. "The fingerprints from his second arrest, the car theft. He told me he'd been arrested when he was young for throwing a baseball through someone's window—he said it was an accident— and that's why the prints were on file."

Marion shook her head. "That never happened."

"In fact," I said, "he beat someone up pretty badly. Broken bones. A concussion."

"It was an unprovoked attack," Marion went on more steadily than I would have given her credit for. "Alan thought the man was interested in his ex-girlfriend."

"The victim was hospitalized for almost a week," I told my daughter.

Gemma shook her head and let out a bark of laughter. "I always thought Dad was a total passive-aggressive, when he wasn't just being annoying. He actually hit someone?"

"He has—at least, he had—a temper."

"I know that," Gemma said. "He gets pissed off all the time at someone from work or the guy behind the counter at the drugstore or someone he thinks is going to cut him off on the road even though the guy doesn't. It all seemed random to me. Stupid, like when he'd get fired for starting an argument, but . . . I guess I never pictured him actually getting violent."

"At least he never hit a woman," Marion said.

Gemma looked at her grandmother as if she couldn't believe what she was hearing. "Does it even matter?" she asked. "Look at what else he's done!"

Marion had no answer to that, and as decently as I could, I suggested it was time for coffee. Thankfully, Marion declined, and a little while later I walked her out to her car.

"Don't be mad at me," she said, opening the driver's-side door. Her face was crumpled with emotion. "I had to do it."

I didn't bother to ask her why she had to tell the truth and why now. The point was that she had.

"I'm not mad," I said, truthfully. "Just—tired."

When she'd driven off, I went back out to the deck. Gemma was still sitting at the table, frowning.

"Did you know about Alan's past when you hooked up with him?" she asked as soon as I'd sat.

We've come this far, I thought. *Why keep the rest a secret now?*

"No."

"But Marion knew."

"Yes."

"Is that why you two fell out? Because when you found out about Dad, it was already too late?"

"Yes, it was. She never told me anything about Alan's problems. That it was a pattern likely to repeat itself. She thought I was different. She thought I could save him, keep him in line."

"That's ridiculous!"

"Yeah," I said. "It is."

Gemma looked furious. "If Alan had known that his father had mental problems, he might have been on the lookout for his own and maybe even gotten some help!"

I thought it unlikely, as someone with mental instabilities might be the very last to realize there was a problem, but I didn't say so.

"Why did they ever have a kid in the first place if Albert was a nutjob?"

Why does anyone have a child?

"I don't know the answer to that," I said. "It's all in the past. Look, Marion is a weak woman. I've had to accept that fact and learn to forgive her for what she did to me. Keeping me in the dark. Putting me at risk."

"And me!"

"Marion is an enabler," I went on calmly. "She probably learned how to be at a very young age, and there's no changing her now. Besides, what's done is done. I know more than most people how hard it is to let go of anger and grudges and old hurts, but sometimes it's necessary for survival."

Gemma half laughed. "So does this mean I'm a nut case too?"

"Of course it doesn't. Gemma, come on. You're one of the most eminently sane people I've ever met."

"I need to go think about this," she said. Suddenly she sounded defeated. Drained.

My heart broke. I watched her go inside the house, and slowly got to my feet to clear away the lunch things. No one, I noticed, had touched the cookies.

Maybe I should have pressed Marion as to why she felt it necessary to tell Gemma about her grandfather's mental illness now. To tell her at all. To tell her about her father's troubled past with women. The need to confess is a strange and very powerful thing and sometimes can't be resisted, even when the confessor knows she might further hurt the one to whom she's confessing.

Chapter 83

When Marion had gone home and Verity and I had talked some more about the bombshell my grandmother dropped smack in the middle of our lunch, I went off to my room, needing to think things through.

I feel bad for the young woman my mother once was. I feel angry with my father for being such a jerk-off. I feel angry with Marion for being such a wimp.

Sure, I always knew Dad was a bit off, a bit quirky, but he was never as bad as the fathers of some of the kids I went to school with—outright drunks or addicts or wife-beaters—so I didn't really care. Dad might be off-balance, but he's also nice, mostly. I mean, he doesn't use foul language. If he sees old people having trouble reaching something on a shelf at the grocery store, he gets it for them.

But he steals, things and people. And he beats people up. And he stalks them. Like stalking is any better than hitting someone in the face? To me, it sounds way more dangerous and totally creepy.

No wonder Ellen pokes fun of Marion and calls her pathetic. I almost can't blame her, though it makes me really uncomfortable when she says critical stuff about Dad. He *is* still my father, even if it's turning out he's not a very good one.

I wonder how much of your life is predestined before birth.

I mean, Verity says I'm eminently sane—her words. I don't know about that, but she says that if I haven't cracked up already, after the crazy shit I've been through, I'm not going to start cracking up now. I hope she's right.

Did Dad even have a choice in becoming the guy he became? Yes. Of course he had a choice! He's not insane!

I tried to remember the few girlfriends Dad had over the years, aside from that one Patty I told Verity about. The one who'd told me that one day I, too, would have to leave the nest—the prison—Alan had constructed around me. And I found I couldn't remember much about any of them. None had stuck around for long. Had they all seen pretty quickly that Dad was a dangerous guy, and run off before he could gain possession of them? Had they all been smart, smarter and more experienced than my mother had been back then? No use. I'll never know what happened to those women. For all I know, one or more of the times Dad and I had to move in a hurry was because some father or boyfriend or maybe even the police were after him for having harassed a daughter or a girlfriend.

I sighed and turned onto my side. The couch isn't really wide enough for me to sleep on my side without opening it out, but it's okay for when I'm just lying here, thinking.

Like thinking that Dad had to have had a good reason for doing what he did, for taking me away from my mother. Wait, what I mean is, I have to believe *he* believed he had a good reason, even if that reason was something as stupid as revenge. Because if I don't believe that, what am I left with? The naked fact that my father is deranged, that he was always deranged, and that he was predestined to go off the edge at some point in his life—taking me, it turned out, with him. The naked fact that I grew up in the care of someone who should have been in a freakin' straightjacket. Huh. I wonder if Dad's defense team is going to try to have him declared unfit for trial.

I got up from the couch and went into the kitchen, where Verity's laptop lives. She wasn't there; I heard her upstairs. I checked the e-mail account she had set up for me back when I first got here. There was a message from Tom; I'd given him my address in my last note. It was just chitchat, like how he and Valerie were feeling fine and how he hoped I was enjoying the summer and that sometimes he missed Maine but not in the winters. I wrote back and told him about meeting my father's cousin and her husband, but said nothing about my kind of complicated feelings about them and all their money. And I said nothing about what Marion had told me about my father. Tom probably knows all that by now anyway. And if he doesn't, it must be because Verity doesn't want him to know. And it's not my secret to tell.

I heard Verity coming down the stairs then, and I closed the laptop.

Chapter 84

Another text from Ellen. I read it—*Great seeing u today*—but didn't reply. In fact, I turned off my phone and put it on the little table by my bed. My couch, whatever. I don't mind her texting me as long as she doesn't expect me to always answer right away. I mean, I have a life.

Even if I'm not sure where that life is going.

Ellen and I went to the Ogunquit Playhouse the other night to see *The Sound of Music*. I'd never been to a play other than the ones at some of the schools I went to, and I have to say it was kind of exciting to be sitting in the second row, close enough to see all the heavy makeup the actors were wearing and to see the scuff marks their shoes made on the wooden stage. One actor spit with practically every word he spoke! (I was glad we weren't sitting in the front row.) The show itself seemed kind of silly and seriously old-fashioned to me, but Ellen seemed to like it a lot, along with everyone else in the theater. The applause at the end was long and loud, and as we walked back up the aisle toward the exit, I heard lots of comments like, "That was fantastic!" and "That was as good as Broadway!"

Afterward Ellen took me to this nice restaurant for "a nightcap." I'd never heard that expression before, but it was obvious what it meant when she ordered a brandy. I had a cappuccino. It came with one of those Italian cookies called biscotti. It was probably the most adult and sophisticated night I've ever spent, and I didn't hate it like I thought I might.

When we were having our nightcaps, Ellen said: "I'm guessing Alan never took you to the theater. He never did have any appreciation for the performing arts." And then she raised her eyebrow like she does. "Then again, he does seem to have acting talent, constructing the role of Jim Armstrong and playing it so well for all those years."

I don't like it when Ellen says something critical or dismissive about my father, but I said nothing in his defense. Honestly, after learning about his past, the restraining orders, the attack on that innocent guy, I don't feel very much like being his knight in shining armor.

I wonder if Ellen and Richard know about Alan's early crimes. I'm certainly not going to be the one to tell them.

Anyway, now there's something even more important to think about than what happened in the past. Now I'm supposed to be thinking about my future.

Here's what happened.

Ellen took me to lunch again today at M.C. Perkins Cove. (That place is not cheap. She and Richard must have a serious amount of cash to be spending all the money they're spending on me.) When the waiter brought our lunch—Ellen always has a salad, and I always go for some kind of sandwich—Ellen asked me if I'd seen the local high school yet.

"Yeah," I told her. "Verity took me there earlier in the summer. We had a tour."

"And what did you think?"

I shrugged. "It was all right."

"But you weren't impressed."

"No, not really." I thought: Why do I need to be impressed? It's only a high school. You go to classes and you come home and then, if you're not stupid, you graduate.

Ellen took a sip of her Prosecco and then said: "How would you like to go to a really good school?"

"What do you mean?" I asked. "Verity said we can't afford a private school."

"But Richard and I can."

Now I thought: So?

"We have an offer for you, Gemma," Ellen went on, resting her fork against her plate. "We'd like you to attend a very good private school in Massachusetts. It's called Greyson Academy. They have an excellent website you might want to explore. It will tell you everything you need to know. But I'm jumping ahead of myself. Richard and I want to pay for your education. We want to pay for you to go to Greyson."

My very first thought was: She's got to be kidding. I mean, I thought she was playing some sort of mean and stupid joke, dangling riches in front of the poor girl but holding them just out of grasp. But then I saw from the look on her face that she was totally serious.

"Have you talked to Verity about this?" I asked.

"Not yet. Richard and I thought you should be the one to tell her, after you've thought some about the offer. And ask me any questions you need to, Gemma. You need to be fully informed in order to make a good decision."

"Where would I live?" I asked, envisioning a dorm room that slept twenty kids, like one of those old-fashioned dorm rooms you see in movies about penitentiaries and boarding schools where they starve and beat the students and where the older, bigger kids sexually assault the little kids. If that was the case, forget about it.

"You would live with us," Ellen said. "We have a lovely guest room with its own bathroom. As soon as you learn to drive, you'll have use of one of our cars. We belong to a very nice country club, and we'll get you a membership, of course. You could take tennis lessons if you like, or Richard could take you out on the golf course. He plays every Saturday morning. We're close to Boston, which is a lovely city. You'll enjoy getting to know it. And we usually go away to someplace warm and sunny around Christmas. You could come with us, of course."

"Like where?" I asked, wondering why I was bothering to ask these questions, as if I really cared about the answers. I mean, me at a country club? Was this woman high?

"Well, we've gone to Aruba and Puerto Rico, but our favorite place to spend the holiday season is Hawaii."

"Oh," I said. And I remembered how a long time ago I'd seen some pictures in a magazine of places in Hawaii, boiling volcanoes and black sand, and I'd thought, *I'd like to go there one day. It looks so cool.* Well, hot but you know what I mean.

Ellen picked up her fork again and speared a bit of lettuce. "We're planning a trip to Paris next spring," she said, "and we'll make sure the dates coincide with your spring break so we three can go together. We'll have to get you a passport, of course, but that's no worry. By the way, lots of the Greyson students go abroad during the breaks." Ellen smiled. "I wouldn't be surprised if we ran into one or two of your classmates in the City of Lights."

I thought suddenly of one of the art books in Verity's studio, one that has pictures of the *Mona Lisa* and this really huge stone sphinx and a statue called the *Venus de Milo*, all in a museum called The Louvre. The Louvre was in Paris.

"I don't . . . I don't know what to say," I told her. *And why,* I thought, *aren't you just saying no? The whole idea is outrageous.*

Ellen laughed. "Of course this must seem so sudden to you and well, it is a bit sudden! Why don't you give it some serious thought? Sleep on it. And talk to Verity, of course. She'll have a few questions that Richard and I will be happy to answer, questions about an allowance for you, which of course we'll provide, and other practical matters. The Greyson semester starts right after Labor Day and I've spoken to the administration about allowing us to get you registered as late as the end of the month."

The end of the month is only weeks away.

I said nothing more after that. Ellen, maybe sensing I was feeling pretty overwhelmed, changed the subject. She told me about a dog they once had and how they were thinking of getting another one and how careful you had to be about breeders. I didn't really listen.

Ellen dropped me off at the bungalow after lunch. "Call me anytime," she said as I got out of her car.

Mrs. Pascoe was watering some flowers in a bed that runs along the front of her house. She waved. I wasn't really in the mood to chat with her, not when I was still trying to process Ellen's insane offer, but I went over anyway.

"Hello, Gemma!" She smiled widely, and I noticed there was some lipstick on her teeth. Bright pink. I don't know how women wear lipstick. I don't know why. The farthest I'll go with makeup is some tinted lip balm. Verity doesn't wear much makeup, and Annie wears none that I can see. Cathy is another story.

"Hi, Mrs. Pascoe," I said. "Your flowers are looking nice."

Mrs. Pascoe then launched into a story of how she learned to love flowers when she was a little girl, and how her grandfather worked as a gardener on some big estate and would take her to work with him sometimes and . . .

I kind of zoned out after that. Finally she let me go, and I went into my house.

She's not a bad old thing, Mrs. Pascoe. And it occurs to me I have no idea if the Pascoes ever had kids and if they have grandkids. I haven't seen anyone visit them since I got here to Yorktide, but then again, it's not like I've been home every single minute of every single day. Verity probably knows if Mr. and Mrs. Pascoe have family somewhere. Not that it matters. I'm just curious.

Chapter 85

"She's with Ellen again," I said, twisting the already twisted cord of the old-fashioned landline around my finger. "That's the third time in the past two weeks. Last Thursday they went to the Ogunquit Playhouse. And Ellen's been texting her too."

"How do you know that?" Annie asked. "You're not spying on Gemma, are you?"

"Of course not," I said, pretending indignation. I hadn't been spying—Gemma had told me about the texts but had made no comment about them, good or bad—but the thought had occurred to me to sneak a look at her phone when she was in the shower.

"So how is Gemma feeling about this newfound friendship? If we can call it a friendship."

"I don't know," I admitted. "She's not saying much. And that's what bothers me. If she came home after an outing with Ellen and told me every detail of their time together, even if she had a blast, I'd prefer it to the silence."

"But Gemma's always been that way," Annie pointed out. "What I mean is, since coming back to Yorktide she's not always been forthcoming about her feelings."

"I know. Look, you don't think the next time you see her you might try to get something out of her? I mean, obviously she doesn't hate this Ellen person. Do you think . . . Do you think Gemma's using Ellen?"

"No," Annie said firmly. "No, Gemma isn't using Ellen. I'm sure it's the other way around, though what exactly Ellen wants with her twice-removed cousin or whatever Gemma is, I don't know. And I can try to get Gemma to open up to me about her relationship with Ellen, but I can't promise she'll spill."

I sighed. "I shouldn't have said that about Gemma's using Alan's cousin. That was unfair. I shouldn't even have considered the possibility. She's a good person. She's too up front to be a manipulator like her father."

"But she is still a child, though not a particularly naïve one, so yes, you're right to keep an eye on things. Just don't panic."

"Me?" I said. "Panic? Never."

Annie laughed. "I've got to go. Marc is pointing at his watch. He hates to miss the movie previews."

I put down the phone, and as I did, I saw Gemma through the window, chatting with Mrs. Pascoe. I'm glad she's progressed to being friendly with the neighbors. Forming relationships, however casual, will definitely help her feel at home here.

Gemma came in a few minutes later while I was taking inventory of our supply of pasta. It's amazing how much pasta Gemma can eat in any one sitting. Luckily, pasta is cheap.

"Did you have a good time with Ellen?" I asked.

"It was okay," she said.

"Where did you go for lunch?"

"That place M.C. again."

I'd been to M.C. Perkins Cove once with David. He'd treated me to dinner for my thirty-eighth birthday. We had a lovely time, and the restaurant has a special place in my heart because of that. Now I wondered if I would always associate it instead with Ellen Burns-Cassidy.

Stop being a drama queen, I told myself.

"What did Mrs. Pascoe have to say for herself?" I asked.

"She was telling me about her garden."

"She's got quite the green thumb. She's taught me a few lessons over the years. I never could have managed the one rosebush I have managed without her words of wisdom."

"Hmm."

I looked carefully at my daughter. "Are you feeling all right?" I asked. She looked tense or troubled. Or maybe something she'd eaten at lunch wasn't sitting well. I remembered there was a bottle of Pepto-Bismol in the bathroom cabinet.

"Verity?" she said. "We need to talk."

Four of the most fear-inducing words in the English language, at least when strung together in that order. "Okay," I said, closing the cupboard I'd been investigating. "What about?"

"About the fact that Ellen and Richard want me to go and live with them."

My stomach sank, and I sank with it into a chair.

Chapter 86

When I got past the first rush of anger over the fact that Ellen had gone behind my back—yes, that's exactly what she'd done!—and made such a totally outrageous offer to my daughter, I found my voice.

"What do you mean, live with them?" I asked. I thought: *If they want to formally adopt her, I'll kill them.*

"Just that." Gemma sat at the table with me. "They want me to live with them and go to some private school. Ellen says they'll pay for everything, tuition and all. And that they'll give me an allowance."

I placed my hands squarely on the table. It took every ounce of my willpower to remain at least outwardly calm, like the rational adult I'm supposed to be.

"How do you feel about the idea?" I asked. "I mean, in general."

Gemma shrugged. "I don't know. It's so . . . it's so out of the blue. I mean, they hardly know me, and they want me to move in with them? At first I thought it was some sick joke."

"But does the idea appeal to you?" I pressed, maybe unfairly.

"I guess," she said. "A little. I mean, she said we'd go to Paris on spring break."

Since when, I thought, has Gemma wanted to go to Paris? And if she has been dreaming about it, why hasn't she told me?

"But you just got here," I blurted. It was a stupid thing to say—my control slipped—but better than what I really wanted to say, which was: *Don't leave me! Please, I'll do anything; just don't leave me!*

Gemma ignored my brief outburst. "The school has a website," she said. "Maybe I should just look at it."

"All right. I'll get the laptop. It's on the coffee table in the living room."

I got up from my seat—yes, my legs held, but I hadn't been entirely sure they would—and retrieved the laptop.

"It's called Greyson Academy," Gemma said when I handed it to her. "Here, this is it."

My heart sank along with my stomach as we viewed images of stately redbrick buildings and well-maintained lawns dotted with massive oaks and firs. The website informed us that the majority of graduates went on to Ivy League colleges and from there, on to graduate studies in law, the sciences, medicine, and academics. There was a strong alumni organization; its current president was a prominent attorney (I recognized his name) and had held public office. There was a swimming pool and tennis courts on campus, as well as a state-of-the-art library that claimed to rival that of many a college. There was, if you can believe it, an observatory.

And then there were the pictures of the students. Some were posed; others were candid. Students in theater productions (the sets, what I could see of them, were astounding); students at city hall, receiving awards for community service; students in formal wear (no tacky prom dresses here); students in graduates' caps and gowns; students in athletic gear, lacrosse and soccer and—good Lord—riding habits; students competing in debates with kids from other schools.

Students in uniform.

"You have to wear a uniform," Gemma stated flatly.

"So it seems."

"I've never worn a uniform. I mean, I've never even been in Girl Scouts."

"I was in Girl Scouts for a few years," I said. "I hated wearing the uniform." Had I really hated wearing it? I don't think I had cared one way or the other. But I know why I'd said what I'd said.

Suddenly Gemma closed the laptop.

"You know," she said, "I haven't told Alan about Ellen and Richard."

"Why not?" I asked, surprised at this bit of information.

"Just because. Because I don't think it matters."

"All right," I said. And I wondered if it didn't matter because Ellen and Richard mean so little to her. If only I could be sure of that!

"You . . . Never mind."

"No, what?" I asked.

Gemma looked down at her hands, clasped in her lap. "When I'm on the phone with Alan, do you ever want to say anything to him?"

Lately Gemma has taken to calling her father by his first name, not Dad. Not all the time, but often enough. "No," I said. "There's nothing for me to say at this point."

Gemma looked up again and half laughed. "I think there's a lot you could say! Like, *What the hell were you thinking?* Like, *I hate you.*"

"But what would be the point? I doubt he could adequately explain his behavior. And I'm pretty sure he hates me and assumes that the feeling is mutual so . . . Though I don't hate him now. Not anymore."

"You feel pity for him."

"Yeah," I admitted. "It's a little bit easier to handle than hate."

"I guess. Look," she said, "we don't have to talk more about Ellen's offer right away, do we?"

"No," I said. "We don't have to talk about it at all." I hesitated and then I said, "We can ignore it."

Gemma half smiled and got up from the table. "I'll be in my room," she said.

First things first, I thought, when I'd heard her bedroom door close behind her. *I have to have a little talk with Ellen Burns-Cassidy.*

Chapter 87

I asked Ellen to meet me at a place where I knew I would feel comfortable—and Ellen, not so much. The home-turf advantage, I guess. I was pretty certain Ellen had never been to Joe's Diner in neighboring Wells and, after our meeting, would never go there again. The mugs are heavy and chipped. The coffee is strong enough to rot the lining of your stomach if you dare to have a second cup. The food is nine-tenths grease. Once a year David and I go to Joe's for a breakfast with the works, from eggs to home fries to sausage to pancakes. We'd go more often if our constitutions could handle it.

I got to Joe's a little before the time we'd agreed to meet. Another small psychological advantage I think I can be excused. I sat in the booth David and I like best, again with the intention of reminding myself I was in a position of power, that I was the person with rights to my daughter.

Ellen arrived exactly at eleven and spotted me immediately. She was wearing much the same outfit as she had been at the party, on the occasion of our first encounter. I don't know what I expected her attitude to be—belligerent and bullying? Lofty and superior?—but it wasn't the ultrasincere, almost subdued woman she presented.

"Verity," she said as she slid into the booth. "I'm so glad you suggested we meet."

Really? I thought. *Does she think this is going to be a comfy little chat?* Hadn't she heard what I'd said to her on the phone? That I was furious about her presumption regarding Gemma and that we needed to get some things settled? Hardly words of welcome.

The waitress appeared, and I ordered a coffee. Ellen ordered a glass of iced tea. She offered no reaction to the surroundings, though I'd half expected her to shudder in contempt at the cracked Formica table or frown at the badly executed prints of forests and shoreline.

When our drinks arrived, I finally spoke. If my silence had made Ellen uncomfortable, she wasn't showing it.

"You had no right to talk to Gemma about your . . . about your plans for her before coming to me first. I'm her mother. I'm her legal guardian. Not you."

Ellen looked me square in the eye. "You're absolutely right," she said. "I'm sorry, Verity. Really, I am. I guess Richard and I are so jazzed about the idea of having Gemma go to Greyson, I just couldn't hold my tongue. I'm afraid I'm a woman of impulse."

I thought: *And will this offer turn out to be a bad impulse? Will Ellen and Richard withdraw the offer as unexpectedly as it had been made? What will Gemma feel then?* Lady Bountiful changes her mind, and the poor are trodden into the mud. It's an old story.

"Yes, well," I said, "in the future, if you have something important to say to my daughter, come to me first."

"Of course. So, what do you think of our offer? I know it must seem overwhelming—"

"To say the least. Why? Why are you doing this?" I wanted to say: *What's your real motive? What's in this for you?* But that seemed too aggressive.

Ellen lifted her slim shoulders in a genteel shrug. "Because we're family. Family looks out for family."

I laughed. "Really?"

"Yes. And Richard and I really want to make up for not having been part of Gemma's life before now."

"You didn't seem to care about her when she was born," I pointed out. "Or, for that matter, when Alan abducted her."

Ellen replied smoothly, again refusing to be riled. "You're absolutely right, Verity," she said. "We didn't know what we had. You know that old expression, 'You never appreciate what you have until it's gone'? That's how we feel now."

It didn't quite make sense—Ellen and Richard had never had Gemma in the first place—but I wasn't there to argue the finer points. Before I could reply, Ellen went on.

"And Gemma really should have two adult figures in her life," she said. "A male and a female figure in the home. That's always best, no matter what anyone says otherwise."

"I think that's debatable," I said coldly. *What a self-righteous, unimaginative prig,* I thought.

Ellen sighed and leaned forward slightly, a gesture of pretended intimacy. "Richard and I couldn't have children of our own, you know. God knows, we tried. And neither of us ever wanted to adopt. It's such a risk. You can never know what you'll be getting, and you certainly can't return them if they're damaged or if they don't quite suit."

I swallowed the revulsion those final words had caused in me. "And?" I demanded. Did she think Gemma could be her child? Did she want to adopt her, a person who might turn out to be damaged goods? I was about to open my mouth and say something I'd regret, like, *Well, you can't have my daughter, you freak show!* when Ellen, still leaning toward me, went on.

"I know that you of all people, Verity, don't want to stand in the way of an opportunity for your daughter to get the sort of fine education she deserves. Gemma is smart, you can see that, can't you? She needs the stimulation of a really good education. She needs the attention of teachers who consistently win awards for excellence in their fields of academic study. She needs quality guidance and direction. Gemma's never had music lessons. That has to be rectified. We have a very good piano at home. And Richard and I can offer her travel. We can introduce her to different cultures and new experiences."

Cultures I can't afford to show her, I thought. And what's wrong with new experiences right here in Maine? There was an entire beautiful state to explore. But I said nothing.

Ellen continued in the more confidential, intimate tone. "I know you think about her future and that you worry about it," she said. "Any good mother would. I know you'll do the right thing by your daughter."

I'll say it right now. Ellen was actually succeeding in making me feel guilty. Bullied, even.

But she had a point under all that snobbery and prejudice and presumption. I thought about those happy, healthy kids Gemma and I had seen on the Greyson Academy website. All the chances for success they'd been given. All the care and concern showed to them. So many people looking out for them, people who held a place of importance in the world, people who could hold out a hand and lead them into the future. What can I give Gemma that can equal all that?

"Promise me you'll keep an open mind about this," Ellen said, breaking into my thoughts.

I didn't promise. But I didn't refuse, either.

Ellen looked at her watch. Cartier. "Look at the time," she said, extracting her wallet from her bag and placing a ten-dollar bill on the table between us. "I'll be late for my hair appointment. I'm so glad we had this chance to talk, Verity. I'll be in touch."

And then she slid out of the booth and was gone.

Ten dollars for a cup of coffee and a glass of iced tea? Well, to be fair, maybe she didn't have a smaller bill. Or maybe she really was completely out of touch with the price of food and drink in a diner. Either way, I hadn't wanted her to pay for me.

Was this how Gemma felt when she was out with Ellen, patronized? *No,* I thought. Gemma would never stand for such a thing. But Ellen was cunning.

I sat at the table for a while, stewing. I contemplated ordering a muffin with Ellen's money—well, I wasn't going to return her change, and I wasn't going to take it with me!—and then rejected the idea as stupid. I left the diner, feeling I'd accomplished absolutely none of what I'd set out to accomplish. *And what is that?* I wondered. Had I intended—at least, had I hoped—to send Ellen and Richard packing? How, exactly? By asking for their pity? By begging them to leave my daughter and me alone?

I know you'll do the right thing by your daughter.

What is the right thing? Force her to go away, to grab what might be an excellent opportunity that will help ensure a successful future? Force her to stay with me just because I want her to? Or let her make the monumental decision on her own?

Chapter 88

Yet another unsatisfactory call from my father. That's a nice way of saying I wanted to strangle him, and if I could have managed that long-distance, I would have. I swear.

This time he went on about how in the past week he'd noticed that "everyone" was giving him "odd" looks. "It's like they know something about me, about something bad that's going to happen to me," he said in a breathless whisper, probably so that the guard couldn't hear what he was saying. "Like someone's planning to get me."

It was all sufficiently vague not to worry me. I mean, no one had laid a finger on him—I asked. And no one had said anything to him—I asked about that, too. In the end, I don't know why I'd wasted my time trying to find some sense in his tale of persecution. In his tale of suspected, imagined persecution.

I wonder if Alan is genuinely paranoid, I mean, certifiably so. Maybe he's always been paranoid. Maybe that partly explains why he took me in the first place, if he thought that the reason Verity had left was because she was out to persecute him. Whatever. Anyway, I didn't tell him what Marion had told me about his father and his own bad behavior. What would be the point? He'd deny everything or blame it all on someone else. And I didn't tell him about Ellen and Richard's offer of a free education. Since he doesn't even know that his cousin is currently in my life, why would I? Again, he'd only take the information and twist it to fit his own weird psychological needs. He'd say Ellen was only showing an interest in me to one-up him, to hurt him.

And maybe he'd be right, that one time. I just don't know.

I've been thinking. None of those kids on the Greyson Academy's website look anything like me. What I mean is, Cathy and Hildy and Becca and Melissa would fit in far more easily than I would, with all their accomplishments and hobbies and, I'm guessing, good grades. I stick out enough here, or I think I do. In a school like that, I'd be notorious in about a second. From the minute I opened my mouth, everyone would know I didn't belong in that world. And if the truth about Alan and my past ever came out, which it probably would, I might be ostracized or bullied or worse, pitied. Why would I want to put myself through that when it's been hard enough fitting in here, where at least I've got Verity in my corner? And the Strawberries, too, I guess. Maybe even David and Marion.

I've always thought I was smart. What if I get to Greyson and find out I'm stupid? What if I can't hack getting good grades in a good school?

But there would be a car and an allowance, and I'd get to travel.

But maybe not if I flunk out. Maybe then Ellen and Richard would send me home, and I wouldn't get to see Paris.

Am I totally shallow after all?

I don't know why exactly I felt like visiting Cathy's house—maybe I should say I felt like seeing Cathy—but I did, so I got on my bike (not the one Ellen had bought for me; that's in the garage, and I'm thinking maybe I could donate it to Goodwill or something, as long as Ellen doesn't find out, not that I'm afraid of her) and cycled off to Maple Street. I found Cathy watering the flowerbed along the side of the house with a long green hose.

"Hey," I said, after I'd propped my bike against one of the white birch trees in their yard. As I did, I noticed how interest-

ing the bark was and thought I'd like to try to draw that sometime and get right all the subtle colors as well as the lines and
textures.

Cathy turned off the hose and began to coil it. "Hey, yourself."

"Did your mom tell you about Ellen and Richard's offer to
send me to that expensive school?"

I hadn't really planned on talking about it, but the words
were out before I could stop them.

"Yeah, she did."

"And?"

Cathy shrugged. "And what?"

Sometimes she can be so freakin' annoying. "And what do
you think about it?"

Cathy hung the coiled hose on a peg attached to the house. "I
think," she said, "that it's a bit weird. I mean, they hardly even
know you, and they want you to live with them? Of course, I
guess it's a generous offer in some ways. I mean, offering all that
money. Mom said the tuition is, like, out of control. But . . ."

"But you wouldn't accept."

Cathy laughed. "First of all, you and I are in totally different situations. But if some long-lost relative of mine suddenly
showed up and asked me to move away with them, I'd say no,
and for all sorts of reasons. Number one, I'm happy where I
am. Why would I leave?"

Happy where I am. I thought about that. Was I ever happy
being where I was with my father? Yeah. A long time ago.

Am I happy being where I am now? What does *happy*
mean, anyway?

"It's probably what Verity wants," I said, "for me to go
away. I'd be doing her a favor if I go to live with Ellen and
Richard. Face it, I got dumped on her. She didn't ask for me."

But even as I was saying those words, I knew it wasn't at all
true, that Verity would want me to leave. I had ample proof of
that, even if I discounted the now shut-down website. Verity is
happy I'm where I am. That much I know.

"That's not fair," Cathy argued, echoing my thoughts. "I know Verity. She does want you. She's always wanted you."

And then I snapped. Blame it on that stupid call from Alan.

"*You* know her? You're not her daughter, her flesh and blood. I might only have met her a few weeks ago, but trust me, I can tell about her."

Cathy didn't say anything for a moment but looked at me intently. It made me nervous.

"What?" I said.

"Nothing. Look, are you really seriously considering saying yes to Ellen?"

Now it was my turn to shrug.

Only later, after I'd been home for a while, did I realize what had really been behind my snapping at Cathy when she'd claimed to know Verity. My attitude toward Verity has changed. I no longer consider her the enemy. I'm not saying I love her or anything, but if I'm honest with myself I can say I like her. I believe her to be a good person. I believe she cares for me, even if I can't yet—maybe ever?—care for her back to the same extent.

Happy where I am.

Things seemed to have been straightening out for a while, but now, since Ellen and Richard came to Yorktide intent on being, in Ellen's words, Fairy Godparents, things are feeling seriously confused again.

After the life I've had, I'm not a big fan of confusion.

Chapter 89

Verity was invited to my Phony Birthday dinner at some new restaurant in Ogunquit called Aquamarine, and I wasn't sure how I felt about that. On the one hand, I guess it was nice of Ellen and Richard to ask her along. But on the other . . . I know Verity doesn't like or even trust Ellen and Richard—and I'm not sure I do, either, at least, not much—and I imagined a seriously uncomfortable time with the three of them, me being the only common link. And with the question of Greyson Academy hanging over us . . .

As it turns out, David had gotten two tickets to hear a jazz trio play at a little club up in Portland that night. The night of my Phony Birthday. When I told Verity about the invitation to dinner, she immediately offered to cancel on David, but I convinced her (it took some doing) that she should go and have fun. I don't know what she thinks Ellen and Richard are going to do when they get me alone. Whisk me off to . . . Oh. I'm almost laughing right now. Verity has a reason to worry about people stealing me. Sorry.

I didn't enjoy myself much, though the food was okay, but the waiters were stiff and they hovered over us, replacing silverware for no reason I could see and refilling the water glasses every time one of us took a sip. Give me The Friendly Lobsterman any day. At one point Ellen asked me if I'd given more thought to their offer to live with them and go to that fancy school. I said that yeah, I had.

"And?" she asked, leaning toward me.

An eager beaver, I thought. I shrugged. "That's it."

Richard spoke up then. "Now, Ellen," he said, "Gemma has a very big decision to make. She needs time."

"But—"

"Ellen."

I was grateful to Richard for controlling his wife—is that a bad term to use about a husband and wife, *controlling?*—and then he started a conversation about who was running for president in the next election. I listened closely, though I've never really paid much attention to politics. It was interesting. Richard is like the exact opposite of Alan, in that he seems to care about what goes on beyond the walls of his own home. I thought then of David, too. David is more like Richard than like Alan—he's not a loser—but he's also different from Richard. David is . . . Well, I don't know what he is, but I like him.

The most annoying parts of the night were the times when Ellen—never Richard—made nasty comments about my father. Not always nasty but definitely critical, like telling me about a time when they were teens (Ellen's a few years older than my father) and he begged her (that was her term) to let him come along with her and her friends to some party and she let him and he got seriously drunk and threw up all over an expensive couch. I wanted to tell her not to talk about him at all if she couldn't say something nice (and clearly, she can't) but like I said, since Marion told me about Alan's violent past, I can't seem to defend him. I'm pretty disgusted with my cowardice, if that's what it is. Or my lack of loyalty. I mean, I'm usually right out there with whatever comes into my mind, and I've always been good at sticking up for me and for Alan.

This is a weird thought, but I wonder if I didn't say anything because Ellen was paying for dinner in that fancy place. Did I allow myself to be bought?

Is that what it would be like if I do for some reason accept the offer of living with Ellen and Richard and going to that private school? Am I going to turn into a wimp?

They gave me a watch. (What are they going to give me next, a diamond ring?) I've never worn a watch in my life, and I don't intend to start now. But I took it and said thanks. I even put it on, though I took it off the minute I got home. Verity wasn't back yet from the concert, which was good because I don't want her to see the watch. I don't know what I'm going to do with it. I can't pass it on to Verity, because she won't wear it. And Ellen will probably want to see it on me, so I can't sell it, though Verity and I could use the money. I wonder if I can return it, nicely. Say, *Thanks, but I don't wear a watch.*

I mean, gifts aren't supposed to come with ties, right? You're supposed to give someone a gift because you like her and not because you want her to give you something in return. But of course not everybody thinks that way.

I feel—weird. Maybe it's the raw oyster Ellen convinced me to try.

Chapter 90

This morning Ellen called and said she wanted us to go for a massage.

"Full body, with hot stones and soothing oils, the whole works," she said. "You'll love it."

I wasn't sure of that at all. The idea of lying naked on a table while some stranger—man or woman—touches me all over gives me the creeps. As nicely as I could, I said no thanks, and then Ellen insisted I at least get a pedicure.

"Every woman should get a pedicure once a month," she said. "It's essential maintenance."

What about men? I wondered. *Don't they need to "maintain" their feet?* But my feet were kind of a mess, so I said sure. I'll get a pedicure.

So we went to a salon in Kennebunkport. The staff spoke in hushed voices, and there was odd but nice music playing really softly. The furniture was in tones of tan and taupe and sand, and there were vases with fat pink flowers. Peonies, I think they're called. I'd never been in a place anything like this salon, and I felt massively out of my element. I mean, people go there to be *pampered*. Pampering isn't something anyone in my old life knows anything about.

My old life. That was a lot about being loud and getting by.

Ellen went off for her massage, and I was led into the room

where they do manicures and pedicures. The pedicure was great, actually. Kind of ticklish at times, but the massage part was amazing—they used hot stones on me, too—and my feet have never looked so good. Ellen had paid in advance, but I snuck a look at one of the brochures stacked on the front desk of the salon. The pedicure cost sixty-five bucks. Unbelievable.

Maintenance is expensive. I wonder when Verity last had a pedicure.

After we left the salon, we went to this little Italian-themed café where Ellen drank, like, four glasses of water before ordering a glass of wine—she said you're supposed to drink a lot of water after a massage. We sat there for a while, and Ellen didn't mention one word about Greyson or Paris or living with her and Richard, though I knew we were both thinking about it, so at one point, after I had eaten half of the tiramisu I'd ordered (good stuff; I'd never had it before), I decided to bring it up.

"What I want to know is, why me? I mean, I know I'm a relative, but that doesn't really mean anything. Why are you offering so much to me?"

"You're family," Ellen said promptly.

"But you have no use for my father," I pointed out. "And he's family too. I mean, you hate him. So why care about me?"

Ellen shook her head. "You're not your father, Gemma. You have nothing at all to do with him. And he has nothing at all to do with you."

Except for the fact that we share DNA, I thought. But I didn't argue. Knowing what I now know about Alan, I'm not in any need of being identified as his flesh and blood.

"I don't mean to sound ungrateful or anything," I said, "but I—"

Ellen didn't let me finish. "After all you've been through, Gemma," she said, "you *deserve* this opportunity. You deserve this opportunity to excel, to show the world what you're made of."

Do I? Does anyone *deserve* good stuff in life? I mean, people who do disgusting things like rape and murder other people deserve to be punished, but life can really suck. And let's say, okay, people *do* deserve good stuff to happen to them, most times it doesn't happen. That's just the way life is.

"I don't think I deserve anything in particular," I said.

Ellen looked at me so intensely, it kind of weirded me out. "Yes," she said, and her tone was fierce. "Yes, Gemma, you *do* deserve a way out. A way up."

The way she said it, like she was determined to convince me no matter what it took that I was worthy of special treatment, of serious attention, kind of shook me.

Maybe, I thought, I am worthy of this life she's holding out to me. This chance.

Maybe.

Chapter 91

"What an ass!" Gemma cried after she'd slammed down the receiver and come stomping out of her room earlier and into the kitchen, where I was answering a few e-mails on my laptop.

"Don't call your father an ass," I said.

Gemma laughed. "What? Seriously? You of all people are telling me not to call my father an ass? The man who ruined your life for seventeen years?"

I winced. "Sorry. Knee-jerk reaction. I was channeling The Spirit of Parenthood. So, what happened?" I had never asked her what she and Alan had discussed during their scheduled phone call. But now it seemed the right thing to do.

"He won't take the plea bargain," Gemma said, yanking out a chair and dropping into it. "I've been arguing with him about it for weeks. Me and his lawyers. He's such an idiot! Do you know what this means? This means he'll have to serve the full sentence the judge eventually gives him. He could be in prison for, like, ten years! Maybe more, I don't know!"

The news didn't come as much of a surprise to me, I'm sorry to say. Alan's lawyers, I thought, must be ready to wash their hands of him. "I'm sorry," I said. And to myself I added: *I'm sorry you wasted your time trying to make Alan see reason.*

Gemma bent over and put her elbows on her knees, hands clasped in front of her. "It's just that I thought . . . Forget it."

"You thought what?" I asked gently.

A long moment later Gemma said: "Even after what Marion told me about his past, I guess I still thought I could *maybe* rely on him to be smart. That maybe the thought of having to spend even more time in jail away from me would set him straight. I was wrong."

I wanted to agree with Gemma that Alan is an ass, but nothing will ever make me change my policy of maintaining a neutral public attitude toward her father. I don't believe in feeding the hate. I can't afford to, especially not now with Ellen and Richard vying for my child's . . . what? Her love?

"Alan," I said carefully, "never really understood his own best interests. We all have moments when we make decisions that are bound to hurt us, but some people, and Alan is one of them, can't seem to make the other sort of decisions, the ones that will benefit him. I don't think he can help it. I don't think we can really blame him for what he's done."

But Gemma was having none of it. "*I* can blame him," she said, looking up at me with an expression of fierce determination, "and I do. In fact, that's it. I'm cutting off all communication with him. The next time he calls, I'm going to refuse to take the call. I'll let the prison people know I don't want anything more to do with him."

"Are you sure it's really what you want?" I asked gently, and I reached over and put my hand on her arm, for just a moment.

"Yeah. I guess you're happy about that."

I felt a tiny sting of hurt, but I reminded myself that she was upset. Disappointed. Angry. She wasn't in full control of her emotions. And it was clear to me that she was wrestling with self-pity, something alien, I think, to her personality. *Well,* I thought, *if anyone deserves to feel self-pity, it's Gemma.*

"Actually," I said, "my feelings are complicated. On the one hand, I'm glad you want to put some space between you and your father. I can't see what real benefit it's been, keeping in touch with him. Then again, I'd be expected to say that, wouldn't I? But on the other hand—don't doubt me, here—on the other hand I'm genuinely sorry it's come to this. I'm sorry it's come to your feeling it's best to put Alan aside for however long you need to. No child of whatever age should be put in the position where she has to choose to break away from a parent." Frankly, I thought, it's heartbreaking. And then I thought of my own father and felt . . . uncomfortable.

Gemma shook her head. "I don't understand why you're being so . . . so generous! He's an idiot. You're sorry I'm rejecting an idiot. That doesn't make a lot of sense, Mom."

Mom. "It doesn't have to," I said, carefully hiding my elation. "Feelings usually don't."

"Yeah. That's the truth."

"Do you want to get out of here for a while? Drive to the beach."

Gemma rubbed her forehead. "No. Wait. Yes."

I got up from the table. "I'll get my keys."

Chapter 92

The day Alan got arrested and I learned who I really was felt like the absolute worst day of my life, a total end to something, to everything. But now, I don't know. Now it feels even more final, like every last stupid little half hope I had of Alan's doing the right thing, the smart thing, of his not letting me down, has been stomped on. Completely shattered. I have no faith in my father anymore, none.

What if, I wondered, by some weird chance, some flaw in the legal system, he was released from prison tomorrow? Would I want to go back to him?

The answer to that is no.

Nothing and nobody can work miracles for you, I figured that out a long time ago, but I wonder if going to Greyson Academy would somehow really, completely stop me from ever going downhill like my father, from being such a total loser and screwing up the lives of the people he had loved, the lives of the people who had loved him.

Ellen said I had nothing to do with my father and that he had nothing to do with me. But that's not right, and she knows it. Everyone knows it. Bad shit is inherited just like good shit comes down through generations.

I think I called Verity Mom when I was telling her about Alan refusing the plea bargain. I'm pretty sure I did. If I did, it just slipped out. She didn't comment on the "Mom," but that's like her. She wouldn't embarrass me by making a big deal out of it.

I never really thought about it like this, but if I go to live with Ellen and Richard, there's a chance Richard might become a sort of replacement father or a father substitute.

Do I want that, someone taking over where Alan left off?

Or David. If Verity marries David someday, he'll be my official stepfather.

But it's ridiculous to think about father figures. I have one father, and he's more than enough trouble. Besides, I'm too old to be influenced by some new guy, too old to be positively affected by his attitude toward me. What Alan did to me is what I'm stuck with, right?

I'm so freakin' confused. I'm thinking like an idiot.

For all I know, Richard doesn't really want me to live with them. He could be just putting up with Ellen's whim or fantasy of a happy family or whatever it is she really wants to make us into. And if Richard is just tolerating the idea of the three of us living under one roof, that could be really miserable for me in the end.

How can I know what's really going on?

How can I really know the right thing to do?

Chapter 93

I wonder if Gemma realized what she'd called me after she'd gotten off the phone with Alan. Mom. I wasn't going to point it out to her at the time, and I'm still not. For all I know, it was both the first and the last time I'll hear that word from her.

Once is better than never.

We drove to the beach after that last call from prison. I keep an old cotton blanket in the trunk, and we spread that out on the sand and sat for a long time, just staring out at the water. And thinking about this strange place in which Gemma and I find ourselves. I know I was.

I wondered if Ellen and Richard had spent a good deal of time at Gemma's Phony Birthday (it's what she calls the birthday Alan gave her) celebration, selling her on their plans for her. She was pretty quiet on the subject of that dinner at Aquamarine, except to say that she likes the Gascoyne family's restaurant better. And when Gemma came home from her spa outing with Ellen the other day, all she talked about was how the pedicure was great. And how the tiramisu was fantastic. She said nothing at all about what she and Ellen had talked about. She did ask if I knew how to make tiramisu. I told her I would find out.

Anyway, Gemma and I haven't outright discussed Ellen and Richard's offer in days. Some moments my heart is in my mouth, thinking she'll accept (lured by the call of a more certain future, pedicures, and tiramisu) and how I'll have to let her go even if I don't want to and I don't. I want her to stay with me. At other moments I feel certain Gemma will turn them down, not so much because she loves me (I don't think she does, not yet), but because she sees Ellen and Richard for what they really are. Not criminals like her father, not evil, but . . . opportunistic. Attention seeking.

I don't think Gemma takes Ellen and Richard's offer very seriously, at least not as seriously as I do, because for her it certainly doesn't represent a threat to anything, like it does to me. Or maybe it *does* represent a threat to her in some way I can't understand. I wish she would talk to me about it, how she feels, what it might mean, her moving away. The few times I've suggested we hash it through, she's said she doesn't want to, plain and simple. I can't force her to talk. But when she does talk, I listen.

"What do you think is going to happen to my father?" she asked, after we'd sat quietly on the sand for almost an hour, surrounded by the laughter of children, the screaming of gulls, the strains of competing pop music.

I looked over at her, my daughter. In profile, I can see Alan in her. I looked back out to the ocean.

"I think," I said, "that he's probably going to be in jail for a long time."

"Yeah," she said. "I think so too."

Chapter 94

Ellen told me she and Richard were giving a party. Another one. I wonder if when they're back home, they give parties all the time, or if it's only a thing they do on vacation.

It doesn't matter.

Verity was invited to this party, and this time she told me straight out she didn't think it was a good idea for her to be there. I can see her point. I mean, I don't think Ellen really wants her to be at the party, and Verity must know that. Still, I bet she'll spend every moment I'm at Ellen and Richard's wondering what they're saying to me about their fabulous life in Lexington, Massachusetts, and the trip to Paris they're planning on taking next spring. A trip I'm invited on. I hope Verity won't sit around, wondering and worrying, but she probably will.

Honestly, I'm not even sure why I went to the party. I thought about asking Ellen if I could bring a friend—Cathy; yeah, okay, I guess she's a friend—but then I didn't ask. Cathy's made it clear, even if she hasn't said it in so many words, that she thinks I'd be making a big mistake if I went to live with Ellen and Richard. She'd be polite and all with them, but I don't think she'd be very good at keeping her opinion to herself. I decided it would be best if I went to the party alone.

Verity dropped me off at the McMansion.

"Have fun," she said.

I kind of smiled and got out of the car.

Richard offered me a beer the minute I got up to the veranda, as if it were no big deal to offer alcohol to someone underage, and honestly, back in my old life, it wasn't a big deal. Maybe it's not considered a big deal in Ellen and Richard's life back in Massachusetts. Anyway, I took it. It was some craft beer I'd never heard of, something made in Maine, Richard said. It was pretty good, and when I was done with the first bottle, I had a second.

Like the first time I'd been at the house, the guests were all adults, a lot of them way older than I am. Richard was sitting at one of the tables with three other men. It looked as if they were talking about something serious; not one of them was smiling. One guy was smoking a cigar. I hate cigars. Ellen was standing by the bar, talking with three women who all looked a lot alike. I mean, they were all blond and slim and wearing white blouses tucked into skirts that came to their knees. The skirts were different colors, at least. Bright pink, bright green, and bright yellow. I wondered if they were members of a club, like a ladies' golf group or something. Ellen was wearing the kind of pants she always wears. All four women were drinking some pink cocktail with a piece of fruit, lime, I think, stuck on the edge of the glass. All four women had sparkly rings on their left hands.

I looked at the almost empty bottle of beer in my hand and wondered if I should get a third one and if anyone would notice or care if I did, when someone put a hand on my shoulder from behind. I was totally surprised and spun around to find this seriously good-looking guy standing there. He was built like Ryan Gosling, slim but with a lot of muscle. I thought he was probably in his twenties somewhere, maybe twenty-six or seven. He was wearing a T-shirt and jeans and a pair of black Converse high-tops. I love those, but they're pretty expensive.

"Hey," he said. "Sorry if I startled you."

I shrugged. "No worries. I'm Gemma."

He told me his name was Brett and that his parents were friends with Ellen and Richard and that they suggested he look them up while he was staying in Ogunquit with some friends.

"Ellen and Richard are my friends too," he said. "I mean, I'm an only child, and I pretty much grew up around adults, so I've got lots of older friends." He smiled. "It helped when I wanted to get into places I shouldn't have been when I was underage."

"Cool," I said.

"So, how do you know Ellen and Richard?"

There was no way I was going to tell this guy about my crazy life, so all I said was, "Ellen's a distant cousin."

Brett nodded. I guess that was enough information for him. "Look," he said, "you want to get out of here for a bit? I've got a room at the house me and my friends are renting for the week. Nobody here will miss us. They've all had at least two or three cocktails by now."

For about thirty seconds I thought, *Yeah, why not?* Maybe it was the beer—I hadn't had a drink since coming to Yorktide and the beer had made me feel a bit high and I know all about how drinking beer can lead to bad decisions—and maybe it was also the fact that I thought if I had sex with this guy for a few minutes at least I wouldn't have to think about this huge decision hanging over my head. Sex as oblivion. It used to work, at least sometimes, like when Dad was going through one of his weird phases and driving me crazy with questioning every single thing I did or person I talked to, or like when we had to move on again because Dad had lost his job and I really didn't want to move on because I liked where we were living. At least during sex, even if it was only for a little while, even if it was in the guy's crappy little apartment or his parents' damp basement, you didn't have to *think*.

And honestly? I was flattered. This guy, Brett, was really, really sexy.

And then it didn't seem like a good idea at all, going off with this guy I'd known for, like, five minutes. Not that I was scared.

It wasn't that. It was that for some reason I felt like I'd be letting Verity down if I did something so—so stupid. So without meaning.

It was weird. I never felt my conscience poke at me like that, so strongly, and never ever about sex. I mean, maybe it's my generation or something; we grew up in such a sexualized culture that it's, like, no big deal.

But I realized I wanted Verity to respect me. I realized I had never cared if Dad respected me. Not really. And I didn't care if Ellen and Richard respected me either.

Just Verity.

"Nah," I said. "Thanks, anyway."

Brett didn't look particularly disappointed. He just shrugged, said, "Whatever," and walked away toward the bar. *He'll probably proposition one of the married women next*, I thought. *Whatever.*

And I wondered what Ellen and Richard would think if they knew one of their friends had come on to me. A minor. I mean, like I said, I wasn't scared and I can take care of myself, but . . .

Would they care?

Soon after that, I asked Ellen to drive me home.

"But the party's still in full swing," she said. "We haven't even broken out the smoked salmon."

"I know, but I'm tired. I think I'm getting a cold or something. Anyway, don't worry. If you can't leave, I can call Verity to come get me."

"No, no, no," Ellen said, already reaching for her bag. "I'll take you."

On the trip back to Birch Lane, Ellen went on about some committee she's on, something about trying to prevent some organization from opening a halfway house a few miles from where they live. I think. I wasn't really listening. I did hear this: "We don't want those people anywhere near us. Do you know what it would do to property values?"

Mostly I was thinking. And what I was thinking was: *I don't think I'm going to take them up on it, Ellen and Richard. I don't think I could stand living under the same roof with this woman—Richard's not too bad—and having to eat dinner with her every night and listening to her talking about her country club or her hairdresser or her grilling me on what happened at school and if I'd finished my homework and if I felt like a success yet.*

Wanting to know if I hated my father. Was hating him going to be one of the rules of the Burns-Cassidy house?

"I'm so glad you were able to come to the party," Ellen said when she'd pulled up outside our bungalow. She seemed to have forgotten what I said about coming down with a cold. It was a lie, an excuse, but she probably should have said something like, *Make sure you take some aspirin,* or *Eat some chicken soup.*

I got out of the car. Before I could close the door, Ellen leaned over. "You probably shouldn't tell Verity about the beer," she said with a wink. "It'll be our little secret."

And, I thought, I won't tell Verity that you had a cocktail before getting behind the wheel. Really, what had I been thinking? Oh. Right. I'd been drinking too.

When I got inside—Verity had left a note saying she was at David's and would be home by eleven—I fired off an e-mail to Tom in response to an e-mail he had just sent me. It included a picture of him and Valerie at some wildlife park, posing in front of a fence behind which there was a male lion lounging on the ground. I told him about Ellen and Richard's offer. I'm not sure why I did. It's not like I thought he was going to influence my decision.

He responded almost immediately. This is the important part of what he said:

Your grandmother chose to name our daughter Verity because she always said that the truth is the most important thing of all. I don't know how these things work, but I do know that Verity has always lived up to her name. She's always been a truthful person, never calculating or deceitful. You could do worse than being Verity's daughter, Gemma. Think hard before you decide about this offer from your cousin.

My first instinct was to show Verity the e-mail. I mean, who doesn't like to hear nice things about themselves? And it's pretty clear her father isn't holding a grudge. Then I considered how she had been estranged from him for so long, and realized she might not be ready to believe her father meant the nice things he'd said. At least not without a lot more evidence. In a way she's being like Alan, not trusting, suspicious.

Adults are weird. Something happens to them along the way. They get a bit—inconsistent. I hope it doesn't happen to me, but it probably will. Why should I be special?

Anyway, I figure I can show her Tom's e-mail some other time. After all, I'm not going anywhere in the fall.

Chapter 95

"You know those sketches you found in your studio earlier in the summer?"

"The anonymous ones," I said. "Yes. What about them?"

Gemma shifted a bit in her seat. "Well, don't be mad, but they're mine. I mean, I did them."

"What!" I put down my fork. I felt . . . I don't know what I felt. "Of course I'm not mad, but . . . I don't understand. You told me you hated art. Back when I first showed you my studio. You said you had no use for it."

Gemma colored slightly. I'd never seen that before. "It was just something stupid to say. What I really meant was that I didn't know anything about it. I still don't."

"But something made you pick up that pencil."

"Yeah. It was actually kind of weird. The drawing just started—happening."

"But why didn't you tell me you were the artist when I talked about the sketches?" I asked.

Now I thought Gemma looked a bit sheepish. I'll take blushing and sheepish over shrugs, whatevers, and a bland expression any day. "I don't know," she admitted. "I didn't want you to get too excited, I guess. I mean, what if I'm not any good? What if it was just luck that I was able to make those drawings?"

She hadn't wanted to disappoint me? Was that it? "Talent doesn't work that way, Gemma," I told her. "Now you know that. Tell me, were you afraid I'd try to force you to study drawing?"

"No. I mean, actually, I think I'd *like* to learn more. I've been doodling—sketching—since I did those first ones at your studio."

"Can I see what you've done?"

"Sure," she said without hesitation. "Wait here and I'll go and get them."

While Gemma went off to her room, I wondered. Was that why Ellen's offer of a trip to Paris had interested her? I'd seen her going through some of the art books at my studio. Clearly, she'd secretly been developing an interest in Art with a capital A. Well, then I'd take her to Paris, I decided. Someday.

You know, I've been worried about the fallout from Alan's latest act of craziness. I know Gemma's more upset than she's letting on, she has to be, but I don't want to force a conversation, not that I would succeed. Gemma doesn't do what she doesn't want to do. But telling me about the sketches seems a gesture of faith in our relationship. And then I wondered if she'd also told Ellen about the sketches. I don't think it's something I can ask without sounding childishly jealous, which of course I am.

Gemma came back to the kitchen with a sketchbook in her hand. I recognized it as the sort I use and wondered if she'd taken it from either of my studios. It doesn't matter. What's mine is hers. Page by page, she showed me her work.

"That's really awful," she said about a sketch of a beach-front house. "The perspective—is that right?—is off. I've been working on perspective."

I turned to the next page. "That's our pine tree," I said. She had covered two facing pages with sketches of its branches and needles. "I see how you were trying to capture the shadows here. Tricky stuff."

Gemma laughed. "I was so frustrated! But I think I got it sort of right eventually."

I pointed to an image at the bottom of the right-hand page. "Here, yes, I see."

A tree trunk battered and washed ashore on the beach. A seagull. Lots of seashells, closely studied. A few roughs of people at some distance. There was one page torn out—a few shreds of paper remained at the margin—and I wondered what had been on it.

The sketches are good. They show talent and energy.

I couldn't help myself. My daughter is an artist, like me. I leaned toward her and put my arm around her shoulders.

She didn't pull away.

Chapter 96

Alan missed his scheduled call this morning. I think both Gemma and I had been nervously anticipating this call, the first after his bombshell announcement not to take the plea bargain and Gemma's subsequent decision to cut him off. A decision I'm not sure either of us felt sure she would keep.

"Maybe he beat me to the punch," Gemma said when a half hour had gone by after Alan's appointed time. We were sitting next to each other on the living room couch. She sounded bitter. "Maybe he's written *me* off. I wanted to be the one to refuse the call. I wanted to be the one to . . ."

"To what?" I asked gently.

Gemma shook her head. "Nothing. It was stupid."

To punish her father. That must be what she meant to say. And it wasn't stupid. Immature, maybe, but totally understandable.

"I'm sorry," I said. I didn't know what else there was to say. Certainly, I had no interest in positing reasons for Alan's silence, good or bad.

Abruptly, Gemma got up from the couch and went into her room. She closed the door but didn't let it slam. I'd almost rather she had shown her usual spunk and temper.

My cell phone rang then. It was Martin McGinty, the head of the art department.

"Martin," I said. "How was Prague?"

"Prague-like. Look, Verity, I have some bad news. We had a break-in here last night."

"Was anyone hurt?" I asked hurriedly. Teachers sometimes work into the night, and security is minimal. Actually, it's nonexistent apart from locks on the outer doors of the building.

"No, thank God."

"My studio?"

"Luckily, minimal damage, one easel broken and a bookcase overturned, but I can't be sure what might be missing. You'll be a better judge of that."

"I'll get there as soon as possible," I told him. "Was anything big taken from the other studios or offices?"

"Computer equipment. And some other random electronics. The police think our thief—or thieves—didn't care at all about art supplies but probably were frustrated when they couldn't find anything they wanted in your studio, so they smashed up a few bits just to say they were there."

I sighed. "Any idea who might be responsible?"

"Well, the police wouldn't tell me anything specific, but it seems there was a similar event last week at a small college on the New Hampshire border. They said they had some leads."

Leads that might go nowhere. I know all about those.

"Okay," I said. "I'm on my way."

"Wait, Verity," Martin said. "I'm afraid I've got more bad news."

"Go on."

"That class you planned out for the fall semester, on the patination of metals? It looks like we might have to cancel it. I'm sorry, Verity. It's a great idea but preadmissions records are showing we've only got three students signed up for it. We need at least ten to make the class worthwhile."

"To make paying me worthwhile," I said. "Sorry. I know it's not your fault."

"Look, there are still a few weeks before the semester starts. Things could change. I just wanted to give you a heads-up."

"Thanks, Martin. I do appreciate it, really."

"And if we do have to cancel the class this time around, we can always try again in spring. Got to run. Roberta and I just got back yesterday, and what with the robbery, I still haven't unpacked."

I said good-bye to the department head. This bit of news meant I'd have to take a closer look at our family budget. I'd been counting on the money from that extra class, not that I'd been foolish enough to spend it before it was earned. And some of the art books I kept at the studio were old and valuable, in a financial as well as a sentimental way. It would be awful if any had been badly damaged. I can't afford to replace them.

I was just about to hunt down my bag and keys and head off for the college when Gemma came back into the living room. "Have you seen my blue hoodie?" she asked. I thought she might have been crying—her eyes were red—but maybe it was her allergies. She'd been sneezing a lot in the past few days.

"Yeah," I said. "It's in the laundry bin."

Gemma rolled her eyes. That was something I hadn't seen in weeks. "But I want to wear it."

"I didn't get to the laundry yesterday." I was about to add my usual *I'm sorry,* but I didn't. The truth was, I wasn't really sorry about not doing the laundry. It wasn't a crime or a sin or an insult.

"How long does it take to do a load of laundry?" she demanded.

"Why don't you do one sometime and find out?"

The words were out before I was even quite aware I'd spoken them.

Gemma folded her arms across her chest. "Ellen and Richard have a housekeeper," she said.

I laughed. "Well, bully for them!" And then I got ahold of my better nature. My adulthood. At least, a bit of it. "Look," I said. "I'm sorry about your father not calling but—"

"This has nothing to do with my father!" Gemma shouted. "I just wanted the freakin' hoodie!"

"Yes, well, you can't have it, not at the moment. I'll do the laundry when I get home. I have to go to my studio for a while."

Gemma snickered. "You care more about those stupid blocks of wood and lumps of clay than you do about me. You promised you'd do the laundry, and you didn't."

Sometimes, no matter how famed you are for your self-control, you can only take so much.

"You understand, don't you," I said, "that I've devoted my entire life to you, even when I didn't know if you were alive or dead, and you can't even show me respect enough to do a load of laundry now and then?"

Gemma looked at me with such hatred and misery then that I shuddered.

"Screw you!" she shouted. "I don't need all your sacrifices. I didn't ask for you to care. I don't owe you a thing!"

"We live here together," I said, my voice shaking. "We both have to participate."

"I don't *have* to do anything. You can't force me to be your daughter!"

"Am I really so horrible that to acknowledge that you're my daughter would make you unhappy?" I asked. Really, all I wanted to do at that moment was throw my arms around her, but I knew that would be a disaster.

"I'm already unhappy," Gemma cried. "I don't need you to make it worse." Then she grasped her hair at the roots with both hands. "God, everything is so messed up! I can't . . . I thought I could . . . Never mind."

Before I could react, she turned around and fled back into her room, this time slamming the door shut behind her. The force dislodged a delicate vase on the shelf over the fireplace, and before I could dash across the room to grab it, it fell to the floor and shattered.

The vase had belonged to Marion's mother.

Gemma's great-grandmother.

Chapter 97

I must have paced from one end of this room to the other and back again about a thousand times in the past few hours. This room that has become mine, however temporarily.

Pacing can sometimes make thinking things through easier.

Here's a fact. I've pretty much lost my father. I mean, he didn't even call today when he was supposed to. Yeah, he could be sick or something, but I know better. Coward that he is, he probably decided he didn't want to listen to me being angry at him. Or, and this is a real possibility, he did something stupid again, like pick a fight and hit someone, and got himself in trouble. Lost his privileges. Proved once again he's an ass.

Whatever the reason he didn't call, one thing is for certain. A life with my father is no longer a possibility. Our future together is gone.

That's his fault.

And now I've lost a future with Verity, too. And that's my fault. After the stupid, hurtful things I said to her, why would she want me to stick around? I mean, of course she doesn't care more about her work than she does about me. What a jerk-off, childish thing to say. And of course I'm not unhappy. Well, right now I am, but I wasn't, not all the time. Not anymore.

It's like I told you earlier. I can be combustible. But there are consequences to that.

Things were going so well. I don't know why I had to ruin it.

Yes, I do. Because I'm stupid like my father. I've got this dumb arrogance. This isolating pride.

And now who's left for me to turn to?

Happy where I am.

I've backed myself into the proverbial corner.

I remembered earlier in the summer when, for about an hour, I was convinced that in the end I was the one really responsible for my parents' breakup and then for Alan's stealing me away. And if that's the truth, that all this crap has happened because of me, whether or not I meant anything bad to happen, and I didn't, how could I, then maybe it would be best for me to walk away from both parents (that's not entirely accurate, but you know what I mean) and let them get over me, the daughter who turned out to be a major annoyance all around. A major disappointment.

But of course, Verity has to agree to let me go. Legally, I'm under her control.

I can guess how she'll react when I tell her I'm going to live with Ellen and Richard. She'll probably be pissed (she'll think I'm an ungrateful bitch after all she's done for me, and I'll have to let her think that, though I am grateful), but she'll also be seriously relieved to get me out of here. There'll probably be another big fight. I'll try to keep my temper this time and not say anything I really don't mean. It's not Verity's fault all this shit has happened.

My mother.

I took my cell phone out of my pocket and called Ellen's number. She answered right away.

"It's me," I said. "Gemma." And then I rushed on, afraid that if I didn't, I'd lose the nerve. "I've decided I'll go to that school and live with you."

"That's fantastic!" Ellen cried. "Oh my God, Richard will be so excited when I tell him!"

"Maybe you'd better wait a bit," I said. "See, I haven't told Verity yet. She might not like it." *Because she's my mother . . .*

"Don't worry about her," Ellen said firmly. "If she makes a fuss, Richard and I will come right over there and take care of everything."

But I didn't want Ellen and Richard in Verity's home. Not because I'm ashamed of it in any way, but because . . . I don't know. It's been nice here, and there's a good feeling. . . . I mean, there *was* a good feeling.

"That's okay," I said. "There's no rush. If she doesn't want me to go, you can talk to her over the phone. Tomorrow."

"All right," she said. "But you call me immediately if you feel she's pressuring you to change your mind. Promise?"

"Yeah," I said. But I knew Verity wouldn't be pressuring me.

"Good. I'm going to call Greyson's admitting office right away and have them send out the application form, though it's only a formality at this point. Richard's taken care of that. Oh, Gemma, I'm so glad you're coming to live with us!"

I almost believed her, but I couldn't tell her I was glad, because I wasn't. I'm not. "I have to go now," I said. "There's someone at the door."

I got off the phone. Ellen had said she and Richard would "take care of" Verity if she tried to stand in the way of my leaving. She had said that Richard had "taken care" of my getting into Greyson.

Dad used to say that all the time when things weren't going right. "Don't worry," he'd say. "I'll take care of it."

I've never liked the sound of those words.

I sank onto the couch. My couch. I put my hands over my face. And then I started to cry.

What's done is done.

Chapter 98

When I got back from the college earlier, both doors to Gemma's room were closed. I could hear her inside. I thought maybe she was talking to someone on her phone, but maybe she was talking to herself. About me?

I poured a glass of wine and went out onto the deck. The sky had been darkening since midday, and now there was the distinct feel of rain in the air. Several inches were predicted. I hoped the repair done to the roof at the end of the winter would continue to hold. It had cost a lot, but a leaky roof isn't something you can ignore.

Money.

With Gemma to support, a good income is more important than ever, so if the course I'd planned for the fall were actually canceled, I'd have to make up for the lost income somehow. I could always wait tables, though with so many restaurants closing down for a good part of the winter, the jobs would be scarce. In the old days, after Alan had absconded with Gemma, I worked as a housekeeper in one of the big hotel resorts during the off-season. I'm not too old or too proud to scrub someone else's floors, but honestly, it's not something I'd looked forward to doing ever again.

More immediate to consider, if less important, is the issue of the damage done in my studio. The broken easel could be repaired or replaced at the college's expense, but the sight of it lying there on the floor, one leg snapped in half, had made me feel incredibly sad. It seemed to symbolize what I was scared might have happened to my relationship with my daughter. And unlike the easel, a relationship could not so easily be repaired, and it could never be replaced.

Marion's mother's vase, I'm sad to say, is a lost cause. I wonder if Gemma heard it fall.

Back to the chaos in my studio. The thief or thieves had indeed overturned the largest bookcase, the one I had built, causing every single book to spill out. The police, after dusting for prints, had righted the bookcase. (Really, I should ask college maintenance to nail it to the wall.) While I was putting the books back onto the shelves according to categories like Greco-Roman art, Medieval European art, and contemporary American sculpture, I found that one of my favorite books, a volume of images from the British Museum's permanent collection, had been badly damaged. The spine had broken, and several pages had been folded and heavily creased. I remember the day I bought that book at a wonderful secondhand shop in Portland, not long after starting my job at YCC. I hadn't bought myself anything unnecessary or frivolous since Gemma had gone missing. I hadn't thought I was worth a gift for having been so stupid about Alan and his intentions, so blind. Buying that book for myself had been a landmark, an act of partial self-forgiveness, and the start of a more normal stage of my life.

If any stage of my life since meeting Alan can be considered normal.

I felt a drop of rain on my head and then another, so I went back inside the house. There was still no sight of Gemma.

I lost my temper with her this morning. That's not an excuse; it's just the truth. All the frustration and fear I'd been feeling about Ellen and Richard courting Gemma, the only half-acknowledged resentment I'd been feeling toward Gemma herself for choosing to spend time with them instead of with me, the one who had waited so hopefully for her for seventeen years, it had all come to a head after that upsetting phone call from Martin McGinty.

I thought everything had been going so well. Had I been fooling myself, thinking we were finally bonding?

No, I don't think so.

It was such a stupid fight, the kind of fight all people who live together experience, no matter if they're married or room-mates or like Gemma and me, child and parent. Would she understand that? That a big stupid fight didn't need to be the end of a relationship?

It's wrong of me to demand love and respect from my daughter—demanding love, if not respect, is Alan's big problem, or one of them. I wonder. If he had called this morning as he was supposed to, would Gemma and I have argued?

If I hadn't gotten the call from Martin, would we be in this sad state of alienation?

Silly questions. And what do they matter now?

Now we have to pick up the broken bits and start over.

Easier said than done.

Chapter 99

She didn't come out of her room for dinner. When I finally went to bed at eleven, she still hadn't emerged. I left a note telling her what there was to eat. When I came down to the kitchen this morning, the note was still there, but nothing in the fridge had been touched. Not even the last doughnut from the bakery in town. The doughnuts had been a treat for Gemma.

I started the coffee brewing and took a carton of eggs from the fridge. And then I heard the back door to Gemma's room opening, and a moment later she joined me in the kitchen. She looked exhausted. She looked as if she had been crying. I wondered if she had slept. I hadn't, not much anyway.

"Hi," I said.

"Hi."

That was a start. "I thought I'd make omelets for breakfast."

Gemma shrugged. "Don't go to any trouble."

"It's no trouble," I said. "Cheese and ham, okay?"

Go gently, I told myself. Slow and careful. I began to assemble the ingredients: salt and pepper, oil for the pan, a chunk of ham, and a few slices of Swiss cheese.

"I've decided I'm going to live with Ellen and Richard and go to that academy."

The knife I'd been using to slice the ham seemed to stop in midair on its own accord.

In the space of less than twenty-four hours, the wonderful life Gemma and I had been building had come crashing to the ground.

I put down the knife and turned to face her, trying very hard to hide the shock and pain and hurt I felt. Gemma wouldn't—couldn't—meet my eyes.

"You don't have to go, you know," I said.

"I know."

Did she, really?

"That fight. It was stupid. I'm sorry."

Gemma shrugged again. "Yeah," she said. Not an apology, but oh, I think she would have apologized to me if she could have! I could feel her sorrow like a physical presence in the room.

This has to be about Gemma, I told myself, *and not about you. Be the adult!*

"I want what's best for you," I said. I could hear the trembling in my voice, but I was too weak to get ahold of it. "I want you to be happy, and if it will make you happy to leave here, then I won't stand in your way. And if it will make you happy to stay here, with me, then I'll welcome you. We can start all over again."

"I already told Ellen. I called her yesterday."

But nothing is set in stone! I wanted to say this, to argue, to plead, but what I said was: "I guess then I should talk to her."

"There's no rush."

"It's only a few weeks until the fall term begins. There'll be a lot to do before—" I swallowed hard before going on. "Before you have to leave."

"I guess. Yeah."

I turned back to the stove and went about preparing our breakfast. Gemma remained leaning against the dishwasher. Neither of us said anything more.

When the omelets were cooked and the bread had toasted, I brought the plates to the table.

"Breakfast is ready," I said. "Come and eat."

Gemma sat in her usual seat. "Thanks," she said, and began to eat, though not with her usual gusto. She didn't once look up at me.

The food was tasteless to me, but I made a show of eating along with her. *Normalize the situation,* I told myself. *Don't create drama.* "I have confidence in you, Gemma," I said, pouring her a cup of coffee. "Confidence that you're mature enough to make an important decision for your future. And for your happiness."

The words were inadequate. I knew that. And I wasn't even sure I believed what I had said, that she was capable of making good decisions for her life. But I felt I had to say something positive.

Gemma didn't reply. I have no idea if *she* believed me.

I think that was the saddest meal I've ever shared with anyone.

Chapter 100

I didn't even feel hungry, which is not like me at all, but I ate the omelet and a piece of toast and drank a cup of coffee like it was any other day in our bungalow on Birch Lane, and Verity and I were going to hang around, doing something fun or nothing more exciting than living our life.

Our life.

She was so calm when I told her I was going to live with Ellen and Richard. Like she had expected it all along, but I don't really believe she did.

I don't really believe she wants me to go. Not all of her, anyway.

Then why is she letting me go through with this decision?

Why isn't she saving me from myself?

See, I think I made a mistake in calling Ellen yesterday.

It was just I was so upset.

I remembered what Verity once said about Alan's being one of those people who consistently make decisions against their own best interests. Maybe I'm one of those people too.

A loser.

Verity said she believes I'm mature enough to know what's right for me.

If she really believes that, she might be seriously wrong about me.

There's this old expression. "You made your bed; now you're going to have to lie in it."

That fight was stupid. Verity was right about that. And she said she was sorry. But I couldn't say I'm sorry to her, though I *am* sorry. Because those words can't change anything now.

I've made my bed.

Chapter 101

As soon as breakfast was cleared away—Gemma had gone back to her room and shut the door, gently this time—I drove over to Annie's house, first writing a note for Gemma and leaving it on the counter by the microwave. *Be home soon,* I wrote. *Call me if you need anything.*

If you need me.

"Why do you think she's doing this?" Annie said, taking a seat across from me at her kitchen table. My confessional.

"That's what I've been wanting to ask you."

"They've been pressuring her. Ellen and Richard."

"Maybe, but I never thought Gemma would succumb to pressure."

"She is still just a kid, remember. And with all that's been going on with Alan? Maybe she just snapped."

"We had a fight yesterday, right after Alan missed his weekly call. It's the first time he's done that. And then I got a call from Marty telling me there'd been a break-in at my studio and that the course on metal patination I proposed for the fall probably won't happen. And then, the next thing you know, Gemma and I were at it."

"Nice timing," Annie said dryly. "What exactly were you at it about?"

"Nothing and everything. Hurtful things were said. Doors were slammed."

"You think one fight might have tipped her over the edge? Do you think she's decided to leave to punish you?"

"Oddly, no, I don't think that's it. She'd be exultant if that were the case. Instead she seems depressed."

"Well, this is a mess."

"I checked them out, you know," I said. "Ellen and Richard. Back when they first came to town. One of the lead detectives on Gemma's case, Bill Morrison, he's retired now, but he was happy to help me dig for some dirt. Except there isn't any dirt. Ellen and Richard are squeaky-clean. No criminal records. Pillars of their gated community. Regular churchgoers. An income that makes me want to choke. There's nothing wrong with them."

"Except that they're not Gemma's parents, and you are her mother."

"Kids do just fine growing up without their biological parents." Whom was I trying to convince? "They do just fine growing up with grandparents or an aunt and uncle."

"We're talking about Gemma. Not anonymous kids."

"I know that! Sorry. I didn't mean to shout."

"If I were you, I'd be screaming."

I think I managed a smile. "We're walking on eggshells with each other. And I'm absolutely miserable."

"You could refuse to let her go. She's still a minor. You could put your foot down."

"No," I said more firmly than I felt. "I have to believe in that idea of loving someone enough to be willing to let her go. Giving her the choice to stay or to leave."

"But what if she doesn't come back to you? Are you willing to accept that possibility?"

"No," I admitted. "But I have to *make* myself willing."

"Does Alan know about this?" Annie asked. "Not that he'd

be of any help to you, or to Gemma, for that matter. Especially not now that he's rejected a plea bargain and proven once again he's an idiot."

"Gemma hasn't even told her father that his cousin is in her life."

Annie sighed. "Have you told Marion yet?"

"No. I think I'm hoping Gemma will change her mind and Marion won't have to know we almost lost her again."

"Do you think Gemma will change her mind?"

I shook my head. "Honestly? No. She's proud. She's stubborn. And for all I know, she really *does* want to get away from me."

"Then maybe you should tell Marion before Ellen does. Marion's delicate. Ellen is not."

"Ellen wants nothing to do with Alan's mother. She won't go near her."

"All right, your call. So, have you spoken to Ellen since Gemma's announcement?"

"I'm going to call her later today. I'm dreading it. I'm not at all sure what I'm going to say. *Congratulations, you won? If you hurt my daughter, I'll kill you?*"

"Do you want me to be with you when you talk to Ellen? Moral support."

I shook my head again. "Thanks, Annie. But this is something I should do on my own. If only I knew why Gemma wants to leave!"

"Maybe she thinks she's doing you a favor." Annie shrugged. "I don't know, I'm just throwing stuff out and seeing what, if anything, sticks."

"But I thought I've made it clear to her that I want her with me. We were getting along."

"You hardly know Gemma, Verity," Annie pointed out. "None of us do. Sorry, but that's the truth. For all we know, she's always been . . . inconsistent."

Would Alan have insight into Gemma's unexpected decision? The thought surprised me.

Abruptly, I got up from the table. "I should get back," I said. "Thanks, Annie."

"I don't know that I've done anything to deserve thanks."

"You listen," I said. "What's better is that you really hear me."

Chapter 102

"I heard Verity and my mother talking. I came right over. Is it true, Gemma? Are you going to live with those cousins in Massachusetts?"

I looked down at my hands. I forgot I'd been wearing one of Verity's rings—with her permission—since yesterday morning, before Alan's non-call. Before our fight. It was silver, set with a small triangular turquoise. I took it off and put it in my pocket. "Yeah," I said.

Cathy, perched on the edge of the lounge chair next to me, shook her head. "I can't believe you're going."

"You sound disappointed."

"I am," she said earnestly. Everything about Cathy is earnest. It used to annoy me. "I thought we were, I don't know. I thought we were all friends."

I cringed. That word again. I'd called Cathy my friend more than once. "Well," I said, "Greyson is a really good school, so . . ."

It was a pathetic reply. Cathy didn't bother to argue it.

"Verity must be devastated. Sorry, Gemma, but I heard her before, at my house."

I thought: *Is she?* Then why did she say sure, go ahead, go live with Ellen and Richard?

Okay. That's not exactly how it happened, but still. She didn't say no.

Had I wanted her to? Had I secretly hoped she would refuse to let me leave, take the choice out of my hands?

"But why?" Cathy persisted. "Why are you leaving when you've only been here a few months? You haven't even given life here a real chance!"

"Don't tell me what I have or haven't done," I said, but there was no real anger behind those words.

She was sort of right, after all.

Cathy got up from the lounge. "I have to go," she said. "I've got a babysitting job at two."

"Okay."

"Look, are you really sure about this?"

I was glad I was wearing sunglasses. Well, actually, they were Verity's backup pair. She'd told me I could wear them if I couldn't find my own.

I was glad I was wearing sunglasses because I couldn't stop my eyes from going all watery. "Yeah," I said quickly. "I'm sure."

When Cathy had gone, I grabbed my bike, the one Verity had bought me, and pedaled as hard and fast as I could down to the beach.

I wonder how close to the beach I'll be living in Lexington. I should look at a map, I suppose. I'll definitely miss being able to hop on my bike and be at the water in fifteen minutes.

The beach was crowded—it was one of those perfect days we seem to get here a lot, and it was almost fully high tide, so there wasn't a lot of sand to go around—but I eventually found a fairly private spot up close to the dunes, what there are of them. (Some bits are restricted because of these little birds that nest there.) I sat right on the sand because I'd neglected to bring a blanket or a towel with me. There was this tangle of seaweed and rope I thought I'd like to draw, but I'd left the house in such a hurry, I forgot to grab a sketchbook, too. *I should keep one in my panniers,* I thought. *And a towel.* And then I realized that when I go to live in Lexington, I'll have to leave the secondhand Tyler and my hand-me-down panniers here with Verity and take the Trek Ellen bought me.

I wonder if Verity will keep the old bike, in case I want it someday. She should try to sell it and get some of her money back.

There's an art department at Greyson. I saw that on the website. But I wonder if every time I pick up a pencil I'll think of Verity and coming here by myself to the beach and how I enjoyed it so much and feel too, I don't know, too nostalgic to work. Too sad. I don't want to stop drawing, but maybe I will. Maybe I won't even have the time to take art classes if it turns out I have to catch up with the other kids in my grade, which is totally possible, given the relatively crappy education I've had so far.

It's all a giant mess.

I pulled up my knees, wrapped my arms around them, and rested my head on my arms. The sound of the surf coming increasingly closer was loud in my ears but not loud enough to drown out the sound of my sobbing.

Chapter 103

When I got home from Annie's, I found the house empty, and for a split second I panicked and was convinced Ellen and Richard had spirited Gemma away.

It was with some difficulty that I got control of myself enough to check for her bike in the garage. The Tyler was gone. The Trek was there.

Lightning doesn't strike twice in the same place. Right?

Actually, I think that's a myth.

I went back into the house and called David at the college, where I knew he would be. And I told him the whole story, from Alan's missed call and Gemma's sad and bitter mood right afterward, to my upsetting conversation with Marty McGinty (of course, David already knew about the break-in at the college but not about the likely cancelation of my course), to the ridiculous blowup that had resulted in Gemma's deciding to go off and live with Alan's cousin. David listened without intrusive comment.

When I finished the tale, I felt exhausted. I am exhausted.

"Well?" I said.

"This is a train wreck," David said promptly. "Sorry, but I can't pretend I think Gemma's going off with those two is a good idea."

"I'm not asking you to pretend," I said.

"And she hasn't given you a reason?"

"No. I can make a few guesses, but I might very well be wrong. As Annie pointed out, I don't really know my daughter, do I?"

"Sadly, Annie's right. None of us really know her. Look, Verity, don't go down without a fight."

"This isn't a contest between Gemma and me," I protested.

"No, it's a contest between you and Ellen. At least that's how she sees it. It's a battle of wills, with Gemma the prize."

"David," I asked, not expecting a definitive answer, "why does Ellen want her?"

"All that matters for us is that she does. Look, is she willing to put anything in writing? Has she brought in a lawyer? What if she gets Gemma down there to Lexington and then changes her mind? Are there stipulations to this arrangement?"

My head was swimming. "David, I don't know the answer to any of those questions. I told you, I haven't spoken to her yet."

"I'd like to know what her husband really thinks of this scheme."

"I wish you wouldn't use that word. *Scheme.*"

"All right, this plan. Does he really care about Gemma's future or is he just letting his bored wife amuse herself?"

Richard had to have consented to the idea of Greyson and all that went with it, I thought. All the money that was involved . . .

"What's in it for him?" David went on. "Why is he taking in a seventeen-year-old girl he barely knows?"

"Stop!" I cried. "I know what you're saying." Of course the black thought had occurred to me, that one or both of them could be a sexual predator. It's why I'd gone to Bill Morrison and asked for his help in vetting Ellen and Richard.

"When are you talking to them?" David asked.

"I'm planning on calling as soon as I get off the phone with you."

"Take some deep breaths first. Seriously, Verity, if you don't feel you can be strong, wait to make the call."

"Okay," I said. "I'll be careful, but wish me luck anyway."
Ellen, the emotional vampire. Is that what she is?

"I'm wishing you more than luck," he said. "And, Verity?
You know I'll do anything you need me to do. Anything."

"I know," I said.

I do know.

I sat very still for a long time after my conversation with
Ellen, hands in my lap. I felt stunned, patronized, and bullied,
much as I had felt at the encounter with her at Joe's Diner.

And I felt guilty, guilty for seeming to want to hold my
daughter back from a chance for a bright and shining future.
Ellen and Richard's version of a bright and shining future.

My manner on the phone was purposefully formal. It seemed
a wiser choice than screaming and yelling at the woman with
whom my daughter had chosen to entrust herself for at least the
next school year. Ellen's manner was upbeat, almost breezy.
Well, why wouldn't it be? She had won. She had gotten what
she wanted, whatever that was in the end.

I attempted to discuss a few practical matters.

"I'll want to visit her, of course," I said. I don't want to ask
for permission to see my own child, but I know I can't just be
dropping in on Ellen and Richard whenever I feel like it. Rather,
whenever I have time to make the two-hour trip there and the
two-hour trip back.

"Of course," Ellen said soothingly. "She will be very busy,
though. It might be best to wait and see how she's adjusting at
Greyson before scheduling too many social calls."

It was an evasive answer, and only the first of many.

"What about the holidays?" I said. "Thanksgiving and
Christmas. I'd like her to come home for the holidays."

"I know you do, Verity. Though there's an awful lot going
on at Greyson around Thanksgiving, a semiformal dance for
one, and an overnight to New York City. Gemma might not
want to miss the activities and the chance to spend some
downtime with her new friends."

"Yes," I said, "but—"

"As for Christmas, Richard and I usually escape to a warm climate for a week, and Gemma did express some interest in joining us. She has almost a full two weeks off then, and I know you'd hate to keep her from a chance to travel." Ellen laughed. "When I told her we love to visit Hawaii, her eyes almost popped out of her head!"

Had they? Gemma has never said anything about Hawaii to me. I couldn't bear to bring up the projected spring visit to Paris.

In the end, I suspect I'll have to let Gemma be the one to decide where she spends her free time. Let her go and see if she comes back. That's the mature thing to do, isn't it?

"There's her clothing," I went on, my manner still formal, if less assured. Inside, I was flailing, losing ground. "We need to discuss an allowance. And what to do about her immediate medical care if she should get sick. She's hoping to start driving lessons this fall. And you know she talks to her father once a week. You have to let her talk to him if she wants to."

"All those things will be taken care of, Verity."

"Her life . . ." I almost couldn't go on in the face of Ellen's continued bland assurances. "Her life needs to be stable."

"And that's exactly what Richard and I can provide. Stability."

Implying, of course, that I could not.

"I'd like," I said, "whatever final agreement we come to, to be in writing."

Ellen laughed. "You don't have faith in me. Oh, Verity, I'm not like my cousin. You can trust me not to do anything to harm your daughter."

"Still," I pressed, "I'd like the arrangement to be formalized in some way, for Gemma's protection and my own peace of mind."

"All right, of course. I'll talk to Richard, and he'll take care of everything."

There was so much more to say, but I had to get off the phone. It was all too much.

Maybe I should ask David to be with me when I next talk to Ellen. Richard should be present too, especially if he's going to "take care of everything," whatever that means exactly. Maybe I should bring along a lawyer of my own. David's good friend in Portland might help us for a rate.

Oh, I just don't know!

One thing I do know for sure: Spending another Thanksgiving and Christmas without Gemma, after the tease of having her with me this summer, will be unbearable.

Simply unbearable.

Chapter 104

"And this," Ellen said, "is a view of the south side of the house. See the trellis? We get the most gorgeous roses in June."

I nodded. "So, you do the garden and stuff?"

Ellen looked shocked. "No, no," she said. "We have a man in to handle the landscaping. And this, this is a view of the solarium out back, and this, this is the interior of the library."

We were sitting at the island or bar or whatever you call it in the kitchen of the McMansion, after yet another lunch out, this time at a place in Kennebunkport called Hurricane. I was dying to peek in the fridge and see if there was anything in there but bottles of the Prosecco Ellen seemed to love and maybe some milk for coffee. Ellen had told me the only time they really cooked was when Richard grilled—he was the guy responsible for the incredible hamburgers. "All the sides at our parties are catered," she explained when I'd asked if she could give Verity the recipe for that carrot raisin salad I liked. "I don't have a clue as to what's in what."

"But what about everyday meals?" I'd asked. "You don't use a catering service for those, do you?"

Ellen laughed. "Of course not! We mostly order in or I throw together a salad."

"What's this?" I asked, pointing to the next picture on her

phone. This picture showed a bow window up high above the rose trellis. I don't think I've ever seen a bow window (how do I even know that term?) anywhere but on the ground floor of a house.

"That's our suite, Richard's and mine," Ellen said. "We did a major reconstruction of our rooms before we moved into the house. We both wanted to maximize the light, and the existing closet space was ridiculously inadequate. Look, here's a picture of our bathroom. We have a Jacuzzi and a Japanese soaking tub. I find soaking in warm water the most relaxing and beneficial thing ever."

I thought of Verity's bathroom back home. Our bathroom, with its shower and no tub.

I've never been a big fan of sitting around in water, warm or cold.

I needed—I still need—to know more about what my life is going to be like in that house with the trellis of roses and the solarium and the library. (I wonder what Ellen reads.) I have to say it's got a lot more character than the house they're renting this summer. I say "character," and now I think what I should say instead is that Ellen's house in Lexington reminds me a bit of a castle, although not a huge one, but definitely a castle, the kind with a dungeon.

I'm not saying I really believe there's a dungeon in Ellen and Richard's house, or that there are actual instruments of torture in its probably ordinary basement. I'm not an idiot. But looking at the pictures of the house made me feel sort of—anxious—about living in it. Like it isn't straightforward or something.

Shit, I don't know what I'm saying!

"Am I going to have chores?" I asked. Dad never assigned me chores. He never had to. I always did a lot of stuff around our house or apartment or wherever it was we were living. Like taking our dirty clothes and sheets and towels to the Laundromat.

Funny. My not helping out with the laundry at Verity's house was what we fought about.

Though of course the fight wasn't really about laundry.

Ellen waved her hand dismissively. "We'll work something out."

"I suppose I could make dinner sometimes," I said. "Or lunch." What I was thinking was: *What can I give in return for all the stuff Ellen and Richard are giving me? What do they really expect from me besides doing well in school and not embarrassing them in front of their rich friends?* Not that they've said I shouldn't embarrass them; I figured that part out on my own.

Ellen took a sip of water. She always drinks bottled water with a slice of lemon. When she's not drinking Prosecco or a pink cocktail. "We'll see how things go."

"I guess I'll have a curfew."

Ellen put her hand on my shoulder and smiled. "Gemma," she said, "you think too much."

Really? I wasn't aware thinking too much was possible!

I tried one more time to get a definitive answer from my father's cousin.

"When I get my driver's license," I said, "do I need to have an eye exam? I haven't had my eyes checked since I was in first or second grade. I had some sort of infection for a while. I had to wear a patch."

Ellen got up from her tall chair and went over to the sink to dump the slice of lemon from her glass. Every time she pours more water into her glass, she adds a fresh slice of lemon.

"Richard will take care of it," she said.

Of course he will, I thought. *Of course he will.*

We'll work something out.
We'll see how things go.
And again, *Richard will take care of it.*

I want to scream. Why can't Ellen give me a straight answer? Verity always does. Why won't Ellen just respect me enough to explain to me how things are going to play out day to day, week to week?

But as annoyed and as frustrated as I was, sitting in the kitchen of Ellen's rented house, I said nothing. As annoyed and as frustrated as I am, sitting here in Verity's kitchen, I'll say nothing.

Too late. It's too late.

Chapter 105

Verity and I went downtown this morning. I didn't have to go with her, of course. I mean, she didn't need me to help her carry heavy bags or anything. She was only going to the little bookstore on Clove Street, The Bookworm, and the post office, but when she asked if I wanted to go along, like she always asks, I said sure, even though we can hardly look at each other. It's not that we're angry at each other. It's just that . . . Wait, why am I presuming I can speak for Verity? All I can say is that I'm not angry with her. I'm just . . .

I just feel like crap.

We'd come out of the post office—Verity bought a book of stamps—when we ran into that woman Aida Collins, the one who showed us around the high school earlier in the summer. Again her resemblance to the characters on that cartoon *Bob's Burgers* struck me, but now I don't find it so funny. Laughing at people because of the way they're made is just wrong. Dad does it, laughs at people with a weird way of walking or a really big nose or whatever, and it always pissed me off, so why am I doing it now?

Aida was pretty bubbly. "I hope you're looking forward to being a student at Yorktide High this fall," she said with a big smile.

"Yes," I said. "I'm looking forward to it."

I could sense Verity's confusion, and I was glad she didn't contradict me.

"We have a fantastic guidance program headed up by the wonderful Steve MacFarland, but if I can help in any way to get you adjusted to the way we do things at the school, just let me know, okay?"

"Sure," I said. "Thanks."

Aida chatted with Verity for a minute, but I wasn't listening to what they were saying. When Aida went off in the direction of the parking lot, Verity said: "You didn't tell her you'll be leaving."

"No."

"Why?" Her tone, by the way, wasn't aggressive or accusatory.

"Just because," I said. "People will know when I'm gone."

It was kind of a stupid answer, but I can't bear the idea of people knowing that The Little Kidnapped Girl is going off again, choosing her crazy father's rich cousin over the mother who spent seventeen years waiting and hoping for her daughter's return. I know people will think I'm a jerk or stupid or ungrateful, and I can't help what people think, but I don't have to look at them while they judge me.

Told you I'm a coward.

"I thought I'd make burritos tonight," Verity said as we headed toward the bookstore. "Would you like chicken or beef?"

My heart felt really bad. (Can you have a heart attack at seventeen?) Only a few weeks ago it used to annoy me when she asked what I preferred and if something was okay with me, and it drove me nuts when she apologized for every little thing, even shit she didn't have any control over.

Now I think I'm going to miss it.

Chapter 106

We had just come out of the bookstore when I heard a woman calling my name. I turned around to see Matilda Gascoyne striding toward us from the direction of the beach, where I know—everyone knows—she's in the habit of taking a brisk daily walk before heading off to work at one of her family's businesses.

"Hail, fellow Yorktiders!" she said. Her face was flushed, and she looked the proverbial picture of health.

"Hi, Matilda," I said. "How are you?"

"Great," she said. "Busy planning the Harvest Festival." She turned to Gemma. "You'll enjoy the Harvest Festival, Gemma. It's a good old-fashioned small-town event. There's an apple-bobbing contest that's supposed to be for children only, but there are some among the adult population who just can't stay away! Which, of course, is unfair, because big teeth have an advantage over little teeth."

Gemma smiled at that. *She's a good actress after all*, I thought. Because I was pretty sure she was feeling miserable.

"And then there's a costume contest," Matilda went on, "also for the little ones, and baked goods and homemade jams and preserves for sale. And there are always a few local musical groups to get people dancing, and when there's enough money in the town's budget, we're able to hire a carnival ride or two.

There's plenty more to the festival, but I won't spoil it for you. You'll have to experience it for yourself."

"It sounds like fun," Gemma said. I thought I heard a wistful note in her voice, but I was probably imagining it. And if it was there, maybe she was faking it for Matilda's sake. What do I know about my daughter, really?

"We're running a special on the scallop dinner at the restaurant this week," Matilda said. "Our new chef makes an excellent potato gratin as a side. You should come in one night."

"Maybe we will," I told her. Sharing a meal in a busy family restaurant might be more tolerable—at least, less painful—than sharing a largely silent one at home. Gemma's and my home.

Matilda was off with a wave, and Gemma and I headed toward the car.

"Maybe you can come—" I stopped myself. I'd been about to say "home." "Maybe you can come back for the weekend of the festival."

Though I doubt she'd have the time. I've seen sample course schedules on Greyson's website. They're brutal.

"Maybe," Gemma said, and that was the last word she's spoken all day.

Honestly, I feel like I can't take much more of this. I almost want her to go away right now, if that's what she really has a mind to do.

But does she?

Chapter 107

Marion never calls after six in the evening.

I snatched up the receiver.

"Is everything all right?" I asked, skipping the preliminary greeting.

"No," she cried, "it isn't." She sounded near hysterical.

"Marion, calm down. What is it? Are you ill?"

"I saw Ellen in Ogunquit earlier. I recognized her right away, even though it's been well over twenty years. I tried to avoid her, but she saw me, she came running up to me. She told me, Verity. About Gemma."

Damn, I thought. I'd been negligent. Scared. I should have told Marion right away. She should have heard this from me.

Ellen has a cruel streak. She told me she wanted nothing to do with Marion, and yet she grabbed the opportunity to deliver news she must have known would cause Alan's mother—Gemma's grandmother—pain.

"I'm sorry, Marion," I said. "I should have told you sooner."

"It's all my fault she's leaving us!"

"No, Marion," I said. "It's not your fault."

If it's anyone's fault Gemma is going off with Ellen and Richard, it's probably mine. Isn't the mother always to blame?

"I never should have told Gemma about her father and grandfather," Marion went on. "I didn't mean anything bad to happen. I just thought that . . ."

Famous last words. *I didn't mean.* And *I just thought.*

Still, I tried to comfort her. "I'm sure Gemma's decision to live with Ellen has nothing to do with what you told her about her father and grandfather," I said. "The school she'll be attending is excellent. Gemma's smart. I think the idea of Greyson Academy appeals to her."

"But why is she going *away*?" Marion asked plaintively. "We have good schools right here!"

"I don't know why," I said. Suddenly I felt utterly fatigued. "Honestly, I don't. Look, do you want me to come over?" Marion is not in what is called rude health.

"No," she said after a moment, and she did sound a bit calmer than she had. Resigned. "I'm fine. I'm sorry I called so late in the evening."

"It's not so late, Marion. And again, I'm sorry I didn't tell you about Gemma sooner."

"Verity?"

"Yes?"

"Remember what I told you about Ellen, back when she first came to town?"

"That she was self-serving and always has been. Yes, I remember."

"I was right, wasn't I?"

"Yes, Marion," I said. "I think you were right."

Chapter 108

I was lying on my bed in my room, staring at the ceiling and letting my mind wander and roam and generally feeling miserable when I suddenly remembered Verity's silver and turquoise ring, the one I had been wearing when we had that big fight. The ring I had put in the pocket of my jeans when Cathy last came by the house.

I jumped up and hurried into the laundry area. If Verity had done the laundry, the ring might have been destroyed in the washing machine or dryer. But the laundry hadn't been done. (Now this seemed like a good thing.) Frantically, I rummaged through the bin of dirty clothes until I found the jeans. The ring was still in the front left pocket. I literally sighed with relief. I thought I should probably put it back in Verity's jewelry box. I thought I probably had no right to be wearing it now that I was leaving her.

But I couldn't give it up. I put it on my finger instead and went back into my room.

I thought about what Cathy said the other day, that she felt we had all become friends. I think she was implying I was betraying the friendship by going off to live with Ellen and Richard. At least, I think Cathy *feels* I'm betraying her, betraying all of them.

Was I? I wondered if I owed loyalty to anyone but myself.

About one thing I was certain. Everything felt . . . wrong. I realized that in a weird way I felt worse right then than I had when I first got to Yorktide. Then I had nothing—no expectations for anything good to come of having to live with my biological mother. But as of a few days ago I had not everything, but a lot. Maybe more than I'd ever had. Until that stupid fight ruined it all, good things had been happening with Verity and me. Okay, slowly and sometimes we'd take one step forward and two steps back, but still, I realized I had been beginning to think I could belong here one day.

That I could belong with Verity. My mother.

And now . . . Now it was all over.

And it was pretty much all my fault.

I took out my stolen sketchbook then—now no longer a secret, except for the stolen part—and began to make a list of reasons I should stay with Verity. Maybe not why I *should* stay, like it's a guilt thing, like I owe her a debt, but reasons why it would be a good thing for me if I stayed. Assuming she would want me to, after I've been such a jerk.

Number One. I've met some of Verity's colleagues. I've seen how she's respected at the college. She's been chosen as Most Popular Teacher three years in a row. I've read some of the reviews of her sculpture. All the reviews are positive. Some are downright glowing. And I saw how many people came to that opening. Since then she's sold two more pieces. What that all means is that she's a genuine artist, a genuine teacher, too. That she works hard and that she cares.

Number Two. I've seen how Cathy can go to Verity for advice, and though for a while this kind of pissed me off, now I realize I was probably only jealous. Because even though I said I didn't want or need Verity's attention, I actually did. I still do.

Three. Verity has really good friends, like Annie and Marc and David. They like her a lot. I like them a lot. And even though I was annoyed Verity didn't tell me David is her boyfriend, it doesn't matter, because I believe she really was trying to protect me. And as it turns out, I think David's cool.

By the way, I did ask Verity what everyone—Annie, Marc, and David—thought about my decision to live with Ellen and Richard and go to Greyson Academy. "Honestly," Verity said, "no one's very happy about it. But they all want what's best for you."

How can anyone ever know what's best for them until they've got it? Or until they've lost it?

Four. Even her father, my grandfather, someone Verity rejected, said those nice things about her in that e-mail, after I'd told him about Ellen's offer. He didn't have to say anything in support of her, but he wanted to.

The fifth reason. Verity didn't make a big fuss about my celebrating my birthday in August, even when I went out to that stuffy restaurant with Ellen and Richard. She could have been all "pity me" about it, but she wasn't. In her place, I probably would have been.

The sixth reason. She really did try to call me Marni before I got pretty sick of the name and told everyone it was okay to call me Gemma.

Reason number seven. There was the time she stayed up almost all night helping those guys who own the local vet, Jack and Hugh, rebuild their Fourth of July parade float after the one they had built caught fire. She was totally wiped the next day, and at one point she fell asleep on the beach during our picnic, but she never complained about it.

Number Eight. I've seen her fight for something that's morally right. The old people who live at Pine Hill Residence for the Elderly need—they deserve—that stoplight.

Nine, and this is a big one. She's actually forgiven Marion for keeping my father's dangerous past with women a secret. She's actually *kind* to Marion, and while at first I thought that was ridiculous, now I think it's impressive. I'm still not sure *I* forgive my grandmother for being so wrong!

By the way, Verity told me Marion is sad about my going away again. Verity didn't go on about it though, just stated it as a fact. I know she wasn't trying to lay a guilt trip on me. I know because she didn't even mention the fact that when I slammed the door of my bedroom after our fight, Marion's mother's vase—my great-grandmother's vase—this old, delicate, almost translucent thing, had gone crashing to the floor and shattered into like a million pieces. I heard it fall. I saw the shards in the trash.

Number Ten. When Alan screwed up by not taking his lawyer's advice and accepting the plea bargain, Verity didn't gloat. She was genuinely sympathetic and even urged me not to completely write him off. It doesn't make a lot of logical sense, being so forgiving and kind, in front of me and everyone else at least (maybe in her heart she's still pissed off), but that doesn't mean it's not a good thing.

Number Eleven. There's the website Verity set up all those years ago. That's proof she never gave up hope I was alive and might come home to her.

Twelve. There's the ritual she performs each year on my actual birthday in March.

And Number Thirteen. There are all the nice little things she does, like letting me have the little plush lamb that was my baby toy; to asking about my favorite foods so that she can make them for me, even when it's obvious she doesn't think I should be eating so much fried stuff (she's probably right); to scolding me for putting my feet on the coffee table without first taking off my shoes (it's a habit I picked up from Dad; no wonder our furniture, what there was of it, was always such a mess); and even to giving me a generous allowance when it's clear she doesn't have a lot of money to spare. Ellen and Richard tossing fifty-dollar bills and designer-brand watches at me is no big deal for them, but I see how Verity sits with the calculator and budgets out expenses for the week and how not once since I've been living with her have I seen her buy anything for herself, like a piece of jewelry (not even a fun plastic ring, the kind Annie wears) or a new T-shirt at that discount place Renys.

I looked down at my hand, at the silver and turquoise ring she lets me wear.

And I thought: *You know what? Of all the adults in my life, the ones who are family, I mean—Alan, Ellen, Richard, Marion, Tom—I believe Verity is the one who truly loves me best, the one who always acts for my happiness first and foremost.* Face it. Everything in my life with Alan was about him. His decision to kidnap me, to go on the run, to stay hidden. And yet look at how Verity reacted to my decision to cut Alan out of my life. She didn't gloat and act all "I won." She suggested I think more about taking such a drastic step as basically abandoning my father.

In spite of what Ellen says about my deserving the opportunity to go to Greyson Academy, in spite of her telling me I'm the one giving her and Richard the gift of my relationship (if you can call it that), that's not really what her offer is all about, is it? It's all about what Ellen wants for Ellen. I don't know her exact motives, but now I know, deep in my gut, that they're basically selfish. If she really wants to give me money for school, why doesn't she just write a check and leave me alone to be with my mother?

Why doesn't she leave me to be happy where I am?

And I remembered what Verity had said to me when I first told her I was going away. About how she believed I was competent enough to make good decisions for myself.

I'll be honest. I've made some pretty stupid decisions in the past. Drinking. Smoking. Having sex without protection. Pissing people off for no better reason than that I could.

I thought about how so shortly after I was born, my life was taken out of my hands. And all I've been doing in my life since then is reacting. And suddenly, sitting there with my sketchbook on my lap, in the home Verity had made for me, I realized I have the power to stop that trend of simply reacting: by taking active control of my life for the first time ever. By doing what *I* want to do. And I knew—I know—without one little doubt, that what I do *not* want to do is live with Ellen and Richard, who, if they really cared about my welfare, wouldn't let me drink and wouldn't want to wrench me away from my own mother!

I closed the sketchbook, tossed the pencil onto the couch next to it, and went to find Verity.

Chapter 109

I looked up from my laptop, suddenly aware I wasn't alone.

Gemma was standing just inside the living room, her hands stuffed into the front pockets of her jeans.

"Verity?" she said. "I mean Mom?"

My heart began to thud in my chest. *What else,* I thought, *what else can there be?* "Yes, Gemma?"

She walked over to the couch where I sat, and perched next to me, just on the edge, as if poised for flight if necessary. But she did look at me squarely.

"Look . . ." she began. "I'm just going to say this. I've decided I don't want to live with Ellen and Richard. I want to stay here with you. I'm sorry. I made the wrong choice."

It was what I wanted more than anything, for Gemma to stay. But I wondered if she was doing this for me and not for her. And that wouldn't be right. I don't need my daughter to make sacrifices for me. I don't. I spoke as carefully as I knew how.

"I want what's best for you, Gemma," I said. "What you feel is the right thing for your happiness."

"I *know* that's what you want for me," she said, pulling her hands from her pockets in what I thought might be a gesture of frustration. "It's why I want to stay with the one person who really . . . Well, I guess the one person who's not trying to buy me or lie to me. So, is it okay if I stay? I mean, I understand if you say no and—"

"Gemma," I said. "It's beyond okay. It's wonderful."

I literally tossed the laptop onto the cushions to my left and then turned back to throw my arms around my daughter. She in turn wrapped her arms around me, and I remembered how, earlier in the summer, I'd told Annie I wished my daughter could cry, at least that she would let me see her cry, and now, holding her and feeling her sobs rack her body, I felt ashamed and humbled and so very, very lucky.

"I was being so stupid," she said when she could speak again.

"No. No, you were not."

And then she broke out of my arms and wiped the backs of her hands across her eyes. "I want to show you something. Can I get into my e-mail?"

I passed the laptop to her, and a moment later she passed it back to me.

"Read this," she said. "It's from Tom. This is what he said when I told him about Ellen's offer."

I read. *Verity has always lived up to her name. She's always been a truthful person, never calculating or deceitful. You could do worse than being Verity's daughter, Gemma.*

Now it was my turn to wipe the tears from my face. *Truthful,* I thought, *but not properly forgiving. Never calculating or deceitful, but not generous enough in understanding.*

My father had suffered too. He lost a wife, then a granddaughter, and then a daughter.

"Thank you for showing me this," I said to Gemma. "I guess I've been pretty harsh with my father. Too harsh. He's a decent man. He doesn't deserve the treatment I've given him."

"Probably not." She smiled. "I mean, if I can manage to keep wacko Alan in my life, you could probably manage to keep Tom in yours. Just saying."

"You're right," I said, more than a little ashamed.

"What was the worst he did?" she asked.

"I guess," I said, "that his only crime was to be kind of emotionally obtuse at times, not able to show me any real support, especially after my mother died." And after Gemma was taken, of course, but I didn't say that.

"Mom, if being an emotional idiot really were a crime, like, ninety percent of men would be in jail!"

I laughed. "Probably."

"Seriously, though, you have to accept a person's limitations if you're going to give them your love or your friendship. You can't punish someone you love for being flawed. So what if Tom isn't, I don't know, isn't David? He obviously loves you."

"Since when did you get so smart?" I asked jokingly.

Gemma shrugged. "I think I was born that way. Or maybe," she said, "I got it from you."

Chapter 110

Annie and Marc and David had all offered to come with us when we confronted Ellen and Richard, for moral support and whatever other support we might need. (What did they expect? That Ellen would try to take me by force?) But in the end Mom and I decided we could handle Ellen and Richard on our own. I mean, who are they anyway that we should feel intimidated by them? Since when has money made anyone a better person?

Not that I don't like money.

Verity sent Ellen a text, asking if we could come by the Mc-Mansion (actually, she just said *house*) to talk. Ellen texted back right away saying, *Of course.*

She was waiting for us on the veranda, a glass of Prosecco in her hand, the bottle in the other. "I thought," she said, "we could share a toast to our Gemma and her future at Greyson Academy!"

Our Gemma? I glanced at Verity, who said, "None for me, thanks. I'm driving. Where's Richard?"

If Ellen was disappointed that Verity wasn't interested in drinking with her, she didn't show it, and then she led us inside to the kitchen, where Richard was sitting at the bar or island or whatever, frowning down at his iPhone.

"Of course," Ellen said, "I can't offer Gemma alcohol. But would she like a seltzer?"

"I don't know," Verity replied with a suspiciously big smile. "Would she?"

I hid a smile of my own and said, "No, thanks, Ellen. I'm fine."

What a liar, I thought. *She's always offered me alcohol!*

"Hey," Richard said, his eyes still fixed on his phone, on which he was busy typing something. Probably, I thought, he's planning a corporate take-over, a move that's going to put hundreds of people out of work. I mean, Verity did tell me he works in "finance."

But maybe I was being unfair. Richard has always seemed like a decent enough guy.

Ellen, who looked exactly like she always did, perfect, chattered on. "I'm so glad the both of you are here," she said. "And I'm so glad, Verity, that you realize our offer of Greyson is the only real way Gemma is going to have a chance to achieve greatness."

Richard finally lifted his eyes from his phone and looked at Ellen with an expression I couldn't read. I wondered if she was drunk or just naturally prone to dramatics. I felt glad I'd probably never have to know.

"Richard's been in conversation with our contractor about making a few alterations to your room at the house, Gemma."

"What's wrong with it?" I asked. I really was curious. Weren't the walls straight enough or something?

Ellen waved her hand. "Nothing's wrong, exactly. I just thought we might open up the space a bit by knocking through the wall that backs onto a linen closet in the hall. We'll lose that closet, of course, but that's no big deal, as there's plenty of cabinet space in both bathrooms, and your room will gain a few more square feet."

Ellen looked from me to Verity and back to me again, as if waiting for our enthusiastic response. When neither of us said anything—what was there to say?—she went on. Richard continued to frown and type.

"And I suppose we should talk about Greyson's homecoming weekend. It'll be on us before you know it, and if we want to be in on the round of parties, then we'd—"

"Ellen," I said. "Stop." I mean, I don't even like the woman, but I was starting to feel bad for her being all excited about something that was never going to happen. That, and Verity was giving me a look that said, "Get on with it." I'd told her I wanted to be the one to break the news to Ellen and Richard.

"What's wrong?" Ellen asked. She finished the glass of Prosecco and poured another one.

"Nothing's wrong," I said. I have to admit, I was a bit nervous. I mean, I knew she wasn't going to take it well, and I really don't like to upset people. Not anymore. "It's just that I've changed my mind. I can't live with you in Lexington. Actually, I don't want to live with you. I'm going to stay here, with my mother."

I watched their reactions carefully.

Richard put his phone down but said nothing. His face betrayed nothing. Not for the first time I wondered how committed he'd ever been to his wife's plan to "rescue" me.

But Ellen. Well, that was another story. The expression on her smooth and perfectly made-up face turned ugly, and she slammed her glass down on the bar, spilling her precious Prosecco.

"What do you mean, you've changed your mind?" she said. Snarled, really.

"Just that. I've decided I want to stay here in Yorktide, with my mother."

Ellen looked wildly to her husband. "I don't believe this!" she cried. "Richard, do something!"

Richard will take care of it.

Not this time he won't, I thought.

Richard got off his stool, went over to the sink for a cloth, and began to wipe up his wife's spilled drink. "It's Gemma's choice," he said. He didn't look at me or at Verity.

"But—"

"But nothing, Ellen," Richard said. "It's over."

Ellen put her hands to either side of her head and then thrust them into the air.

"You've ruined our plans!" she cried. "You're the most self-ish, ungrateful person we've ever encountered. If you don't agree to come live with us and enroll at Greyson Academy, we'll cut you out of our lives—and out of our will. We've told everyone back home that you will be living with us. Now we'll look like fools."

Verity opened her mouth—no doubt to defend me—but I shook my head at her. And then I laughed. "Look," I said, "I'm sorry you're disappointed. But do you really think I care about your money? Okay, at first it was kind of fun, taking your presents. I'll give them back if you want. But I know I made the right decision, choosing to stay with my mother. She doesn't try to buy me, for one. And if you really care so little about the two of us that you'll walk away, fine, do it. Good riddance. Right, Mom?"

"Right," she said. I thought she looked like she was going to cry. But she also looked happy.

Ellen waggled her hand at me dismissively. "I don't want any-thing from you. Keep the phone and the bike and the watch. People like you will probably need the cash before long."

For a split second I thought I was going to fly at her and punch her in the face. But then my willpower got to work, and I unclenched my sudden fists and loosened my tense shoulders. "Thanks," I said.

Ellen wasn't finished. "You'll never make anything of your-self without our help."

"You interfering—"

"Mom."

Verity's lips tightened, and I thought, *Yeah, it's costing her a lot to keep quiet.*

"I'll make something of myself," I told my father's cousin, and my voice was like steel. "My mother did everything she's done with her life with no help from anyone. Certainly not from your family. And I'll be a success too. Watch me." I turned then to Verity. "Let's get out of here, Mom."

When we were almost to the door, I stopped and turned back. Verity put her hand lightly on my shoulder.

"Wait," I said. "One more thing. Why, Ellen? What was your point in all this? Or do you even know?"

Ellen seemed to sag then. Literally, she slumped onto one of the stools and hung her head.

"I think," Richard said, "that you both should go."

We did.

Chapter 111

The beach was crowded with people young and old, with their blankets and chairs and umbrellas and coolers and kites and Frisbees. Seagulls were screaming. Toddlers were squealing. Music was playing. Lovely, happy chaos.

Somehow, it seemed good for us to be part of it all after what Gemma and I had just been through.

"Well," Gemma said, as we headed down the beach toward Wells, the cool ocean water lapping around our ankles, "that was nasty."

"You handled it beautifully. Better than I could have in your shoes. That woman is toxic."

"Ellen's a bully," she said. "And I've had my share of experience with bullies."

"Still, I—"

"Let's not talk about it, okay?"

"Sure," I said, though there were things about which I had questions. Like, is Ellen mentally unbalanced, and what really is Richard's role in that marriage? An enabler? A caretaker? Not that Gemma would have the answers to those questions.

Gemma bent down and picked up a shell the color of slate. "I want to start a collection of shells too," she said. "Unless that's, like, invading your territory."

"Of course not. We could also start a sea glass collection. I don't know why I haven't already."

We walked along in silence for a while, and I felt so very aware of the fact that this is what I'd dreamed of for years, to simply spend time with my child, to walk along the shore, to share meals together, to know that she chooses to be with me. A life lived side by side. It's all worth so much more than what money can buy.

I know it won't go on forever. I know someday she'll move on and she should. She'll become an independent adult, and that's a good thing. But for now, well, for now, I'll cherish this greatest of gifts.

"No regrets?" I asked after a time.

"No regrets. You're going to teach me to draw, right?"

"Right. How about we celebrate at The Friendly Lobsterman?"

"Celebrate what?" Gemma said. "My freedom?"

"That's as good a way to put it as any."

Gemma smiled at me. "You know, you could probably get me to do all the housework if you promised me a plate of their onion rings once a week. Hey, I'm not above a little bribery."

Chapter 112

Alan called this morning, right on time. He had no excuse for not calling last week. At least, I guess he didn't because he didn't mention it. Neither did I.

Anyway, I had decided I would take the call, but I know now for sure that the magic in our relationship, such as it was, is gone. And if I stick to the decision to keep him in my life, I'm going to have to accept his severe limitations. (I can't preach to Verity about her relationship with her father if I don't follow my own advice!) I'm going to have to live without expectation of his making smart choices for himself. I'm going to have to live with the expectation of disappointment. Maybe, someday in the future, I'll stop even being disappointed by Alan. Maybe I'll have learned how to abandon every last little bit of emotional connection. Who knows?

He asked how I was doing. I said fine. He asked if it was hot. I said yes. I asked him if he'd gotten his annual summer cold yet. He said no. I didn't ask anything about his case.

We were off the phone in record time. When he said, "Love you," just before hanging up, I said, "You too." I think I still mean it.

See, even though my feelings for my father are damaged, not what they once were, I do feel bad that he's all alone in the world. *Really* all alone. I mean, I certainly can't help him, not from out here and not when I can't even handle knowing all the details of his day-to-day life in case they make me too upset. And Mom and Marion (I'm going to call her Gram; I think it will make her feel like I'm not mad at her for lying about Alan) can't help him, either, even if they wanted to, and I know Marion—Gram—wants to rescue him somehow. Some people might say my father doesn't deserve help, supposing there was any real help to give. But I don't know about that. I don't think Alan Burns deserves to be abandoned. I just don't.

I guess I don't think anyone deserves to be abandoned.

I was thinking last night about that poster in Verity's studio at the college, about what that guy Sir Francis Bacon said about "strangeness in proportion" being what makes something really beautiful. And I was thinking, that's one of the problems with Ellen Burns-Cassidy. I'm not talking about her physical appearance as much as I am about the way she presents herself to the world. Too perfect. Everything right where it should be. But when you really look at perfection, you see that it's not only boring, it's also sometimes ugly.

That said, I do hope Ellen will be okay. That Richard won't abandon her. But what if he needs to save himself?

Not my problem.

By the way, Verity gave me the silver and turquoise ring to keep. I love it. And the minute she gave it to me, it dawned on me that I'd never asked when her birthday is! I mean, how self-centered am I? Anyway, I was too embarrassed to ask her, so as soon as I could, I e-mailed my grandfather, who got back to me right away. October seventeenth is the answer. I so won't forget it.

We're all going out this afternoon to celebrate the end of The Ellen and Richard Show, which is what I'm now calling their time in Yorktide. They've gone back home, by the way. I guess they lost money, abandoning the McMansion they'd paid for through the very end of the summer. I don't care. And I gave their bike to that place for old people, Pine Hill. Not everyone there is ancient and incapacitated, and the staff person Verity and I talked to when we dropped it off said she thought there'd be a fight for its use. Well, she was smiling when she said it, and anyway, Verity said the administration sets up schedules for the use of all the recreational facilities and stuff. There's still no verdict on the stoplight, by the way, but the fight's not over.

As for the watch Ellen and Richard gave me, we sold it. Not that we *need* the money the way Ellen implied, but we want it and are going to have fun with it. Five hundred dollars! It's splurge money, Verity says. Now all we have to do is decide what we want to splurge on. And the phone, well, I'll hang on to it, because someday my old one is going to break or get lost, right?

Anyway, like I said, Verity, David, Marion, and I, and the Strawberries (I really should stop calling them that) are going to a lobster pound right on the water (duh, where else would it be?) in Kittery Point. After that we're going to an outdoor concert with a local jazz band. I don't know anything about jazz, but I know I'm going to have a good time.

I really know it.

Epilogue

Greetings from Yorktide, Maine!

It's just over a year since I came to live with my mother. Can you believe it?

Where to begin?

Well, I got through my first New England winter without killing anyone or, more important, without killing myself. People here joke about that sort of thing—cabin fever and stuff—so it's okay if I do too now. I'd never seen so much snow in my life, outside of the movies, I mean. It was pretty gorgeous and also kind of overwhelming in a frightening sort of way, especially when you looked out over the ocean right after a storm and all you could see was—monochrome. The sea and the sky and the rocks and the sand were all tones of white and gray and black. No spot of color anywhere. It was pretty eerie, like something out of a movie about ancient mythical lands populated by wizards and trolls and half men/half beasts. Even though I'm still a novice with the art thing, I had to try to draw and even to paint those bleak but beautiful winter landscapes. Some of the pieces came out okay. Some, not so much. Manipulating paint is hard.

And the cold! Whoa. Everyone here walks around dressed in, like, a million layers, and no one seems to mind that they look

like the Michelin Man. Mom had to teach me how to dress—
like I was a little kid again!—because if you don't know about
layering and what winds off the ocean can feel like (sandpaper
scraping over your skin) and SmartWool socks, you'll be seriously sorry and probably get frostbite. And the minute the
temperature climbs to, like, forty, people start wearing shorts, and
some even wear flip-flops when there's still snow and ice hanging
around in dirty patches. I was as eager as anyone to get back into
T-shirts and to put away my thirty-pound L.L.Bean boots (which
I got at a secondhand shop), but there was no way I was going
to expose any part of my body below my neck before the temperature got up to at least sixty-five. Which it finally did in,
like, May. It was just one more adjustment to make so that I'd
learn to fit into my new world. Like getting used to having
home-cooked meals in place of frozen dinners, and a washing
machine and dryer actually in the house so that you didn't
have to drive miles to the local laundry place and hang out
with a random bunch of people, most of whom were as annoyed as you were to be there, while your clothes got destroyed by a crappy industrial-strength machine.

And then there's the whole winter sports thing. Mom and I
don't really have money for skiing, which is crazy expensive,
but Annie and Marc found this great deal for a day at some
mountain in New Hampshire, and one day in January they invited me along. You know how I feel about sports, but the idea
of skiing seemed kind of cool—the scenery, I thought, would
be good—so I borrowed some of Annie's old equipment, and
David gave me a fleece scarf/hat thing he said he'd never worn.
He says he doesn't look good in bright blue. Men can be so
vain! It was really nice of Annie and Marc to offer me the opportunity to go with them—all expenses paid, if you can believe it—but in about a minute I realized skiing just isn't for
me. I kind of knew it wouldn't be, like I said, but I thought,
what the hell? I'll give it a try. And then I was on my butt more
often than I was on my feet, and Cathy and her parents and all

these little kids were whizzing by me and laughing while I tried to get back up onto my feet without impaling myself somehow on the tips of my skis.

Bottom line—I suck. Really suck. It's a freakin' miracle I didn't break my head or something. Never. Again.

I have to admit I got a little sentimental around Christmas. It was the first one I'd ever spent without my father and the first one I'd ever spent with my mother, and if that isn't enough to unsettle even the most hard-hearted person, I don't know what is. Mom seemed to sense my mood though, and she was sensitive enough, as usual, not to press me to "share." I mean, I had a good time overall. Yorktide and the other towns around here were totally decorated in pine boughs and big red ribbons, and almost every house had at least a few strings of colored lights around the windows and over the front door. And don't forget the wreaths. It's hard not to feel upbeat with everyone you meet in the convenience store and the post office and even the gas station, if you can believe it, passing around gifts of homemade candy and cookies. We had dinner with Annie and Marc and Cathy and David at the Strawbridges' house on Christmas Day, but on Christmas Eve, Mom and I went to midnight mass (which was actually at ten o'clock) at an Episcopal church she told me she used to go to sometimes ages ago, and I was so surprised by how peaceful I felt, almost like I was in another, much better world. Maybe it was the music and the incense, but by the time the service was over, I felt kind of high, in a good way. The mood lasted even after we'd left the church and gone home, where we sat around for a while, drinking hot chocolate and listening to an old CD Mom has of a Christmas album some singer named Johnny Mathis made in the sixties or something. I've always been suspicious of any experience even remotely warm and fuzzy, but right then I was happy enough to hum along to "I'll Be Home for Christmas."

Still, I thought a lot about all the Christmases I'd spent alone with Alan, and how he would buy these packaged Italian-style cookies with pink and green icing (I loved those cookies) and how he'd stuff my stocking (really just a sock) with candy (of course) and silly little things he'd get at the dollar store or from the gum ball machines at the grocery store: little plastic monsters and marbles and bead bracelets that would break by the end of the day. One year he found a silver tinsel tree on the sidewalk, obviously thrown out by whoever had once owned it, and he brought it in. It was about two feet high, and though its stand was half broken, we managed to sit it on our kitchen table, though it made eating there kind of difficult. We decorated the tree with tiny candy canes and round red glass balls we got at the hardware store for, like, two dollars a box. Finally, after about four or five years, the tree just fell apart (and most of the balls had gotten broken by then) and we had no choice but to throw it into the garbage. Dad really loved that tree, even more than I did. I thought of him, alone in his cell (but for the snoring cell mate he complains about), probably without any glittering decorations and certainly without any presents and Annie's amazing roast goose and Mom's homemade chunky cranberry relish (I'd never seen cranberry relish that didn't come in a can!), and I tried to remind myself that Alan Burns was where he was because of his own choices, and I shouldn't feel sorry for him. But it was no use. I did feel sorry for him. I didn't let it ruin my own Christmas season though, and I didn't feel guilty for that.

Mom got me a silver and turquoise bracelet to go with the ring she gave me last summer, and I got her this new modeling tool she wanted (I asked David to find out for me what she secretly wished for). She told me I didn't need to get her anything (she said I should save my money), but come on, like I could sit there, tearing open a gift from her and not give her something in return. I'm not a total jerk. Anymore.

About making friends.

I feel like Cathy and I are friends by default, and she probably feels the same way, but that's okay. I never really had a close friend before coming here to Yorktide, at least, never a close friend for very long, what with all the times we moved and with

Dad's being so obstructive about my social life—when he wasn't oblivious to it. I guess I never knew how to make and keep a real friend. It's still not really an easy thing for me to do, and Mom tells me that when she was young, she had trouble making and keeping friends too. She's told me how Dad managed to isolate her from her college friends and the artists she'd hung around with, but she says she doesn't blame him for that anymore. She says she was responsible for her life—if only she had known it then! Anyway, aside from Cathy, there's this girl I met at YCC when I was hanging around one afternoon, waiting for Mom to get done teaching a class. I was in the library, sitting in one of those big faux leather chairs they have (a lot of them are cracked, but whatever), flipping through one of those huge coffee table books (this one was on the symbolism of churches and cathedrals), when this girl sat in the chair close to mine and said hi. LaJuana—that's her name—was also waiting for *her* mother, who teaches American history, and we got to talking. She doesn't go to my high school and she lives in Bermondsey, which is a few towns away, so she doesn't spend a lot of time in poky little downtown Yorktide (which is actually kind of sweet), so that's probably why I hadn't seen her around. We kind of hit it off—she's snarky in a funny way—so we hang out sometimes. (She drives and has her own car. I drive now, but Mom and I share a car.)

And a few times I've hung out with Daisy Higgins and Sophie Stueben, girls I first saw at Mom's opening last summer but didn't get to meet until school started. Sophie's got a past almost as dramatic as mine, and Daisy's been through a lot too, losing both of her parents so young. Sophie and Daisy are really tight, so it's more like I'm just an acquaintance than a friend, but that's okay. It's not like I need a lot of friends or even that I want a lot of friends. I still sometimes feel a bit overwhelmed by all that's happened in my life since last spring when Dad stole that car. I feel like there are enough new people around already for me to get to really know—Mom and Marion, David and the Strawbridges, and even Tom, long-distance.

As for guys, even though there are a few cute ones in school, I've decided not to get involved with anyone—not even just for sex—for at least a few years. And when I do decide it's time to be open to a relationship, I think I might want to find someone a bit older, someone who's seen more of life than the average pampered kid, someone who's handled bigger problems than not being able to afford a pair of fancy sneakers. But who knows? Maybe I'll wind up falling for the boy next door. Not that there is one older than little Michael Gallison, but you know what I mean.

I just finished my junior year with good grades overall and a certificate of excellence in art. Yeah, turns out I'm a prodigy or something. Just kidding, but I do have talent. I know you're thinking, *Why is she eighteen and still in high school?* It's because Alan held me back from going to first grade with everyone else my age. He said he didn't think I was ready. *He's* the one who wasn't ready.

Whatever.

I got along okay with most kids in my class. The fact that, like Cathy said, the school doesn't tolerate bullying and has that group called Respekt Yourself helped! And I've found that kids—young people—make a lot less of a stink about things than most adults. I mean, only two people said anything to me about my past, and neither was obnoxious about it. Anyway, that was way back last September, just after school started. By now I'm just one of the crowd. Fine by me.

Back to my father. It's not great news, but no big surprise, either. Because he wouldn't accept the plea bargain, in the end he got a pretty severe sentence—ten years jail time and fines, though I don't know how he'll ever manage to pay the fines because he's broke. There's some chance for an early release. I don't know the details—once I would have wanted to—but knowing Alan, he'll blow that somehow and wind up serving the entire decade. The trial and sentencing was reported in the local papers, and for about a week I was the hot topic again in Yorktide. But this time I took my celebrity in my stride, and soon enough it was over. I've had too many fifteen minutes of fame for one person, thank you very much. Now I'd like to live the rest of my life quietly.

Like that will happen!

Marion—like I said, I call her Gram; it makes her happy—is pretty devastated by the ten-year sentence. She writes to Alan every week. I saw an unfinished letter on her kitchen table once when I was visiting her. When she came into the room about half a second later, I pretended I hadn't seen it, and Gram stuffed the piece of paper into the pocket of her sweater. I'm not sure if Mom knows Gram writes to her son, and I have no idea what Gram tells him or even if he writes back. I could ask, I suppose, but I don't. I don't really want to know.

I write to him now, also. It's easier than talking on the phone and hearing that too familiar note of whining and per-secution in his voice. But he is, after all, my father, so I guess I owe him something. I tell him about school and the weather and keep as neutral as I can, only occasionally mentioning Mom. It's not easy, believe me, and a part of me feels like I'm doing wrong by my mother by pretending she's not now a huge part of my life. But it is what it is. I'm trying not to get further dragged into the melodrama I was born to be a part of. I don't want to have to hear any rantings or self-defensive lies on Alan's part if I talk too much about Mom.

One thing I did tell him though. I told him she's teaching me to draw and to paint. He said: "Is she forcing you?" I wasn't surprised at his reaction. I wasn't. Still, I was a bit hurt. He doesn't care about me, not really, just his limited version of me. "No," I told him. "I asked her to teach me. I like it." To that he said nothing, and I won't mention it again. Nor will I send him anything I draw or paint. He'll only see it as being from Mom.

Anyway, Alan is Alan, and I have no illusions at all about his worth to my life. When he gets out of prison—if he man-ages not to get himself killed before that—I suspect he'll want to see me, but right now I don't know how I feel about that.

Nothing would be the same as it was before he stole that car, and now I know what we had together was largely a lie.

I know I have the power to make the decision to see him or not, and I'll think long and hard before making that decision. A big factor is what it would do to Mom if I agreed to meet with him. Of course I know Mom would never stand in my way if I did want to see Alan—she's proven beyond a shadow of a doubt that she's got my best interests in mind and that she's a fundamentally fair person—but still, I don't know. Alan Burns really hurt her, almost destroyed her, and the sacrifice of Mom's peace of mind just might not be worth any happiness or satisfaction I might get out of seeing my father face-to-face. We'll see when the time comes.

After last summer we never heard from Ellen and Richard again, not a peep. It still kind of freaks me out when I think about how they just swooped into my life—into our lives— expecting me to just go off with them. And I almost did! That was a seriously close call. I try not to think about that whole disaster of that stupid fight with Mom and then telling Ellen I'd go to live with her and Richard, and then of how I was miserable until I worked up the nerve to tell Mom that I'd changed my mind and wanted to stay with her in Yorktide. I feel embarrassed when I think about all that, even though I'm only embarrassed in front of myself, which is somehow bad enough. You don't need other people around to make you feel like an idiot.

Money's an issue for Mom and me—though compared to how Alan and I lived, I feel rich here with Mom, and in more ways than one. So even though it was kind of tough getting used to juggling homework with after-school activities—hey, I might not like sports, but here I'm required to do something athletic if I want to graduate—I managed, and then, back in January, I got a job watching Molly and Michael next door one night a week so that Peter and Grace can get out on their own for dinner at one of the bazillion clam shacks around here or to a bowling alley they like in South Berwick. The money isn't much, but it helps, and I like spending time with the twins. And because I live right next door there's no commuting! This summer, though, I'll be working at—you guessed it—a clam shack in town. Sophie Stueben got me the job—she's been working at The Clamshell for a while now—and though a portion of what I make will go to our household fund (that's my idea), I have a plan to buy a piece of turquoise like the one I saw at that Native American museum when I was a kid. Maybe I'll wear it as a pendant, to go with my ring and bracelet from Mom. Note: Tourmaline is Maine's official stone, and it can be green or pink or a combination of both, watermelon tourmaline, which is pretty cool. But I like to wear turquoise as a reminder of my childhood in the Southwest. After all, there were some good times.

Oh, more about our financial situation. Even though Verity's class on the patination of metals went ahead for both the fall and spring semesters, it's not as cheap for two to live as it is for one, so I've decided to go to Yorktide Community College for two years, work my butt off, avoid taking any classes by Mom because that would be weird, and apply for every scholarship I possibly can. I think I'd like to stay in Maine after that, maybe go to Adams College in South Berwick or Maine College of Art in Portland so I can come home on holidays without it costing a fortune.

Home. Yorktide, with Mom. It's not such a bad place to live after all. By now (except for that week when the results of Alan's trial were made known) people have pretty much learned to ignore the fact that I was The Little Kidnapped Girl. At least, they leave me alone—even that obnoxious Mirelle Turner turns the other way when she sees me coming—and only speculate about the first seventeen years of my life behind closed doors. I haven't decided what I'll do about my past in my future, by which I mean, will I tell new people I meet in places far away from Yorktide that I was kidnapped by my father when only an infant and returned to my mother seventeen years later? I suppose I'll have to come clean. It is, after all, *my* life and while I'm not thrilled it started out the way it did, I'm not ashamed of it. I'm not even ashamed of Alan, though I doubt anyone would criticize me if I were. He's obviously got a screw loose, to put it mildly, and you don't *choose* to be a few sandwiches short of a picnic, to put it even more mildly.

Thank God, not all my family is screwed up. I keep in touch with Tom, and I tell my mother about what's going on in his life, like the time he sprained his ankle while he was mowing the lawn and the fact that he and Valerie are going to Aruba on a packaged trip next year. But Mom also exchanges e-mails with him sometimes, and they've even talked on the phone once. She said it was an awkward conversation but that she was glad she had called. He's invited us to visit him in Florida anytime, and I told Mom I thought we should go. I think she's almost to the point where she's going to say okay. I mean, Tom's a nice guy. On my birthday—my real birthday—he sent a check for twenty-five dollars, and I spent it on taking Mom and me to dinner at Flatbread one night, this amazing pizza restaurant. (We went to the one in Portsmouth.) Well, the bill was more than twenty-five dollars, but the money helped and we had a good time. We shared this completely decadent chocolate brownie dessert, too, and both of us felt jittery after from all the sugar. It was awesome, the dessert, I mean—not the jitters. By the way, I've cut way down on coffee. Not so much sugar, as you can see!

I really like David. He's a good guy, and he's so into my mom and not just because she's kind and talented and can make even simple ingredients like a can of cream of mushroom soup, some onions, some cut-up chicken, and a box of noodles taste fantastic. And face it, he's hung around since I've been home, and I haven't always been easy to put up with. A lot of other men would have gone running from a woman whose screwed-up (through no fault of her own) teenage daughter suddenly got dumped on her doorstep, but David didn't. Plus, he's smart, and I like talking to him about all sorts of things, from movies (we both really like *Pulp Fiction* and *Fargo*; in fact, David introduced me to them) to all the crazy shit that's going on in the world on any given day, like wars and terrorist shootings and weird sex scandals among politicians. I guess I wouldn't mind if he and Mom decided to get married, though that would mean we'd have to move out of this house, which is way too small for three people, and into David's, which is just about big enough for three people. Or maybe we'd have to sell both houses and buy a new one. Anyway, before too long I'll be out on my own, and it would be nice to have a place to come home to when I lose a job or get kicked out of an apartment by a roommate from hell. Not that I would ever take advantage of their welcome. I'm not the type to be pathetic like that. Mom knows that. Well, it's up to them, what they do, though I've hinted pretty broadly to Mom that she's got my okay if she wants it.

For the first time ever I celebrated my real birthday, the actual day of my birth, March 26. I asked Mom what she remembered of that day, and no big surprise, I guess, she remembers every little detail—well, until she was too tired to even notice what was going on, and that was after I was born and it was noted I had the requisite number of arms and legs, etc., and it was okay for her to basically pass out.

Mom asked what I wanted to do to celebrate my eighteenth birthday and honestly, because it was such a strange thing to think about, having a birthday in March, which is still really winter here, I said I just wanted to stay home and have a cake, just the two of us. Mom suggested maybe we should also have Gram, and I said okay to that. So it was just we three. Gram brought along the pictures she'd already showed me a million times, the ones she'd taken of me and Mom in the hospital, and Mom made a cake with—get this—homemade vanilla icing, which I'd never had before, and chocolate ice cream, and given my well-known sweet tooth, I was pretty content. I got cards, too, from David, and from the Strawbridges, and from Tom. Of course, Alan didn't acknowledge the day, and I didn't expect him to. Honestly, I'm not sure what he thinks is real at this point. Clearly, he's come to believe an awful lot of his own lies, and so what's the point in reminding him I was really born in March and not August when his brain might not be capable of comprehending that?

Even though I've joked with Mom about celebrating two birthdays every year now—meaning, I get two cakes—I don't think I'll go ahead with that plan. I mean, why? Maybe it's better to keep as much as I can of my false life before Yorktide firmly in the past. Alan's a huge reminder, of course, and maybe he's enough of a reminder. And if he sends me a birthday card this August, well, I can't help that. His reality was never anyone else's reality, was it?

Overall I feel a lot calmer than I did at this time last year. Well, that makes sense! I mean, at this time last year my world was exploding, and the pieces were falling back to earth in all sorts of random bits. Now those pieces have sort of solidified, and there's structure where there had been none. People need structure. Which is not to say I'm calm all the time. At least once in every conversation I have with my father, I can feel my pulse start to speed up, like when he says something so unbelievably stupid, like getting into one of his paranoid fantasies again. And even—though I kind of hate to admit this, after all she's done for me and keeps on doing—Mom can get on my nerves, like when I sneeze and she starts running for the aspirin. But then again, it's human to be both happy and sad, both calm and agitated, right? As long as you don't let the sadness and agitation turn into something nasty that makes you attack the people who love you. That's the hard part.

But it's not impossible.

Gemma Elizabeth Burns-Peterson has been living here with me, her mother, for just over a year. My daughter. And my hero.

I mean, really, to have gone through all the unexpected upheavals and radical changes she's gone through in the past twelve months or so and to have come out the other end so strong and so steady . . . Well, it's a pretty big achievement.

Still, I worry. It's a mother's habit, and it won't be shrugged off. I wonder if Gemma's really as happy and as adjusted to this new life as she appears to be. I don't mean I think she's consciously hiding unhappiness or discontent—Gemma is nothing if not real—it's just that she's come so remarkably far, or has seemed to, that sometimes I fear a sort of backlash. I fear she'll finally collapse after all and, I don't know, run wild, run away. And then I think, *no,* that's not my daughter. For whatever mysterious reasons, Gemma, the girl Alan called Marni, is so much stronger than I was at that age and certainly so much stronger than her father ever was at any age.

We celebrated her eighteenth birthday on March 26, the first time we'd celebrated her birthday together. I wondered if there was any point in my going down to the beach at dawn, as I had done for all those years in a row, to perform my annual ritual of hope. Because now there was no need to launch a promise of remembrance and love out into the wide world, not with Gemma right here with me, flesh and blood. But I found it too hard to let go, so in the end, before Gemma woke that morning, I did go down to the shore and this time, instead of sending another little missive onto the waves, I said a very heartfelt thanks to who or whatever forces had helped to bring Gemma home to me. The air was raw—we were expecting a snow squall later that day—and I stood there shivering on what little there was of the sand (it being high tide) until I felt sure someone or something out in the universe had heard me. Then I went home, passing on my way a few local fishermen already back from their run out to sea. I suspect this solitary ritual, now one of gratitude, is something I'll be doing for every year of my daughter's life, no matter where the future takes us.

When I got back to the house, Gemma was in the kitchen, making a pot of coffee. The look she gave me let me know she knew where I'd been and probably why. Neither of us said anything about my excursion, though, and we went on to have a very pleasant day, culminating in Marion's joining us that evening for dinner, cake, and presents.

I spoke to David that night from my bedroom, with the door closed and my voice lowered. "How did it go?" he asked. "And are you all right?" I *was* all right, I told him, and Gemma seemed to be all right too, though she had been a bit subdued all day. Of course, Ellen and Richard sent no acknowledgment of Gemma's birthday, not that we had expected them to. They had sworn to cut us off, and so far they've been true to their word. All I can say is, if they ever come sniffing around my daughter again, well, I won't hesitate to send them packing with a few choice words. To have cared so very little for Gemma not to even have pretended to accept her decision to stay with me with some degree of grace, some show of goodwill . . . I shudder to think what her life with them would have been like. But all that's gone into the past. Amen.

David and I have talked again about marriage, but I'm still not entirely sure it would be the right thing to do for Gemma's sake. If we had lived together as a run-of-the-mill single mother and child, I'd still hesitate before settling into marriage—I'd consider carefully the quality of the man I was bringing into the life of my child—but given Gemma's and my odd situation, I find myself cautious about introducing another big change to her life. David understands this as he's understood so many other things about me through the years. He's even promised me that if we married, and if Gemma wanted it, he would be more than happy to officially adopt her. Close to a saint he might be, but still, he has a right to live a happy and fulfilled life, and I can't keep him hanging around for much longer without making a decision either way.

I *want* to marry him. I believe he thoroughly respects my relationship with Gemma, and I want to spend the rest of my life at his side, and with him by mine. But sometimes Gemma will be standing in between us, and how that will really feel to David, he can't know for sure until it happens.

I know. A leap of faith is what's required now, faith in myself, in David, and in Gemma. I'm not the same person I was the last time I contemplated marrying someone—and thank God for that—and David is as far from Alan as a man can be. Thank God for that, too.

Gemma, my wonderful daughter, has been key in my reconciling with my father, in helping me to forgive him for not being able to help me when I needed help the most. I've come to understand why I reacted so negatively to my father's fumbling attempts at consolation back when Alan (it was supposed) made off with Gemma, and I think I can be forgiven those negative feelings, but that doesn't mean my decision to keep him at arm's length was the right one. And the only thing Valerie ever did wrong was to not be my mother. The only crime she ever committed was to love my father. I've been unfair to her, too. Anyway, Gemma and I are hoping to get down to Florida for a visit next February, when YCC and the high school have a weeklong break from classes.

I'm very happy to say that Gemma's nascent artistic skills are advancing rapidly, and it thrills me to see how she embraces each step of the journey, understanding that failure is part of success and that nothing worthwhile ever comes easily.

Ain't that the truth!

I don't know if she'll pursue a career in art—that's entirely up to her—but I do hope she continues to live her life with art. Art makes life so much more bearable and meaningful.

That's something Alan could never understand.

What is there to say about Alan? He's made his bed and now he's lying in it. A harsh sentiment, but it's true, at least to a great extent. Alan's poor choices—to the extent of which he was capable of making choices independent of his mental or emotional problems—landed him behind bars for the next ten years. We all live and die alone—another harsh reality—and in the end Alan will be the only one facing his truth head on, that he stole a child from her mother and deserved what he got in return.

Poor Marion is taking Alan's sentence badly, as any mother would, of course. But she's long since given up making excuses for him, and so I hope she can achieve some peace of mind soon. Gemma is good to her grandmother, visiting her once a week (mostly on her bike, as we're sharing one car at the moment), and getting her out of the house for walks and fresh air, not something Marion is likely to do on her own.

Gemma has also made a few friends here in Yorktide, and she sometimes hangs out with a girl named LaJuana, whose mother also teaches at YCC. Cathy, of course, is still in the picture, but as I suspected a year ago, before Gemma came home to stay, Cathy and her friends are just too different from Gemma to allow for a really close fit. As long as Annie's daughter and mine aren't tearing each other's hair out, all is good.

When I ask about boys, which I do on occasion, Gemma informs me I'll be the first to know if she's interested in someone but that I shouldn't hold my breath. Like I want her to get involved with a boy! No, I'm happy about her celibacy, believe me.

I'm happy about a lot of things.

For so long I thought I would never be able to say my life was whole, complete. But now it is. Whole. Complete.

Lovely.

I think I am quite possibly the most grateful person on this earth.

Please turn the page
for a very special Q&A
with Holly Chamberlin!

Q. What made you decide to write about a teenage girl who had been kidnapped at infancy?

A. My editor came across an article about a stolen child and he asked if it would be a topic I'd be interested in exploring. I said sure. I mean, talk about a subject ripe with opportunity. Once I started the preliminary research into cases of abducted children and the damage done to the family left behind, I was hooked. It's a fascinating and, unfortunately, an all too common crime.

Q. Talk about your biggest challenge in telling this story.

A. The biggest challenge was to make Verity, the mother, more than merely a sad and depressed victim. Yes, she spends every day since her baby was taken grieving her loss. But in order to be a compelling character, one with whom a reader actually wants to spend time, she also had to have an interesting and successful life. Equally as challenging for me was to make Gemma, the daughter, more than just a bundle of fury and rejection.

Q. Gemma is tougher and more experienced, if not necessarily more mature, than most of the teen characters you've created in past books. And she's certainly lived a more difficult life, even going hungry at times. Was it fun to write her?

A. Maybe not fun, exactly, but I very much enjoyed creating Gemma. She's smart and a survivor. She's tough, yes, but she's basically a decent and caring person with a conscience. It was a challenge to show how her feelings for her father change from the time of his arrest to a year later, after his trial and sentencing. It was also a challenge to show how her feelings for her mother change over this period. As for Gemma's relationship with Ellen, her father's cousin, I wanted to show that while Gemma is savvy, she's still a child, susceptible to a cunning or even just a pushy adult, and full of self-doubt at the same time she's full of bravado. When Gemma decides to go off with Ellen and her husband, she really believes she's choosing the only path still open for her. She really believes on some level that she's to blame for the mess that is her life. Why? Because she's a vulnerable child who's been lied to consistently by the adult who raised her. Her sense of identity has been badly undermined. Frankly, my heart broke writing those chapters between the time Gemma declares that she's leaving Verity until the time she finds the strength to tell her mother that she wants to stay.

Q. In *Seashell Season* you deal for the first time with a truly criminal character. What was it like creating Alan Burns, aka Jim Armstrong?

A. In spite of the fact that Alan's criminal behavior kick-starts the story, I don't see him as much a hardened criminal as I do a deeply weak and troubled man. Of course, what he did to Verity and to his mother amounts to a sort of psychological torture, and what he did to Gemma—stealing her from her mother and creating an utterly false identity for her—is also terribly cruel. We never really know what prompted Alan to abduct his daughter in the first place—revenge against Verity for leaving him, a genuine though delusional belief that she was going to hurt the baby, or a combination of both—and that's because in my conception of him, Alan doesn't really understand his own motives.

Q. What's next for Holly?

A. Another novel! This one is set at Christmas and is called *The Season of Us*. I'm really excited to revisit the characters I introduced in *The Summer of Us* many years ago. So many readers have asked for a sequel to that book and now they'll have one!

SEASHELL SEASON

Holly Chamberlin

ABOUT THIS GUIDE

The suggested questions are included to enhance
your group's reading of Holly Chamberlin's
Seashell Season!

DISCUSSION QUESTIONS

1. When her father is arrested and his crimes uncovered, Gemma is thrust into the middle of a full-blown identity crisis. When she explores the website her mother created in the interest of discovering her whereabouts, Gemma feels deeply disturbed by the imagined portraits of her through the years. Talk about how much of our identity is given to us—by family, culture, neighbors, and friends—and how much is left for us to invent or discover. What part does a name—given or chosen—play in creating our identity? What is the true relation between Marni Armstrong and Gemma Peterson-Burns?

2. Verity tells Gemma that the community of Yorktide has been invested in the story of her abduction since the start, and that it feels the need to celebrate her return. Talk about how communities react to local tragedies and triumphs, how a community feels ownership of its members for better or worse. When does genuine interest and concern on the part of one's neighbors become voyeurism and mere nosiness?

3. Verity describes Marion as an enabler, someone mired in the need to protect and keep secret the weaknesses of those they love. Talk about how Marion's behavior and choices regarding her husband might have negatively affected her son. If she had been honest with Alan about his father's history of mental breakdowns, might Alan have had a happier and more productive life? Do you believe that Marion had a duty to warn Verity about her son's problems when the two first started to date? When does a mother's loyalty to her child become a liability and a danger to others? Do you understand Marion's desire to have a relationship with her son, now in jail, even

after the pain he caused her by his actions, including, in effect, his abandoning of her?

4. In relation to the question above, do you think that Marion's revealing to Gemma her husband's mental fragility and her son's angry past regarding women was the right thing to do? Was it the right thing at the wrong time? Earlier Verity wonders if Gemma ever need know the extent of the Burns family's damage. How does Gemma's knowing the full story of Albert's and Alan's troubles affect her subsequent decisions, both good and bad?

5. Verity often contemplates the question of nature versus nurture, one of life's greatest puzzles. Gemma wonders how much of a person's life is determined before birth— that is to say, how influential a person's family history really is. Talk about how Verity and Gemma have been influenced by their parents' behaviors and about how they have tried, succeeded, and perhaps at times failed to overcome a negative legacy—or to have embraced a positive one.

6. Do you think Gemma makes a wise decision when she decides to continue contact with her father, or do you think it would have been smarter for her to cut him off and move on? Talk about Verity's decision to largely ignore her father since shortly after the abduction. Do you think she was at all justified? Consider Verity's decision to forgive Marion for her deceptions and to welcome her back into her life. How can one possibly know when the healthiest thing to do is to walk away from a familial relationship?

7. In relation to the question above: Is love still possible when like has turned to dislike? Gemma is no longer

under any illusions about the extent of her father's odd-ity and she knows that he is not a man to be trusted or relied upon. Still, she has some fond memories of their years together, and she acknowledges his generally de-cent care of her. Are good memories perhaps enough to allow for a relationship to progress into the future?

8. Cathy and her friends seem like foreign creatures to Gemma, and she wonders where they derived their self-confidence, interests, and ambitions. She wonders if their energy and optimism are results of having grown up in a stable home where a child knows she can trust a parent completely. Talk about the notion of sta-bility in the home ensuring—or not ensuring—a suc-cessful life. Consider that although Alan was not the most reassuringly stable parent, Gemma, long aware of this, is in many ways a strong and balanced young woman. Nature? An instinct for survival? Or was Alan's love for his daughter—as warped as it might have been—enough to give Gemma the seed for a good and produc-tive life?

9. Talk about the possible motives behind Ellen Burns-Cassidy's desire to take on the education—and the up-bringing—of her cousin's daughter. When Gemma asks Ellen why she is being so generous, Ellen says that Gemma deserves this opportunity—not really an answer as to why Ellen feels she's the one who needs to provide it. Then, after Gemma declines the offer of a full ride at Greyson Academy, she asks again what prompted Ellen to pursue so close a relationship with her, a stranger. Ellen can't or won't answer. Do you think Ellen fully understands her own motives in inserting herself into Gemma's life? Verity and Gemma wonder what part Richard played in his wife's "scheme," as David calls it. What do you think?

10. Money is an important theme in the book—how too much can corrupt and too little can damage; the suspicion of its power and the desire for the relief and pleasures it can bring. Inherently, money is meaningless, its value determined only by what it can or cannot perform in the practical world. Talk about the role money plays in the lives of the main characters.

Against the picturesque coastal Maine setting that she evokes so well, bestselling author Holly Chamberlin creates a heart-felt story of family bonds and new beginnings . . .

It came as no surprise to anyone in Yorktide when glamorous Carol Ascher fled the little Maine town for New York City. While Carol found success as an interior designer, her younger sister, Bonnie, stayed behind, embracing marriage and motherhood. She even agreed to take in Carol's teenage daughter during a tumultuous patch. Now both their girls are grown and Bonnie, recently widowed, is anticipating the day she'll retire to Ferndean House, the nineteenth-century family home on the rocky Maine coast.

But forty-five years after leaving Yorktide, Carol suddenly announces that she's moving back—into Ferndean. Bonnie is indignant. She's the one who kept the homestead in order and tended to their dying mother. Now Carol expects to simply buy her out? As far as Bonnie is concerned, Ferndean is part of their heritage—not just another of Carol's improvement projects, to be torn apart and remade according to her whim.

The entire Ascher family is in flux, uncovering secrets that upend their relationships. Carol's longing to be welcomed home is fueled by a painful truth she's carried for years. It will take an extraordinary summer—in a remarkable place—to lead these women back to each other, buoyed by the tides of friendship and forgiveness.

Please turn the page for an exciting sneak peek of
Holly Chamberlin's
ALL OUR SUMMERS
coming soon wherever print and e-books are sold!

Chapter 1

It was a beautiful, early summer day in the town of Yorktide, Maine. The temperature was politely hovering around seventy-five, the humidity was low, and the pink and white peonies were in magnificent bloom.

Summer was Bonnie Ascher Elgort's favorite time of the year. It didn't matter that she was spending the day at Ferndean House, her family's homestead, dusting and polishing furniture, vacuuming rugs and draperies, keeping an eye out for spiders, and checking for burned-out lightbulbs. The windows were open and the cooing of a pair of mourning doves filled the air. Life was good.

Bonnie leaned over the deep kitchen sink to scrub at a mark on the backsplash. The motion caused an ache in her shoulder. At sixty-two, Bonnie was heavier than she had ever been. She knew she had lost about half an inch in height; she could see how her shoulders were slightly hunched. It didn't bother her; she still felt strong, and that was what mattered. Her medium-brown hair had dulled a bit over time, and since her husband Ken's illness and death it had become threaded with gray. This didn't trouble Bonnie. She had been told by friends that she had a youthful air about her, though she wasn't really sure what that meant or if it was important. Probably not.

What really mattered in life was on the inside. Unlike her

sister, Carol, Bonnie had never been particularly interested in clothes. It had been years since she had worn a pretty dress and carried a fancy bag, and that had been at the wedding of a friend's grandson. And, of course, there had been Ken's funeral a year ago come September. As the grieving widow, form had required her to make a certain appearance and she had, in the only skirt, blouse, and jacket that still fit her. Shoes had been a problem. Her daughter, Julie, had taken her to one of the outlets in Kittery, where after a grueling hour or two they had finally found a pair of tan low-heeled pumps. Bonnie had not worn them since the funeral. Maybe she would wear them to her granddaughter's high school graduation in a few years.

Bonnie moved from the kitchen into the dining room, where she ran a dustcloth over the carved bits of the massive oak sideboard that held pride of place. It was one of Bonnie's favorite pieces in the house. No one was quite sure who had brought it to Ferndean or when, but the sideboard had been there as long as Bonnie could remember. Truth be told, almost every single piece of heavy furniture, every knickknack no matter how cracked or otherwise damaged, every painting darkened with age and lack of professional care, every plate and saucer decorated with a pattern long out of fashion, held special meaning for Bonnie.

Which was why it had not been difficult for her to come to a decision about her future. She would sell the cottage in Yorktide in which she and Ken had lived for all of their married lives and move permanently into her family home. Ferndean House had been left equally to Bonnie and Carol by their parents, Shirley and Ronald Ascher, but Carol lived in New York City and had done since she was nineteen. Ferndean meant nothing to Carol Ascher. It meant the world to Bonnie. It was a member of the family. It was alive.

Ferndean House, located at 23 Wolf Lane, was situated on twenty acres of land that boasted a good-size pond (a stop-off for migrating birds in autumn and home to peepers in early spring); monumental oak, pine, and maple trees; and a profusion of native ferns, high and lowbush blueberry bushes, and flowering shrubs such as azalea and rhododendron. The house itself was about three thousand square feet with two floors of rooms and an attic that had formerly served as servants' quarters. There was a big stone fireplace in the living room; a charming front porch that ran the entire length of the house; a back deck that had been added at some point in the 1940s; a large flower and kitchen garden; and the puzzling remains of a stone structure set at one end of the large lawn that stretched behind the house.

Ferndean had been built by Carol and Bonnie's great-grandfather for his much younger third wife. He had named the structure after the house in *Jane Eyre* where Jane and the blind and crippled Mr. Rochester were reunited. The novel—only recently published—had been his wife's favorite; indeed, it was Bonnie's favorite novel, too. Marcus and Rosemary's wedding portrait, taken in June of 1848, still hung in Ferndean's living room, in what Bonnie had been told was its original frame.

After Shirley Ascher's death some thirty years earlier, Bonnie and her sister, in a rare instance of accord, had decided to rent the big house during part of the summer season. It would be a good source of income, most of which would go toward the upkeep of the old place. What was left over was pure profit; that profit benefited Bonnie and her family enormously, but Carol, who didn't need an additional source of income, routinely put her share back into the fund kept for the maintenance of the building and grounds.

Taking up full-time residency at Ferndean House would eliminate the income from seasonal renters, but Bonnie wasn't concerned. She would have cash from the sale of the cottage. Besides, she was not an extravagant person. Her needs were small, and she was used to living on a tight budget. All would be well going forward.

It would have to be well, Bonnie thought as she left the dining room, because she thoroughly believed that she was entitled to full possession of Ferndean. She was the one who had cared for Shirley Ascher in her dying years. She was the one who had helped to raise Carol's troubled daughter, Nicola. She was the one who had handled the management and maintenance of the family homestead for the past thirty years.

Who had changed Shirley Ascher's soiled sheets, prepared her meals, and taken charge of administering her medicines? Who had attended Nicola's school events from the time she came to live with her aunt in Yorktide? Who had cleaned up when Ferndean's pipes had burst? Who had mowed the lawn, planted the flowers, harvested the herbs and vegetables? Who had repainted the kitchen and bathrooms every ten years? Who had dealt with the summer tenants—finding them, vetting them, cleaning up after them?

Bonnie fondly patted the curved wooden banister of the grand staircase that led to the second floor. Yes, after all these years as full-time caretaker of her family homestead, Bonnie Ascher Elgort was entitled to be Mistress of Ferndean. It was something she had been dreaming about for a long time, pushing aside Carol's claim to the house and reigning supreme. But Ken had always held her back from making waves with her sister. Ken, the calm and reasonable husband, the broker of peace, the man who had wholeheartedly accepted Carol's troubled child into his home. And Carol Ascher hadn't even had enough respect for such a wonderful man to attend his funeral.

But now that Ken was gone, there was no one to keep Bonnie from achieving her dream. That the dream was largely fueled by ancient sibling rivalry didn't make it any less desirable. On the contrary, ancient sibling rivalry gave Bonnie's dream its incredible power.

In the living room now, Bonnie straightened the framed photos that were grouped on a table draped with a yellowed lace cloth. The entire family was represented, from Marcus and Rosemary to Bonnie's granddaughter, Sophie. Bonnie was especially fond of her parents' wedding portrait. Both looked so young and so solemn! And here was a photograph of Bonnie and Carol taken when they were quite young, three and six, Bonnie guessed. The girls were wearing bulky snow suits; behind them, Ferndean House, laced with snow, rose in its classic New England majesty. The image was a bittersweet reminder of the happy, almost idyllic childhood the sisters had shared at Ferndean, long before Carol had abandoned her home and her family for fame and fortune in New York City.

The distinct sound of a key in the front door caused Bonnie to turn from the table of photographs. It was probably Nicola, Bonnie thought, though her niece usually knocked before entering when she saw her aunt's car in the drive.

"Hello!" Bonnie called out as she made her way to the door. She felt a smile come to her face. She always felt like smiling when Nicola was around.

The door creaked loudly as it opened inward and a woman's figure stepped inside. The dustcloth Bonnie had been holding fell to the floor. She felt her stomach drop along with it. Her right hand went to her heart.

Chapter 2

New York City
Two weeks earlier

The past few days had been unseasonably warm; heat seemed visibly to rise from the concrete sidewalks and to shimmer in waves above the busy streets. Even though she would be comfortably seated in an air-conditioned, chauffer-driven town car, Carol was glad she didn't have to commute from her home on the Upper West Side to her office in Chelsea and back again.

The reason that Carol Ascher was able to avoid the steamy streets of Manhattan was because a month earlier she had sold her business—Ascher Interior Design—to her long-time, dedicated, and very talented junior partner. There was no doubt in Carol's mind that the company she had birthed and raised would find as much success in the future as it had found in the past. Still, there were several moments each day when Carol effectively forgot that she was no longer at the helm. When she realized with a start that she was no longer needed. When she found herself worrying about things for which she was no longer required to worry.

Carol passed through the hallway that led from her bedroom at one end of the apartment. As was her habit, she glanced at her image in the Art Deco mirror that hung over a black lacquer occasional table just outside the living room. She was pleased with what she saw. She hated that awful term sometimes used to describe a woman who appeared younger than her biological age. Well-preserved. Like a bit of dinosaur bone at the Museum of Natural History. What Carol was, in fact, was well taken care of. She got regular therapeutic massages; attended Pilates and yoga classes; had her hair professionally cut and colored every five weeks; and took her vitamin, calcium, blood pressure and cholesterol pills as recommended by her doctor. At sixty-five she was as tall and straight as she had been at nineteen, when she first arrived in New York City.

Even as a child Carol Ascher had instinctively known that appearances were important. As an adult, her wardrobe was highly curated; she favored a small handful of well-established designers. Her jewelry collection was comprised of basics from some of the big houses— Bulgari; Van Cleef & Arpels; Tiffany & Co.—as well as unique creations by several contemporary independent designers. She owned a Hermès bag that had cost more than she guessed her sister, Bonnie, had spent on bags, shoes, and coats in her lifetime. She owned a vintage Cartier diamond ring that had cost almost as much as the four years of Nicola's college tuition.

Like most responsible parents, Carol intended to leave the bulk of her estate to her child. But given the kind of woman Nicola had become since moving in with her aunt and uncle ten years earlier, Carol highly doubted that she would get any pleasure from the Hermès bag, the Cartier ring, or the Chanel suits. The paintings and sculptures she might admire. But maybe not. In many ways, Nicola Ascher had become a stranger to her mother.

With that in mind, Carol had begun to consider that it might be worth leaving a few of the precious or particularly meaningful items originally intended for Nicola to someone who would truly enjoy them. It was at this point that she met an impediment. She had no godchild. She was not close to the children of her acquaintances or colleagues. As for the other members of her family, well, with the possible exception of her seventy-year-old cousin, Judith, there was no one who appreciated good design and craftsmanship like she did.

Carol was bothered when she realized this. It was human nature to want to leave a legacy, to pass along a skill, a passion, a treasured object to a person you cared about. There was, of course, her former junior partner, now owner of Ascher Interior Design. But the truth was that Carol and Ana had never been close outside of the office. Carol had wanted it that way.

From the living room, Carol passed into the library. It was her favorite room in the apartment, light and airy in spite of the thousands of books, the carefully selected objets d'art, and the grand piano that had once belonged to one of the most prestigious of Old New York families. This morning, however, only one item was of interest to Carol. She picked up a card that sat on the three-legged, marble-topped table by one of the windows. The card was a note from a client and her husband, expressing gratitude for Carol's having made a generous donation to the research foundation seeking a cure for the childhood illness that had recently taken their seven-year-old son.

The boy's death had hit Carol hard. Very hard, even though she had met little Jonathan only once. Jonathan had been a charmer. Bright, socially adept, physically beautiful. His death—untimely, unfair, ghastly—had brought home to Carol with the force of a thunderclap the fact of her relative isolation in the world. Forget about who would cherish her possessions after her death. The more important question was: who would mourn her?

Because this vital question had been haunting her for weeks, Carol had finally decided it was time to make peace with her family. That might be easier said than done. Carol had not heard from Nicola since a phone call Christmas morning. Nicola's tone had been markedly cold. And there had been a sharp decline in Bonnie's correspondence since Ken's death the

previous September. Carol had not been able to attend the funeral; she had been in India on business. Maybe she should
have visited her sister upon her return to the States.

But she hadn't.

Well, Carol thought, returning the card of thanks to the
marble-topped table, she was going home now. To Yorktide.
Better late than never.

Still, she had yet to put her apartment on the market though
she knew realtors would eagerly line up for the chance to sell
the home of famous interior designer Carol Ascher, a perfectly
appointed, nine-room apartment with views of Central Park.

The reason for her procrastination was both simple and not
so simple. Nicola's bedroom. Everything in the room was exactly as it had been the day Nicola had gone to live with her
aunt in Maine. To dismantle the room would be in some way
to dismantle the most precious part of Carol's past. Nicola's
childhood.

Carol straightened her already straight shoulders and
briskly banished the mood of melancholy that was suddenly
threatening to overwhelm her. She would sell the apartment as
soon as possible. A person was more important than four
walls and a jumbled assortment of dolls, board games, and
sparkly headbands.

Nothing would stand in the way of her homecoming, Carol
thought as she strode from the library to her home office, not
even her family's possible—probable?—refusal to see her if
they were given advance warning. To that end, Carol had decided to show up in Yorktide unannounced, where Ferndean
House, the family homestead, awaited. Carol still had a key.
And the house was currently empty; for some unfathomable
reason Bonnie hadn't booked summer renters yet. But that
was perfect; the sooner Carol could get started with major ren-
ovations on the old place the better. For all she knew parts of
the building were structurally unsound, in spite of her brother-
in-law's assurance that Ferndean continued to pass inspec-
tions.

Carol sat at her desk and opened her laptop. She was fully aware that taking your enemy by surprise might be considered a power play.

Enemy? Carol frowned. That was the wrong word. Adversary? That was a bit harsh, too. Well, whatever the term, Carol expected some resistance to the idea of her occupying Ferndean House. Bonnie could be contrary where Carol was concerned, but that didn't really worry her. Once Bonnie heard her sister's more than generous offer for her share of the Victorian wreck that had been left to the Ascher girls she would happily sign on the dotted line.

Successful, wealthy, universally admired businessperson that she was, Carol Ascher was sure of it.

Connect with Us

Visit us online at
KensingtonBooks.com
to read more from your favorite authors, see books
by series, view reading group guides, and more.

for sneak peeks, chances to win books and prize packs,
and to share your thoughts with other readers.

facebook.com/kensingtonpublishing
twitter.com/kensingtonbooks

Tell us what you think!

To share your thoughts, submit a review,
or sign up for our eNewsletters, please visit:
KensingtonBooks.com/TellUs.